SECURITY RISK

JANIE CROUCH

ADIRONDACK ATTACK

JENNA KERNAN

MILLS & BOON

First Published in Great Britain 2019
by Mills & Boon, an imprint of HarperCollins*Publishers*
1 London Bridge Street, London, SE1 9GF

Security Risk © 2019 Janie Crouch
Adirondack Attack © 2019 Jeannette H. Monaco

ISBN: 978-0-263-27431-8

0819

MIX
Paper from
responsible sources
FSC™ C007454

FSC
www.fsc.org

This book is produced from independently certified FSC™ paper to ensure responsible forest management.

For more information visit: www.harpercollins.co.uk/green

Printed and bound in Spain
by CPI, Barcelona

SECURITY RISK

JANIE CROUCH

This book is dedicated to the ladies in the Crouch Crew.
Thank you so much for all your support and
encouragement. I couldn't do this without you!

Chapter One

The noose around his throat slowly strangled Tanner until gray blurred the edges of his vision. At the very last moment before he lost consciousness, he forced his weight onto his legs, providing blessed air. He knew the relief was short-lived. One leg was broken, the other almost useless after the hours of trying to support his weight on just his toes on the stool where he balanced precariously.

"Tell us who the cop is, and this can all end."

Tanner could barely see through his swollen eyes. "I already told you." The words were garbled whispers—blows to the face and the trauma to his throat had ensured that. "I'm the cop."

Someone pushed his leg out from under him, causing the rope to tighten around his neck once again, his hands tied behind his back rendering them useless. Airflow immediately ceased, although he didn't jerk or move unnecessarily. He'd learned after the first hour that flailing didn't accomplish anything but using up more energy and oxygen.

He had a limited supply of both.

"Which one of them is the cop? We know you were communicating with one of them."

The voice was referring to the two men also tied up

with Tanner, but sitting in chairs, one barely twenty-one years old. Tanner couldn't see them. Couldn't hear them. Could only try to survive this moment.

Someone helped him plant his good leg back on the stool so he could relieve the tension on his throat. At least they'd finally figured out he couldn't talk while they were attempting to suffocate him.

He breathed in as much as his swollen throat would allow. "I wasn't communicating with one of them." That was the truth. He'd been communicating with both of them. All three of them had been sent undercover together. "It's just me."

The blow to his stomach caught him completely unaware and had him coughing up blood and struggling to balance on the stool. Tanner didn't know how much more he could take. But he would do whatever he had to if it meant Nate and Alex would walk out of here.

Tanner definitely wouldn't. He'd already made peace with that.

Before he could prep himself for another blow, someone ran into the opposite side of the warehouse screaming curses that would make a sailor proud.

"Cops! They're everywhere outside!"

For a split second Tanner felt hope. They were going to make it.

The hope died a moment later at the simple instructions the leader of the syndicate gave his men.

"Kill them all."

It echoed over and over in Tanner's head.

Kill them all.

Kill them all.

At the first blast of gunfire and thump of a body, Tanner used all his strength in one last Hail Mary attempt to dive from the stool. He could barely believe it when

*the rope gave way, snapping from the ceiling rather
than ending his life. He crashed to the floor and—
ignoring that agony lighting through his entire body—
forced himself onto his feet.*

*And turned just in time to see one of the syndicate
members point his Glock at twenty-one-year-old Nate
Fletcher's forehead where he was strapped to a chair.*

Tanner dived for them.

EIGHT HOURS LATER the nightmare still felt slick and
slimy on Tanner Dempsey's skin. The flying motion
had woken him up. It was what had woken him up, often
violently, hundreds of nights since what happened in
that warehouse three years ago.

Tanner was never in time to save Nate in his dream,
just like he hadn't been in time to save him in real life.
He'd watched as the life of a promising law enforcement officer—and human being—had been snuffed out.

Tanner had been too late to save Alex, the other
undercover officer, too. He'd died with the first bullet
when Tanner had still been strung up.

The place had been swarming with cops not a minute later. Almost everyone in the Viper Syndicate, a hu-
man-and-weapons-trafficking cartel, had been caught
or killed that day, too.

But not in time to save Nate or Alex.

Tanner scrubbed a hand over his face. He was sitting
in a Denver courthouse, having finished giving his testimony in a drunk-driving case. Normally, he would've
already left after providing his info, but he was staying to catch the prosecuting attorney during the court
recess for lunch.

Ryan Fletcher, Nate's brother.

Maybe knowing he would be seeing Ryan today was

what brought the nightmare back last night. Although, after three years' worth of required visits with the department psychiatrist, Tanner knew there didn't necessarily have to be a reason for his subconscious mind to start dwelling on what had happened that day. Sometimes his mind just went there of its own accord. Some PTSD triggers were visible, but many more were hidden.

He and Ryan had become not quite friends, but more than just professional colleagues over the last year since Ryan had moved to Colorado and become one of the district attorneys. When Tanner was in Denver, or Ryan was in Grand County to see the sheriff, they sometimes got together to spar at the gym. Ryan might be a lawyer, but he kept himself in good shape.

And Tanner had worked damn hard to come back from what had happened at that warehouse. Tried to use his wounds—both physical and mental—to make him a better police officer. He demanded it of himself. As captain of the southeast department of the Grand County Sheriff's Office—which included his hometown of Risk Peak—he would do whatever it took to keep the people in his care safe.

A half smile popped up on his face before he could stop it. Risk Peak now included Bree Daniels, the woman who'd been causing smiles to pop up on his face unbidden for months.

She'd run out of money, and hope, in Risk Peak three months ago while being chased by a terrorist organization. Normally, Tanner wasn't thankful for bad guys, but the fact that these had led the socially awkward yet breathtakingly beautiful Bree to his front door was enough for him to make an exception.

"We haven't won the case yet." Ryan walked up to

him and slapped him on the shoulder. "You might want to save grinning like an idiot for when we do."

Tanner reached out to shake the man's hand. "Think there's going to be any problem getting a conviction?"

"That would be a definite no. Guy was on a suspended license and ran from the police. Plus, I've got Dr. Michalski providing his professional evaluation of the defendant this afternoon."

Tanner nodded. "Dr. Michalski is good." Tanner should know—he'd been seeing the man for three years. Tanner wasn't a huge fan of his sessions—sometimes it felt like he had a million other things to do than just sit around and talk about the past, but he couldn't deny that Dr. Michalski was a good psychiatrist.

"Yeah, he's definitely better on the stand than the last department psychiatrist I worked with in Seattle. Jury responds much better to him." Ryan grinned. "Of course, he's never going to be as good as putting you on the stand. Anytime I know you'll be testifying, I try to get as many women in the jury as possible."

Tanner rolled his eyes. He'd been teased about his looks before, by both the district attorneys and his colleagues in the sheriff's department. But as far as he was concerned, there was only one person whose opinion of his looks mattered. And it definitely wasn't anybody in a jury.

"Anything I can do to help get bad guys off the street."

"Speaking of." Ryan's easy smile slid from his face. "You heard that Owen Duquette got released on parole last week?"

Tanner swallowed a curse and nodded. "I made my objections known to the parole board. Strongly. Both in written form and in person at the parole hearing."

"It just feels like a slap in the face, you know? Duquette might not have been in the warehouse that day, but he knew what was going on. He was complicit in Nate's death. I'm sure of it." Ryan's fist tightened around his briefcase handle.

But they both knew that knowing something and *proving* it in court were two entirely different things. Duquette's ties to the Viper Syndicate had been tentative at best, legally. The district attorney at the time had only been able to charge Duquette with relatively minor trafficking charges, not murder.

But still, to get out after only three years? Tanner was angry. He couldn't even imagine how Ryan felt, knowing someone they both highly suspected was connected to his brother's murder was now back out on the streets.

"I'll make it my business to keep an eye on him," Tanner said. "And not just while I'm in uniform. The second he steps out of line, I'll make sure he goes down."

Ryan nodded. "Thanks. It's just…you know. Nate would've been twenty-five this month."

Tanner had to look away. If he had just snapped that rope a few seconds earlier, maybe Nate would've been here.

But that was Tanner's burden to bear. "Duquette will get what's coming to him. Don't doubt it."

A career criminal like Duquette wouldn't stay on the straight and narrow very long. Tanner would use whatever resources he had to know the moment Duquette stepped in the wrong direction.

Ryan nodded, then looked over Tanner's shoulder. "Oh, hi, Dr. Michalski. Got a moment to go over a couple of last-minute details?"

"Sure, Ryan." Dr. Michalski stepped up beside Tanner and offered his hand to shake. "Tanner, good to see you. It's been a while."

Translation: *You missed your last required appointment.*

Response: *Sorry, it just happened to be scheduled when I was off saving the country from a terrorist group about to illegally access cell-phone data all over the world.*

Neither man actually said it.

"Doc. Good to see you, too."

"Everything okay? No anger…problems?"

The good doctor had obviously heard Tanner's discussion about Duquette.

"Yeah, I'm fine. Just a little frustrated when my job gets harder because of criminals getting released early."

"Maybe we can talk about that sometime."

Tanner resisted the urge to roll his eyes. "Sounds like a plan. I'll let you guys get to your discussion."

Ryan smiled. "Tanner, thanks again for your work on the stand. Stellar, as always. Next time bring a cowboy hat in case we need an extra push with the lady jurors."

Tanner shook hands with both men before saying his goodbyes.

Because there was someone else he knew for a fact found him attractive in a cowboy hat. Someone who barely came up to his chin and had waves of thick brown hair running down her back. Someone to whom it never occurred to wear makeup, but it didn't matter because her natural beauty could give a cover model a run for their money any day of the week.

One look into her green eyes would have him forgetting about psychiatrists, witness stands and even the ghostly itch of a noose stretched around his neck.

Chapter Two

He watched Tanner Dempsey leave the courthouse just like he'd watched him all day. He'd silently observed, no one discovering what he was really doing. What he was really planning.

Had Dempsey realized he was watching? Of course not. Because Tanner Dempsey was so full of himself he couldn't possibly conceive that someone might watch him with contempt or scorn or disdain.

The handsome cop with the charming smile couldn't possibly devise that someone didn't fall under the spell of his charisma.

The man felt bile churning in his stomach as he saw how friendly other people were with Dempsey. It was impossible to understand how everyone surrounding the cop in the courthouse wasn't sickened by his arrogance. How he obviously thought himself better than everyone.

And then people shook his hand, smiling and friendly. Fooled. They couldn't see the truth right in front of them—that Dempsey was fooling them all.

It had taken every ounce of restraint the man had to not stand up in the courtroom and scream out that Dempsey was a fraud.

Dempsey thought the rules did not apply to him. Thought he could just do whatever he wanted. That everyone he arrested and testified against was no better than a bug beneath his shoe.

But soon they would all learn the truth about Tanner Dempsey's conceit. He would get what was coming to him.

It was time for the lawman to fall from grace. And the man would make sure that happened.

Chapter Three

"Order up, Bree!"

Bree Daniels smiled at Gayle Little sitting at the table in front of her. "So then what did Mr. Little do?"

Mrs. Little frowned. "Dan just yelled for you. Don't you need to go get the food?"

Bree smiled gently at the older woman. Mrs. Little came in a few times a week since her husband of sixty years had passed away recently. Bree knew Dan would much rather Bree stay out here and talk to Mrs. Little—to listen to her tell a story Bree had already heard—than to rush back and get the food.

"Don't you worry about Dan. He'll take the food out himself if I don't get back there in time."

There would've been a point not long ago that Bree wouldn't have realized that staying and talking to Mrs. Little was more important than getting the food from the kitchen. She wouldn't have realized there wasn't a single customer in the Sunrise Diner who wouldn't gladly eat a lukewarm meal if it meant seeing Mrs. Little—a woman most of them had known all their lives—forget her sadness for a spell.

It had only been over the last few weeks of living here in Risk Peak that Bree had begun to understand the nuances of interacting with people. It wasn't something that came easily for her.

She was probably the only genius-level hacker in the world working at a mom-and-pop diner in the middle of nowhere, without a computer in sight. Most people would say it was a waste of her talent, but Bree didn't care. If she never saw another computer, that would be just fine with her.

Computers, and her talent with them, had gotten her tortured as a child, gotten her mother killed and had nearly cost her her life a few months ago. So working as a waitress was just fine with her.

"And then he surprised me by getting down on one knee right then and there and asking me to marry him. On our third date," Mrs. Little said, a dreamy look in her eyes.

Bree's smile was genuine, feeling no urge to tell the older woman she'd heard the story before. It was so sweet and romantic.

At least she no longer sat tensely through every conversation worried that however she responded would be wrong or inappropriate.

While Bree didn't miss working with computers, she had to admit she found them much more simple than people. Coding held no subtext—it was straightforward, inputs and outputs, and for Bree as basic and simple as breathing.

Relationships and people, on the other hand? They were the opposite: full of unspoken rules and expectations and subtext.

Simple things other people took for granted, like talking and joking and, heaven forbid, *flirting*, were causes of darn near panic attacks in Bree. Part of it was from growing up without any friends and a mother terrified they'd be taken back into captivity at any moment. The other part of it was just how Bree's brain worked.

Like a computer.

Mrs. Little patted Bree's hand as she finished her story, and Bree turned back toward the kitchen. Sure enough, someone had already taken the food out to the table where it belonged.

For just a moment she tensed, second-guessing herself and whether she'd made the wrong decision by talking to Mrs. Little rather than concentrating on the job she was being paid to do. But both Dan and Cheryl smiled at her when she turned back toward the kitchen, so Bree decided not to worry about it.

She had bigger things to worry about. Tanner was on his way to come get her. Said he had a surprise for her this evening.

Bree did not do well with surprises.

She knew he'd been in Denver today providing testimony in court. The fact that she couldn't call him and ask him for more details about this evening had just ratcheted up her anxiety.

What did it mean when a man said he had a surprise, but that it wasn't a date and that she should definitely not get dressed up?

What did that *mean*?

"You okay, honey?" Cheryl came and stood beside her and rubbed her arm.

Not too long ago that sort of casual touch would've been completely foreign to Bree. Living a lifetime without anyone touching her had made all touches feel odd.

Judy, the other full-time waitress, came and flanked Bree on the other side, knocking Bree's hip with her own.

"You've been staring at that pitcher of tea for a full

minute. You thinking about asking it out on a date? Tanner would probably be jealous."

The sound of his name just made her abdomen muscles tighten more.

"I'm scared," she finally whispered.

Saying it, talking personally about herself, was still so difficult. But these women were her friends.

Friends. Still such a foreign concept.

Both women immediately pulled in closer. Cheryl wrapped her arm around Bree's waist. "Scared of what, honey? Do you feel like someone is watching you again? Do you think it's the Organization?"

"They're gone," Judy assured her. "They may not be in prison yet, but none of them are free. Especially not Michael Jeter. He's not going to get anywhere near you."

Bree shuddered at the name of the man who'd kept her and her mother captive and hurt them both to force Bree to use her computer talents to further his agenda. Her mother had never fully recovered from his torture. But they were right—Jeter was currently awaiting trial and couldn't hurt her anymore.

"No, not Jeter," she whispered. "Tanner."

"You're afraid of *Tanner*?" Judy asked.

This was why Bree didn't like talking. She always messed it up. She could feel herself withdrawing, falling back into old, bad patterns of retreat that were more familiar.

But Cheryl got right up in Bree's face. "Hey. Talk to us."

Bree looked in the older woman's eyes. There was no judgment there, just acceptance and kindness.

"Order up," Dan yelled from the kitchen window a few feet away.

"In a minute!" both Cheryl and Judy responded in sync. Dan sighed.

"Why would you be scared of Tanner? Did something happen?" Judy asked.

Spitting it out was probably the best option. "He's coming to get me in an hour. Said he had a surprise and not to get dressed up."

"A surprise isn't bad, Bree." Cheryl rubbed her arm again. "Granted, that boy should know better than to think you're going to like surprises, but it's definitely not something to be afraid about."

"But he told me not to get dressed up! That means he doesn't want me to go to any trouble with my hair and makeup if he's just going to tell me it's over."

The other two women met each other's eyes.

"Or…" Judy drew the word out. "He has something else planned and he doesn't want you to worry about a dress or fancy shoes."

Bree's forehead wrinkled as she considered that. "Like what?"

"I've got another order up, gals," Dan said from the window again.

"In a minute!" Now Bree joined the battle cry. She looked to her friends with a little more hope.

"Maybe a hike," Judy said. "I know it's colder out, but you both like to hike."

Cheryl took the pitcher of tea from Bree's hands and set it down on the counter. "Maybe stargazing. That's romantic. He wouldn't want you to get dressed up for that."

Judy gave a one-shouldered shrug. "A motorcycle ride. I know he doesn't have one, but maybe he borrowed one."

"The point is, the words *surprise* and *casual* are

not bad. Tanner Dempsey is nothing if not straightforward. That man is never going to blindside you." Cheryl kissed her on the cheek, and then both women smiled and headed toward the kitchen to keep Dan from having a fit with undelivered food.

Bree turned and made her way back over to Mrs. Little, pouring her some more tea.

She wasn't convinced surprises weren't bad. She'd had a lot of years where the unknown meant dangerous or painful.

But one thing they said was definitely true: Tanner wouldn't blindside her.

He'd spent the last month helping her with damn near everything. Helping her move back into the Andrewses' small apartment on the outskirts of town. Helping her learn how to interact with others. Helping her figure out how to navigate her life now that she wasn't on the run anymore.

And most important, helping her deal with the crippling loss of the twins she no longer had to care for. She knew Christian and Beth were back where they belonged, in their mother's—Bree's cousin Melissa's—care. But after nearly three months of being their sole caretaker, losing them so suddenly had left a huge gap in Bree's life.

Tanner had distracted her with dates and horseback rides at his ranch and kisses that curled her toes.

So Judy and Cheryl were right. Bree wasn't exactly sure where her relationship with him was going, but if he had something bad to say, he wouldn't beat around the bush.

The door to the diner chimed as it opened, and as if her thoughts had conjured him, Tanner was there—all long legs and big, broad shoulders that almost filled the door before he made his way inside. Her gaze continued up to his face, his thick dark hair cut short. That square jaw covered in what seemed to be an almost perpetual five o'clock shadow.

Those brown eyes.

Bree couldn't stop staring. Even knowing she was standing there holding a pitcher of tea in the middle of a restaurant and just *staring*, she still couldn't stop.

But at least he was staring at her, too.

He closed the distance between them, stopping when he was a few feet from her. "I know I'm early. I just had to see you. Today has been…"

She took a step closer. "Are you okay? Did anything happen?"

Every single part of her body seemed to clench as he reached out and trailed his thumb down her cheek. "It's all fine now."

She couldn't look away from those brown eyes. It wasn't so long ago that she found it hard to look him in the eyes, but more often than not now she found it impossible to look away. "Fine. I mean, good. I'm glad it's fine."

He took her awkwardness in stride as always. "I'll just sit out here until you're finished and chat with Dan and folk, if that's okay."

Sure. The word formed in her brain, but she couldn't seem to get it out of her mouth as his thumb trailed down her cheek again. She nodded abruptly then turned away, almost running back toward the kitchen.

Judy and Cheryl were both grinning like idiots.

"Yeah, I'm definitely going to go with 'not a bad surprise' for my final answer," Judy said.

Cheryl turned Bree around so Bree's back was to her.

"What are you doing?" Bree said as she felt the knot of her apron loosen.

"Dan's basically been running the whole restaurant by himself for the last half hour anyway. We don't need you here." Cheryl pushed her gently between the shoulder blades back toward the front of the restaurant. "You've got a gorgeous man out there who couldn't bear to wait one more hour to see you. Go get changed out of your work clothes. Whatever his surprise is, you want it."

Chapter Four

It didn't take Bree long to figure out where they were going, and the last of her tension eased away. He was taking her to her favorite place on the planet: the ranch Tanner shared with his brother, Noah, about thirty minutes outside Risk Peak.

She'd stayed here when she'd been on the run, and it was impossible not to fall in love with this place. Horses and quiet and mountains. No people ever around except for Noah, who rarely made his presence known at all.

She and Tanner usually came here on the weekends. He'd taught her how to ride and care for the horses. But they'd never come in the evening.

Her heart clenched a little as he led her around the house. Of all her memories of the twins, waking up and seeing them both outside in Tanner's big, capable arms as he walked and showed them the horses was forever ingrained in her psyche.

"Hey, what's that sad look for?"

She gave a one-shouldered shrug. "Just… Beth and Christian. I miss them."

"Have you Skyped this week?" He took her hand, his long fingers stretching securely over hers.

She nodded. "Of course. Melissa and Chris know if they don't call me as scheduled, I'll never let them hear the end of it. But it's just not the same." She couldn't help her little sigh. "They're happy and safe and together as a family, and I want that for them."

"But you miss them."

"Crazy, right? They were never mine to begin with." She'd tried to warn herself of that, but those babies had stolen her heart.

"Not crazy at all. But maybe my surprise will help make it better." He led her over to his barn.

"Did you guys get a new horse?" Now, that would be a wonderful surprise. Bree loved interacting with all the animals here, since she'd never had any sort of pet growing up.

"Better." He took her hand and pulled her toward a stall in the far corner.

She rounded the doorway so she could see and couldn't stop her near squeal of pleasure. "Corfu had her puppies!"

"And one is yours, if you want it."

"Really?" It was all she could do not to jump up and down and clap her hands. She knew she was acting like an idiot but couldn't help it.

A puppy.

It wouldn't be the same as having the twins, but it would be a *puppy*. And it would be hers.

Tanner took her hand and led her closer to Corfu— a mixed-breed dog who'd just shown up on the ranch a year ago. "They're nearly a week old already, since Noah didn't see fit to mention the fact that Corfu had given birth to me until yesterday."

The four pups were lying snuggled next to Corfu, who lifted her head and sniffed at Bree as Bree crouched beside her.

"Is it okay to pet her?"

Tanner crouched down, too. "Sure. She knows you're her friend."

Bree scratched the dog's head gently, smiling as she leaned into Bree's fingers.

"They're so little!" She touched one gently. "Which one is mine?"

"There are three boys and one girl. You'll have to decide."

"Boy," she said instantly. "I want that one. I'll name him Star." She pointed to the one in the middle—black, with a large white spot on its head.

Tanner laughed softly and scooped the puppy up. "I'm afraid you'll have to make a tough decision."

"Is he already spoken for?" It was ridiculous to be disappointed. Any puppy would be great.

"No, you just can't have a boy pup *and* this one. Star is a girl." He held the pup out to her.

"A girl," Bree breathed then smiled, taking the tiny pup in her arms. "Of course you're a girl. You're a beautiful, sweet girl, and we'll be best friends."

They played with the pups a few more minutes before Tanner said they should let Corfu and the babies rest.

"I can't take her with me tonight?" The thought of having the pup around in her apartment that always seemed too quiet was so appealing.

Tanner slipped an arm around her shoulders and pulled her close as they walked out of the barn and toward his house. "It'll be another five weeks before she's weaned. No sleepovers until then."

Five weeks wasn't that long. Hell, before a couple of months ago, she'd spent years without talking to anyone or having any human contact. Surely she could survive a little over a month without a dog.

He spun her around to face him as they got to his

house. "It's been harder than you've let on, hasn't it? Being by yourself."

She shrugged. She didn't want to be a whiner. "I was by myself for a lot of years, even before my mother died. Seems silly to complain about it now when I'm finally *not* alone."

He took a step closer, his hands dropping to her waist. "I know I'm not as cute as those twins, but you really aren't alone. I'm always here if you need me." His forehead dropped against hers. "Okay?"

She couldn't worry about anything when Tanner was this close. All she could do was breathe in the scent of him, woodsy and fresh and undeniably male.

She rose up onto her toes when his lips moved toward hers. Her mind might work like a computer, but her body was all woman when she was around him. She shivered as his thumb brushed over her jaw, then felt like she was melting out of her own skin as he kissed the side of her mouth before running his tongue over her lower lip.

He kissed her gently like that until she couldn't stand it anymore and she threaded her hands into his hair at his nape and pulled him hard against her. She gasped as the pleasure radiated through her, heard him groan and knew he was feeling the same. They both surrendered to the heat between them, lost in sensation.

When they finally broke away, both of them were breathing hard. His forehead fell against hers again. "I think I better get you home."

She wanted to ask him to stay with her tonight. To take that next step their kisses had been moving them toward for the last few weeks. Every time they were pressed up together, it was abundantly clear he wanted her. If she gave him the go-ahead, would he make that next move? Would he finally give her whatever it was her body needed to ease the restlessness and heat that seemed to thrum through her every time he was around?

If he were just waiting on her, she'd tell him she was ready right now, this very moment. She might not have experienced sex before, but she wasn't afraid. Not with Tanner. He wouldn't hurt her. She knew that more than anything else.

But it was more than just her own natural hesitation. Something was holding him back, too. Something she was too bad at interpreting interpersonal cues to figure out. He never made her think it had anything to do with her. But still…

She was missing a lot of the emotional components other women—*normal* women—weren't. Women who hadn't been born with a brain that worked like a computer and sentiment that sometimes didn't seem to work at all. Women who hadn't had to shut down emotionally because they'd been tortured. Women who hadn't been on the run for half their life with no interaction with other people.

All those things left some pretty large gaps in Bree's emotional development. Maybe subconsciously Tanner was realizing Bree wouldn't be able to provide all he would need, and he wanted to keep from taking that last physical step that would make it harder for them to break apart if they needed to.

Why else would he be stopping, when his body still pressed up against hers made it clear he wanted her? At least physically.

"Let's get you home," he whispered.

The ride back to Risk Peak was mostly in silence, but not uncomfortable. Tanner's hand never left hers, bringing her fingers up to his lips to kiss every so often.

It just made Bree more confused. The urge to blurt out all her questions was overwhelming, and a few months ago she wouldn't have been able to stop herself. But she forced herself to remain quiet rather than demand answers for things that didn't make sense to her.

The fact that there were more kisses after he parked at her apartment on the outskirts of town, and the fact that her body was fairly humming by the time they pulled away from each other, didn't help with her confusion.

He took the key she offered and unlocked the door, checking her apartment for any threats before letting her inside. He always did that, even though there hadn't been any sign of trouble since they'd disbanded the Organization almost two months ago. But she didn't mind him doing it. The fact that he put himself between her and any potential danger made her feel cherished.

He kissed her forehead. "I'll see you tomorrow?"

Stay.

She screamed at herself to say it. To just tell him outright that she was ready. That she wanted him. Wanted *this*.

But before she got up the nerve, with one more kiss to her forehead, Tanner was gone.

She sighed and called herself every type of idiot for not voicing her desires. How was it she couldn't seem to get herself to *shut up* when she was blurting out something inappropriate for a situation, and now couldn't seem to force herself to *speak up* when there was something legitimately good she wanted?

She eventually got ready for bed, but once she was there, she couldn't sleep. After thirty minutes she gave up even trying. She couldn't do anything about Tanner, but she could research puppies.

Maybe that would take her mind off everything else.

She went over to her desk, running her fingers across her laptop. Even opening it caused her to tense, but researching something as innocent and fun as this didn't need to bring back any of the bad memories.

Once she got started, habit took over, and all discomfort from using a computer was left behind. Within an hour she had read multiple articles on canine physical, mental and emotional development. Then she researched and made a list of everything she would need to buy the next time she was in Denver. It was probably a good thing she had five weeks before Star could come home; there were a lot of things a puppy needed. She wouldn't be caught off guard this time, like she had been when the twins had been thrust into her care.

She was still wide awake when she got to the recommended square footage of outdoor space a dog that size would require. She had a small plot of backyard, which would need a fence. She would have to talk to Dan and Cheryl about that. But more important, would it even be big enough to meet the recommended size? Would she still be allowed to get the dog if it wasn't?

Knowing her brain would never let her sleep until she knew the exact square footage in her backyard, Bree slipped on a pair of sweatpants with her sleep shirt and some shoes. Grabbing a tape measure and her phone so she could type in the measurements, she headed outside.

She was glad she didn't have any neighbors around to see her out measuring her yard in the middle of the night. Using the tape measure, she began marking off quadrants, typing them into her phone as she went. She was at the farthest point from the apartment when she took a step backward and tripped over something.

Cursing, she slid back, turning on the flashlight on

her phone so she could see what had tripped her. She didn't remember there being any logs or large rocks in her yard. Although they weren't necessarily bad—a dog might like them.

But when she shone the light, she realized it wasn't a log at all. She'd tripped over a *person*. She couldn't see the face of the person passed out facedown, but it looked like a man by the size of him.

"Hey, are you okay?" she said. She poked his shoulder when he didn't respond. "Excuse me. Wake up."

When he didn't move at all, fear began to crawl along her belly. She reached over to take the guy's pulse.

His skin was cold to the touch, and there was definitely no pulse to be found.

She hadn't just tripped over a person. She'd tripped over a *body*.

Chapter Five

Tanner groped for the phone, his mind becoming instantly alert as it rang on his bedside table. After ten years in law enforcement, he'd gotten used to having it go off at any and all hours of the day or night.

But when he saw it was Bree, his heart began to gallop. She wouldn't call at four o'clock in the morning without reason.

"Bree, what's wrong?"

Her breath sawing in and out didn't ease his fear in any way. He was already getting out of bed and putting on his clothes. "Bree? Talk to me, freckles."

"Tanner? There's a…body."

He cursed as he zipped and buttoned his jeans. "Are you okay? Are you hurt?"

"No. I'm not hurt."

He pulled on a shirt and began buttoning it. "But someone was inside your apartment?"

"No, I found the body outside."

He had no idea why she would've found a body outside in the middle of the night. Maybe someone was drunk and passed out on her lawn. Maybe it wasn't a body at all.

"Are you inside? Safe?"

"Y-yes." The barely whispered word didn't reassure him.

"Just stay where you are, okay? Don't move. I'm at my place in town. I'll be to you in less than five minutes."

He hated to hang up but had to so he could call the station and get Ronnie Kitchens, the deputy on duty tonight, out to the scene. Tanner would meet them there. He was pulling up to Bree's place by the time he got off the phone with Ronnie.

Weapon drawn, he approached her front door, keeping an eye out all around him.

He knocked. "Bree, open up, sweetheart. It's me." He kept his eyes pinned out in the darkness, looking for any sign of movement.

The door creaked open just slightly. "Tanner?"

He hated to hear the fear in her voice, so much more noticeable because it had been conspicuously absent for the last month. "Yeah, freckles. Let me in, okay?"

The door opened wider, and he stepped inside, holstering his weapon and pulling her against him in a one-armed hug. "Are you all right?" He looked around the room. Nothing seemed out of place or destroyed.

"Yes, i-it's out back. Outside. I tripped over it." A shudder racked her small frame.

"I want you to stay here. Ronnie will be here in just a minute, and we're going to check it out." He led her to the kitchen table and helped her sit in a chair. "Why were you outside in the middle of the night?"

"I was measuring the yard to see if it was regulation size for a dog."

Even with the gravity of the situation, Tanner almost smiled. Measuring a yard in the middle of the night for her new puppy? That totally made sense in a Bree world.

"Sweetheart, not that I doubt you, but are you sure it was a body?"

"Yes. I tried to get him to move before I called you. In case it was someone who'd fallen asleep or something."

That didn't sound good.

"Okay." He rubbed his hand soothingly over her hair. "Stay here. I'm going to check it out."

The lights from Ronnie's squad car were reflecting in the windows, so Tanner went outside to meet him.

"We definitely have a body?" Ronnie asked as he exited his car, a little slower than he'd once been after narrowly escaping a body bag himself a few weeks ago.

"Bree says it's out back. I haven't confirmed. Said she tripped over it when she was measuring the yard for her new dog."

Ronnie stopped and stared at him. "Do I even want to ask why she would be doing that in the middle of the night?"

Tanner shrugged. "It's Bree. Once she gets her brain set on something, there's no way around it."

The whole town was getting used to that response. Ronnie was no exception. "Let's go check it out."

They grabbed high-powered flashlights from the squad car and moved quickly to the back of the house, firearms once again drawn. Bree's patch of land wasn't that large, and it didn't take them long to realize Bree hadn't been mistaken.

There was very definitely a dead body.

Ronnie muttered a curse and kept him covered with his weapon as Tanner rushed over. As soon as he touched the cold skin of the male body lying on his stomach, Tanner knew there was no way the guy was alive. But he checked the pulse anyway.

Dead.

"We need to get the crime lab out here. Definitely dead—for a while, it feels like." Tanner stood, backing away from the body to try to keep the scene as pristine as possible.

"Natural causes?" Ronnie asked.

Tanner shone his light on the back of the guy's shirt. It was covered with blood. "Nope. Nothing natural about this."

TANNER STAYED OUTSIDE as forensics made their way onto the scene and began processing, using the floodlights they brought. It didn't take long to realize the guy not only hadn't died of natural causes, he'd been murdered. The multiple stab wounds covering his back were testament to that.

Tanner kept Bree inside the house. She was curious, but coming face-to-face with this sort of violence under the glaring lights wasn't something he'd suggest for anyone. Not to mention it was now an active crime scene that shouldn't be contaminated.

It wasn't long before he was having to give that excuse to more than just Bree. The lights had woken folks up, and before long there were curious bystanders from all over town stopping by. It wasn't every day someone was murdered in Risk Peak.

Ronnie was doing his best to shoo them along, thankfully having set up the crime scene tape far enough back to keep this from becoming an online media sensation.

"Captain Dempsey." Owen, one of the crime lab techs, jogged over to him. "We've done all our preliminary processing and are ready to turn the body over."

Time to find out if they had a dead local on their hands. Tanner prayed he wouldn't be making a dreaded trip to the house of someone he knew to tell them a loved one had been killed.

He and Ronnie both joined the two techs as they reached down and rolled over the body. Ronnie let out a relieved breath. "That's nobody from Risk Peak, right? Thank God."

Relief flooded Tanner, too. "Yeah, I think you're right. I don't recognize—"

Tanner stopped. Because he *did* recognize the dead man, although it wasn't someone from here. He let out a blistering curse.

"What?" Ronnie asked. "Is it someone we know?"

Tanner crouched down beside the body. "Someone *I* know. Joshua Newkirk. He was arrested four years ago, and then he got out on early release six months ago. He's from farther north in Grand County. Raped a woman there. I was part of the team who arrested him."

And now, four years later, he was out and might have been on his way to attack Bree. The MO was similar. Newkirk had broken into the other woman's house while she was alone.

Tanner stood back up. "Damn it, I told the parole board he should be kept in prison. That the risk of repeat offense was too high."

Just like he'd said about Owen Duquette earlier today. Different parole board, same situation. It was hard to keep the community safe if they were going to continue letting offenders back onto the streets so soon.

Ronnie stepped back so the crime lab could continue their job. "Well, he won't be attacking any more women now, that's for sure."

Tanner shook his head. "I can't even pretend I'm

going to lose sleep over Newkirk's death." Damn well not, since they'd found the man on Bree's lawn.

"That didn't give someone the right to kill him." Ronnie shook his head.

Tanner scrubbed a hand over his face. "No, of course not. We'll bring that person to justice. But damn it, Ronnie, the guy was twenty feet from Bree's door."

Owen the crime tech looked up. "I don't think this guy was planning to attack the lady who lives here."

Tanner focused in on Owen. "Why?"

"I don't know if this is going to make it better or worse, but this guy wasn't killed here. There would've been a crap ton of blood."

Ronnie raised an eyebrow. "Crap ton? That a clinical term?"

"I'm just saying that if this guy was stabbed here, there would be blood pooling around him."

Tanner looked around. He didn't see any blood, either. "What does that mean, exactly?"

"One option is that guy could've been stabbed closer to town and just made it this far before giving up the ghost, pardon the pun. We'll look for blood traces and see if we can follow it anywhere. Might get lucky and lead us to the actual murder scene."

"That would be highly useful. But there's another option?" Tanner asked.

Owen's brows furrowed. "Well, the body could've been placed here. Unless we find some sort of blood trace leading from somewhere, then I would assume that the body was dumped here by the killer."

Damn it, that was almost as bad as thinking a rapist had been on his way to Bree's house. "Why would someone dump a body here?" Tanner barked. "Specifically at this apartment?"

Owen shrugged. "That I can't tell you. Maybe because it's pretty far at the edge of town and this just happened to be a convenient place, but..." He trailed off.

He wasn't going to like what Owen was going to say, but the younger man still needed to say it. "You can tell me, Owen. I'm not going to kill the messenger."

"You only dump a body in someone's yard if you want it to be found. Otherwise, there's ten thousand acres of national forests all around us. Why not drag it in there and leave it? Could be years before anyone found him."

"So it was some sort of message to her?" Ronnie asked. "Does she have any connection to Joshua Newkirk?"

Tanner shook his head. "I've got no reason to think so, but I'll ask."

"For what it's worth—" Owen crouched down next to the body again "—it's a lot more likely that this has nothing to do with her. Somebody could've killed Newkirk and just decided to dump the body here before going any farther. Like I said, her apartment is on the edge of town, so dumping it here, in the dark, makes sense. I'll know more in a few hours."

Tanner and Ronnie stepped back farther so he could go to work. Ronnie slapped Tanner on the shoulder. "We'll get answers."

Tanner nodded. "I'll ask Bree if she knew Newkirk."

He turned back toward the house and found Bree standing in her back door, fully dressed but still with a blanket wrapped around her as if to ward off a chill. And who could blame her? There was a dead rapist a couple dozen feet from her house.

Tanner walked up to Bree. God, he hated that pinched look that was back on her features. It had been there so much when he'd first met her but had been gone for a while.

He wanted it gone again.

"Was it someone from around here? Someone we know?" she asked.

Tanner wrapped his arms around her. "No, freckles. Not anyone from around here." He could feel some of the tension leak out of her. "Do you know someone named Joshua Newkirk?"

She pulled back so she could look him in the eye. "No. Should I?"

He believed her. She had no reason to lie about it, and he didn't think Bree was very good at lying anyway.

"That's the dead guy's name. I was able to ID him pretty quickly because I arrested him a few years ago. Evidently, he's made a few enemies since getting out of prison six months ago."

And while Tanner was grateful a rapist hadn't been on his way up to Bree's back door, he didn't like how any of this was feeling to him.

He prayed Owen's last statement would be correct, and that Bree's yard had just been a convenience. That it was just a coincidence that the body had been placed here.

Tanner wasn't prone to believing in coincidences. Anger and frustration pooled inside him. She'd been through enough. He'd brought her to Risk Peak to keep her safe, and now this. The worst could've happened, and he wouldn't have been able to prevent it.

He felt her small hands close over his fists.

"I'm okay. Whatever's going on in that head of yours didn't happen. You'll figure out what's going on and put a stop to it. Give yourself time."

The trust in her eyes gutted him. He stroked his

knuckles down her cheek. There were so many things he wanted to say to her, to assure her of, but the phone rang in his pocket. He grabbed it and saw it was Sheriff Duggan, his boss.

Bree waved at him to get it and turned and walked toward her bedroom.

"Sheriff Duggan."

"I hear there's a body in Bree Daniels's yard."

Tanner wasn't surprised word had already reached her. Grand County wasn't big enough that a murder wouldn't be a big deal. "Yes, there sure is. I'll do you one better. The body is Joshua Newkirk."

"The convicted rapist?" She let out a curse. "And he was killed in Miss Daniels's backyard?"

Tanner filled in his boss on all the details, including the lack of blood on scene.

"Tanner, I need you to be straight with me," the sheriff said after he'd finished. "It's no secret you're involved with Bree. Do I need to pull you off this case? I'm worried you can't stay neutral."

"The guy is dead. I'm not sure my neutrality makes any difference."

"You still have a killer to find, and it's no secret you weren't a fan of Newkirk's."

Tanner swallowed a curse. "I hope nobody was a fan of Newkirk's. Just because I'm not sad he's dead doesn't mean I won't bring down his killer."

Sheriff Duggan was quiet for a moment. One of the things Tanner appreciated the most about the woman he'd worked for for over ten years was that she thought things through before she spoke.

But when she did speak this time, it wasn't something he wanted to hear.

"I'm going to send Richard Whitaker out there. And

before you start arguing with me, because I know you will, this is not a punishment or because I don't trust you. He's fresh eyes, and he doesn't have a history with either Bree or Newkirk."

Tanner knew this was what was best, but it still rankled. Not to mention nobody got along well with Richard Whitaker. The guy was a grade-A jerk.

"You know I don't like it, but I'm not going to fight you on it."

"Good. Because someone has been murdered. And whether we liked the dead guy or not, our job is to find out who did it."

Chapter Six

Richard Whitaker, Tanner's counterpart in the northern part of Grand County, showed up an hour later. Tanner and Ronnie met him out front as he pulled up.

"Whitaker." They both shook the man's hand.

"Dempsey. Kitchens." Richard nodded at them before tilting his head toward the crime scene in the back. "Sheriff said you finally had a little bit of excitement out here."

Tanner caught Ronnie's eyes roll in his peripheral. He couldn't blame the man. Everybody tended to want to roll their eyes around Richard Whitaker. The guy had moved here from Dallas six or seven years ago because his wife was from this area and wanted to return. Ironically, when they'd divorced eighteen months back, Richard had been the one who'd stayed and his wife had been the one who moved away.

Whitaker was a good cop. He had gotten quite a bit of experience in his years with the Dallas PD—a fact he never let anyone forget. But his disdain for small-town life and police work was pretty evident. Sometimes it was hard to understand why he stayed.

"Yeah. Victim's name is Joshua Newkirk. He was a convicted felon—a rapist." They walked toward the crime scene. Owen and his colleague were now searching for any blood traces that might show where Newkirk came from if he stumbled here on his own.

"Based on body temps," Ronnie continued, "looks like he's been dead a little over six hours. Body was called in a little over two hours ago."

"But Miss Daniels didn't call 911. Is that correct?" Whitaker looked pointedly at Tanner.

Tanner crossed his arms over his chest. "Yeah, that's right. She called me. She knows me. It's not a huge stretch."

"Maybe. But when I was on the Dallas force, a lot of times we would find the person who called in a crime had something to do with it. Seems like they thought it made them look more innocent."

Tanner stiffened. "Well, you're not in Dallas, and Bree didn't have anything to do with this."

Whitaker tilted his head to the side. "And that right there is the exact reason why the sheriff sent me out here. You're not neutral, Dempsey."

Tanner's teeth ground together. He stopped walking. "Just because I'm not going off chasing wild rabbits doesn't mean I'm not capable of finding out who did this to Newkirk."

Ronnie stopped next to him. "I'm not involved with Bree, so, by your definition, I'm much more neutral, and I concur with Tanner. I don't think she has the physical prowess to get the drop on someone Newkirk's size. Plus, I definitely don't think she's stupid enough to drop a body in her own backyard. The woman has an IQ of 832."

Whitaker looked like he was going to argue the point further, but finally he just nodded. "Fine. We won't concentrate on Miss Daniels at the moment. But if evidence suggests she had a part in this, I can damn well promise you I'm going to bring her in. Just because Risk Peak is a small town and everyone knows everyone else doesn't mean we're going to ignore facts and proper procedure."

Tanner could feel Ronnie rolling his eyes again. "Yeah, we get it," Tanner said. "Facts and solid procedure are the same regardless of whether you're in a big city or small town. But Bree didn't do this."

Whitaker gave another hard nod and walked the rest of the way to the body.

Tanner stayed behind and turned to Ronnie. "Can you finish up here with him? I'm going to take Bree out to the ranch so she can get some rest. I'll be back in this afternoon."

Ronnie slapped him on the shoulder. "Absolutely. I wish this hadn't happened in her backyard. Literally. She's been through enough."

Tanner scrubbed a hand over his face. "I know."

"Go take care of her."

The one good thing about Whitaker being here was that it allowed Tanner to leave with complete peace of mind, ironically, because of the man's big-city police force expertise. Whatever inexperience Ronnie may have working with a murder, Whitaker made up for. And the sheriff was right: two sets of eyes were always better than one.

But Whitaker was still a jerk.

Tanner walked through the back door of Bree's apartment and found her sitting at the kitchen table, hands wrapped around a mug. Exhaustion seemed to drip from her features. She looked more like she had when he first met her months ago—tired, haunted.

He hated it.

"Hey," he whispered. "You doing okay?"

Those green eyes that had enthralled him from the very first time he'd seen her looked up at him now.

"I'm okay. Just tired."

"Why don't you pack a bag? You can't stay here. I want to take you to the ranch."

Those eyes lit up a little. "Really?"

"Is that okay?"

She nodded with more energy. "Let me get my stuff."

A few minutes later, they were headed out to Tanner's SUV. "I'll just bring you in to work later. Is that okay? Then you can get your car. I know the drive will be a hassle, but I don't want you staying in town on your own."

"That's fine."

He opened the door for her, then went around and got in himself, starting the vehicle and pulling away.

He kept glancing over at her as he drove, waiting for some sort of outburst from her. But she actually looked a little happy.

"Why do you keep looking at me like that?" she asked when they were about ten minutes outside town.

"Occupational hazard, I guess. Just want to make sure you're all right. I wouldn't blame you if you were upset. Hell, I convinced you to move to Risk Peak because it was supposed to be a *safe place*. And now this happens."

She actually smiled at him. "I was most concerned the dead person was someone we knew. When you told me it wasn't, that was a huge relief. Plus, now I get to stay at the ranch. I'll get to see Star every day rather than having to wait five more weeks."

He couldn't help but smile back at her. That was Bree, wasn't it? She never quite reacted the way people would expect someone to.

It was one of the many reasons he was falling in love with her.

But then the smile fell off her face. "That's wrong, isn't it? How I'm feeling. I should be upset that someone is dead."

"Believe me, you not being hysterical is helpful in this situation."

She turned to look out the window and was silent for a long while. "But it's not normal. Once I found out it wasn't anyone we knew, I didn't really care that there was a dead body in my backyard. It was more stressful that there were so many people at the house than anything else. And it can't be normal that I care more about getting to the ranch and seeing a dog."

He grabbed her hands she was twisting in her lap. "Bree—"

She turned to him, face distraught. "I don't have correct emotions, Tanner. I'm broken."

He flipped on his hazard lights and pulled the SUV over to the side of the road, then turned to her, cupping her cheeks with both hands.

"I don't ever want to hear you say that again. Your emotions are just fine. Just because you're not hysterical doesn't mean you're broken. Never feel bad for how your brilliant mind fortifies you so you can survive."

"But—"

"No buts." He reached between them and kissed her briefly. "You survived what would've broken most people. And you're amazing just the way you are."

He wasn't sure if she believed him, but he meant every word. He waited until she finally nodded before releasing her and pulling back on the road again.

It wasn't long before they were arriving at the ranch. He grabbed her overnight bag, and they walked inside.

"We both need to get a few hours' sleep," he said. "I'll take the couch and you can have the bed."

She walked toward the bedroom but turned at the door. "Come with me. Just to sleep together like before." Those big green eyes studied him as she reached her hand out toward him.

There was nothing he wanted more than to curl up with her in his bed. But with his anger and frustration so close to the surface, he couldn't discount the fact that he might wake up swinging. The thought of Bree being the recipient of his night terrors made him break out into a cold sweat.

"Never mind," she said quickly, misreading his hesitation, hand falling back to her side. "You don't have to."

Damn it, he'd rather never sleep again than see that wounded look in her eyes from something he'd done.

He stepped toward her. "I want to. Trust me, there's nothing I want more. But… I just don't want to take a chance on waking you up if I get called back in to Risk Peak early." That was at least a partial truth.

The haunted look fell away from her eyes, and a shy smile broke on her face. "I don't mind. I'll take a shorter amount of sleep if it means I get to sleep next to you."

He would have given her anything in the world to keep that sweet smile on her face. He took her hand, and they walked into the bedroom together.

They took turns changing into sleep clothes in the bathroom, then got into the bed together. The act was so innocent and yet so intimate.

Tanner rolled over onto his side and pulled Bree's back against his front. He breathed in the sweet scent of her hair as her head rested in the crook of his elbow. His other arm wrapped loosely around her waist.

She was out within minutes, her smaller body relaxing against him, trusting him to shelter and protect her while she slept. Tanner wouldn't betray that trust, even if that meant protecting her against himself.

Besides, sleeping was overrated when he could be awake and feel every curve that had been haunting his dreams for months pressed against him.

Definitely worth it.

Chapter Seven

"Coffee?"

The fact that Ronnie was already at Tanner's desk with a cup of the steaming brew right under his nose before Tanner even realized he was in the room was testament to Tanner's exhaustion.

It had been a hell of a week. He'd spent all day every day working the Newkirk murder case. Running into dead end after dead end.

And then night after night near Bree, loving being around her but trying not to let her get too close. It was a fine line he was walking with her. They needed to have a long conversation about his PTSD as soon as this case was done.

Because there was no way he was going to be able to keep his hands off her for much longer.

Tanner took the cup from Ronnie and nearly scalded himself as he swallowed a gulp. "I was looking over the suspect list again, hoping something might jump out at me this time."

Ronnie grabbed the tennis ball that rested on Tanner's desk and began bouncing it. Bounce the ball as they bounced around ideas. They'd been doing it for as long as they'd been working in this building together.

"Maybe Whitaker will have some insight after talking to Newkirk's family again."

Tanner nodded. At least the other cop was out of their hair. He'd finally left yesterday after being in Risk Peak for three days.

The few details they had about the murder were set out in the case file on Tanner's desk. Joshua Newkirk had been stabbed in the back six times. He'd definitely been wrapped and transported into Bree's yard. The crime lab team had not found any traces of blood anywhere around the body. So there was no way he could've stumbled into her yard of his own accord.

Whitaker had not taken Tanner's insistence that Bree was innocent at face value. Only after thoroughly investigating any possible ties between her and Newkirk and coming up empty had Whitaker deemed her cleared. He'd even brought her in for questioning, which Tanner chalked up to just wanting to piss him off.

He set down his coffee cup and held up his hand so Ronnie could toss him the ball. "Why Bree's place? That's the only thing about this that doesn't sit right with me. Why dump the body in Bree's yard?"

Ronnie nodded. "It's not like there's any shortage of people who might want to kill Newkirk. Guy has enemies all over the state. But nothing to do with her."

Tanner bounced the ball back to him. "And he had no real ties to Risk Peak. I was part of the group who arrested him, but I was helping to work the case up north. I didn't even have a major role in any of it."

Ronnie flipped the ball back and forth between his hands. "Yeah, I don't get it, either. I'm hoping Whitaker comes up with something after today."

Tanner sighed. "As long as it doesn't mean he has to come spend three more days here."

"Maybe we could start a pool to guess how many times in a day Whitaker will say the words *Dallas* or *big city*." Ronnie tossed the ball back to him.

He chuckled. "I'd be down for a piece of that action."

"Is Bree doing okay? I can't blame her for not wanting to move back into her apartment. Hell, Cindy would make us move to an entirely new place altogether if a body showed up in our yard."

"Bree's doing good. I don't think she'll have any problem moving back into her apartment. I just want to give her however much time she needs." Tanner set the ball back on his desk.

He'd brought up the topic of moving back into Risk Peak very casually with her yesterday. He didn't want her to feel like he was forcing her away from the ranch.

It would probably be best for her to move back to town. That way she wouldn't have to drive so far to get to work every day, and he could get a good night's sleep in his own bed without having to worry about hurting her.

But hell if he wanted that. He liked having her on the ranch. Definitely because he knew she was safe, but also because he liked having her around. For meals. For coffee in the morning out on the porch. For watching her play with that damned puppy.

But he couldn't go on the way he'd been going. He was way past burning the candle at both ends—his life was more of a roaring bonfire at both ends. He wasn't getting the sleep he needed, and knowing that Bree was wondering about the distance he kept between them ate at him.

Definitely time for a talk about what had happened to him on that undercover op three years ago. How it had affected and changed him. How PTSD might be something he had to live with for the rest of his life.

But it was something he hated to talk about. Just ask Dr. Michalski. He'd been trying to drag details out of Tanner for three years.

Tanner also didn't want to talk about it with her since Bree had known such pain in her own young life. He didn't want to add to her burden by asking her to help carry his trauma also.

But not talking wasn't going to make it go away. Bree was part of his life now. The biggest and most important part. If he couldn't get his PTSD under control, then it was something that he had to share with her so she understood what was going on.

But damn it, he wished he could be someone who just came to her with no baggage. She deserved that. Deserved someone who could help her carry her own.

"Until we hear from Whitaker, I'm just going to put the Newkirk case on the back burner."

Tanner looked up at Ronnie. "Yeah. Nothing we can do."

"Also, high on the fun scale…we've promised Mr. Dunwoody that we would stake out his auto shop over the next week and try to discover who's vandalizing him. So I'm going to be out there for the graveyard shift tonight."

Dunwoody's auto repair shop was on the southeast edge of the county, in the middle of nowhere. Much to Mr. Dunwoody's chagrin, someone kept breaking into his shop and painting rainbows everywhere. Mr. Dunwoody threatened to wait for it to happen again with his shotgun ready, but Tanner had talked him into letting them try to catch the vandals first. Especially since it was probably teenagers from the nearby high school.

"Great. I guess I'm lucky and get tomorrow night's shift, then."

Ronnie rolled his eyes. "Maybe we'll get lucky and I'll catch them tonight. Pacify Mr. Dunwoody."

Ronnie gave a little salute and walked out of the office. It was time for Tanner to go also. All the stuff involving Newkirk, Mr. Dunwoody or any of Risk Peak's other problems would have to wait. Even the hard talk he needed to have with Bree would have to wait.

Tonight he was leaving this behind. Taking Bree to possibly his favorite place on earth. It was exactly what he needed, and he was looking forward to it. Tonight would be the opposite of what the rest of his week had been. It would be fun, relaxed, easy.

TONIGHT WAS GOING to be a total disaster.

Bree sat in the living room of Tanner's house, smoothing her palms along her skirt. It was a cute skirt, a flowy navy blue with little white flowers. It came down to just above her knees and looked great with the matching white blouse. Tanner had loved it when she'd worn it for a date a couple of weeks ago, but now she just wanted to rip it off and throw it away.

Of course, that probably had less to do with the outfit and more to do with the fact that Tanner was taking her to have dinner with his family. How could this go any way but poorly?

Before she could think of an excuse not to go, Tanner pulled up.

The way his breath whistled out between his teeth and he stared at her made her feel better. But only for a moment. "You look absolutely edible."

Whatever argument she was about to make to try to get out of dinner disappeared when he stalked toward her. That was the only word for it: *stalked*. Like he was a predator and she was his prey.

And he had every intention of eating her up.

It should scare her, make her wary, but all it did was light up the most feminine parts of her.

He was on her in just a second, one strong arm wrapping around her hips and spinning her until she was pressed up against the living room wall. He pressed up against her, and all thoughts fled from her head when he claimed her lips.

His mouth was demanding as he tilted his head, moving hers with it, giving him the angle he wanted. She moaned as his tongue traced the seam of her lips, and she opened for him. The kiss deepened, his tongue sliding over hers, tasting her. Claiming her.

When his hand fisted her skirt, sliding it up, and she felt his fingers skim along the outside of her thigh, she pressed herself closer. Trying to concentrate on the kiss was impossible with the lines his fingers were trailing up and down her hip and thigh.

"Damn it." He was breathing as hard as she was as he pulled away a few minutes later, his forehead dropping against hers. "We've got to stop this or we're going to be late and my mother will kill me. I've got to change and shave. My five o'clock shadow is a little out of control."

She reached up and touched his cheek. "I like your scruff. It's sexy." It made him look a little dangerous.

His hand covered hers on his cheek. "We met because of this scruff, you know. I caught you shoplifting in the drugstore because Mr. Vanover keeps my special razor refills in the back aisle. If he didn't, I probably never would've been back there or seen you."

She ran her fingernails along the short whiskers. "I'm

glad you caught me," she whispered. "It's the best thing that ever happened to me."

Heat seemed to pool in his soft brown eyes. The hand that wasn't covering hers on his cheek wrapped around her waist, anchoring her against him.

She could feel the hardness of him pressed up against her. For just a second she was tempted to throw caution to the wind and see if she could seduce him into staying. But she quickly pushed the thought aside. She didn't want their first time to be because she had emotionally manipulated him in order to get out of a dinner.

Not to mention she didn't know how to seduce a man anyway.

He groaned and pulled back. "You're going to be the death of me."

"Is that a good thing or bad thing?"

"The very best of things. Now, you wait right here five minutes. It's time for the most important people in my life to get to know each other better."

Chapter Eight

Bree wanted to run; she really did. She wanted to run when Tanner made it back to the living room four and a half minutes later looking mouthwatering himself in jeans and a button-down shirt.

She definitely wanted to run when they pulled up to his mother's house thirty minutes after that.

Bree had met all of Tanner's family before. Noah at the ranch, of course. Mrs. Dempsey and Tanner's sister, Cassandra, came to town sometimes and to the Sunrise. It was impossible not to have met them in a town the size of Risk Peak. But this was the first time she was facing them as Tanner's girlfriend.

Grasping the box filled with Mrs. Andrews's lemon pie from the Sunrise Diner, she walked stiffly with him toward the door.

He slid an arm around her shoulders and pulled her close, kissing her temple. "You're going to do great. They're going to love you."

Bree was not nearly as sure about either of those things. This situation was pretty much her worst nightmare—a small group where she was expected to interact and banter wittily.

So basically to act like a normal person with normal personal interaction skills.

Yeah, this was not going to go well.

Dinner actually went by without her making any terrible faux pas. Between Tanner and Cassandra's constant bickering, with Noah and Cassandra's husband, Graham, occasionally chiming in, there wasn't much conversation that was expected from Bree. Every once in a while, Mrs. Dempsey would try to bring her brood under control, but it was easy to see that the fighting was in good fun. Graham and Cassandra's three kids, all between the ages of eight and twelve, ate as fast as they could then begged to be excused to go back out to the fishing pond. Cassandra agreed, sending them with the cookies she'd baked.

As soon as they were gone, she turned back to the adults at the table. "I'm no idiot. I made cookies for the kids so there's more pie for us."

"Damn it, I thought I was the smartest one in this family," Tanner muttered.

When everyone got up and started carrying their dishes into the kitchen, Bree grabbed hers and followed suit.

"How are you enjoying living on the ranch?" Mrs. Dempsey asked. "It's always been too isolated for my tastes. Is it the same for you? It must be much different than Kansas City."

Bree's life in Kansas City had been pretty isolated also. She'd been surrounded by people, but still alone.

"No, I actually like the isolation. Sometimes a lot of people can be a little too much for me."

"Amen to that," Noah muttered. "Give me horses over people any day."

Tanner smiled and kissed her on the top of the head as he passed by with some dishes.

"Yeah, but what's it like living with my idiot

brother?" Cassandra elbowed Tanner as she walked into the kitchen.

Bree wasn't sure what to say. They weren't really living together. Would Mrs. Dempsey think Bree was some sort of freeloader? "I'm only living there because of the crime scene at my house and the puppy."

Cassandra grinned as she and Tanner sat back down. "Not if Tanner has anything to say about it."

Bree could feel heat rising in her cheeks. She had no idea what she was supposed to say to that. "Um…"

"Ow!" Cassandra glared at Tanner. "Mom, Tanner just pinched me under the table."

Mrs. Dempsey turned to them. "You two behave. Bree, why don't we leave the infants alone and go cut the pie."

They could hear Cassandra and the boys yelling and laughing as they left.

"Are they really arguing?" Bree asked.

Mrs. Dempsey rolled her eyes. "Cassandra is the baby. She likes to stir up trouble when both her brothers are here. Do you have siblings?"

"No, it was just me." She'd barely even had a mom growing up.

Mrs. Dempsey began cutting the pie. "My son doesn't bring someone home for a family dinner lightly. He's quite smitten with you."

"I… I…" Some days Bree wasn't sure he was. For the past days, even though she'd lived in the same house as him, he'd seemed to keep himself so distant. Not like he resented having her there, but like she was a guest who he liked but wanted to keep a respectful distance from.

But then today…that kiss against the wall. There had been nothing like that all the other days. Nothing like that, ever. Where he'd kissed her like he was about to lose control.

And she'd loved it. She could still feel the ghost of his fingers on her outer thigh.

But was Tanner *smitten* with her, like his mother suggested? "I don't know. Sometimes, I just don't know."

Mrs. Dempsey looked up from the pie and studied Bree. "Tanner has his own demons—pretty significant ones—and his own way of handling them."

"He does?" He was so laid-back and friendly. He seemed so likable and approachable. It had never really occurred to her that he might have demons like her.

"He doesn't talk to you about stuff?"

Bree shook her head. "Some. But no, not stuff like that."

Mrs. Dempsey's tone hadn't been judgmental in any way, but the words themselves made Bree recognize once again that maybe she wasn't meeting Tanner's needs. Maybe that was why they still hadn't slept together.

Mrs. Dempsey reached over and squeezed Bree's arm. "He's protective of you. I can't blame him—you've got something special that makes him want to take care of you. To fight all your battles for you. Tanner's dad felt that way about me."

Mrs. Dempsey didn't look like someone who needed protecting. She looked like she could fight her own battles.

"Of course, I had to set Clifford straight pretty early on in our relationship. Because it was never going to be enough for me—or for him—to let him wrap me in cotton wool. It is enough for some women and some relationships, but it wasn't what either Clifford or I needed. Is it what you need, Bree?"

Bree's answer was immediate. "No. I've been taking care of myself for a long time. Probably longer than I should've. I'm strong."

Mrs. Dempsey smiled at her. "I believe that. You've definitely got a core of steel. You're probably going to need to convince Tanner that you're strong enough to be what he needs, though."

What did Tanner need? Bree wasn't sure. She might've asked Mrs. Dempsey if shouting hadn't started from the dining room.

"We want pie! We want pie!"

Mrs. Dempsey sighed and grinned. "Looks like the natives are getting restless. Shall we?"

All of the Dempsey siblings began eyeing the pie in Mrs. Dempsey's hand as soon as she walked in the room.

"Hey, Mom," Tanner said, innocence all but dripping from his voice. "Is there any pie left in the box, you know, for after we're done? Asking for a friend."

Mrs. Dempsey's eyes narrowed. "If I say yes, are you going to forget every manner I ever taught you?"

"No, ma'am," all three Dempsey siblings and Graham responded at the same time.

She just rolled her eyes. "Then yes, there's one piece left."

Bree's jaw dropped as Tanner, Noah and Graham accepted their pie and began scarfing it down. She glanced over at Cassandra, but she was eating hers at a more humanlike rate. She shrugged. "I gave up my horse in this race when I got married. I might've been able to outeat one of my brothers, but there was no way to beat them and Graham. Although sometimes if I promise hubby here sexual favors he'll give me some of the pie if he wins." She wagged her eyebrows. Graham gave her a thumbs-up with one hand and kept piling in pie with the other.

Bree just smiled, watching the eating with wonder. "Tanner tried to explain the whole pie thing to me once. But really you have to see it in person to truly understand."

As soon as the men finished their pie—within seconds of each other—they made comically polite excuses before rushing toward the kitchen. This entire process was obviously a time-honored tradition.

Cassandra and Mrs. Dempsey just shook their heads, both eating their pie at a much more leisurely pace.

"So," Cassandra said. "How are you liking waiting tables at the Sunrise Diner?"

"Cass," Mrs. Dempsey said quietly.

Cassandra shrugged. "No harm in me talking to her about it."

Bree didn't mind talking about her job. Did Mrs. Dempsey think she was sensitive about it?

"I like it. Dan and Cheryl have always been very supportive."

"Do you miss working with computers?" Cassandra asked.

Bree stared down at her pie. Tanner probably hadn't told his family very much about her past. This conversation had turned stressful amazingly quickly. What was the most appropriate way to answer Cassandra's question?

She brought a piece of pie to her mouth, more to buy herself time than anything else. How did she feel about computers? Pinpointing it wasn't easy.

"It's complicated," she finally said.

"How so?" Cassandra asked.

"Cass…" Mrs. Dempsey said again.

"I'm not doing any harm, Mom. Just trying to understand."

Bree was somehow causing tension between Cassandra and her mother. She didn't want that. "I'm good with computers, but because of some of the stuff that happened when I was a kid, they sometimes hold triggers for me."

Cassandra nodded, her eyes narrowing. "Do you think you'll ever work with them again?"

Bree shifted in her chair. She wasn't sure why Cassandra was asking her that. Were they worried she might do something illegal and drag Tanner down with her? They had to know that she had ties to the Organization. Did they think she was involved with the evil stuff they'd done?

Before Bree could think of what to say, Cassandra continued. "I'm a hairdresser by trade. I have my cosmetology license."

Bree blinked at the change in subject. "Oh. I've never seen you working in town."

"I don't, at least not very often anymore. I stay home with the kids now. But I'm starting a part-time project. A mission, sort of."

The guys came back in from the kitchen, all three of them grinning but looking a little disheveled. "We shared."

"Is my kitchen still in one piece?" Mrs. Dempsey raised one brow.

"Yes, ma'am," all three said dutifully.

"I was just telling Bree about the shelter," Cassandra said. "I had an idea and wanted to get her opinion."

Tanner sat in the chair next to Bree and put his arm

along the back, playing with the hair at her nape. Everyone in his family noticed the possessive touch, but none of them seemed upset about it. That was good, right? It meant they liked her?

"What did you want Bree's opinion about?" Tanner asked.

Cassandra ignored his question and looked at Bree. "I'm part of a privately funded group in Grand County that is starting a women's shelter. We are just far enough outside Denver to help women from there trying to get out of domestic violence situations."

Bree nodded, still not quite understanding what opinion Cassandra wanted from her, but if it was enthusiasm for this venture, Bree could definitely give that. "That sounds amazing."

"A friend of ours in Colorado Springs—" Cassandra gestured between herself and Tanner "—Keira Weber, started one there. Not only is it a safe place for women to stay, she teaches them a trade, how to cut and style hair."

Bree nodded. That was a great idea, too. Logical. Practical. It not only helped the women get back on their feet, it provided them a means to provide for themselves long-term. "It sounds like a very noble venture, and a smart way of going about it."

Cassandra smiled. "I wanted to get your opinion about offering some basic computer classes to these women. Providing them skills that would be most useful in an office workplace."

That was also a good idea. Bree was just about to say so when Cassandra continued. "And I wanted to see if you'd be interested in teaching the classes."

Bree jerked ramrod straight and stared at her for

a moment before a slightly hysterical laugh fell from
her lips.

That was a terrible idea. She would be a horrible
teacher. Standing up in front of a group of people, trying to explain things? Definitely not a good plan.

She glanced down at her hands. But…these would
be women who needed help. People who were like her,
or how she'd been when she first wandered into Risk
Peak. Alone, desperate, broke. Their situation wouldn't
be exactly the same, of course, but still… Similar.

Could she do it? Could she figure out a way to help
these women the way people in Risk Peak had helped
her?

A clanging of a plate against another brought her attention back to the table. Cassandra had stood up and
was stacking the remaining pie plates on the table.

"Cass," Tanner said. "You should've talked to me
about this first."

Cassandra turned to Bree. "Sorry you think the
idea of women learning computer skills is laughable. I
thought maybe you could see the bigger picture."

"No, that's not what I meant." Bree gave a panicked
look at Tanner before turning back to Cassandra. "I *do*
think it's a good idea."

"Cass, you don't have all the facts here," Tanner said.
His phone buzzed at his waist, and he grabbed it and
looked down at it. "Damn it. This is the station. Gotta
take it."

Tanner walked out of the room, leaving Bree with
his family.

"Cassandra, I…"

"You know what? Don't worry about it." Cassandra
took the plates and walked into the kitchen. Graham
followed her in with an apologetic shrug.

"Just ignore her," Noah said. "That's what we do."

Mrs. Dempsey reached over and patted Bree's arm. "Don't worry about it, honey. Cassandra is very passionate and her heart is in the right place, but she doesn't always think everything through."

"I wasn't trying to say the *idea* was bad, just the idea of me teaching it may not be so great."

The older woman smiled. "We'll talk to her and explain. Nobody wants you to do anything you're uncomfortable with."

Bree almost laughed again but caught herself. If they knew she was uncomfortable just having a regular conversation like this, they'd probably think she was an idiot.

But before Cassandra came back in and Bree could try to explain her communication faux pas, Tanner entered the room.

"Sorry, Mom. I'm going to have to cut things short. Ronnie has some sort of food poisoning, and we promised Mr. Dunwoody we'd scope out his shop tonight. Try to figure out who is vandalizing it."

Bree all but jumped out of her chair. Leaving seemed like a great option, since she'd already ruined the evening.

Tanner hugged his family, and Cassandra caught Bree just before they went out the door.

"Listen, I hate it when my husband is all logical and stuff, but he pointed out that I blindsided you. And he's right. That wasn't fair."

Bree nodded rapidly. "I do think it's an excellent idea. I just don't think I'm a good teacher. You could do much better."

Cassandra smiled. "Actually, I don't think we could

do better. Tanner says you're a genius with a computer. And he doesn't throw that word around lightly."

Bree just shrugged.

Cassandra grabbed her hand and gave it a squeeze. "Just think about it. What you know and could teach these women could make a huge difference in their lives. Not only because of what you would teach them, but because you understand some of what they're going through. You're right—a number of people could teach them computer skills. But it's *you* who could really make a difference."

Chapter Nine

Tanner woke up the next morning—he glanced over at the clock, nope, the next *afternoon*—feeling better after a few solid hours of sleep.

He'd stayed outside Dunwoody's shop until just after 4:00 a.m. There had been absolutely nothing going on near there, and despite multiple cups of coffee, Tanner had been falling asleep in his vehicle. Finally, he'd just decided to give up and head home. Evidently the wicked rainbow painters weren't out that night.

He'd hoped to catch Bree here, but she'd already gone to work, which was probably for the best. After that kiss yesterday afternoon, Tanner didn't know if he could lie in the same bed with her again and not do anything about it.

He wasn't a man given to fancifulness, but the skin of her thigh had been so soft he could damn near write poetry about it.

Seeing her around his family hadn't cooled his ardor, either. He liked watching her with them, seeing how she fit in, even when she was uncomfortable and unsure of herself thanks to Cassandra. His sister could be a lot for anyone to handle, and he wanted to wring her neck for dropping the computer-teaching bomb on Bree.

Bree might have gotten upset initially, but they'd

spent the entire ride home talking about what computer skills would most help the women at the shelter. Bree had a basic syllabus all but planned out by the time they'd gotten back to the ranch. It was easy for him to see that, despite her hesitation, she was going to teach the class. Now he just needed to wait for her to realize it, too.

Watching her face her fears and step up to help others was pretty damn amazing. *Bree* was pretty damn amazing.

So yeah, it was probably better she hadn't been there this morning, or else he definitely wouldn't have been keeping his hands off her.

Tanner made himself a sandwich for lunch, washing it down with a big mug of coffee. He was outside checking on Corfu and the pups when Noah came riding up on one of his horses. He got off and quickly put the horse in the corral.

"You expecting company?" Noah asked.

"No." Most people knew better than to come out here without being invited or calling first. Noah was not a people person.

"Looks like one of the Grand County sheriff's vehicles."

Tanner grabbed his phone out of his pocket to see if he'd missed any calls. Nothing. "I have no idea. They haven't tried to contact me."

Noah nodded then faded back into the wooded area surrounding their property, making himself unnoticeable. But Tanner had no doubt he'd be out in a second if he was needed.

Less than a minute later, the vehicle arrived outside Tanner's door. Noah had been right—it was a Grand

County SUV. But it wasn't any of Tanner's regular colleagues who was driving; it was Richard Whitaker.

"Dempsey," he said as he got out of the vehicle.

Tanner raised an eyebrow. "You lost, Whitaker? Dallas is about eight hundred miles south of here."

The other man pointed to Tanner's cup of coffee. "Just now waking up?"

"As a matter of fact, yes. The stakeout I was on last night didn't amount to anything, so I left. I called in that I was going home."

Whitaker crossed his arms over his beefy chest. "I know."

For the first time Tanner was a little more worried than confused about Whitaker's appearance at his home. "Why are you here?"

"Sheriff wants to see you in her office."

"Why? Has there been a break in the Newkirk case?"

Whitaker shrugged. "Possibly. I'll let the sheriff talk to you about that. Did you go anywhere else besides your high-crime stakeout?"

Tanner ignored the small-town barb. "No. I'd already put in a full day then came back to work someone else's shift."

"You must've been tired. Why'd you come all the way out here rather than your place in Risk Peak?"

Tanner wasn't going to discuss his relationship with Bree and that he'd wanted to see her. It was none of Whitaker's business. "Why are you asking so many questions? Why are you here at all? The sheriff could've just called me herself and asked me to come in."

Whitaker shrugged. "I'll let the sheriff answer that, too. I'm just here to make sure you get to her with no problems."

That was definitely not a good sign.

Tanner gave a curt nod. "I'll follow you in."

Less than an hour later, he was sitting across from Sheriff Duggan in her office. She'd invited Whitaker in also and then closed the door.

"I'll cut straight to the chase, Tanner." She walked back and took a seat in the office chair behind her desk. The same chair that had once been Tanner's father's when he'd been sheriff. "Peter Anders is dead."

A low curse fell from Tanner's mouth, although he could admit he wasn't terribly surprised. Anders had been in and out of prison for the entire eight years Tanner had known him. Tanner had been the one to arrest him more than once.

He scrubbed a hand over his face. "When? How?"

Sheriff Duggan looked over at Whitaker before bringing her eyes back to Tanner. "Roughly nine hours ago. The body was found about an hour later. He was stabbed multiple times in the back."

"Like Newkirk," Tanner said.

Whitaker crossed his arms over his chest. "Yeah, exactly like Newkirk."

Tanner shifted to look at him. "I hope you're not considering Bree as a suspect again." Because Tanner damn well wasn't going to stand for it.

Whitaker's eyes narrowed. "No, *Bree* isn't our suspect."

The implication was clear, but Tanner turned back to the sheriff, wanting to make sure he understood. "What exactly is Dallas PD implying over here?"

Before she could respond, Whitaker spoke again. "Is there anybody who can verify your whereabouts last night?"

"I was on a stakeout at Dunwoody's auto shop in the

southeast corner of the county. They've had some vandals. We think it's high school kids and wanted to put a stop to it before Dunwoody decided to take matters into his own hands with buckshot."

"Anyone see you out there?" Whitaker demanded.

"No. There was nothing happening, so I went home." Tanner looked over at the sheriff. "I called everything in. It's all logged."

Whitaker shifted his weight in the chair, looking over at Tanner, eyes narrowed. "You went all the way back to your ranch when you could've just gone to your place in town."

Damn it, Tanner still wasn't going to drag Bree's name into this. Especially since he hadn't actually seen her this morning and she couldn't provide an alibi anyway. "Yes. I have a place in town, but the ranch is my home. Everybody knows that."

"It's also a lot more isolated," Whitaker quipped. "You're quite a bit less likely to be seen there. If, say, you needed to wash up or something."

Tanner jerked out of his chair, nearly knocking it over in his fury. "What exactly are you saying?"

"Hey, I'm just—"

"Enough, Whitaker," the sheriff cut in.

Tanner ran a hand through his hair, getting himself under control, but he was too agitated to sit back down. "Fine. I get that someone else whose arrest I was involved in is dead, and that sucks. But to jump straight into accusing me of washing blood off my hands? What the hell?"

The sheriff held out one hand toward him. "You're right, Tanner. And I don't believe you had anything to do with Anders's death."

"Her belief is the only reason you're not in cuffs in an interview room rather than in an office," Whitaker muttered.

Sheriff Duggan slammed her palm down on her desk then pointed at Whitaker. "You watch it. The Dempsey reputation is multigenerational and stellar. So you can either present the facts with respect and let your colleague provide his refutation or you can get the hell out of my office."

Whitaker shrank a little in his chair. "Yes, ma'am."

And somehow, even though it should make him feel better, that exchange made Tanner even more concerned.

"Sit down, Tanner," she said. "Tell us about your relationship with Peter Anders."

He rubbed a hand down his face as he sat. "I first arrested him eight years ago. He's been in and out of prison since then. Tends toward violent crimes. Assault. Assault and battery. Has—*had*—a pretty nasty temper."

"And like Newkirk, you also reported to Anders's parole board that you thought he shouldn't be let out." Whitaker's more reasonable tone didn't reassure him.

He met the sheriff's eye. "Look, I'll be honest—I do that with a lot of people. I get these requests for my opinion from review boards, and I give it honestly. Most of the time I do think the criminals should serve closer to their full sentence. A lot of times it feels like we're fighting a losing battle if the prison system just dumps them back on the streets too soon. But..."

"But what?" she asked.

Tanner sat forward and leaned his arms on his knees. "Peter got out almost a year ago after his latest charge—a bar brawl where he put a guy in a coma. But this time Peter seemed different. He'd found religion or something. I don't know. I really thought he was trying to change."

"So you've been in contact with him?" Sheriff Duggan asked.

Tanner shrugged one shoulder. "Some. Trying to help him get a job and get away from the people and situations that always seem to land him back in prison."

"You ever been in Anders's car?" Whitaker asked.

Tanner nodded. "Yes, a couple of weeks ago. He wouldn't come inside the station to talk, so I went out to him."

Whitaker gave a tiny snort of disbelief. "Convenient."

Tanner turned to glare at the man. "If anything, that shows I wasn't trying to kill him."

Sheriff Duggan nodded. "I can see that. But here's the real problem. We found this." She tapped on an electronic tablet then spun it around so Tanner could see it. "This is a copy of all Anders's texts for the last few days. We need you to address one in particular, Tanner."

Tanner looked down at the one she was pointing to.

Peter: I can't get rid of this Dempsey cop. He's on my ass all the time.

Bugaboo2: Just tell him to go to hell.

Peter: Cop is scary. He's threatening me. Seriously. So I'm a no-go for this weekend. Sorry.

Tanner tensed. "That's not what it looks like. I knew some of his old friends were pressuring him back into the lifestyle he was trying to get out of. I told him to use me as an excuse to say no."

Whitaker raised an eyebrow. "Convenient that it's your word against someone who can't say anything further."

Tanner turned to the sheriff. With every passing minute, this was looking worse and worse for him. "Do I need a lawyer? I feel a little like I need a lawyer."

The sheriff shook her head. "You're not being formally charged. I already talked to Ryan Fletcher this morning. He has no interest in pursuing this case at this time. Says it's all circumstantial. And, like me, he doesn't think you had anything to do with it."

Tanner nodded.

Whitaker all but threw up his hands. "We've got Dempsey's fingerprints in the victim's car. A text from the vic claiming Dempsey was threatening him. And he's got no alibi. *Worse* than no alibi."

Tanner's eyebrows narrowed. "What the hell is worse than no alibi?"

He expected Sheriff Duggan to jump in, too, but she didn't. When he glanced over, her lips were tight.

"Worse than no alibi is that the place you were supposedly staking out was vandalized last night," Whitaker said. "Guess you missed it, if you were even there at all. Of course, *not* being there would've given you plenty of time to drive to get to Anders, even if he was across the county."

"Or I stayed at the Dunwoody shop like I said, and the vandals came in after I left around four in the morning."

Whitaker held both hands out in front of him and shrugged. "Just sayin'. Anybody else would already be in a holding cell."

"But we're not dealing with someone else," Sheriff

Duggan interjected. "Tanner has no motive for killing either Newkirk or Anders."

"Except they were both violent criminals that kept getting put back on the streets," Whitaker said in a low, reasonable voice. That voice was so much more dangerous than his yelled threats. "Dempsey said it himself. Sometimes you feel like you're fighting a losing battle. Maybe he decided to do something about it."

Sheriff Duggan steepled her fingers in front of her lips. "Like I said, I don't think you did this. But until we get it sorted out, you're going to need to go on admin leave. I need your badge and your gun, Tanner."

He remained silent, not even glancing at Whitaker as he took both off his belt and slid them across the desk.

The sheriff took them and put them in a drawer. "I still need you to schedule a visit with Dr. Michalski. He told me you've missed the last couple of scheduled sessions."

Tanner gritted his teeth. "I was busy."

Whitaker gave a slight cough/laugh. Tanner wanted to punch him in the face but refrained, knowing it wouldn't do anything but get him more admin leave. He stood.

"We'll be in touch soon, Tanner," the sheriff said. "Give us a chance to work on your behalf. Take this time to get caught up on your appointments with Dr. Michalski and any reports you're behind on. That way when the dust clears, you're able to hit the ground running. We're all on the same side."

Tanner gave a terse nod then walked out into the hallway, still wanting to punch someone.

Finding Dr. Michalski standing right there did not diminish that feeling.

"What are you, waiting for me to come out of the principal's office?"

"You missed our last two sessions." The psychiatrist's expression and tone were even. The way they always were.

But seriously, did the guy have his ear at the door?

Tanner stuffed his hands in his pockets, conspicuously aware of the lack of familiar weight his gun and badge usually placed on his waist. "Sorry, Doc. I had real police work to do. Thought that took priority over rehashing past events in my life that can't ever be changed."

"I understand police work, Tanner. And I would've thought nothing of it if you'd just rescheduled like you're required to do. The rules apply to you, too."

Tanner grimaced. Because damn it, the man—and his goddamned even tone—was right. But hell if he was going to admit that right now, when he'd just basically been told that while the sheriff didn't think he was guilty, she didn't think he was innocent enough to keep wearing the badge.

"Yeah, I'll get around to it."

Dr. Michalski just nodded. "Be careful. That sort of arrogance can get you killed in this line of work. We work together as a team or everything crumbles quickly."

Tanner took his hand out of his pocket and rubbed his eyes. The thing was, he totally agreed with the doctor. Mental health was important. Just as important as physical health. The country was figuring that out the hard way.

The work he'd done with Dr. Michalski had helped him come to grips with some of what had happened in that warehouse three years ago. Tanner didn't always enjoy the company of the other man, but he had to admit their sessions had been valuable.

"Fine," he mumbled, brushing past the doctor. He couldn't do it right now. He just needed to get out of here.

"Make an appointment," the doctor said in a just slightly louder but still even tone. "And keep it this time."

Chapter Ten

The man couldn't keep the smile from his face.

And why should he even try? There was something downright delightful about knowing Tanner Dempsey was on his way down.

There wasn't enough info against him to arrest Dempsey—*yet*. But the seeds of doubt had been planted in the minds that counted in the most delicious way possible.

How had it felt to Dempsey to be summoned from his own home to the sheriff's office, like the criminal that he was?

How did it feel to Mr. High and Mighty to know that people doubted him? To realize they were starting to see the crack in his veneer and would soon know him for what he really was: a fraud and a lying, judgmental bastard.

Oh, and a killer.

How did it feel when the pedestal he'd placed himself on started to show signs of rust and decay? Was he unable to sleep at night, knowing he was going to fall?

Did he worry when he realized the blood on his hands and deceit in his heart would become visible to everyone soon?

Including the woman who occupied Dempsey's every

thought. He'd had the gall to move her in with him, even knowing what he was.

But no worries. She would see the facts soon, along with everyone else. No one would be able to ignore the truth any longer. She would watch as Dempsey was finally sentenced for his sins and spent the rest of his life rotting in jail.

She would be sad, but maybe the man could step up and comfort her. That would be a beautiful full circle.

So yes, the man's smile was huge. He had to keep his colleagues from seeing it and asking him what was going on.

Because he just might tell them.

Justice was finally about to be served.

Chapter Eleven

When Bree pulled up to the ranch, she found Tanner chopping wood. He'd chopped enough wood in the past three days to last all of Risk Peak through the winter.

Being on suspension obviously did not sit well with Captain Sexy Lips.

He'd explained that the sheriff didn't actually think Tanner had committed the two murders, so that was good. It was just a matter of staying out of the way while the other people in the department worked the case. But he definitely did not like being kept in the dark about what was going on with the investigation.

For the past three days, the fact that she had no idea how to help him had eaten at her. Just another glaring spotlight on her lack of interpersonal relationship skills. Usually it was *him* helping *her* figure out how to sort through feelings. But for the last three days, the shoe had been on the other foot.

Not a good fit.

Bree had tried her best to cheer him up or take his mind off his problems, but she didn't really know how. Wasn't sure what was best or appropriate.

Your mind works like a mainframe.

She could hear Michael Jeter's—head of the organization that had helped her develop her computer skills to the point of genius, and who had also made her life a living hell—voice in her head. But it was nothing short of the truth. She did think analytically, rationally and logically, just like a computer.

Not the way to help someone going through an emotional crisis.

Ironically, it had been her own emotions—feelings of inadequacy and incompetence—that had been blocking her mind from realizing the truth.

Tanner didn't need her to help him emotionally. He needed the part of her brain that worked like a computer. He needed her to help figure out the real killer so he could get back to the job he loved. Emotion had nothing to do with that.

As soon as it had become clear to her, she'd asked the Andrewses for the rest of the day off, and tomorrow as well. She'd gone home and grabbed the computer she generally tried to avoid, the one she hadn't touched since looking up details about owning a puppy last week.

It was time to work the problem. There was no one better at doing that than her.

Tanner turned from the wood he was chopping to look at her as she got out of the car. She tried not to swallow her tongue at the sight of him clad only in a cowboy hat and jeans—chest bare.

She was never going to get tired of looking at him. It was more than just his strong chin and carved jaw that already had a hint of shadow to it even at this hour. More than his broad, powerful shoulders that tapered into trim waist and hips. It was more than those deep brown eyes that seemed to notice everything.

It was all of it. The whole package put together that made up Tanner as a whole.

He walked toward her. She liked the way he walked. Not graceful. Not aggressive, but…powerful.

"You're home early," he said. "It's still midmorning."

She finally tore her eyes away from his torso to look up at his face. "Yeah. I brought pie. It's good at any time, even morning."

He reached over and tucked a strand of hair behind her ear. "Pie is a very distant second to the reason I'm glad you're here."

Her eyes dropped back to his naked chest. She wanted to close the inches that separated them and lick it.

She wanted to get them back to the passionate kisses where he slammed her against the wall. *That* kiss had been leading somewhere she desperately wanted to go.

But there hadn't been any kisses like that since he'd been suspended from the force.

The words were out of her mouth before she could stop them. "I want us to get back to the slamming against the wall, so I brought my computer." She grimaced. That hadn't come out the way she'd meant it to.

He chuckled. "You might have to throw in a little more information for me. I didn't quite follow your brain that time."

She decided to leave out the part about passionate kisses against the wall. Especially when she was a second and a half from licking his chest.

She took a breath. "You're frustrated about being suspended from the force. I can't help much with the emotional part, but I can help you with my computer and my mind."

His eyes narrowed. "Whitaker is on the case. He has experience with this sort of thing. He'll eventually get it figured out."

She rolled her eyes. "The same guy who thought I killed Newkirk? It could take him weeks just to figure out how to get his head out of his ass. I'll never get any more kisses if we're depending on him."

Tanner chuckled again and stepped closer. "I seem to recall kissing you this morning before you went to work."

Oh gosh, why did his sweat smell so good? So clean and male and *Tanner.* "I want the *other* kisses," she whispered. "Like the one before we went to your mom's house."

His brown eyes darkened, and his hand slid down to wrap around her waist, pulling her against him.

Every single part of her insides seemed to clench. *Yes.* This was what she wanted.

But before his lips touched hers, he seemed to withdraw back into himself. His fingers that had been grasping her waist with an almost bruising force a moment ago loosened.

He stepped back, rubbing his hand over his eyes. "Bree—"

She sighed. She'd become used to the distance between them. "I know. You're upset about what's happening, and doing romance with me is the last thing on your mind. That's okay. I—"

His mouth was on hers and she was backed up against the car—just like she'd been against the wall—before she knew what was going on. She gasped, and he took full advantage of it, thrusting deeply into her mouth with his tongue before withdrawing and coaxing hers to play. She sank into the kiss, her mind going blank as his lips ravished hers.

When he finally backed away, all she could do was stare at him.

"*Doing romance*, and doing a hell of a lot more, is always on my mind when it comes to you," he whispered. "Don't ever think I don't want to be around you any way I can get you, no matter what is going on with my job."

"O-okay."

They both stood there for many moments, breathing unsteadily.

"But I know how much your job means to you," she finally said. "And Risk Peak needs you back. So I want to help. Please let me help."

"What did you have in mind?"

She slid over and opened the car door, grabbing her laptop.

"You know I have a computer, right?" he asked. "You don't have to bring yours."

She shrugged. "This one is...better."

He shook his head, a half smile pulling at the corner of his mouth. "I'm not even going to ask."

"Probably a good idea."

He led her inside, and she sat down at the kitchen table, staring at her laptop.

Tanner stayed next to her as she breathed through her anxiety. Opening it up was tough. Her history with computers in a serious way—beyond researching puppy facts—was tied to being physically and emotionally tortured. She had to remind herself that the computer itself couldn't hurt her in any way.

"You okay?" he asked.

"I used it a few months ago when I helped bring down the Organization. This should be quite a bit easier than that."

He crouched down next to her so they were eye to eye. "You had to do that in order to save the world. You don't *have* to do this. I'll be just fine, you know.

Whitaker will eventually crack who really killed those two guys."

"No, I'm okay. I want to do this. The computer can't hurt me. Jeter can't hurt me anymore, either."

He reached over and kissed her knee. "That's the damn truth."

He straightened, and she opened the laptop, allowing it to boot. The first few keystrokes into her search were the most difficult, but then her brain let go of its fear and she dived in.

This was what she was most gifted at in the world.

Gaining access to the Colorado state system to find out more information about Peter Anders and Joshua Newkirk didn't take her long at all.

"I'm going to shower while you work. It's probably better if I don't know too much about what's going on here."

Her fingers continued to fly over the keyboard. "I'm not breaking any laws." *Yet.* "Have you been cutting wood since I left this morning?"

"No. Ironically, I had to go into the main sheriff's office earlier for a couple hours. I had an appointment I couldn't get out of." He paused. "With the police department psychiatrist."

Now her fingers stilled on the keys. "Oh. Because of being on suspension?"

"No. Something else. Something that happened a few years ago. Something you and I should probably talk about."

That didn't sound promising. She looked over at him. "Right now?"

"No. It's not something easily explained."

She nodded. "A complicated past is something I understand. So whenever you're ready."

He kissed the top of her head. "Thank you."

He walked off toward the shower, and Bree found herself staring at the screen without really seeing it. Mrs. Dempsey had been right. Tanner had demons— ones big enough to need required appointments with a psychiatrist years later.

Not that she thought less of him for seeing a psychiatrist. She was very aware she'd be much more emotionally well-adjusted if she'd been able to talk to someone about what she'd gone through.

It just…stung a little that she'd been living under the same roof as Tanner for almost a week—seeing him nearly daily for over a month—and he'd never mentioned an event traumatic enough to need psychiatric care.

What did it say that he hadn't felt like he could even mention that to her? Especially after everything she'd told him about her past.

Bree forced the thought aside. It would have to wait. She needed to focus on the mission in front of her now: discovering whatever she could about Anders and Newkirk. She started with all the legal ways she knew of gaining information and searching public records. Then slid into slightly more morally gray area, but still not technically illegal.

Both Anders and Newkirk had lived colorful and violent lives. Both had had run-ins with the law before they'd gotten arrested for the specific crimes they'd actually gone to jail for. But they didn't seem to have run in the same circles or have known the same people.

Both had spent time in prison, although they hadn't served at the same place at the same time. Both had gotten out of prison earlier than they should have, although Bree couldn't find out why without definitely crossing into the illegal-hacking area.

It was easy to see why Tanner was a suspect. As arresting officer, he definitely was the most obvious link between the two dead men.

It took Bree another two hours of searching—a pretty damn long time given her skills—before she finally found someone else in common. And even then it wasn't easy to spot.

Both Anders and Newkirk had been a cell mate of a Darin Carrico. Newkirk for six months. Anders for less than a week.

It was a weak tie, at best. But it was all Bree could find unless Tanner wanted her to really jump into illegal territory. She doubted he would be comfortable with morally gray, much less morally pitch-black.

Besides shoving a sandwich in front of her at lunch, Tanner had stayed out of her way. He knew what she was like when she was working—he'd seen her in action a few months ago. How focused she stayed. He hadn't bothered her.

She was filtering through sites and databases at a rapid clip and wanted to make sure not to miss anything. But as it became more and more evident she wasn't going to find much of anything online, she admitted that some relationships and associations didn't show up in a computer. Even ghosting through the men's social media accounts hadn't turned up anything to link the two of them. Sometimes there just wasn't a visible electronic trail, even for two people who knew each other.

And if she couldn't find anything except a weak tie to an old cell mate, she could damn well imagine no-

body at the Grand County Sheriff's Department was
going to find much.

She sighed. This did not mean good news for Tanner.

Chapter Twelve

An hour later Bree pushed back from the computer and turned to Tanner. "Okay, I've got bad news and worse news."

"That doesn't sound promising." Tanner held a hand out to her from where he sat on the couch. She stood and walked over to him, smiling as he grabbed her wrist and pulled her down next to him.

"There aren't very many overt ties between Newkirk and Anders. I've pretty much tapped out all legal channels. But if you'll just give the okay, I can—"

His fingers threaded through hers. "No. I don't want you breaking any laws. I didn't kill those men. The circumstances with how it went down were damn unfortunate, but they're not going to charge me. So, let's not do anything illegal."

She nodded. "Okay. Well, we do have one possibility. The only other connection I could find between Newkirk and Anders was that they were both cell mates, albeit very briefly, with a man named Darin Carrico."

"I don't recognize the name."

She stood, pulling Tanner with her over to the laptop at the table. With a couple of keystrokes, she had Carrico's arrest record pulled up.

"Darin Carrico, age twenty-five, arrested for trespassing, burglary and illegal sale of handguns as well as a long list of misdemeanors. He's been in prison for four years and has another three to go."

Tanner leaned over her shoulder to get a better look at Carrico's mug shot. "Yeah, I still don't recognize him."

"Newkirk was his cell mate for six months. Anders was his roomie for five nights."

Tanner let out an audible sigh. "That's a pretty thin connection."

"But it is something. And Carrico is currently incarcerated at Colorado Correctional Center. That's less than an hour away."

"I can't question him in any sort of official capacity. Not while I'm on suspension."

Bree spun around in her chair so she could face him. She'd already researched this, too. "But your badge could get us in, right? That's all we need. If we leave right now, we can catch him today. Otherwise we'll have to wait until this weekend. I know you can't ask him anything official, but at least we could see if he tips his hand in any way."

Maybe this would lead to nothing. Maybe Carrico had nothing to do with it. But if this was something that helped Tanner to feel like he was more in control of his own fate, then it was worth the drive.

It didn't take much to convince Tanner of the plan, and a little over an hour and a half later, they'd made it to Camp George West, the nickname for the Colorado Correctional Center. They were searched, signed in and waiting for Carrico at a table in the large visiting room.

"Why don't you let me do most of the talking," Tanner said, giving her hand a squeeze.

She rolled her eyes. "Do you really think I'm going

to argue with you when you tell me I *don't* have to interact with someone else?"

He chuckled softly and leaned over to kiss her temple. "I guess not."

There was no recognition whatsoever in Carrico's face as a guard escorted him to the table. Since Colorado Correctional was a lower security level, Carrico wasn't in any sort of shackles. He did have on an unattractive orange jumpsuit that hung off his thin frame.

"You guys Jesus people?" Carrico asked as he sat down across from them at the table, his thin lips twisted in a sneer. "Because no offense, but I'm not interested."

"No," Tanner said. "My name is Tanner Dempsey, and this is Bree. We wanted to see if we could ask you a few questions about Joshua Newkirk and Peter Anders."

A dark, bitter look overtook Carrico's face, and he muttered a vile curse. "You're cops. Why the hell are you coming in here like you're visitors?"

Tanner shook his head. "I'm not here in any sort of official capacity. I'm just here to talk."

Carrico leaned back and crossed his arms over his chest. "But you are a cop, right, pig?"

Tanner just shrugged. "I work for the Grand County Sheriff's Department, yes."

"And why exactly should I help you?"

"All I want to know is whether you know Anders and Newkirk. That's all."

Carrico shook his head. "You obviously know that I was cell mates with both of them, or you wouldn't be here."

"You had any contact with them since they got out?"

"Yeah, we're pen pals. I get a perfume-scented letter once a week from both of them." Carrico rolled his eyes. "No, I haven't heard from either one of those bastards, not that I expected to. They weren't my friends. Although, if you run into either of them, ask them who the hell's ass they had to kiss to get their early release."

Bree wondered if Tanner would bring up that no one would be asking them anything since they were dead. That was probably what Bree would've blurted out. But he kept his cool. "Why? You looking to get out early?"

"You kidding me?" Carrico scoffed. "There's no way I think I'll get out early. I just want to stop your cop bastard friends from sending me to Colorado State Pen."

Tanner leaned closer to the table. "Why are you getting sent up to a level-three facility? You get into trouble here? A fight?"

"Hell, no. Look, man, I got a daughter. A little girl. I get to see her twice a week right now, but I won't ever get to see her at a supermax security. You can't take a kid in there. I'm just trying to do my time and get out, but somebody screwed me over."

Bree might not be good at reading interpersonal cues, but Carrico was visibly upset about being sent to this higher-security prison.

"You're in on nonviolent charges, right?" Tanner asked, eyes narrowing. "If you got sentenced here and you haven't done anything to merit being sent up, then there shouldn't be any reason why an appeal won't go through."

"Yeah, well, already tried that, and it didn't work. Somebody has it in for me, and I don't know who or why." Carrico slouched over on the table, smirk on his face. "Grand County, huh? I even talked to your department's shrink when he came here yesterday. Dr. Michael whatever. Thought for a minute he was going to help me, but shouldn't have gotten my hopes up."

Tanner sat up straight. "Wait—are you saying Dr. Craig Michalski was here yesterday? He came to see you?"

"Yep."

Tanner glanced at Bree before turning back to Carrico. Holy crap. Was Michalski the same department psychiatrist Tanner had gone to see this morning? Had Michalski realized the connection between Carrico and the two murder victims? If so, he obviously hadn't mentioned it to Tanner at their appointment.

"What did he say to you?" Tanner asked.

"You both work for the same department. Why don't you ask him?"

Tanner's lips pressed together to a thin line. "Was he asking about Anders and Newkirk?"

"Dude, nobody cares about your boyfriends but you." Carrico turned to Bree. "Honey, he obviously isn't giving you what you need. Sorry I can't help you from in here, but I know some people if you're looking for real men who know how to treat a woman right."

Her skin crawled, and she shrank back into herself as Carrico leered at her. Tanner's palm slammed down on the table. "Eyes on me, jackass."

Carrico held out his hands in front of him in a gesture of—obviously false—submission. "Sorry, Officer."

Tanner visibly got himself under control. "Why don't you tell me what Dr. Michalski was here to talk to you about and I will look into why they are moving you into a higher-security prison. No promises, but if there's been some sort of mistake, I can help rectify that. I can make sure you stay here, where you can have visits with your daughter."

Carrico snorted. "You know what? I don't believe for one second that you're really going to help me. You cops ain't done nothing but screw me over. But you know what? I'll try, just in case—"

"Carrico." A guard walked over, interrupting them. "You've got a visitor. That okay, Deputy, or you want us to have him wait?"

Tanner nodded and a few moments later a man who looked almost exactly like Carrico, except more skinny—hard to believe that was even possible—and pale, walked over to their table. If Bree had been asked which one was in prison just based on looks she would've said this new guy, who was obviously Carrico's brother. Carrico's *sickly and pale* brother.

"Who the hell is this?" the guy asked as he reached over and squeezed Carrico's shoulder.

"This would be Grand County officer of the law Dempsey, and his lady friend."

The new man's eyes narrowed. "Why are you here?"

"Who are you?" Tanner asked.

"I'm Glen, Darin's brother. I'm here twice a week to see him. I don't think you can say the same."

"No. I'll be honest—before this afternoon I wasn't even aware Darin existed. I'm here, completely off duty, to ask him about Joshua Newkirk and Peter Anders."

Glen shook his head. "God, you cops are all the same. Always taking, never giving. You're about to send my brother up to a max security prison. Why the hell should he help you with a damn thing?"

"I've already made my offer to Darin to look into it. I can't make any promises, but maybe there's something that can be done."

Glen just turned to his brother. "Darin, no. We've heard this before. No more help to these bastards until they help you first." The pale man spun to stare at Tanner and Bree. "My brother's done talking to you. Don't come back here. Or I'll be filing a complaint on my brother's behalf."

Tanner stood and Bree stood with him. Tanner turned to Darin. "If you change your mind, look me up. Tanner Dempsey. You have my word that I'll look into this, even if you can't help me with my questions."

Carrico shrugged. "Well, like I said, if Anders or Newkirk have some words of wisdom about who to talk to about stopping this transfer, I'd be glad to hear it."

Tanner said nothing, just led Bree out with a hand at the small of her back.

"Well, that was a bust. Sorry," she said as he opened the door for her and she climbed into the passenger seat.

"Not totally."

"Because you think he might talk to you? Glen was going to allow that over his dead body, which, admittedly, looked like it might be relatively soon."

Tanner shook his head. "No, I doubt I'll hear from him."

"Then how did it help?"

"Well, for one, Darin definitely didn't recognize me when he first saw me. Didn't know my name."

Bree nodded. "Yeah, he would have to be one hell of an actor if he did."

"Also, I don't think Darin knows Newkirk and Anders are dead. Admittedly, he could be playing us, but I honestly don't think he wanted anything more but to ask them who could keep him from going to Colorado State Penitentiary." He scrubbed a hand across his face. "Not that any of this is going to help me get reinstated."

She hated that Tanner looked even more defeated as he started the car and pulled out of the parking area. She'd really wanted this to make a difference.

He grabbed her hand and pulled it up to his lips.

"Thank you for bringing us out here. Even if Darin has nothing to do with what's going on with me, somebody still needs to look into what's going on with him, because the situation doesn't sound right. So good comes out of this no matter what."

Bree's heart gave a little tug. That he would be up to his eyeballs in his own problems and was still going to make it a priority to find justice even for a criminal…

How the heck was she supposed to keep herself from falling in love with him?

Chapter Thirteen

They got back to the ranch and ate dinner, but Bree wasn't done looking into this. If there was one thing all her experience with computer coding had taught her, it was that when the coding led to a dead end, you had to step back until you could find a way around whatever had trapped you.

Carrico seemed to be a dead end, but maybe Bree just needed to find a way around him and see if anything else was there. Perhaps the guy was just what he appeared to be: someone who wanted not to be sent to a supermax prison so he could continue to receive visits from his daughter.

But Bree had spent a big chunk of her life within an organization that had fooled the entire world into thinking they were good and altruistic, when really they were emotionless, sadistic bastards.

Tanner was a good man who wanted to believe the best of everyone. He got that from his parents. Bree had heard the story of how his father had been killed in the line of duty because he'd trusted someone who had then shot him.

She didn't think Tanner was gullible in any way, shape or form. But she was going to look more closely at Carrico before giving him the benefit of the doubt.

Research him impartially and dispassionately to make sure he was truly a dead end and not involved in all of this somehow.

And she wasn't afraid to bend a few laws to do it, regardless of Tanner's opinion.

Her emotional stuntedness was working to her advantage in this case. She didn't give a rat's ass about Carrico's sob story if it meant clearing Tanner's name.

A couple of hours later, she was glad she'd stayed the course, despite Tanner's repeated attempts to get her to put away the computer for the night.

When she found it, she could barely believe her eyes.

"Tanner, I found something."

He looked up from whatever type of sporting event he was watching. Football, maybe? She wasn't good with sports.

"I don't even know what you've been looking for the past two hours."

"I think our friend Carrico may not be as innocent as we thought."

Tanner flipped off the television and walked over to her. "What makes you say that?"

This was where it got a little bit tricky. "Because Carrico is currently in a lower-security prison, he has access to email. It's monitored, but he sent a message to two separate guerrilla mail accounts—which are temporary and completely anonymous addresses—one eight nights ago and one four nights ago."

"The nights before Anders and Newkirk were killed."

Bree nodded.

"What did the emails say?"

"The first one said, Last fall the beautiful flowers made me smile although they soon withered and flew away. The second, Every laugh makes me think of pudding."

"Okay, definitely weird. But the messages don't sound suspicious or dangerous to me."

Bree had recognized the foursquare cipher as soon as she'd read the email. It had taken her a little while to break it, but not very long. "There's a code. A cipher."

Now she had his full attention. "You're sure?"

She turned the screen so he could see the words the highlighted code provided.

Newkirk tomorrow.

She scrolled down so he could see the other one: Anders ASAP.

Tanner let out a low curse. "Who did those messages go to? Is there any way of finding that out?"

"The proxy is anonymous, so I can't get much more information without significantly more illegal effort, and even then it's iffy. It's an anonymous, encrypted email that uses a VPN to reroute and hide the IP address. Sites like these are utilized when people are trying to be…covert."

He collapsed down in the chair next to her, still staring at the screen. "Covert. In other words, illegal."

"Not always. Maybe they're cheating on a spouse or something. But yeah, illegal in this case. I know the words themselves don't prove anything…"

"But the fact that they were sent within hours of both men being killed, and that Carrico knew both of them, is significant. More damning than what they have on me."

She smiled. "That's what I thought, too. That's good, right?"

"It's definitely a start." His eyes narrowed as he looked at her more closely. "You said we can't get the other email without you being *more* illegal? That means even getting this much was illegal."

She shrugged. "Yeah. But just a little. And if it leads us to the real killer then who cares, right?"

"A judge is going to care."

She cringed. She wasn't used to thinking about things like judges. "You don't have to give the sheriff's department specifics, just point them in the right direction. Even Whitaker couldn't be dumb enough to miss this if it's staring him in the face."

He laughed, and it sounded more carefree and Tanner-like than she'd heard most of the week. Her heart did another tumble.

He brushed a finger down her cheek. "Damn it, woman. What am I going to do with you?"

His hand reached into the hair at her nape, and he pulled her into his lap with a quick tug. She hardly let out a little laugh of her own before his mouth was on hers.

The kiss started out light, playful, with Bree draped over the back of one of his arms and the other moving in gentle circles on her hip. But before long the kiss turned much hotter and demanding.

The needs in her body were hot and demanding, too.

She wanted Tanner.

She hooked an arm around his neck, pulling him closer, deepening the kiss herself, not that he seemed to mind. When his lips moved down her jaw to her neck, she couldn't stop the moan that fell from her lips.

She hadn't even known it was possible to feel this way. Like everything was on fire and burning and there was nothing more she wanted than to be consumed by the flame.

Tanner wrapped one of his big arms around her waist

and stood, raising them both easily with his strength, and took a step toward the bedroom.

Finally.

She wrapped her legs around his hips, her arms clasped tightly around his neck as his lips moved back to hers. Keeping her pressed against him as he walked.

He slowed momentarily as he moved them through the bedroom door, and she tensed. She didn't want him to stop. She felt like she'd been waiting for this her entire life.

She brought her lips back to his, kissing him deeper. It was the only way she could think of to let him know without words how much she wanted this. She threaded her fingers into his thick dark hair and kept their mouths fused.

Whatever it was she was trying to communicate, Tanner understood. His fingers on her hips gripped her closer—strong, secure, confident.

She knew he would take her wherever she wanted to go.

A FEW HOURS LATER, Bree woke up. She stretched, not even for one second trying to keep the smile off her face.

She'd had no idea.

No idea that two people could be as close as she and Tanner had just been. The things that lawman could do with his hands and lips ought to be illegal.

And was she supposed to have known that there were spots on her body—*innocent* spots on her body—that he could use against her so succinctly?

The backs of her knees.

The spot just below her ear.

Her navel.

And he'd found—and paid attention to—every single freckle she had.

She was never, *ever* going to be able to look at her body the same way after what they'd done.

And they hadn't even had sex, technically. When Tanner had laid her on the bed and told her there was a lot more he wanted to show her tonight that didn't include intercourse, she'd been skeptical. Thought it was just another way he was trying to keep distance from her.

She'd been so wrong. He'd definitely not been trying to keep his distance from her.

Afterward, he'd carried her exhausted, sated body into the shower. The water had perked her up a little, and she'd convinced him to show her what *he* liked.

It was only after the hot water started to run out that they'd finally left the shower. Tanner had dried them both off and tucked her body next to him in the bed, turning out the light.

Curled up next to him, she'd drifted off to sleep cognizant that she'd never thought she'd ever have this sort of intimacy with someone, much less someone she cared about as much as Tanner. Never thought she would feel as cherished as she did right in that moment. She'd fallen asleep happier than she'd ever been, Tanner wrapped around her like her own personal blanket.

But when she reached over for him in the bed now just a few hours later, he wasn't there.

She waited a couple of minutes to make sure he hadn't just gone to the bathroom, but it didn't take her long to realize that wasn't the case.

She glanced over at the clock. It was almost 4:00 a.m., too early for him to be out doing any chores or getting ready for work. Maybe he'd gotten hungry. She grinned again. They'd certainly burned enough calories. She wouldn't mind a bite to eat herself.

But when she came out of the bedroom, she found him asleep on the couch. And not just in the accidentally-sat-down-and-fell-back-asleep stance. He had taken out a pillow and a blanket and made himself a little bed.

Away from her.

"Tanner?"

He'd been a cop for too long to wake up groggy. Even in the dim light, she could see awareness in his eyes. "You okay, freckles?"

"Why are you out here sleeping rather than in the bedroom with me?"

Suddenly everything she'd been feeling—all the closeness and intimacy she'd been celebrating—melted away. Obviously, he didn't feel the same connection between them, or he wouldn't have come out to the couch to sleep as soon as he could untangle himself from her.

He shook his head. "Whatever you're thinking, stop. This isn't what it looks like."

She wrapped her arms around her middle, trying to fortify herself. "It looks like you were sleeping out here rather than sleeping with me. Is that not the case?"

He let out a sigh. "Yes, but not because I didn't want to be next to you. Believe me, there is nothing more I wanted than to sleep with you tucked against me, especially after the things we just did together."

Honestly, she wasn't sure whether to believe him or not. Tanner wasn't a liar. She knew that down to the very marrow of her bones.

But years of insecurity and knowing how bad she could be at interpersonal situations ate at her. All the possible mistakes she could've made and not even have been aware of it.

"Did I do something wrong?" she whispered. Except for in the shower, she'd definitely been more on the receiving end of pleasure than the giving end. "Was I too selfish? I didn't do enough for you?"

He flew off the couch and pulled her into his arms. "No, Bree. Hell, nothing like that. It was amazing for me. *All* of it—especially watching you come apart in my arms like that—was amazing for me."

She could hear his heartbeat under her ear, but it didn't reassure her the way it had when he'd pulled her against him a few hours ago.

The urge to flee was overwhelming. To get away and be by herself. It was so hard to feel like she'd grown so much only to see herself spiral back down into the need to run.

But maybe that would be the best thing. "Look, I should probably go. Maybe stay at my house since everything seems to be working out for you professionally-wise."

His hands came up to cup her cheeks, tilting her head back until she was forced to look at him. God, looking at him right now was so hard.

"No. No more running. I want you here. I want you with me."

She sucked in her breath. "I don't understand."

He kissed her forehead. "Just give me a chance to explain it to you, and if you still want to leave, then I won't stop you."

Chapter Fourteen

Tanner wanted to kick his own ass. He'd just experienced the greatest night of his entire life—bar *none*—and now he had made Bree feel like she'd done something wrong.

He looked down into her green eyes that seemed so wary and guarded now. He would go the rest of his life making sure he never put that look in her eyes again.

He was thirty-three years old and hadn't lived like a monk. He knew what had just happened between him and Bree in the last few hours had been special. It had been the type of connection many people searched for their whole lives, but few ever found.

Tanner wanted to spend the rest of his life getting to know all the nooks and crannies of this woman's body. Find every single place his lips could touch that made her gasp, sigh or moan. And then stick around those places until she was calling out his name.

But he couldn't do that until she knew the truth.

"I suffer from night terrors. Sometimes I wake up and think I'm trapped in a situation somewhere else, and I come out swinging."

He knew enough about Bree to know that cutting right to the heart of it was the best way to communi-

cate with her. She was never going to be one for sub-
tlety or sugarcoating.

Even now he could see her mind trying to turn over
the facts and put them in their proper place. "You were
afraid you would hurt me."

He smiled. Of course she came to the correct as-
sumption immediately. She was brilliant. But then his
smile faded. He trailed the back of his knuckles down
her cheek. "Yes. You've already been through so much
violence, freckles, I didn't want to add to your burden.
I couldn't stand the thought that I could hurt you coming out of my nightmares and make you afraid of me."

She sighed and nodded. "We'll come back to that.
Can you tell me specifically what causes the night terrors, or is it something more general?"

He could almost see her mentally making a check-
list of things to research.

A slight shiver shook her frame, since she was nearly
naked in the cold living room. He reached down and
snagged the blanket off the couch, wrapping it around
her. Then he picked her up, blanket and all, and sat
down with her in his lap. He *needed* her to be close just
as much as he *wanted* to be close to her.

"It's PTSD from an undercover case gone impossibly wrong three years ago."

She listened in intense Bree fashion as he explained
about the Viper Syndicate. How he'd been discovered
as undercover, and Nate Fletcher and Alex Peterson
had also been with him. He left out a lot of the gory
details of his physical beating and torture. She didn't
need to know that. She'd lived through enough of her
own horrific violence. But telling her about how it all
ended? The nightmares that still plagued him? That,
he owed her.

"They were trying to force me to tell them if I was working with someone else. I figured there was no way I was walking out of there alive, so I might as well not take down two other good men with me."

He felt her arms wrap around him through the blanket. He tucked her head more firmly under his chin and forced himself to tell the rest of the story.

"SWAT raided the building and spooked the Vipers. They killed the first officer, Alex Peterson, immediately." He sucked in a breath. "I broke the noose around my neck and was diving for the guy about to execute Nate Fletcher, but I was too late."

She sat quietly for a long time, her arms wrapped around him like she would fight anything or anyone that dared to want to harm him. "The night terrors… What are they about mostly? Being strangled? Being helpless?"

Tanner closed his eyes and breathed in the scent of her. She understood. Maybe more than anybody else he'd ever talked to about this, because of her own experiences. She'd probably suffered from night terrors herself after what she'd been through.

"All of it. The pain, the fear, but mostly my inability to save Nate. If I had just broken that noose sooner. Just found the strength to do that, it might've been enough. A young man with his whole life in front of him might still be here."

"Or you might have died right along with him. It's like what you told me about what Michael Jeter did to my mother. We can only make the best choices we have in the circumstances we are in." She rubbed her chin against his chest. "I know that doesn't make it any easier to take. But I know if you could go back right now

and save Fletcher's life, even at the cost of your own,
you would do it. There's something to be said for that."

How many times had Dr. Michalski tried to tell him
the same thing? That Tanner had done the best he could
in the situation he was in. That maybe he could've broken that rope around his neck sooner, but there was no
guarantee it would've made any difference whatsoever.

Tanner didn't blame the SWAT team for not coming in two minutes earlier, so why was it okay to blame
himself?

He understood that; he really did. But at the end of
the day, like Ryan Fletcher had pointed out, Nate wasn't
around to celebrate his twenty-fifth birthday this year.

"The night terrors have been worse this week because of my frustration about the murders and being
suspended," he said. "Believe me, I wanted to be with
you in every way a man can be with a woman, but I
don't want to hurt you further."

She nodded and let out a breath. "I know I'm not
good with emotional stuff. I'm never going to be good
with emotional stuff."

"Freckles—"

She kissed his chest. "No, let me finish."

He shut up and kept his arms around her. "I'm not
good at the emotional stuff, but I'm not weak, Tanner.
My past may have been brutal, but it made me strong.
I know you and I haven't really talked about exactly
where we are going with our relationship."

He wanted to stop right there. Wanted to explain to
her that, especially after earlier tonight, he was all in.

All. In.

There was nothing he wanted more than to spend
the rest of his life with this woman. But he was older
than her by nearly a decade. He had seen and done so

much more than she'd been able to do, living on the run most of her life. He was willing to take however long she needed—to wait forever—for her to feel ready to start a life with him.

"You've been so patient with me," she continued. "Taking things slow and going at a pace I'm comfortable with. And I so appreciate your willingness to do that."

Now he had to stop her. "Because you're worth it." He kissed the top of her head. He meant every word.

She squeezed him then moved back so they could look eye to eye. "It means the world that you think so. And I feel the same. But if we are ever going to go forward as a true couple, you've got to know that *I don't break*. At least, not very easily."

She was right, of course. He'd been doing them both a disservice by hiding this from her. Keeping it a secret had forced him to carry too much and insulted her by implying she wasn't strong enough to help lift his burden.

He reached down and framed her face with both hands. "I've never thought you anything but incredibly strong. But what I did was downright stupid, and you're right to call me on it."

The tiniest of smiles lit up her face. "I don't get to do that with you very often, Captain Dempsey. You're a pretty smart guy. But I want to help you. We can work out your triggers together. And hell, if I take a shot to the jaw from you in the middle of a night terror, you'll just owe me one."

He raised an eyebrow. "You mean you'll want a return shot to my jaw?"

"No. But after the last few hours, I can think of *many* different ways for you to work off any guilt. And we haven't even gotten to the really interesting stuff yet.

Imagine what I can come up with once you teach me how sex really works."

She shifted so she was straddling his lap. There was nothing separating them but the thin blanket.

She grinned, and that beautiful smile was all woman. Tanner felt his heart tumble over into an abyss he knew he was never coming back from.

He gave her his own smile. "You know, for someone who feels like she doesn't know how to say the right things, you do a pretty damn good job."

Because she had. Just by being Bree, she had shifted some of the weight he carried. Helped disseminate it more evenly between the two of them.

They were a team. And he was head-over-ass in love with this woman.

"Good. You won't break me, Tanner. I promise."

He kissed her. He meant it to be a kiss of reverence and thanks. But it soon turned into something much more passionate.

"I think we better head back to the bedroom and practice some of those apology moves, just in case you need them. Especially the ones that involve you kissing right here." She pointed to the spot on the side of her neck just below her ear.

"I've created a monster."

Wrapping his hands under her hips, he stood and carried her back into the bedroom. He'd be kissing her there and a lot of other places. And when they fell asleep afterward, he'd be right there by her side, where he belonged.

Chapter Fifteen

Bree rode with Tanner to the sheriff's office in the northern part of Grand County the next morning. She still had the day off work and wanted to be there in case Whitaker was too oblivious to see what was right in front of his ass.

She offered to write it down for Tanner in case he needed a direct quote.

Tanner had no intention of allowing Bree to admit any illegal doings to Whitaker. He didn't trust the man not to lose sight of the bigger picture—finding the murderer—and arrest Bree just out of spite.

It would take a while for Whitaker to follow up on everything Tanner would present. Tanner didn't expect to be reinstated today, although he was hoping the wheels would be turning enough that maybe he'd be back tomorrow.

But today both he and Bree had the day off. Too bad it was cold and rainy out, or else he'd spend it convincing Bree to move in with him permanently at the ranch and hauling the rest of her stuff.

He wanted her there. He'd never met someone who belonged at the ranch and loved it as much as he and Noah. If it were up to Tanner, Bree wouldn't spend another night away from him for the rest of their lives.

So much for trying to take it slow for her sake. At least he hadn't dragged her off in front of a county judge to get married.

The thought had crossed his mind.

"What do you want to do today?" she asked, smiling over at him from the passenger seat. "My vote is for going back to bed and—"

She gasped and gripped the door handle as a car cut in front of them on the rainy road, way too close.

Tanner let out a low curse. Not only had the guy cut him off, he was now hitting his brakes. Tanner slowed down, then tried to go around him, but the guy swerved again so they were trapped behind him.

"What the hell?" Tanner muttered.

The driver continued to tap his brakes, forcing Tanner to slow further behind him. He flipped on his blinker and pulled to the side of the road. Tanner pulled off also.

He reached over into the glove compartment and pulled out his backup firearm that he had a concealed-carry permit to keep inside his vehicle.

"What just happened?" Bree's green eyes were huge.

"Stay here. I'm going to talk to this guy and see what the hell is going on."

He reached over and gave her hand a squeeze before opening the car door and stepping outside. At least the rain had reduced itself into a mist.

The door of the car in front of him opened and Tanner stopped, firearm ready but pointed at the ground. Then Tanner saw who it was.

"Ryan?" Tanner relaxed his grip on the gun. "You nearly gave me a heart attack. Why the hell did you almost run us off the road?"

Even through the low light and heavy mist, Tanner

could see the tension radiating through Ryan Fletcher. It was unlike the lawyer to be so discombobulated. Every time Tanner had seen him in the courtroom, he'd been completely unflappable.

"Tanner, thank God I caught you. Sorry for the vehicular dramatics. I just didn't know how else to get in touch with you."

Tanner tucked his Glock into the back waistband of his jeans. "How about a telephone. That would work."

"I couldn't call. There couldn't be any trace of a call."

Now Tanner was getting concerned. "What's going on?"

"You can't go in to the sheriff's office. They're going to arrest you."

Tanner shook his head. "No, it's all been taken care of. We found some other evidence. Doesn't clear me outright, but it at least provides another link between the two dead guys besides me."

"I just came from Sheriff Duggan's office. Now there are *three* dead guys. Another body showed up this morning. Stabbed in the back again."

Damn it. "Well, I have a pretty ironclad alibi for last night." Bree would be able to provide a statement that he'd been with her for the entire night.

He rubbed his hand over his face. Except she *wouldn't* be able to attest to that in all honesty, would she? She had no idea how long he was gone from the bed before she came out and found him on the couch. She'd be willing to say he'd been in bed with her all night, but there was no way he was going to allow her to lie and commit perjury for him for that.

Tanner gritted his teeth. "I'm assuming this third victim is tied to me also, if they are threatening to get a warrant?"

"They've already got the warrant, Tanner. Judge issued it immediately based on the evidence. And the guy is tied to you and me both. Owen Duquette."

Tanner's curse was low and foul. "I wanted that bastard in prison, but I didn't kill him."

Ryan ran his hand through his hair. "Look, I'm not going to be shedding any tears over Duquette's death. Honestly, if you *did* kill him, I'm not even sure I would care, after how he was tied to Nate's death. But I don't think you did, and that's why I'm here."

He heard the car door open and held his hand out to Bree without even looking behind him. This affected her, too.

"Is everything okay?" she asked.

He pulled her to his side. "Bree, this is Ryan Fletcher. He works in the district attorney's office."

"Fletcher?" she asked softly.

Tanner nodded. "Nate Fletcher's brother."

Ryan stepped forward and held out his hand. "Nice to meet you. Sorry it's under these circumstances."

"What circumstances?"

Tanner wrapped an arm around her shoulders. "There's been another murder. Somebody else connected to me."

Bree's curse echoed his from a moment ago. "I don't understand what the hell is going on."

"When it was just Anders and Newkirk, I was willing to accept that it was a nasty coincidence. But three people tied to me?"

"This is some sort of setup," Ryan finished for him.

"I'm not big on conspiracy theories, but three dead guys that I arrested? That I lobbied pretty hard to keep in jail and am on record for being frustrated when they were let out? That's really starting to look like pretty good motive." Tanner scrubbed a hand down his face.

"But motive shouldn't be enough. Not for someone like you who has a stellar reputation in law enforcement," Bree said.

Ryan nodded. "She's right. Nobody would think about trying to arrest you based just on potential motive, even if it was good."

Tanner wasn't so sure. Whitaker didn't seem to need much more than that to be convinced of his guilt.

"But there's more than just motive," Ryan continued. "Your DNA was present at Duquette's crime scene. It was also present in Anders's car and at Newkirk's body."

"I've already admitted to being in Anders's car, and I was first on scene at Newkirk's death, so that would explain both of those. But I definitely haven't been anywhere near Duquette since he got out of prison."

The three of them looked at each other, the truth unavoidable. Someone was trying to frame Tanner for murder.

"Who would do this?" Bree whispered.

He wrapped his arm more tightly around her. "I don't know. But I'll talk to the sheriff, and we'll start gathering some possibilities. She and I have known each other for a long time. She worked for my dad. She'll give me the benefit of the doubt."

"Sheriff Duggan may not have that luxury," Ryan said. "I was at her office first thing this morning, because I got a call directly from the governor. Evidently, there's some concern that the sheriff may not be able to consider you objectively."

Tanner and Bree both cursed. Tanner had to smile when hers was quite a bit more colorful and descriptive.

But Ryan didn't have anything to smile about. "I

just came from a meeting with the sheriff, Whitaker and Dr. Michalski."

"Let me guess. Whitaker was the one leading the charge for my arrest."

Ryan rolled his eyes. "Actually, he seemed excited that there was *real* police action going on. It was Dr. Michalski who provided the most damning information. He overheard us talking after court last week. Remembered you saying Duquette would get what was coming to him."

Tanner threw up his hands. "As in, put back in jail as soon as he broke the law again, not murdering him."

"The sheriff asked Dr. Michalski point-blank if he thought you were capable of killing someone. Michalski said yes."

"*I'm* capable of killing someone," Bree muttered. "Actually, I don't have to kill them. I can just get into a computer system and make their entire identity—"

Tanner lifted his hand off her shoulder and wrapped it over her mouth. Ryan was his friend, but he was also the district attorney.

"She didn't get a lot of sleep last night. Just ignore her."

He shot her a warning look then removed his hand, a little afraid she might bite him. But she kept quiet.

"Look, your worst problem is your DNA showing up at Duquette's murder scene. Psych opinions and possible motive play a very distant second fiddle to that. I don't have all the details. I was just trying to get out of the sheriff's office and to your ranch so that I could warn you. If you go into that building right now, you're not coming back out a free man. Not today, at least."

Tanner hated the look of fear in Bree's eyes. "He's right," she whispered.

Tanner shook his head. "I've worked in law enforcement for a decade. My dad did for twice as long. I trust the system. It's not perfect, but it works, by and large."

"Unless you have someone working that system against you." Bree's small hand squeezed his. "I spent a good chunk of my life running from people who used the system against me."

"I'm not telling you to run," Ryan said. "As far as anybody in Grand County thinks, you don't know anything about this. Why don't you go off grid? A lovers' getaway, where no one can get in touch with you. Use that time to see if you can discover further information. I'll do the same."

Damn it. Tanner didn't want to run. It only made him look guilty.

"You can do a lot more for yourself out of a cell than you can inside one," Ryan continued. "Whoever is doing this has a pretty big reach. If you're inside, you're leaving others unprotected." His eyes shot to Bree.

She immediately shook her head. "No, I can take care of myself. I've been taking care of myself for a lot of years. If you feel the best thing is to turn yourself in right now, you should do that. I'll be doing what I can to help you from out here."

Which would undoubtedly be illegal.

While he had no doubt that Bree could and would take care of herself, he'd made her a promise a few months ago that she was no longer in this—in *life*—on her own. That was doubly true after last night.

Ryan was risking a significant amount by trying to warn Tanner. Tanner didn't take that lightly. The man could lose his job or even go to jail for obstructing justice.

He was being given a gift. A head start on figuring out who was hunting him. He'd be a fool not to take it.

"Okay, I won't go in. For forty-eight hours, seventy-two at most, just to try to get a bead on who's after me."

The hunter was about to become the hunted.

Chapter Sixteen

"We need to go to my apartment," Bree said from inside the SUV as they watched Ryan pull back onto the road. "This SUV is too conspicuous, not to mention they probably have some sort of means of tracking it."

Tanner looked a little like he was in shock. She knew he wasn't one hundred percent on board with this decision to run. But if they didn't get moving right now, the option was going to be taken out of their hands.

Running, keeping away from people who were looking for you, was definitely in Bree's wheelhouse. God knew she had enough experience at it.

Tanner was still staring out the windshield into the rain.

She reached over and squeezed his hand. "Dempsey, let's go. Get safe first, fall apart later."

Yep, she'd just quoted her mother.

Tanner gave a brief nod then pulled onto the road and drove toward Risk Peak. Thank goodness they'd dropped her car off here yesterday on the way to the prison. They were going to need it and what she had in her apartment.

"I'm not even sure where we should go." Tanner's knuckles were white as he gripped the steering wheel.

"We're going to my apartment first. I have some things that will help us."

And at least they still had her computer with them. They were going to need that most of all.

She put a call in to Cheryl and Dan at the Sunrise Diner to let them know she wouldn't be in for a couple more days. She told them that Tanner had kidnapped her and taken her somewhere secluded and romantic, and she wasn't even exactly sure where she was.

She felt a little bit guilty at how excited they seemed at the thought. But Ryan was probably right. The best thing she and Tanner could do right now was make it seem like they had a reason to be out of pocket. And *not* look like they were on the run from the law.

She half expected Tanner to change his mind and decide to turn himself over to the sheriff, and fight this head-on. If he did, she wouldn't try to stop him or discourage him in any way.

Head-on was Tanner's way. And it was one of the things she loved most about him.

But he didn't. As a matter of fact, the closer they got to Risk Peak, the faster he drove, like he realized that they needed to get the hell out of Dodge quick.

"We won't have very long before they have an APB out on me. We've got to be out of town by then. They're going to be able to trace things like credit cards and ATMs, and I don't have that much cash on me."

"I've got everything we need in my apartment. Get me there, give me five minutes, maybe even less, and we can be on the road."

She'd struggled with the fact that she still had a bug-out bag packed and waiting in the corner of her closet, even though the Organization wasn't hunting her anymore. She told herself it made her a coward to keep it around, that it encouraged the bad habit of running when she got scared. But she hadn't been able to force herself to get rid of it.

And now she was glad.

Ten minutes later they were pulling up in front of her apartment.

She handed him the key to her car. "Grab anything useful from in here, and definitely my computer. I'll meet you at my car in five minutes."

He looked at her, expression tight. He was still white-knuckling the steering wheel. "You're running again. I never wanted you to be forced to do that. And now I'm dragging you into breaking the law with me."

He was about to be arrested for murder, and he was worried about *her.*

"We haven't actually seen the warrant out for your arrest, so technically we're not breaking any laws yet. Let's run away for a romantic getaway, just the two of us." She smiled. This was so much harder for him than it was for her.

He hit his palm against the steering wheel. "Fine. Three days, that's it. If we haven't figured out who's behind it by then, I'm turning myself in, back from our *romantic getaway.*"

"Deal." If they didn't have any further info in three days, they were in a lot of trouble anyway.

"And when this is over, I'm taking you for a *real* romantic getaway, off grid, just the two of us."

She grinned. "Making an honest woman out of me—I like that."

"Trust me, if I'm not starting a thirty-year prison sentence in the next few months, I plan to make an honest woman out of you in every possible way."

She only got a second to gape at him before his fingers twisted in her hair at the nape of her neck—the way he seemed to like to do so much—and he pulled her in for a quick kiss. "Go get your magic bag of tricks. We don't have a lot of time."

"Three and a half minutes at my car." She was out the door without another word.

The bug-out bag was exactly where she'd left it. Thankful for the preparation and evasion skills her mother had instilled in her, even though they'd been so painful at the time, Bree grabbed it. It wasn't meant for two people, but it would give them a much better head start than law enforcement would be expecting.

Her phone buzzed in her purse. She took it out and looked at it.

Ronnie Kitchens. The deputy who worked with Tanner every day in Risk Peak.

Bree knew better than to answer it. She left the phone on her kitchen table and hefted the large backpack onto her shoulder. They'd be coming here soon looking for her and Tanner. *Accidentally* leaving her phone would give credence to their claim that they were on a romantic getaway.

And she would not, under any circumstances, think about Tanner's comment about making an honest woman out of her. She needed to focus on getting them through this situation and keeping Tanner out of jail.

Not focusing on what it would be like to become Mrs. Bree Dempsey.

She was back out of her car with a few seconds to spare on her three and a half minutes. Tanner was already there, looking more grim. "Ronnie just called me."

She got in and he started the car. "You didn't answer, did you?"

"No. I'm sure he wants to know why there's an arrest warrant with my name on it coming across his desk."

"He called me, too. I left my phone on the table, so it will just look like I forgot it."

Tanner handed her his phone. "Do whatever you need to make sure they can't track me with this."

She ran her fingers along his old-fashioned flip phone. The fact that he didn't have a smartphone was what had saved her life a few months ago. She opened the back panel and removed the battery and the SIM card. It was doubtful they could've traced it, even as a whole unit, but keeping these pieces separate would definitely stop them.

She dropped the separate pieces into the cup holder in the console of her late-model gray Honda. It was one of the most popular cars in the United States, which was precisely why she owned it. This vehicle would blend in with every other car on the highway.

"Got any particular direction you think we should head?" he asked.

"Just out of Risk Peak, definitely not in the direction of the ranch, and probably not toward any of your family's houses, either."

He nodded. "Yes, those will be the first places they'll look."

They drove toward Denver, deciding that the more vehicles around, the less conspicuous they would be. As they approached Aurora, a suburb just outside Denver, they started running low on gas.

"We're going to have to stop," Tanner said. "But we can't run any credit cards. I have eighty-seven dollars in my wallet. That's not going to get us far."

"That's okay. I have about two thousand in my backpack."

He nearly gave himself whiplash as he spun to look at her before returning his eyes to the road. "Why the hell do you have two thousand dollars in your backpack?"

She shrugged. "It's my bug-out bag. Do you know what that is?"

"I was raised in Colorado and have a brother who's always one step away from disappearing. So yeah, I know what a bug-out bag is. But most people have camping supplies and waterproof matches. Not two grand."

The term *bug-out bag* had been coined by survivalists to mean a bag that contained whatever emergency gear someone kept available and ready to go at a moment's notice—in case they needed to *bug out*. Most people thought of it in terms of wilderness survival.

Bree's bag was completely different. It did have some traditional supplies—a Mylar blanket, changes of clothes and a small first-aid kit. But Bree had never planned to be heading to the wilderness if she had to survive on the run. Her kit was for *urban* survival.

"Actually, I have something we should probably use now that we've cleared Risk Peak. Can you pull over at that rest stop ahead?"

Tanner nodded tightly and did as she asked. He definitely didn't look any more relaxed as she took a license plate out of her backpack.

"The first thing any police officer will do if they're looking for a car like mine is run the license plates. These will come up clean."

"Why do you even have those?"

She gnawed on the side of her lip. "Actually, six months ago I had five different clean license plates, to use if I had to run from the Organization. I got rid of all but one."

He scrubbed a hand across his face. "Well, I'm glad you only have one illegal set."

"In the interest of full disclosure, I also have a credit

card and ID under another name." She flinched at his thunderous look. "I—I… I'm trying, Tanner, I promise. But running and disappearing was my whole life for so long."

She didn't want him to be disappointed in her, and she'd tried to force herself to get rid of the bag multiple times, but she just couldn't.

His face relaxed, and his hand reached for hers. "I know. And who am I to judge, considering you're using all this stuff to help me? But let's try to keep the illegal activities as much to a minimum as possible. And when we get all this cleared up, how about getting rid of all the illegal stuff."

She nodded. Maybe by then the thought wouldn't send her into a panic.

He took the license plate from her and changed it out. Then they got back on the road.

"We need to come up with a plan," she said after a few more minutes. "Driving around puts us at unnecessary risk. I know you don't want me to use the fake ID or credit card, but that will allow us to get a hotel room. All we need is somewhere with good internet and I can start to look into the situation."

Which would involve more illegal activity, but she didn't want to bring that up.

But she wasn't fooling him. His lips tightened. "What systems are you going to hack?"

She sighed. "I was going to start with the sheriff's office. I should be able to find all the details of the latest murder there. Then cross-reference them with Darin Carrico and see if there's an association. I also want to see if he sent out another email before Owen Duquette was killed."

Tanner nodded, not giving her a hard time about the

hacking she would need to do. At this point, there was no way around it. They needed info and they needed it fast. The best she could do was promise to only access the info they needed.

She was capable of so much more.

"Will Grand County be able to trace where the hack is coming from? Find you?"

Bree actually laughed out loud at the absurdity of that statement.

A half smile lit his face. "I guess that's a no."

"Believe me, there's very few people outside of the ones from the Organization we put in prison a few months ago who would be able to do a back trace on me."

"Okay, because if we've got to bend some laws, I want to make sure none of it comes back on you."

"Believe me, it won't."

"Then I've got the perfect place for us to go. We'll actually have to circle back toward Risk Peak, but it's far enough away that we won't run into anyone. A cabin, but with security and Wi-Fi. I'll have to make a call first to some of Noah's former Special Forces teammates."

She nodded. "Okay, we can get a burner phone when we stop for gas. Any truck rest stop off the interstate will have them."

A few minutes later, they were pulling up to a gas station. Bree grabbed two baseball caps from her bag.

She handed one to him. "Stay in the car and keep this as low over your eyes as possible. Don't look around, just look down at your hands like you're messing with a phone. I'll get the gas."

She could tell right away he didn't like that. "No."

She rolled her eyes. "I'm much less conspicuous than you are, Tanner. I've got more experience blend-

Janie Crouch 127

ing in, plus I'm not half a foot taller than everybody else around me."

His lips pressed together in a mutinous line, but he finally gave her a brief nod.

Bree got out of the car, pumping the gas then going inside to pay and find a burner phone. She kept her head down and eyes averted—not a problem for her.

She was going to have to work quickly once Tanner got them to the cabin. He said he'd give it three days, but she was betting after two he'd be ready to turn himself in.

Tanner Dempsey was never going to be good at hiding. It went against his nature. Even when he had worked undercover, she was sure they hadn't used him as someone who blended in.

But she would find out what was going on. Because there was no way she was letting him go to jail.

Chapter Seventeen

"We're going to need to break into the sheriff's office."

Tanner's head flew up at Bree's words. It was after 2:00 a.m., and she'd been working nonstop for the last twelve hours, digging up whatever she could about the three murders.

If he had thought he felt helpless when he was just supposed to keep out of the way of the investigation, it was nothing compared to how he felt knowing someone was out there actively trying to frame him.

That was where they'd started in their research: Who held some sort of grudge against Tanner?

Ended up that was a pretty long list when they'd included everyone he'd arrested or stopped from completing some sort of nefarious plan.

"Break into the sheriff's office?" he asked. "Adding to the list of crimes I'm wanted for doesn't seem like the best of plans," he responded, walking over and rubbing her shoulders. She leaned her head back against his stomach. "Is it some sort of information you can't get to electronically?"

"Evidently, Sheriff Duggan has pretty important info that she's not entering into her normal computer system. Is that strange?"

He nodded. "She's got a separate computer in her

office, without any sort of internet connection to it at all. She calls it her diary."

Bree's eyes narrowed, but she obviously had respect for Sheriff Duggan's tactics. "Smart."

"Definitely. Not to mention she knows what you're capable of. She knows that any information stored in a computer connected to the internet can be accessed by you if you put your mind to it."

Bree reached back and grabbed his waist with her hands, tilting her head back so she was looking at him, upside down. "I only found out about it because she mentioned it in an e-memo to her assistant. Do you think Sheriff Duggan thinks you're guilty now?"

"I hope not. But me not being there to explain myself is certainly not helping."

He knew word had gotten around Risk Peak that there was a warrant out for his arrest. He couldn't even think too much about how that made the people who knew him feel. They trusted him to uphold the law. To now be on the opposite side of the law was almost unfathomable.

"I should turn myself in. I might have to sit in a cell for a couple of weeks, but we'll get this cleared up."

Bree stood and turned so she was facing him, climbing up onto the chair on her knees. "I support you. I really do. But let's see what's in the sheriff's office. If it's nothing important then, heck, you'll already be in the building, and you can turn yourself in then if you want."

Bree was still working the Carrico angle—had been all day—but she hadn't come up with anything to tie him to this third victim. He and Duquette had never served any prison time together or seemed to have any ties any other way. Bree hadn't found any email sent by Carrico concerning Duquette.

She'd spent more time looking at the first two emails concerning Newkirk and Anders, convinced something wasn't right, frustrated when she couldn't figure out what it was.

She pulled back to return to her computer, but he grasped her hips and kept her in place in front of him. "Okay, we go to the sheriff's office and see if there's anything that throws major light on the case. In for a penny, in for a pound, right?"

As far as Bree had told him from the "watchful eye" she was keeping on the sheriff's office in Risk Peak, they believed that he was making the most of his administrative leave and had gone on that romantic getaway. For once, small-town rumor was working in his favor.

But if they figured out that wasn't the case, it would become a manhunt. So figuring out what the sheriff was keeping on her private computer was probably a good idea, even if the thought of it was distasteful.

An hour later they were going through a basement side door into the Grand County Sheriff's Department office. It should've had a fire alarm on it, but Tanner knew some of the guys had disconnected it because it provided an easy way in and out for a smoke break.

He grimaced as the door made a loud creak as they opened it. If they got caught, it wasn't technically illegal to be using that door, but it sure as hell was going to raise a lot of questions.

Fortunately, there wasn't anything happening in these administrative offices in the back of the building at this time of night. There was more life on the south side of the building—a holding cell and the night officers' offices. But they shouldn't need to go there for any reason.

He kept a hand at Bree's back as he led her down the

darkened hall toward Sheriff Duggan's office. She had her laptop gripped tightly in her arms. She hadn't offered a reason why she'd brought it, and he hadn't asked.

Sheriff Duggan's office door wasn't locked, which only made him feel marginally better about opening it and ushering Bree inside. At least so far he hadn't actually had to break in. But he was committed now. If there was fallout, he'd have to deal with it. He wasn't going to second-guess himself any more.

Bree immediately moved over to a laptop sitting at the corner of Duggan's desk. "This is it."

"Work as fast as you can."

Bree was pretty damn fast.

She had the sheriff's computer opened and had hacked her way past the password in under two minutes. "Got it."

He whistled through his teeth. "You're scary fast there, freckles. Passwords don't seem to give you any trouble."

She smiled. "Passwords are nothing more than a security blanket for the general public. They definitely don't keep any true hackers from getting what they want."

He shook his head. "Promise me you'll always stay on my side of the law."

Of course, which side was his right at this moment? Tanner didn't examine that too closely.

"Okay, Sheriff Duggan," Bree whispered to the computer. "Tell dear diary what's on your mind."

A few minutes later, Bree reached a hand out toward him without looking back at him. "Oh my gosh, come look at this."

"Is it bad?"

She shook her head. "No, it's definitely not bad. She's

kept a record of dozens of phone calls, messages and meetings she's had today. All about you."

"What?" He rushed to her side.

She showed him what she was talking about on the screen. Sure enough, at least a dozen people, from Risk Peak and other parts of Grand County, had contacted the sheriff basically as character witnesses on his behalf. Obviously some of them didn't have all their facts straight—gossip was fast in a town Risk Peak's size, but rarely accurate—but they'd all rushed to his defense when they'd heard about the arrest warrant.

"She's keeping a very meticulous list of everyone defending you," Bree said. "Some of these are pretty impressive character witnesses."

He was honored and more than ever wanted to clear this up so he could get back to serving the town he loved so much.

Bree started clicking away on the computer again. "Okay, let's see what else is going on inside the sheriff's mind. Because as touching as that is, it's not going to help clear your name."

Tanner resumed his lookout through the cracked door as Bree went back to work. It didn't take long for her to find the other info.

"There you are," she whispered. "The sheriff doesn't want to say it publicly, but she has some concerns about someone in the office. She discovered someone else who was a connection between all three victims."

"Who?"

"Hang on." She clicked a few keys, then paused. "Dr. Craig Michalski."

Shock ricocheted through his body. "What?"

"He was the official county psychiatrist for both Newkirk and Anders. Was even asked to come in for a second opinion for Anders for the parole board. That was one of the reasons Anders was released—because Michalski suggested it."

Tanner rubbed his eyes. He had known Michalski had visited Carrico, although still didn't know why. The fact that he'd been the psychiatrist assigned to Newkirk and Anders wasn't really surprising. Dr. Michalski was part of a lot of cases. "Okay. Keep going."

"Says here that the sheriff approved the doc's request to talk to Duquette about eleven months ago while Duquette was in prison." She looked up from the computer and met his eyes. "Because Michalski was trying to understand more about you."

Tanner scrubbed a hand over his face. A year ago he'd hit a particular rough spot with his PTSD. He'd been angry, for sure, frustrated at his inability to just move past everything. Had been frustrated at the lack of noticeable progress in his therapy.

"Dr. Michalski and I haven't always seen eye to eye. But I'm going to be the first one to argue that just because you happen to know three people doesn't mean you killed them."

She nodded. "Granted. But Sheriff Duggan has some concerns. She's afraid Dr. Michalski has some sort of personal problem with you. She also says he's been acting erratically over the past three months. Enough for her to have real uneasiness."

"Damn it," he muttered.

"That's basically all that's on this computer." She closed it. "Tanner, I know you don't want to jump to conclusions, but Michalski would've known how to taint a crime scene with your DNA. He told the sheriff and Ryan Fletcher that he thought you were actively capable of committing murder. What if he has some sort of vendetta against you or something?"

Had that been true and Tanner had just missed it? There was definitely no love lost between him and Dr. Michalski, but would the man murder people in order to frame Tanner?

A light flipping on in the far hallway caught his attention.

"We've got to go, now," he said, holding out his hand for Bree.

She closed the computers, and when he heard footsteps in the direction they needed to go, he rushed her out the door and down the opposite direction they'd come in. It would force them to circle back, but at least they'd be able to do that undetected.

Tanner picked up speed and rounded the corner, Bree's hand in his.

And ran straight into Dr. Michalski.

"What the hell?" Tanner let go of Bree, placing himself between her and the doctor. "What are you doing here, Michalski?"

This was one of the most isolated sections of the building. There wasn't much reason for Dr. Michalski to be down here at all, and especially not in the middle of the night.

The doctor shifted back and forth, more agitated than Tanner had ever seen him.

"What am *I* doing here? What are you doing here, Tanner? Do you know there's a warrant out for your arrest?"

Tanner grabbed the man by his shirt and pressed him up against the wall. "Actually, yes, I do know that. And part of the reason for said warrant is because of your statement to the sheriff that you thought I was capable of murdering those guys."

"I did nothing more than offer my honest opinion of whether you had the mental and emotional capacity for the act. Whether you want to admit it or not, you are capable of it."

Tanner didn't disagree, but that wasn't the point. He didn't let go of the other man's shirt.

"But in the context of when and why it was being asked, you just threw me under the bus, Doc. Knowing there was a connection between me and all three victims and how it would look."

Michalski shifted nervously again. His eyes darted all over the place before finally settling back on Tanner. "I was just offering my professional opinion. Valuable information."

"Really? Then why didn't you offer other valuable information, too? Like the fact that *you* had contact with all three victims."

The doctor cleared his throat. "My job brought me in contact with all three of them."

"So did mine." Tanner had to force himself to keep his voice down. "I didn't do this. I didn't kill those men, as much as circumstantial evidence and your opinion of my psyche might suggest otherwise."

"If you're not guilty, just turn yourself in. All this will get sorted out."

"Speaking of guilt." Bree peeked out from around Tanner before he could stop her. "Why are you here at three o'clock in the morning?"

"Especially in this part of the building?" Tanner added. "There's no reason for you to be back here at all if you're not up to something."

The other man's eyes bolted around nervously again.

"No offense, but I'm not the one who has a warrant out for my arrest. I don't have to give a reason for being here."

Tanner was about to argue the point none too gently with the doctor when a ping came from Bree's laptop behind him. A second later she grabbed his arm.

"Whitaker just logged in to a computer on site. We need to go."

What the hell was Whitaker doing here at three o'clock in the morning? He didn't work night shifts, either.

"Tanner," Michalski said, his voice returning to the soothing tone he was more familiar with. "Just turn yourself in right now. There's been a ton of people who've come in or called to speak up on your behalf. If you didn't do this, trust your colleagues to find the real killer."

"Yeah, Doc? Well, you're a colleague and you certainly didn't speak up on my behalf. So I think it might be to my benefit to prove my own innocence."

Tanner dragged the older man down the hallway and threw him into a closet, bolting the door from the outside. Michalski would be able to get someone's attention tomorrow when the administrative offices filled up.

He looked over at Bree. "You okay?"

She nodded. "Yeah, but let's get out of here. The turning-yourself-in plan doesn't seem like such a good one anymore."

A door clicked open at the other end of the hallway. Tanner grabbed Bree's hand, and they ran in the opposite direction, barely making it around the corner without being seen.

Tanner didn't slow down. If Michalski made enough noise, whoever was around would undoubtedly hear him. And if it was Whitaker—although why would Whitaker have a reason to be in that part of the office at that time of night, either?—the chase might be starting immediately.

They needed to get out of the building right now. But the only way to do that was going back the way they'd come.

"We're trapped, aren't we?" she whispered.

He let out a low curse. "Whoever that is, it won't take them long to get to the closet I stuffed Michalski in."

She nodded and dropped to the floor, opening her computer and resting it on her crossed legs. Within just a few seconds, an alarm was going off at the front of the building.

"What is that?" he asked her.

She shrugged, getting up. "I triggered a window alarm near the northeast side corner of the building. It won't buy us much time—"

He pulled her in for a quick, hard kiss. "But it will be enough."

They were getting out of here and figuring out exactly what the hell was going on.

Chapter Eighteen

The man looked at report after report after report that had been shown to him. Reports of how Tanner Dempsey could not be guilty.

He was their hero.

He was incapable of wrong.

How could the people here be so blind? Dempsey had managed to completely pull the wool over everyone's eyes. Convinced them he was infallible.

He was so, so fallible.

The people in this town, this county, obviously couldn't see what was right in front of them. Their letters proved how much Dempsey had fooled them. They argued for his innocence out of hand, never suspecting that Dempsey was the epitome of everything wrong with law enforcement.

Tanner Dempsey wasn't a hero; he was a villain. He should be shunned, not cheered. If it were anyone else who was accused of three murders, there'd be a statewide manhunt, rather than everyone sitting around twiddling their thumbs, waiting for Dempsey to come back from his *romantic getaway* and explain himself.

As if he could explain away the darkness that encompassed his very soul.

The man realized he had miscalculated. Dempsey

was never going to be taken down this way. Never going to rot in prison like the man had envisioned. There were too many people who would insist on his innocence even if he walked up and stabbed them in the chest.

Dempsey was certainly capable of it; the man knew that without a doubt.

The thought that Dempsey wouldn't pay for his crimes was unbearable.

But every day that he was allowed to run free, he came closer to clearing his name.

Because of that woman. The one who looked at him with such devotion in her eyes.

First, Dempsey fooled everyone into believing that he was an upstanding man of the law. And now he would also get to fall in love? To have a life and a happy ending with a beautiful woman? To not pay for his sins in any way?

It was time for a game change. Life in prison was too good for Dempsey.

Instead, Dempsey would lose *everything*. Starting with the woman and ending with his life.

Chapter Nineteen

They hadn't even made it back to Bree's car and gotten
back on the highway toward the cabin before she had
her laptop open and was researching Dr. Craig Michalski. He was the key to all this.

She used a mobile hot spot from the burner to gather
data on the drive, frustrated when it couldn't provide
her information fast enough. When they pulled up to
the cabin, she went inside without a word, still carrying the laptop with one hand and typing with the other.

Tanner was smart enough to just stay out of her way.

"Sheriff Duggan is right to be worried about Michalski. About four months ago, his behavior and financial
patterns changed. He started spending a lot more money
and spending a lot more time away from home."

Tanner was pacing behind her at the cabin. "That's
not necessarily a sign of guilt. Could be a midlife crisis
or something equally benign."

That was true. "But it also could be an indication that
he was mentally or emotionally snapping."

Tanner's hands rested on her shoulders. "Do me a
favor. Come at this as if you're trying to prove Dr. Michalski is innocent rather than prove he's guilty."

"Why?"

He kissed the top of her head. "Because that's what

I would want someone to do for me. Plus, it might provide you a new way to look at things. Not to mention, if Michalski wanted to frame me, he could've done it long before now."

Bree actually wanted to growl, but refrained. How the heck did he expect her to prove *him* innocent if she was trying to prove everyone else innocent, too?

"Best I can do is neutral," she muttered. "Definitely not treating him like I think he's innocent."

"Fair enough."

"Assuming that Michalski's behavioral changes have nothing to do with the three dead bodies he had contact with and failed to mention…then what really doesn't fall in line is Carrico."

Tanner resumed his pacing behind her, but she kept her eyes on her computer. "You're right," he said. "Michalski had legitimate reason to be around all three victims, but we don't know why he was talking to Carrico."

She pulled back up the encoded emails Carrico had sent. "Do you think they could be working together? That Michalski is on the other end of that guerrilla email account?"

"Is there any indication that Michalski and Carrico know each other?"

Bree split her computer screen so she could see the prison guest log on one section and Michalski's phone record on the other. She wrote a tiny program very quickly to search through both for the commonalities they were looking for.

It didn't take long for the results. "Nothing obvious. If Michalski called him, it wasn't with his cell, office or home phone. Three days ago was the only time he's ever visited Carrico. No obvious phone calls or emails from Colorado Correctional."

He shook his head. "I've got to believe that if the two of them were working together, Dr. Michalski would be too smart to go visit Carrico so overtly like that. Especially right in the middle of all this going down."

She shrugged. "Or maybe it never occurred to him that we'd make the connection. It was pretty thin. But…"

"But what?" he asked, standing behind her again.

"There's something not right about these emails Carrico sent. The ones with the cipher codes." She couldn't quite put her finger on it, but she knew she was missing something.

"Are you sure you cracked them correctly?"

"Definitely. I just feel like I didn't look at the source code thoroughly enough. I took the messages at face value, because it was showing me what I wanted to see—that you were innocent." She tapped her temple. "I should know better."

She had all this skill when it came to computers, but when it mattered most she couldn't seem to figure out whatever it was she was missing.

Why was Dr. Michalski talking to Carrico? The others were legitimate connections, but there was no reason he should've been talking to Carrico.

And these emails from Carrico to whoever was on the other end of that burner email. Something was off about those, too. Carrico didn't strike her as someone who would use a cipher to communicate. The delicate nature of the code just didn't seem to be his style.

"It's time for me to turn myself in," Tanner said. Except for bouncing information off the other, he hadn't spoken much since they got back to the cabin. He'd stood looking out the window. She'd known it was just a matter of time before those words would come out of his mouth.

"They know I'm running now," he continued. "Michalski, guilty or not, will sing like a canary. So they'll up the search. They're going to put pressure on my family, call Noah in for questioning. I can't let the people I care about pay the price." He walked over and kissed the top of her head. "I can't let *you* pay the price. If we go back in now, there shouldn't be many repercussions for you."

She sighed. If that was what he wanted to do, she would support him. But if he would just give them a little more time…and do something she knew he was going to fight.

She stood and wrapped her arms around his waist. "I know I might sound like a broken record, but before you turn yourself in, there's one more thing I want us to try."

"What?"

"Let's go visit Carrico again. He's the key to cracking this open. There's too much about his situation—the emails, his ties to two of the victims, but not three—that's illogical. But most important, why was Michalski there talking to him just three days ago?"

Tanner let out a harsh breath. "I can't go inside the prison. My ID will ping law enforcement immediately and let them know I'm there. Plus, Carrico hates cops anyway. He's not going to talk to me."

She backed away a little bit and pointed to her chest. "But he might talk to me. I'll go. Maybe I can figure out whatever it was we missed the first time."

Tanner backed away, crossing his arms over his chest and leaning back against the wall. She'd known he wasn't going to like the idea.

"No," he said. "And before you ask, it's not because

I don't think you can do it, but because it's not worth the risk. Your name is probably tagged in the system, too. As soon as you show them your ID, it's going to tip off the same people as if I had done it."

If he hadn't liked the first part of the plan, he definitely wasn't going to like the second. "Or... I can use the ID I had in my bug-out bag. It's never been utilized—it's completely clean. It definitely won't raise any red flags."

Tanner didn't move from where he was standing. Those brown eyes of his were shuttered. "Still no. Carrico could be a killer. Sending you back in there does nothing but put you on his radar. Three men are already dead. I don't want to put you at risk, too."

She walked over until she was standing right in front of him and raised her hands until they were caressing the outside of his biceps under his Henley shirt.

"I don't think Darin is the killer. All this played out just a little too nicely, don't you think?"

"He's our most likely suspect and we can't ignore that. Just because he might have gotten someone else to do it rather than pull the trigger himself wouldn't make him any less of a killer. I feel for him in his situation with his daughter, but that doesn't mean I can deny the evidence we found."

"But that evidence has holes. Like it's leading us somewhere that's definitely going to be a dead end." She squeezed his arms. "If you could get in there to talk to him without letting law enforcement know where you are, would you think it was worth it to talk to Carrico one more time?"

She could almost see his teeth grinding in his jaw. "Maybe."

"What does your gut say about Carrico?"

Tanner let out a sigh. "Fine. You're right, okay? Right up until the point where you found those encoded emails, I was completely buying into his story. But somebody framing him and me? We're really getting into conspiracy-theories territory here."

"Tanner, just let me talk to him and find out what Dr. Michalski said. I'll do it today while he's still at Colorado Correctional and we can still get in contact with him. If he's really about to get moved up to the max-security prison, it will be harder to get info from him there."

She could see him struggling with the idea.

"Team, remember?" she said. "I'm not arguing with you about turning yourself in. I know you think that's the right thing to do, and I support that. But let's do it with as much information as possible."

His arms came around her and jerked her to his chest. "I don't like it, but I can't deny what you're saying."

Thank God.

"Let's start some coffee. We've got a few hours left before visiting starts. Let me see what else I can find out about Michalski."

Tanner kissed the top of her head and pushed her toward the laptop, then went to make both coffee and breakfast for them. Bree didn't waste any time. She immediately hacked back into the Grand County Sheriff's Department system. She quickly wrote a program to send her a message anytime Tanner's name was used by anyone in any department.

It didn't take long to figure out they definitely knew Tanner was evading them now. There was a full search going on for him.

She winced as a new alert came across her screen.

"What?" he asked as he refilled her empty coffee cup.

"You were right. Whitaker brought Noah in for questioning."

Tanner gave a brief nod. "Not surprising. We share a residence, and everyone in town knows how close we are."

She knew how much Noah loved the outdoors, how much he hated people. "Will he be all right?"

"Noah can handle himself. He'll keep it together however long he needs to. It helps that he doesn't know a damn thing about what's going on, not that he would hesitate to lie to help me." Tanner's tone was light, but there was a heaviness to his stance now.

She reached up and cupped his cheek. "I'll work faster."

He gave her another tight nod then turned back toward the kitchen.

Bree dug deeper into every file she could find. She had to be more careful; the sheriff's department had obviously brought in some sort of computer specialist to try to help track her.

It almost provided a challenge.

In the end it was Tanner's advice to treat Michalski as if he *wasn't* guilty that led her in the direction she needed to go. And it definitely hadn't been what she'd been expecting.

"Tanner, look at this."

She turned the screen so he could see it more easily and brought up a backdoor list of all Dr. Michalski's patient files. Including Tanner's.

Tanner began to read.

"What exactly am I looking for here? Something specific?"

"This is a relatively sophisticated back channel into

Michalski's files. I should have needed to build this grouping one file at a time, but I didn't."

"What does that mean?"

"It means someone has already hacked Dr. Michalski's files. It's impossible for me to tell who from here. I'd need access to his computer. All I can tell you is that it was a reasonably well-done job."

Tanner rubbed his fingers over his eyes. "This case just keeps getting stranger and stranger. Like there's some puppet master pulling the strings that we can't see."

She couldn't have agreed more. "Then we start yanking on strings of our own and see what happens. And I think we should start with Carrico."

Chapter Twenty

Kelsey Collins entered the Colorado Correctional visitors' area right when it opened that afternoon. Bree wasn't surprised when none of the guards who had checked her in a few days ago recognized her. Her brown hair was tucked up under a short blond wig. Her freckles were covered by a pound of makeup. Her whole posture was different than how she normally carried herself.

And they all matched the ID she'd handed the guard as she checked in. The guard had scanned it and handed it back to her when it came back clean.

Bree had not doubted it would.

Tanner, on the other hand, was a half step above a nervous wreck waiting out in the car. For a few minutes—especially when she'd come out of the bathroom in full Kelsey Collins gear—she hadn't thought he was going to let her do this. Could almost see him trying to find a way that he could take the risk on himself rather than allow her to do it.

The fact that he *really* didn't want her doing this had actually made her desire to do it even greater. She could practically feel Tanner's concern and need to protect her surrounding her like a cocoon.

It was…nice.

So much more than nice. It was what she'd been waiting for her whole life and never thought she'd find.

Damn it, she wanted to help clear Tanner's name so they could go on that getaway he'd talked about. Whoever this master puppeteer was, he needed to be stopped, not only because of all the bad murderer stuff but because he was getting in the way of Bree's love life.

She'd never had one before, and now that she did, she was tired of waiting.

Bree kept her Kelsey Collins persona wrapped around her as she walked to an empty visitors' table, just a couple down from where they'd met with Carrico last time. She refused to let her fears—not that she would get hurt, but that she wasn't capable of doing this—get the best of her. She would talk to Carrico, study every bit of his nonverbal behavior that she could and get the answers she needed.

The Kelsey Collins disguise didn't fool Carrico very long. He hadn't been across from Bree more than a few seconds before his eyes narrowed.

"You're looking a bit different than the last time I saw you, cop lady friend, not that I mind the blond. Where's Mr. Cop today? You decide to trade up for a real man?"

Carrico was slouched in his chair, face set in a half smirk. Bree forced herself to look deeper at the man, beyond the surface conceit and attitude. To study him the way Tanner would if he was here.

Carrico's thin face was even more gaunt than it had been a few days ago. Dark circles had taken up residence under his eyes. The man was worried. Not nearly as flippant as he pretended to be.

She needed to get through to him and keep him from becoming defensive. Otherwise he'd never talk to her.

She didn't have any sort of interrogation training. She barely had any sort of *conversation* training.

She decided to go with what she did have: the truth.

"I owe you some thanks. Because of you I figured out I was in love with Tanner."

One of his eyebrows shot up almost comically. "And how is that, exactly?"

"Because after we left here three days ago, Tanner planned to help you with your situation regardless of whether you'd given him any useful information to help him out or not."

Carrico shrugged, not looking impressed.

"Tanner has his own problems," she continued. "Believe it or not, ones just as big as yours, but he still planned to help you—even though he doesn't know you and you acted like a complete jackass when we talked last. He wants to help you because that's just the type of person Tanner is. Someone who does the right thing, even when it doesn't benefit him personally."

He'd done that with her, too. Risked everything to protect her and get her out of a situation where she would've died.

Tanner Dempsey was courageous, strong, smart and just a little bit broken. Bree didn't know a lot about feelings, but she knew with absolute clarity that she was in love with him.

"Yeah, well, I'm still going to Colorado State Penitentiary, so I'm not feeling like your boy is such a golden angel."

She leaned forward. "He has to get himself out of trouble before he can help you. But he will help you, Darin."

"My brother says not to trust cops. Not to talk to anyone else."

"Believe me, I know what it's like to trust no one but yourself. But I promise you, if Tanner can get himself clear of his own charges, he will do what he can to help you. Don't you want to be able to know you did everything you could to be able to see your daughter?"

He didn't say anything, but she felt like she was getting through to him. "I can tell you're not sleeping well—I know that feeling, too. Staying awake, trying to figure out if you missed anything. If anything can be done to change the situation you're in. I know what it's like to sit alone with my own desperation, Darin. Tanner will help you. He's a man of his word. I've bet my whole life on it."

He let out a sigh and leaned in toward the table. "Fine. What do you want to know?"

"Why was Dr. Michalski here last week?"

Darin shrugged. "He was my last resort. I knew he'd talked to both Anders and Newkirk, and that he was part of the reason they'd gotten paroled early. I never could get Dr. Michalski to come talk to me, though, to see if there was anything that could be done about my transfer. Finally, my brother Glen convinced him."

"Do you know how Glen convinced him?"

"Not really. Maybe used the cancer card." His face tightened in grief. "Glen has Stage IV lung cancer. So maybe he played on the doc's sympathy."

Stage IV cancer. That would explain why Glen had looked even more gaunt than Darin when she'd seen him.

"Did Dr. Michalski say anything about Tanner when he was here?"

Carrico rolled his eyes. "Are you kidding? No. The guy would barely even talk about my situation. All he wanted to know was about how Glen knew his wife.

How the hell am I supposed to know that? All I know is about what's in here. Glen has his own life."

This was it. The piece they'd been missing. "Glen knows Dr. Michalski's wife? How?"

He snorted. "I can't really keep track of my brother's whereabouts from in here. But whatever. I think they both work in the courthouse together or something. Both of them do IT computer stuff."

Which meant Glen could definitely have been the one to hack Dr. Michalski's files.

"Do you think Glen tried to blackmail Michalski into coming to talk to you?"

The rest of Darin's tough-guy facade fell away. "Glen has taken care of me since we were kids. He hates that I'm in here. He was helping my ex take care of Sharon, my daughter, sending them money and stuff. Keeping an eye on Sharon and making sure my ex treats her right."

"He sounds like a good guy."

"He's the best. But now with the cancer, he's…" Darin trailed off, shrugging, obviously unable to say the word *dying*. "I don't know what I'm going to do without him. Especially once they send me to max security, he won't be able to visit because he's so sick. He didn't say that, but I could tell. And he's only got a couple months left anyway."

It wasn't difficult to see Glen was pretty damn sick. "So he got Dr. Michalski here to talk to you to see if he would recommend an earlier release for you like he had Newkirk and Anders."

Darin nodded. "I wasn't even hoping for early release, just maybe to see if he could get me kept here."

"Did Dr. Michalski mention an Owen Duquette when you talked to him? Or do you know him?"

There was no light of recognition in Darin's eyes. "No. Who is he?"

She shook her head. "Nobody important. So you don't know how Glen finally got Dr. Michalski here to visit?"

"Nope. All I know is that the good doctor sure as hell wasn't interested in helping me with my situation."

Bree had been wrong. It was *Glen* Carrico they needed to talk to, not Darin. But there was still one thing that didn't make sense—those emails she'd discovered with the cipher. The more she talked to Darin, the less sense it made.

She decided to come at it from a side angle rather than directly. "How old is Sharon again? Do you get to talk to her a lot right now? Phone? Email?"

Darin rubbed his hand across his face. "She's four. We talk a little on the phone—twice a week. No email, but that's probably more me than her."

"You guys don't get email in here?"

"No, we do, but computers are Glen's jive, not mine. I haven't touched one since I've been in here."

She stared at him. Was he lying? She didn't think so but couldn't be sure. What he was saying made more sense than the complexly coded emails that seemed to have come from him. "Never? You've never emailed any friends or former associates? Your brother?"

Darin shook his head. "Nah. They know to call me if they want to talk. I can't type worth a damn."

It was time to ask him straight up. "So you never sent anyone a message about Anders or Newkirk?"

"Why does everybody care about them so much? I barely knew the guys when they were here, much less now. I can't even remember what Anders looks like."

"Everybody cares because they're both dead. Murdered." She hoped she wasn't making a big mistake by telling him this.

Darin's eyes got wide before he sank back hard against his chair. "They are?" Panic fell over his features. "Wait—do the cops think I had something to do with it?"

She shook her head. "Actually, the cops suspect Tanner did it."

He relaxed a little. "Oh. Your man does have some pretty big problems, then. Why are you asking me about them?"

Bree believed Darin was legitimately surprised at the news of their deaths. "You're the only other person who seemed to know them both, besides Dr. Michalski and Tanner. I was hoping you could remember talking to anyone about them."

"No, only to Glen when we were trying to figure out a way to keep me here, rather than going up to state pen. I just remembered that Anders and Newkirk had both made deals that had gotten them out early."

Glen again. Time was running out, and they needed to talk to him.

"That other guy you mentioned. Duquette. He dead, too?"

There didn't seem much point in lying. "Yes. Unfortunately."

He whistled through his teeth. "Then no offense, but glad I don't know him."

Even though it went against her nature, she reached over and touched Darin's hand. "I've got to go. But I promise Tanner will look into what's going on with your transfer."

"Sounds like your man has trouble enough of his own to worry about."

She nodded and let go of his hand. "He does. But I'm going to make sure that gets cleared up. And once I do, he won't forget about you."

He just gave a one-shoulder shrug. "I won't hold my breath. I've been forgotten by damn near everyone."

Before she could say anything further, he stood and walked toward the door.

THE HOUR BREE was inside the prison was one of the longest of Tanner's life. He alternated between cursing himself for allowing her to do this at all and remembering that she was a genius and had handled circumstances worse than this since she was twelve years old.

Still, seeing her walking toward him with her unnaturally blond hair meant he could finally let out the breath he'd been holding for the past hour. Her gait was leisurely, and she was pretending to talk on the telephone—both smart. Nothing about her drew any sort of attention. She could be one of any hundreds of women her age walking across a parking lot.

He forced himself to stay in the car. It was the least he could do in order to help her sell her act.

But it took every ounce of his control not to grab her and pull her into his arms and never let her out again.

"Any problems?" he asked when she got in beside him.

"We have all sorts of problems, but if you're asking if I had any trouble getting inside, then no."

Thank God. Tanner started the car and pulled out of the parking lot. "Okay, so what were the problems?"

She began taking out the pins that held her wig in place. "This is probably going to sound like I'm just trying not to start my sexual experience as part of a conjugal visit with you...but you can't turn yourself in yet."

He swallowed a bark of laughter. This woman. "Colorado doesn't allow conjugal visits, but I'll still hear you out on why I can't turn myself in yet."

"I think this is all more complicated than we even thought."

He didn't even try to stop himself from rolling his eyes. "Of course it is. What did you find out?"

"I don't think Darin Carrico had anything to do with the murders. I told him Anders and Newkirk were dead, and he legitimately seemed surprised."

"What about the emails he sent?"

"I don't think he sent them at all. Someone just made it look like he did. If I look a little deeper, I wouldn't be surprised if I found the emails hadn't originated from Camp George West at all. Damn it, I should've looked into that further rather than take it at face value. It was stupid."

He reached over and placed his hand on hers, which had curled up into fists on her lap. One of his hands could cover both of hers. "Hey. You're doing the best you can under much less than optimal circumstances. If it wasn't for you, I'd be sitting in a cell with zero information about what was going on."

"It was still a careless mistake."

"Yeah, well, your mistakes are still providing us forward progress, so let's focus on that. If you don't think Carrico has anything to do with the murders, then who do you think is involved?"

"I think all the answers might be with *Glen* Carrico, not Darin. Evidently he somehow knows Michalski's wife, and I think Glen might be the one who hacked the doctor's files."

"And he's setting up his brother to look like the murderer? They seemed pretty friendly a few days ago."

"No, I don't think so. I'll have to dig deeper about the emails. But I definitely think Glen is the puzzle piece we've been missing in all this."

He squeezed her hands. "Then you're right. It's time to pay the other Carrico brother a visit."

Chapter Twenty-One

Glen Carrico's house was far away from damn near everything. The longer they drove down his isolated drive, the more uncomfortable Tanner became.

"What do we know about this guy again?"

Bree had held her computer in her lap since they'd pulled away from the prison almost an hour ago.

"Glen Carrico. Older brother of Darin. Thirty-two years old, never married. No known significant other. Has lived at this address pretty much all of his adult life."

"And he and his brother are close?"

Bree side-eyed him. "Juvenile records are a bit trickier to…access, but from what I've seen, yeah, they are definitely close. Looks like Glen took on responsibility for raising Darin when their mom took off. Glen was eighteen years old at the time. Darin was eleven. Glen pretty much gave up a lot of his future to take care of his brother."

Tanner grimaced. "Glen got any sort of record himself?"

Bree shook her head. "Nothing. Honestly, it looks like he was a good kid. Got accepted to Colorado State with a full scholarship, but declined. Did his best trying to raise his troubled brother."

"He couldn't have been very happy that Darin ended up in jail."

"Definitely not, and even more upset when they gave notice two months ago that they're transferring him to max security. He's written memos to just about every person with a pulse in the Colorado law enforcement system, trying to get Darin's situation changed."

Tanner grimaced. "I'll be honest—I don't really understand what Glen has to do with any of this. He doesn't have any ties with the victims and has never been in trouble with the law."

She nodded. "And Glen is dying of cancer. Only has a couple months left to live, according to Darin."

Tanner muttered a curse under his breath. People with nothing left to lose sometimes couldn't be trusted. Added an extra layer of risk he and Bree definitely didn't need.

A small, run-down house finally came into view. Tanner parked in front of it, then reached over and got his Glock from the glove compartment. It didn't look like anyone was home, but Tanner wasn't taking any chances.

"Any possibility I can talk you into staying in the car?" he asked her.

Her sour look answered him before she even got the words out. "Any chance hell is freezing over in the next thirty seconds?"

He chuckled. "Fine, but be careful."

"Yes, sir, Captain Sexy Lips." She gave him a little salute.

Keeping her close to his side as they approached the front door, Tanner untucked his shirt and placed his weapon in the front waistband of his pants. He didn't like approaching the door without his weapon in hand, but he didn't want Glen mistaking his gun as an act of aggression and responding in kind.

"Glen Carrico, this is Tanner Dempsey. I'm not here in any official capacity. I'd just like to ask you a few questions." Tanner said the words as they approached the broken steps leading up to the door. He listened for a second, but there was no answer.

"Maybe we can talk about Darin and if there's some way I can help him," he called out again.

Still no answer, and as they got closer to the door, Tanner realized it was open just the slightest bit.

He brought his arm out and scooped Bree behind him, pulling his Glock out and pointing it at the ground by his leg.

"Glen?" he called out again.

He dropped his volume. "I really think you ought to consider waiting in the car." He had a very bad feeling about this.

Bree's hands squeezed his waist. "Do you think he's dead?"

"I think it's mighty quiet, and his door is cracked open in the middle of the day. That's not a good sign."

"I'll be okay. I don't want to leave you."

He nodded—he didn't really want her out of his sight, either—and continued forward, weapon raised. He wasn't acting in any sort of law enforcement capacity, but years on the force still had him identifying himself once more at the door. "Glen, I'm coming inside. Your door is open, and I'm worried something is wrong."

Tanner swept Bree over to the side against the house, then nudged the door open with his foot. He gave her a pointed look and mouthed the words *stay here*.

She nodded, and he had to trust she would keep her

word. He moved inside, weapon now raised to eye level.
He glanced around the room quickly but saw nothing
posing danger. Keeping his back to the wall as much
as possible, he walked quickly into the small kitchen.
Nothing. It didn't take him long to clear the rest of the
house.

There wasn't any danger here and, even more important, no dead body.

"It's clear, freckles. You can come in."

"Anything bad?"

He shook his head. "No, thank goodness. I was expecting the worst, and I'm happy not to have found it."

He tucked his gun back into the waistband of his
jeans, and the two of them began looking around. There
didn't seem to be anything out of place or any sign of
foul play, even with the door cracked open.

Hell, this house was in the middle of nowhere. There
was much more chance a wild animal would wander in
here than people.

It wasn't till they were near the back of the house
and Bree passed by an open window that they heard
the music coming from a large shed a couple hundred
meters from the back of the house.

"That music wasn't playing when we got out of the
car. Maybe Glen is out there," Bree said.

They started the whole process once again. Tanner
tried to keep Bree shielded as much as possible as he
called out to see if Glen was in the shed and identified
himself.

He reached the door and had convinced himself that
the man had just left the radio on when a shot fired from
over their shoulder and blew out the window at the front
of the shed, not five feet from where they were standing.

Bree gave a little scream and Tanner dived for her,

knocking them both to the ground, as another shot rang out, this one going a little more wide.

Keeping Bree tucked behind him, Tanner pulled out his gun and fired once in the direction the bullets had come from. There was no way he'd be very accurate from this distance, but it would buy them a second or two.

"Stay low and get inside."

Bree immediately began crawling toward the shed door.

He fired once again, only one time, wanting to save as many bullets as he could in case he needed them, but also wanting to give them a little bit of cover to make it.

Another shot rang out, this one going too high. Bree was inside already, so Tanner dived for the door, yanking it closed behind him.

The shed looked like it hadn't been cleaned out in years. There was stuff everywhere—from stacked tires to old tools to piles of plywood. But the junk worked in their favor.

"Stay low and try to get behind something," he said, guiding her to a spot behind the stack of tires. "If Glen starts shooting blindly the walls won't stop bullets, but the other stuff will."

"Are you sure that's Glen out there? Why's he shooting at us?"

"Maybe he saw me with my gun and got nervous."

Or maybe they'd just found their killer.

"I'll try to give him the benefit of the doubt," he continued. "Mostly because Glen is either a really bad shot or he wasn't trying to hit us. If he had wanted us dead, he could've done it the moment we stepped outside his house, from the angle he was at."

Tanner stepped closer to the door. "This is Captain

Tanner Dempsey," he called out. "We just want to talk. Whatever's happening here is a miscommunication."

"I know who you are, cop." That was definitely Glen Carrico's voice.

"I know I had my weapon out, Glen, but that was because your front door was open and I thought there might be danger. It wasn't intended in an aggressive nature toward you. So let's just both put our weapons down and we can talk like reasonable adults."

Glen scoffed. "I don't think I have ever known a cop to be reasonable my whole life. Somehow I don't think today is going to be my lucky day."

"I'm not here as law enforcement, just as a regular person. I just want to talk."

"Tanner Dempsey, hero of Grand County, not here as law enforcement?" Carrico gave a bitter laugh. "I know all about you, Dempsey. And you're not going to get away with what you've been getting away with."

"I don't know what the hell you're talking about, Glen. I didn't kill those guys, so I'm not getting away with anything."

For a long time the other man didn't say anything. When he finally did, Tanner had to strain to hear him.

"You're here earlier than I thought. I thought I had more time."

"More time for what?" Tanner called out when Carrico didn't say anything else. "Glen, come on. Let's talk this out. I'm willing to chalk up the bullets in our direction as a miscommunication. We can still discuss what we're here to talk about."

"What if I don't want to talk to you? Did that ever occur to you, you conceited pig?"

Bree winced from her place crouched behind the tires.

"Fine. Then just let us out. You don't have to talk to us at all. We'll leave."

"No can do, Dempsey." Carrico's contempt was clear the way he spit Tanner's name.

"You can't keep us here. And you don't want to shoot a cop. That will bring all sorts of heat down on you."

"Even if I shoot *you*, Dempsey? My understanding is that you're wanted for murder right now. What if I just say I thought you were trying to attack me and that it was self-defense? After all, you are on my property."

The man did have a valid point.

"I don't think that's really what you want to do, is it, Glen?" Tanner said in the most soothing voice he could muster and still get the volume he needed. "If you'd wanted to kill us, you could've done it already."

Silence followed. Then more silence.

"Do you think he left?" Bree finally asked as the quiet around them dragged out further.

Tanner moved over so he could peek out the window. "Maybe. If he did, we should leave before he changes his mind."

She nodded. "I'm all for that."

Tanner eased the door open. "Glen, we're coming out. Hold your fire. We just want to get to our car and leave."

They both stayed far away from the door as Tanner pushed it open with a stick in case it was a trap. Then held the stick out to see if that would draw fire.

Nothing.

Gritting his teeth, he stuck his hand out long enough for Glen to fire at him, praying he'd be pulling it back with all his fingers still attached.

He did.

It was now or never. He held his hand out to Bree. "Let's go before Glen changes his mind."

Keeping low, they ran out the door. But they weren't two feet away before a shot rang out and the door frame above their heads splintered.

With a low curse, Tanner grabbed Bree around the waist and spun them both back into the shed, slamming the door behind them.

"Yeah, sorry. You leaving isn't going to work out for me after all," Glen yelled.

Chapter Twenty-Two

Tanner's curse was foul. He wasn't sure what had just happened out there, but he knew things had gone from bad to not-going-to-get-out-of-here-alive bad.

"Glen, c'mon, man. Don't do this," he yelled.

"You weren't supposed to come here, Dempsey. Not yet. Damn it, I thought I had more time."

"More time for what?" Tanner yelled. "To help your brother? Do you know who killed Peter Anders and Joshua Newkirk? That's all we want to talk about. We want to figure out what's going on."

"Snitches get stitches, haven't you heard?" Glen sneered.

"Oh my gosh, did he kill them? Is that what he's saying?" Bree's green eyes were big where she crouched behind the tires again.

"I hope not." Not because Tanner wasn't ready to close this case and prove his innocence, but because Glen had the tactical advantage right now with them trapped in the shed. If he was admitting to murder, he definitely wasn't planning on letting them go free to tell the world about it.

"Don't say anything else, Glen," Tanner called out. "Let's just wait and talk things out reasonably."

"I killed them," Glen yelled. "I killed Anders, Newkirk and Owen Duquette."

The words were breathy and quick, like he was relieved to get them off his chest.

Damn it. Tanner ran a hand over his face. He had to get Bree out of this shed. He pulled out his phone. It was time to call in the cavalry.

Proving his innocence wouldn't do him any good if they were both dead.

"Are you calling 911? How long will it take them to get here?" she whispered.

"A while. But I'm not calling them. If they come in here guns blazing, Glen is just going to open fire on this place. I'm calling Whitaker."

She made a sour face. "That guy is an ass hat."

Ass hat or not, Tanner trusted him to have the experience needed for this sort of situation.

Whitaker answered on the first ring. "If it isn't the man on the top of my personal most wanted list."

"Yeah, well, maybe we can go out for dinner and dancing sometime," Tanner quipped. "I need you to get to this address." He rattled it off.

"Glen Carrico's place?"

What the hell? "Do I even want to know why you know that?"

"You're not the only person around here who can do detective work, you know. I'm actually on my way out to talk to him right now."

Tanner wanted to know exactly how Whitaker had figured it out, but that would have to wait until later. "Good. Because Glen just admitted to killing all three of the victims. He's got Bree and me trapped in a shed and is firing at us."

Whitaker let out a curse. At least he was taking this seriously. "I'm probably twenty minutes out."

"Okay, we'll hold him off until then. Hurry." Tanner clicked off the phone.

He looked around. There was stuff piled up everywhere, but only one door. He moved away from the cover the piles of wood provided and eased toward the back of the shed. He wasn't going to wait for Glen to decide he was done talking and ready to start shooting. They'd be sitting ducks.

"Do you think my brother's really going to survive in a max security?" Glen yelled. "He can barely hack it at Camp George West. Those guys I killed gave up information on other people in order to get out of jail. They were scum. Criminals who then ratted out others in order to save themselves."

Tanner shifted a large metal shelf. Was that a small window up near the ceiling at the back? It had been blacked out, but maybe it would still open. It was going to make a lot of noise trying to get to it.

"Try to keep him talking so he can't hear me."

Bree nodded, watching him with wide eyes. She moved closer to the door.

"How did you know that they snitched on others?" she called out.

"The precious psychiatrist's files told me everything I needed to know. All three of them had to be cleared by Michalski before their sentences were reduced."

"What did you use to hack the files? Doxing? A Trojan horse or what?"

Tanner moved the large cabinet again, wincing as it made a loud scratching noise.

Meanwhile Bree looked like she was actually interested in how Glen had hacked the files. She probably was.

"Neither," Glen responded. "I did it the old-fashioned way. I bought the information from somebody else who hacked it. Michalski's own wife sold me the files."

"Why would she do that?" Bree whispered to Tanner. He had no idea, just continued to move furniture so he could get to the window.

"You want to know what the irony is?" Glen asked. His voice was sounding weary now. "I wrote, emailed and called Dr. Michalski for weeks, trying to get him to come evaluate Darin when we first got word of the transfer. Guy wouldn't even give me the time of day. You know how I met his wife? Because I was going to ask her if she might be willing to put in a good word with Michalski for us. We worked in the same building, but I didn't know her. It was my last shot."

While Glen continued to talk, Tanner finally muscled the furniture so that he could climb up it and reach the window.

Good news, it could be opened.

Bad news, there was no way he was going to fit through that. It was going to be tight, even for Bree.

"Ends up Mrs. Michalski hates her husband," Glen continued. "Evidently, he's been known to sleep with a patient a time or two. She couldn't put in a good word for me with him since she'd kicked him out of the house, but she was willing to give me his files for free so I could blackmail the good doctor into doing whatever I wanted."

"That would explain why Michalski was in the sheriff's office at 3:00 a.m. He probably doesn't have a home to go to right now," Tanner muttered as he pried open the window as wide as he could. Which still wasn't going to be large enough for him to fit, no matter how big he got it.

But at least Bree would be getting out.

"And did it work?" Bree yelled out. "Were you able to get Michalski to help you?"

"That bastard cop is just as bad as all the rest of the bastard cops. Didn't care about me. Didn't care about my brother or what would happen to him."

Glen's voice was clearer. He was getting closer.

"Tanner…" Bree whispered.

"I hear him. He's coming toward us. Climb up here."

She nodded but turned back to the door first. "What about the emails? Why would you make your brother look guilty if you were trying to keep him out of the maximum-security prison?"

"I didn't do that!" Glen scoffed. "I would never do that. It must've been Michalski's way of making sure he didn't actually have to do what I want."

Tanner helped Bree climb up to where he was.

"I want you to go out the window."

She shook her head. "There's no way you're going to fit through that thing."

"I don't need to fit through. All we have to do is keep Glen talking until Whitaker gets here. He should be here in another ten or fifteen minutes."

They both knew Glen wasn't going to wait that long. "But…"

He kissed her quickly. "Freckles, if there's going to be a shoot-out, it's better for me to be here by myself. Knowing you're undefended makes you vulnerable and splits my focus. By myself, I can keep him pinned. And—"

He stopped talking as a red electronic timer on the

workshop table over Bree's shoulder blinked on. It hadn't been on a second ago.

And then it started counting down from two minutes.

"What the hell?" he muttered.

He let go of Bree and climbed down to take a closer look. She immediately followed. He traced the cord attached to the timer and lifted a greasy sheet that covered a large table. When he saw what it was attached to, his heart stopped.

The timer didn't.

"Oh my God," Bree whispered beside him. "Those are explosives."

Glen began yelling from outside again, much closer. "You shouldn't have come here, Dempsey. You weren't supposed to be here."

Tanner didn't waste any time. He grabbed Bree's arm and propelled her back up toward the window. "You have to get out, right now."

"But—"

"Situation is still the same. If I have to face Glen guns blazing, doing it by myself gives me a better chance."

"I don't want to leave you," she whispered.

"I know, freckles. But do it anyway."

She nodded.

Relief flooded his entire body. They didn't have time to fight this out. Knowing she was safe would allow him to focus. He kissed her hard once more then hoisted her up and through the impossibly small window.

"Get out of the blast range and stay hidden until Whitaker gets here," he told her as she wiggled her hips through. Once she made it, he winced as she fell forward. It was a long way to fall and no good way to catch herself.

But at least she'd be alive.

He couldn't see out the window to make sure she was all right, but it wouldn't have mattered anyway—he was running out of time. Only forty-five seconds left on the countdown. If he had more time, he might have tried to call in support and see if there was any way he could disarm it, but there was no way that could happen now.

"Why are you doing this, Glen?" he called out. "It doesn't need to be this way."

He didn't actually expect Carrico to answer, but he did. "This wasn't what I wanted. Any of it. I just hope it's worth it in the end."

Tanner was done with the cryptic statements from this guy. He wasn't waiting any longer. Bree was safe.

He shot at the front window once to try to get Glen's attention focused in that direction, and then he stormed the door.

Chapter Twenty-Three

She and Tanner really were going to need to have a long talk about exactly what it meant to be a *team*. Team did not mean one person stayed in jeopardy while the other ran for her life.

But when the clock was ticking and some sort of bomb was about to blow up the whole building, it wasn't time for an argument. So she kissed him and wiggled out that tiny window and fell what felt like a thousand feet to the ground.

But she damn well didn't run to safety. Instead she immediately grabbed the biggest stick she could find and headed around to the front of the shed.

If Tanner was coming out of there guns blazing, then she was going to help him by coming from the back, club swinging.

As she sprinted around the building, Glen's attention was caught by the front window of the shed shattering. She ran as fast as she could toward the skinny man, even as Tanner came bursting out of the shed door, firing his gun in Glen's direction.

Glen was hit by one of Tanner's bullets, but only in the arm, not enough to take him down. And then he was firing, too. Tanner, out of bullets, dived to the side to get away from the shots firing his way.

She knew it wasn't going to be enough.

"No!" She screamed to get Glen's attention before he could fire at Tanner again and continued to run at full speed, branch raised.

Glen spun around to face her, and she knew he was going to get the shot off before she could hit him. She prepared herself for the feel of a bullet, but when the shot rang out, no pain came.

Instead, it was Glen who fell from a shot to the head. Bree spun to see what had happened. Did Tanner have another bullet she didn't know about? He was running toward her, leaping over Glen's body and pulling her against his chest and behind one of the larger trees.

Not two seconds later, the shed exploded, sending pieces of wood and metal flying out as shrapnel. The tree saved them from it ripping into their bodies.

Tanner held her away from him and looked down at her, fear clouding his brown eyes. "Are you okay?" He began patting her down, looking for wounds.

"I'm fine. How…? Did you shoot him?"

"Excuse me. Can I get a little help over here?" The voice was coming from the other side of where the shed had stood. They both rushed over through the smoke and debris to find Ryan Fletcher leaning up against a tree, gun next to him.

"Fletcher? What the hell are you doing here?" Tanner rushed to his friend's side and helped ease him to the ground.

"I was on my cell phone with Sheriff Duggan when Whitaker called in what was going on. I was closer, so I rushed over here. Made it just in time to shoot someone I've never met then get blown to kingdom come." He smiled. "Everybody always says an attorney's job is bloody."

Tanner smiled. "Well, you don't have any projectiles sticking out of your body, so I think you're going to be okay. Maybe a concussion."

"Pretty sure you've punched me harder than this, sparring."

Bree reached down and squeezed his shoulder. "You saved my life. Thank you."

"Anytime. I'm glad you guys don't have to run anymore." He smiled and leaned back against the tree.

About ten minutes later, Whitaker finally showed up, just in time to be of no real use whatsoever. An ambulance came for Ryan, but he refused to leave, even though he probably needed to get a CT scan.

Tanner stayed glued to Bree's side, and to be honest, she didn't want him far anyway. They'd come too close to losing each other.

They waited with Ryan on Glen's rickety front porch steps as some of the other sheriff's deputies arrived—including Ronnie Kitchens, who hugged them both—and began searching the house.

Whitaker came out a few minutes later. "Well, as far as I'm concerned, you're cleared, Dempsey. We found access to a huge stack of Dr. Michalski's files on Carrico's computer, cross-referenced with a list of all the people who'd gotten reduced sentences because of giving up info on others. Looks like Carrico planned to take them all out."

"Unbelievable," Ryan muttered.

"Would've liked to have known why he chose me to set up for the fall," Tanner said.

Bree pulled him closer. "And how he could possibly think this would help his brother's case. If anything, this will just make it harder for Darin to stay at the minimum-security facility."

"Guy had cancer, right?" Ryan asked. "He's pretty young. That couldn't have been easy. Maybe he just snapped."

"I guess so." Tanner rubbed his eyes then looked up at Whitaker. "You already knew about this place when I called. How'd you figure it out?"

"Michalski. I found him after you broke into the sheriff's office last night and locked him in that closet." He shot a sideways look at Bree. "After I figured out that the window alarm was false, of course. Michalski was just spitting mad that you had snuck into the building."

Tanner raised a dark eyebrow. "Didn't make *you* mad that I had snuck into the building?"

Whitaker leaned against the porch rail. "Don't get me wrong—I would've arrested your ass if I had caught you there. But I also couldn't think of many reasons you would be there at all if you were guilty and on the run."

Tanner shrugged. "I wasn't guilty."

"What I couldn't easily figure out was why *Michalski* was there at three in the morning. Started checking building logs, and it seemed he'd been there all night for multiple nights. Started looking further and figured out there was a lot going on with the doctor that he wasn't telling. I went to the sheriff, and she and I confronted him this morning with our concerns. He admitted his wife was divorcing him and had hacked his files. She'd been selling them to whoever she thought could do the most damage to Michalski's reputation."

"He should've been up front about that from the beginning," Bree said. "There were ways to do damage control. Hell, I could've tracked down anyone she'd sold the info to and destroyed it."

Whitaker nodded. "I think Michalski understands that. He's the one on administrative leave now. I'm sure you'll be reinstated as soon as the sheriff sees you, between what we found here, Carrico admitting to the killings and Fletcher finding him in the middle of attempted murder."

Tanner stood. "Good. Then the sheriff can expect to see me first thing tomorrow. Right now, we're going home."

Home. That was definitely where she wanted to go. She wanted to check on Star and Corfu and make sure they were doing okay. She wanted to sleep for a hundred hours in Tanner's big bed.

Beside him.

Bree and Ryan stood with him. Bree's grin was huge, Ryan's a little more painful as he rubbed his head. But he slapped Tanner on his back. "Congrats, buddy. I'm glad you're no longer the hunted. I'm going to help make sure the people who really deserve the blame for this get what's coming to them."

Tanner shook his head. "No, nobody in the department is to blame. It was just some unfortunate circumstances. I'm just ready to get back to the job."

Bree squeezed his hand. "And I know Risk Peak wants you back, too."

Ryan nodded. "If you say so. I think I'm going to take a few dozen aspirin and call it a day. I'll catch you guys later."

Tanner and Bree headed toward their car, too. Tanner still hadn't let go of her.

She smiled at him. "Looks like you get to go back to being Captain Sexy Li—"

She never finished the sentence as his mouth slammed against hers and he backed her against the car. She moaned, gripping at his hair and clutching him to her, totally not caring that his colleagues might be able to see them.

When they finally broke apart, he leaned his fore-head against hers.

"You scared me to death. You're not great at following directions, you know that? You were supposed to run to safety. Not charge a fully-armed man with just a tree branch."

"Well, you're not great at understanding the whole concept of *team*. In a team, one person doesn't run for safety while the other gets riddled with bullet holes or blown to smithereens. So how about we call it even?"

He smiled. "How about we go home?"

"Sounds perfect to me."

Chapter Twenty-Four

"You know you don't have to do this. I know we joked about it when we were on the run, but I never actually expected us to go on any sort of romantic getaway."

Tanner reached over and grabbed both Bree's hands that were wringing nervously in her lap. He brought one to his lips.

"I wanted to do this. Wanted to take you somewhere romantic and secluded. And where I didn't have to compete for your attention with a certain dog and her pups."

The case had been closed now for nearly a week. Dr. Michalski was on extended administrative leave while law enforcement got the rest of the hacked-files situation under control.

Darin Carrico had been devastated by his brother's death, but true to his word, Tanner had looked into the situation surrounding Darin's sudden prison transfer. Once he started questioning it, nobody seemed to be able to provide a real reason for why the transfer was occurring. Tanner made a special request, and with the help of Ryan Fletcher, it looked like Darin was going to be able to stay at Camp George West for the remainder of his sentence.

It seemed a waste for four people to die in order to

make something happen that should've happened with just a phone call.

Bree reached over to cup his cheek. "Hey, what's that frown about?"

He turned his head so he could kiss her palm, loving the way she pushed her own discomfort aside because she was worried about him. "Nothing. Just thinking about how all this could've been avoided if Darin and Glen had felt like someone would listen to them. None of this had to happen."

She nodded. "I wish it hadn't happened this way. Even though the dead guys were criminals, they still didn't deserve to die. And the thought of Glen being so desperate… I feel like he only became a killer because he was backed into a corner."

"Yeah. Under different circumstances, his life would not have ended up this way. And I'm going to try to help Darin as much as I can once he gets out. God knows that family needs some proof that not all law enforcement is bad. Maybe I can help him get a job. Get visitation with his daughter."

It was the least he could do, because if the system hadn't been broken in the first place, all this might have been avoided.

She nodded. "Good. Because he's going to be lost without Glen. But still, I can't help but be glad there are a few good things that came from all this."

"Like what?"

"Like the fact that you and I might have danced around your PTSD for months before we talked about it outright. It could've festered and grown into something a lot more difficult to surmount."

"You're definitely right about that."

She nodded. "And of course helping Darin, like you

said. Everybody needs a way to be heard. Speaking of, I talked to Cassandra about the computer class she wants me to teach for the shelter. I've decided to do it. To teach it myself."

He grinned. He'd known it was just a matter of time until she'd come around. "I think you'll be great at it."

She shrugged. "If they can find the guts to leave their abusive situations, certainly I can find the guts to help teach these incredible women a new skill."

"Have I told you how absolutely amazing you are?"

She grinned and waggled her eyebrows. "I'm hoping maybe we can take this weekend and both find some ways to show each other that."

Sheriff Duggan had insisted Tanner take the entire weekend off. He'd been working twelve-and fifteen-hour days since he'd been reinstated. Just the paperwork involved with everything that had happened had been a full-time job, plus everything that had fallen through the cracks while he'd been away.

The sheriff hadn't needed to twist Tanner's arm to take a whole weekend off. He'd been more than happy for two full days to devote to Bree. He'd barely seen her all week. Except for the night immediately after Glen's death, when he'd taken them to the ranch, they'd both been staying at their own places in Risk Peak.

But he planned to talk to her about moving in with him by the time the weekend was over. He wanted her with him.

They pulled up at the resort in Estes Park—an ornate place with remote bungalows meant specifically for romance and privacy.

He hadn't told Bree where they were going, and her eyes grew big now as they parked and walked inside the main lodge to get their key. "Wow, this is fancy."

He pulled her up against him. "You deserve fancy."

She deserved *everything*.

The sun was setting as they checked in and walked down the lovely path that led to their private bungalow.

"It's a different view from the ranch, but the ranch is gorgeous in its own way," she said. "Maybe you guys ought to consider opening a resort."

He chuckled. "Noah would love that. He says I already owe him a week's worth of winter chores for having to spend three hours in the sheriff department's interrogation room avoiding answering questions about me."

She laughed. "You know he's going to wait until the middle of a blizzard and then call in his marker."

"I have no doubt about it."

He opened the door and escorted her inside with his hand at the small of her back.

"Man, this place really is *bougie*."

He raised an eyebrow. "*Bougie?* Is that bad or good?"

"Do you not ever talk to any of the teenagers in town? They taught it to me. *Bougie* is fancy good. I finally researched its origins and found out it's from the word *bourgeois*."

He shook his head. "I'm obviously not up on my slang. I'll work on that."

Once they were both inside and had looked around the bedroom and the living area with windows that opened out to a stunning view, Tanner wasn't exactly sure what to do.

He'd brought her here to make love to her. Because he wanted the first time to be absolutely perfect for her, to make up for everything she'd gone through in the last week.

He hadn't let himself get too close to her this week

because he hadn't wanted their first time to be rushed or ordinary. He wanted it to be...*bougie*.

He'd wanted to make love to her for so long, but now that the time was here, with no obstacles in their way and in a wondrous, romantic spot, he was actually a little nervous.

"I'm not sure what I'm supposed to say right now," she said. "Is everything okay? We don't have to do anything if you're not ready."

Enough. His own indecision was making *her* nervous. He snagged her around the waist and pulled her up against him. "Isn't that supposed to be my line?"

She smiled, winding her arms around his shoulders. "It's been a long week for you. And I know it all turned out okay in terms of your job, but we don't have to do anything tonight if it's just not the right time."

"An isolated room with a giant bed and nobody interrupting us? Oh, I think this very definitely *is* the right time for you and me."

His lips had barely touched hers when the phone rang on the bedside table. He ignored it, much more interested in the feel of Bree's lips than whatever was going to be said on the phone.

But when it kept ringing, Bree finally wiggled away from him and answered it herself.

"Hello?" He continued to kiss down her neck as she answered. He could hear the voice speaking briskly.

"So sorry to interrupt you, Mrs. Dempsey. This is the front desk."

"I'm not Mrs. Dempsey, but I'm here with Mr. Dempsey." Tanner loved how she was breathing hard and struggled to get the words out as he continued to kiss her neck.

"My apologies. We have a bottle of champagne, for

the Dempsey party, courtesy of the Grand County Sheriff's Department, waiting for you at the front desk. We would normally deliver it to your room, but our bellboy just got sick and had to go home."

"That's okay. I'll walk up and get it." She squeaked out the last word as he bit down lightly on the side of her neck.

She barely got the phone back in its cradle before he had her pulled up against him. Her arm reached back, fingers threading into his hair, throat tilting back as she leaned her head on his shoulder, giving him better access.

Her back was completely pressed up against his front. He used one hand to keep her neck tilted at the angle he wanted, and the other to find all the places on the front of her body that he could play with until she gasped.

He found many.

And didn't stop until she was bucking against his hand and calling out his name.

"You stay here, and I'll go get the champagne," he whispered in her ear as she finally caught her breath and recovered from the shudders racking her body.

She turned and snuggled against him like a little cat, rubbing his chest with her nose. He loved to see her so sated and happy like this.

And the weekend was just getting started.

"No," she whispered. "I'll get it. I know you wanted to shower. You get going on that, and be ready when I get back with the champagne." She slipped away from him. "You better hurry, because if you're not done, I'm going to have to join you in there."

He pulled her in for a quick kiss. "You're going to have to work on your threatening skills."

"Oh yeah?" she asked. "Then how about this as a threat?"

He nearly swallowed his tongue as she whispered some of the things she planned to do to him once they were both naked.

"But I need a couple of sips of champagne first," she finished with a smile.

"Good gravy, woman. Hurry up and get that champagne."

The sound of her laugh as she ran toward the door ranked right up there with his favorite things on the planet.

He made a beeline for the shower, because although he wouldn't mind her joining him in there, that could wait. The first time they made love, he wanted it to be in a bed, where he could take his time.

For just a second, he had a moment's pause. Their first time really should've been in his bed back at the ranch—where everything started for them. But he shook it off. There would be plenty of time to make love to her there, too.

He was out of the shower five minutes later and slipping on the sleep pants he'd brought but had no plans to be sleeping in and walked back into the bedroom. No Bree.

It was only after another ten minutes had passed that he began to get concerned.

He picked up the phone on the bedside table and dialed the front desk. "Did anybody come by yet to pick up the bottle of champagne left for the Dempsey party?"

He could hear papers shuffling around before the woman at the front desk answered. "I'm sorry, sir. I just arrived for my shift. Can you give me just a moment and I'll call you right back with an update?"

"Sure." He hung up.

Had Bree gotten lost on the path to the front desk? It was a pretty straight shot, but she had been known to get distracted by things. He wasn't worried, but he'd just go look for her. He slipped on a shirt and pair of shoes.

He saw the envelope as soon as he came out of the bedroom. The bloodred color of it was almost garish against the snowy white of the rug it lay on. Tanner tore it open.

Bungalow 42. I have a surprise for you.

What the hell? What in the world had Bree done? Had she figured out where he was going to take her—not that that would be difficult for her, since he'd put the reservation on his credit card—and had planned something of her own?

This woman kept him on his toes, that was for sure.

Ironically, bungalow 42 was the one he'd wanted. It was the most isolated, with the very best view. But it had already been booked.

Tanner smiled. Looked like now he was going to get it anyway.

He slipped out the door. Of course, if Bree had hacked his credit card account, they were going to have to have a long talk.

But first they were going to have a long time *not talking.*

He half jogged to the outskirts of the property, smiling the entire time. His grin grew bigger when he saw the door was cracked open and candles lit inside. Who would've thought Bree would have her own romantic side.

He pushed the door open. "Freckles, you are in so much trouble. I'm going to show you how to—"

Tanner stopped talking when he heard a voice from the far corner, obviously not Bree's.

"Dempsey. I thought for a second I had misplayed this, that you weren't going to come."

Ryan? What in the hell was going on?

"What are you doing here, man?"

In the dim light of the candles, he could see Ryan reach over for a light switch on the wall. "It's a little dark in here, isn't it?" Ryan asked. "Let me shed a little light on the subject."

He flipped a switch, and all the oxygen was sucked out of Tanner's world when he saw Bree, strung up by her neck, struggling to keep stable on a chair balancing precariously on its back legs.

"Does this situation feel familiar at all?"

Chapter Twenty-Five

Fear was a fist in Tanner's throat, blocking his airway. He let out a vile curse. "What the hell is going on here, Fletcher?"

Tanner rushed toward them, but Fletcher pulled out a knife and held it against Bree's ribs. "No farther, or she'll be dead before she hits the floor. Oh, wait—she won't hit the floor. She'll just dangle there in the air."

Tanner stopped his approach. He didn't want to tip her balance in the chair or cause Ryan to do anything to hurt her further.

"Fine." He held his hands out in front of him in a gesture of surrender, wishing desperately he'd brought his weapon.

Bree's arms were restrained behind her back, and there was a piece of industrial tape covering her mouth. Her beautiful green eyes were wide and frantic as she struggled to keep her balance with her toes on the chair.

Yes, this was a very familiar scene, and Tanner knew exactly what she was going through.

"Hang in there, freckles," he said in a low voice.

Ryan laughed, the sound cruel and ugly. "*Hang in there?* That's a pretty poor choice of words if you're trying to provide her any comfort."

"I don't know what kind of sick game you're playing, but it ends now. Cut. Her. Down."

Fletcher's handsome face contorted into a sneer. "No, I don't think so. Not after all the trouble I went through to get us to this place. I think it's about time that you learned what it's like to lose someone."

Tanner's body twitched with the need to move as Ryan took the point of his knife and ran it down Bree's bare arm.

"My original plan involved you rotting in prison for a few life sentences, but it didn't take me very long to realize how deeply you have everyone fooled. Everyone in this entire damn county thinks that you're some sort of hero. They have no understanding of what you really are—a murderer."

Tanner tried to wrap his head around what Ryan was saying, while keeping his eyes glued to Bree's face. "I didn't kill those guys. Glen Carrico admitted to it."

Ryan shook his head. "Glen Carrico had about twenty-three more seconds to live and was willing to do whatever he could to keep his baby brother from being transferred to big-boy prison. I was happy to scratch Carrico's back if he scratched mine."

It was all starting to make sense to Tanner. "*You* are behind the whole thing from the beginning. Did you kill Anders, Newkirk and Duquette yourself?"

Tanner grimaced when Ryan gave the chair Bree was balancing on a little push, causing her to rock haphazardly. Tears squeezed out of her panicked eyes.

He made his peace right then and there that he was going to have to kill a man he thought was his friend.

And he wasn't going to hesitate.

He let out the breath he'd been holding as Bree finally found her balance again. He knew the terror she was going through. Knew how tired the muscles in her legs would be from trying to hold her weight at an awkward angle and just on her toes. It wouldn't be long before her calves would begin to cramp and seize.

He could feel the phantom noose around his own throat like it was yesterday.

"Yeah, I killed them." Ryan raised an eyebrow. "So what? The world should thank me for removing people like them from the streets. Hell, you were the one who stated outright that they should stay in jail."

"But that didn't mean I thought they should be killed."

Ryan shrugged one shoulder carelessly. "They were just a means to an end, anyway. Their deaths were supposed to be your fall from grace. But nobody was willing to believe the great and mighty Tanner Dempsey could possibly be the bad guy."

There was no point in trying to argue that Tanner hadn't actually killed anyone and that was why no one believed him capable of it.

"Why are you doing this, Ryan? Because of Nate? Why now? You and I have been hanging out for years."

"And never once during that time did you mention the fact that if you would've broken that rope around your neck sooner—tried a little harder—you could've saved Nate's life."

It all became clear to Tanner.

"You got into Dr. Michalski's hacked files." That had to be it. Besides Noah and Bree, Michalski was the only other person he'd talked about Nate's death with.

And he'd said those very words. Felt that very guilt. That if he'd just made an effort and snapped the rope sooner, he could've stopped Nate from being shot.

"Michalski's files are what brought Carrico and

me together. All the times I talked with you, I always thought you had done everything you could to save Nate. That you weren't to be blamed. But I was wrong, wasn't I? You are to be blamed, yet no one ever did. Not even so much as a mark on your file."

"Ryan—"

"Don't try to talk your way out of this. Don't forget I've had plenty of time watching you work people on the stands. I used to admire you for it, how smooth you were. But that was before I realized that you were a murderer. Then it was like my blinders were ripped off and I could finally see you for what you really were—an egotistical bastard who thinks he's better than everyone."

"Ryan, please believe me. I would've saved your brother if I could've—"

"Liar!"

Tanner watched in horror as Ryan pulled the chair out from under Bree's outstretched leg. Without its support, she fell forward and the rope began to strangle her. She began to flail, her body instinctively trying to do whatever it could to ease the pressure on her throat and allow oxygen in.

Tanner rushed toward them but stopped when Ryan brought the knife tip up to the side of Bree's neck. The way she was jerking caused her to jab herself into it. Blood soon began trickling down her throat.

"Stop, or she dies this second."

"Get the chair back under her legs, right damn now." Tanner could feel every muscle in his body tensed to attack. Could he get to Ryan before he dealt Bree a fatal blow with a knife?

He relaxed the slightest bit when Ryan pulled the knife away from her neck and placed the chair back under her legs.

The pressure was off her throat now, but she was still panicking, unable to breathe under the tape.

"Ryan, take that tape off her mouth."

Bree's chest was moving at a way too rapid pace for the amount of oxygen she was able to get in. She was going to hyperventilate, and that would be deadly in her current state. Passing out might lower her breathing rate, but it would also mean she couldn't keep her balance on the chair.

"Freckles," he said, trying to keep the panic out of his voice. "Look at me. You can do this."

He didn't even know if she heard him. Her eyes were still wild and darting all around the room, her chest heaving.

"Goddamn it, Ryan, if she passes out, you won't have any leverage over me whatsoever." And Tanner was damn well going to kill him. "Take the tape off *now*."

Ryan let out an annoyed sigh. "Fine." He reached up and ripped the tape brutally off her face.

Bree flinched, then began sucking in big gulps of air. They weren't out of danger yet. The oxygen now flooding her system could make her just as dizzy.

"Freckles, I need you to slow down your breathing. If you pass out, there's nothing to keep you balanced on that chair. Look at me."

Those green eyes finally settled on his face. She watched him, and he took slow breaths with her, getting her to match his. "That a girl. You're amazing."

Ryan just watched the entire exchange, shaking his head. "You know, *she* is the reason I really couldn't tolerate this anymore. It's bad enough that you fooled everyone who knows you into thinking you're some sort of hero. Then you actually get to fall in love? Have a wonderful future with someone? Nate didn't get to have that. So it was totally unacceptable to me that you would."

"So your grand plan was to frame me for murder?"

"It wasn't enough just to kill you." Ryan was so angry, spittle flew from his mouth as he spoke. "The world needed to know the truth about you. That you're the enemy and to be feared, not to be revered."

Tanner took a slight step closer. He needed to keep Ryan distracted long enough to be in diving range. And he had to be able to tackle him from an angle that would lead him away from Bree.

"I guess I played right into your hands by running. That was a nice touch."

Ryan shrugged. "It definitely would've been more difficult to pin all this on you if you had been there to answer all their questions. It's so ridiculous how much people wanted to believe you were innocent."

"Even Whitaker?" Tanner took another slight step forward. He wanted to look at Bree, to reassure her, but he knew he needed to keep Ryan's attention focused on him.

"Especially Whitaker. I thought for sure that guy wouldn't be blinded by your halo since he's not from around here, but he fell for your lies just as much as everyone else."

Ryan wasn't actually interested in the truth. Whitaker didn't like Tanner much at all, and he definitely wasn't blind to Tanner's faults. If Tanner had been the real killer, Whitaker wouldn't have hesitated for a second to take him down. But all Ryan could see were the lies he'd convinced himself of.

"So when it became apparent I wasn't going to be able to convince the people around here of your deceit and depravity, I decided I had to change my tactics. I wouldn't have the joy of seeing you rot in prison for the rest of your life, but I could still put Nate's ghost to rest by killing you." ·

"Then kill me. But leave Bree out of this. She has nothing to do with you, me, Nate or any of it."

"Tanner…"

Hearing her shredded voice absolutely gutted him. It had been weeks before his own voice had recovered from his ordeal. Weeks of not being able to swallow without pain.

Ryan turned to her but thankfully didn't move the chair again. "Did you know your boyfriend was a murderer? Did you know that if he just tried a little harder he could've saved my brother's life? That Nate would still be here?"

"No," Bree whispered.

Tanner took another step forward while Ryan was focused on her.

"Yes! He said so to Dr. Michalski himself."

"The things he said to Michalski are his worst fears, not the actual truth. He said them because he blames himself." Her voice was soft but steady. "He's spent hours of his life trying to figure out if it would've made a difference if he had pulled on that rope harder earlier. Sometimes he can't sleep at night knowing that if things had been different—just the slightest bit different—your brother would still be here."

"He should have tried harder!" Ryan screamed.

"Tanner would be the first person to tell you that. But you know what he wouldn't tell you?"

Tanner was about to take another step, but he froze just in time as Ryan looked back at him. "There's a hell of a lot he wouldn't tell me. Stuff he's left out for years."

"Well, I'll tell you something he wouldn't tell you.

He wouldn't tell me, either, but I hacked the hospital files to see how badly he'd been hurt. Do you know that Tanner was tortured for hours to get him to give up the other police officers he was working with? Do you know that your brother didn't die in agony because Tanner took all that punishment on himself and never cracked? Broken bones, burns, knife wounds. Did your brother have any of those, Ryan? If not, it's because Tanner took everyone's share."

He hadn't wanted her to know those details, hadn't wanted for her to be responsible for carrying them. But once again he'd been underestimating what she could handle.

The woman who argued she had no interpersonal skills certainly seemed to have them now. Ryan was actually listening to her. Maybe there would be a way out of this without someone leaving in a body bag.

And he would take up the hospital file hacking with her later.

He got another step closer before Ryan turned to look at him again. "Is she telling the truth?"

"I didn't want anybody to die that day. But honestly, I didn't think there was any chance I was walking out of there alive. The Viper Syndicate already knew I was a cop. I figured if I could stop Nate and Alex from suffering the same fate, it was the best I could do."

"But they died. Nate died." Ryan's hand with the knife lowered. For the first time it seemed like he wanted to understand what had really happened.

But Bree's legs were shaking. She wasn't going to be able to support herself on that chair for much longer.

"Yes, they died. And part of that is always going to be my fault. Bree is right. It wakes me up at night, the fear that I could've done something differently that would've gotten those two men—especially Nate—out alive."

For a moment, Tanner really thought it was going to be enough. That the sensible man and razor-sharp lawyer he'd always known Ryan Fletcher to be was going to see reason and realize that what he was doing right now—hurting Bree—was desperately wrong.

But then something flickered in his mind. Tanner could almost see the exact moment when the anger or bitterness or sheer madness—whatever it was—overcame his friend again.

"No," Ryan said, knife coming up in his hand once more. "You don't get to talk your way out of this with your charming swagger. You don't get to live while Nate doesn't. You don't get to have a happily-ever-after with a beautiful woman while he rots in the ground. You're going to know what it's like to watch her die, and then you're going to die your—"

Tanner didn't wait for him to finish. He knew what was coming next—Ryan had just announced it. Instead, Tanner launched himself at Ryan as hard as he could.

He was coming in from too far, at the wrong angle, but at least that knife was nowhere close to Bree. Instead it sliced straight into Tanner's shoulder as he crashed into Ryan, sending them both rolling to the ground.

Tanner grunted through the pain as Ryan pulled out the knife to try to stab him again with it.

He caught Ryan's wrist on the downward swing, stopping the knife from where it would've landed in his jugular. He threw his weight to the side, trying to roll Ryan with him, farther from Bree. But they had sparred too many times and Ryan was too well aware of his tactics to be taken by surprise.

Instead, Ryan pushed in the opposite direction, bringing the blade down and catching Tanner on the biceps.

He ignored the burn of the new cut, clocking Ryan in the jaw with his elbow before spinning around and catching him in the face again with an uppercut.

Ryan was dazed but didn't let go of the knife. Both men got to their feet, staring at each other, ready to do battle. Tanner knew it wasn't just his life he was fighting for. If Ryan took him out, he would definitely kill Bree, too.

Tanner braced himself for another attack with the knife, his mind working out possible scenarios based on what he knew about Ryan's fighting style. Ryan wasn't as strong as Tanner, but he was deadly fast and eerily precise in his strikes. In a fistfight that made them just about even. But the knife in Ryan's hand definitely gave him an advantage, not to mention the wounds that were already dripping blood everywhere and would soon be slowing Tanner down.

But the lightning blows he'd expected never came. Instead, Ryan pivoted and slid to the side of Tanner. Tanner quickly caught him, but not before the other man threw out his leg in a slide kick and knocked over the chair Bree was balancing on.

He could hear Bree's strangled groans behind him as the rope once again cut off her source of oxygen. Tanner dived for the chair, but Ryan tackled him, knocking him out of the way.

He felt the sting of the knife again and again as he threw Ryan off him and crawled toward Bree. His side. His calf. Tanner kicked out blindly behind him as his fingers brushed the leg of the wooden chair. He just needed a few more inches and he'd be able to right it back under her.

Then he couldn't stop his cry of pain when the knife stabbed him deep in his waist. Unlike the other blows that had been slices, this one had done definite damage.

The whole room was starting to get a little fuzzy around the edges. Tanner was losing too much blood. He didn't have much time.

He was working at a disadvantage because Ryan was using Bree against him as a weakness. As a chink in his armor. As long as Tanner kept trying to protect her, Ryan had Tanner exactly where he wanted him.

But if there was anything the last couple of weeks had taught him, it was that Bree was his partner. She was nobody's liability.

They were a team. She'd said it herself.

His fingers wrapped around the edge of the chair again. He knew Ryan expected him to crawl toward her with it, to try to get it back under her.

But Bree was strong. She could make it. And that wasn't something Ryan had taken into consideration.

Instead of moving toward her, Tanner spun with the chair in hand and slammed it against Ryan's head. Caught completely off guard, the man fell to the ground, dazed.

Once Ryan was down, Tanner stumbled the couple of feet toward her, lifting Bree's weight by her thighs, taking the pressure off her throat.

She sucked in a couple of gulps of air then croaked out, "Finish him."

She had to know Tanner would need to let her go to do that. Even setting her back down as gently as he could, it was the hardest thing he'd ever done.

This time she didn't flail as her oxygen cut back off. She trusted him to do what he had to do.

He trusted her to survive as he did it.

A team.

Tanner turned back toward Ryan, reaching down and grabbing a leg of the chair that had broken. Ryan was starting to recover from the blow to the head, but it wasn't enough.

Ryan spun the knife toward Tanner again, but with one blow of the chair leg, it went flying from his hand. Three blows with the chair leg later, and Ryan was unconscious on the ground. The sickening thud from the third blow probably meant Tanner had broken his jaw or cracked his skull.

Tanner didn't care. Ryan was down and was going to stay down.

Tanner took a step toward the knife, his foot sliding in whatever liquid was covering the ground. He let out a low curse when he realized the liquid was blood, most of it his.

The room was spinning, his vision reduced to a pinprick now. He fought to hold on to consciousness and knew if he didn't get that knife and get Bree cut down, she would strangle there.

That was damn well not going to happen.

He got the knife and tried to crawl back to her, but everything had turned so dark he couldn't seem to find her.

"Tanner." Her voice was a hoarse whisper, but it was enough.

He forced himself to his feet and took drunken steps toward her. "Freckles?"

"Tanner."

He wasn't sure if it was her voice that led him to her or sheer blind luck. But he ran into her hanging form a moment later.

Using the last of his strength, he lifted her. There was

no way he was going to be able to cut the rope from her neck. It was all he could do to stay upright.

After a moment of breathing, she whispered, "Just cut my hands, baby. I'll do the rest."

He couldn't see the tape on her wrists, couldn't see anything at all. He just prayed he wasn't cutting her too badly as he kept one arm wrapped around her legs, supporting her weight, and used the other to slice through the tape.

"You did it," she whispered. She took the knife from his hands. "We can do this, Tanner. You've always held me up, in every possible way. Now just do it for a couple more minutes."

Her voice seemed like it was coming from a great distance, but no matter what, he would do it.

"Won't let go." His words sounded mumbled and unintelligible, even to his own ears. But she understood.

"I know you won't."

He drew on every iota of strength he had to hold her weight while she cut herself down. In the end it was thoughts of Nate, and the rope he would've sworn he didn't have the strength to break and yet had, that kept him in place.

Sometimes you didn't know how strong you were until strong was the only option you had left.

He felt Bree's weight collapse against him and knew she'd managed to cut through the rope. They both fell to the ground, tangled with each other.

And the black that he'd fought for so long consumed him.

Chapter Twenty-Six

All Bree could do for the first few moments after falling to the ground with Tanner was breathe.

Every breath seemed to stab her lungs like a blade, but at least she had air. He'd saved her, by finding the superhuman strength to support her while she hacked at the rope.

"Tanner!" She yelled his name when he didn't move at all, but the sound was barely more than a whisper. She felt for a pulse, sobbing silently in relief when she found one.

The bungalow floor was covered with so much of his blood. Way too much of it. She didn't want to leave him for a second but knew she had to get help here as soon as possible. She crawled over to the phone and called the front desk, screaming as loudly as she could—which still meant they could barely hear her—for them to call for an ambulance.

She struggled back to him, forcing down the panic every time she slipped in his blood, and pulled his unconscious form into her arms, holding pressure on his wounds as best she could. There were so, so many.

She was going to lose him.

She struggled so often with finding the proper emotions for a situation. But not this time. This time she knew exactly what she felt: mind-crushing fear.

But his heart kept beating. She whispered everything she could think of in his ear as she held him waiting for the paramedics to arrive. Promises of everything she wanted to do with him. Marry him. Have babies with him. Travel the world but still always come home to the ranch. She wanted to be there with him when Star had puppies, and her puppies had puppies.

And she wanted sex. There was so much sex she wanted with him.

She told him over and over that she loved him and he was her hero.

When she ran out of promises, she moved on to threats. Threatening to illegally hack into every database in the country if he died and left her alone. To send secret messages to Whitaker about what she was doing so he would come arrest her.

Finally, after what seemed like an eternity, the paramedics arrived.

Letting them take Tanner from her was the hardest thing she'd ever done. How could she will his heart to continue beating if he was out of her sight? But she knew she had to let them take him. Help him.

"We are a team, Tanner Dempsey!" She was trying for a yell, but her ravaged voice came out as a croak. "It takes *both* of us to be a team."

A second set of paramedics insisted on looking at her wounds and refused to let her drive when she tried to stumble toward the door and get to Tanner's car. She wanted to scream at them to leave her alone, but her voice was completely useless by that point.

When they started talking about taking her to a different hospital than they'd taken Tanner, she began to panic. She couldn't communicate without her voice, and no one was willing to listen to what she was trying to say or figure out what she wanted.

She wanted to be near Tanner. She didn't care if the other hospital had strangled-people specialists. She had to be near Tanner. She could feel the agitation building at her inability to communicate. When her tears fell and she began to pull away from everyone, they thought she was in shock and started talking about sedating her.

As if she couldn't *hear* as well as couldn't speak.

Ironically, it was Whitaker, who showed up a few minutes later to help process the crime scene, who finally made the difference. He got down on the ground next to her where she sat, covered in Tanner's blood, and asked her what she needed.

Tanner. She mouthed it to him over and over until he finally nodded.

After Ryan was cuffed and taken away in his own ambulance, Whitaker left the crime scene to his colleagues, since it wasn't his jurisdiction anyway, and rode with Bree in the ambulance to the same hospital as Tanner.

The paramedics had once more tried to talk her into going to the other facility, but it was Whitaker who'd laid a hand on her shoulder and firmly told the paramedics no. So as far as she was concerned, Whitaker no longer held the status of ass hat.

Of course, he made her get checked out by the doctors before taking her to see Tanner, so he was still in the general ass vicinity. But maybe just jackass.

The doctor had checked out her throat, declared her very lucky to not have a crushed windpipe, announced it would take weeks of discomfort and blah, blah, blah, but that Bree should make a full recovery.

As soon as she knew her injuries weren't life-threatening, she'd demanded to use Whitaker's—whom she couldn't seem to get rid of now—phone and typed out one word.

Tanner.

She already knew her throat was in bad shape. She could feel the razor blades every time she swallowed or breathed too deeply. She'd wanted to be with Tanner. She agreed to let them admit her so they could treat her throat and help her manage the pain, as long as they agreed not to keep her from Tanner if he needed her.

She didn't even know if he was alive. Would someone have come and told her if he'd died? She began getting agitated again.

Whitaker sighed and procured a wheelchair to wheel her into the trauma waiting room, while Bree went into the bathroom and cleaned as much blood off herself as possible.

It wasn't until she was on her way into the waiting room that she wished she had her computer. They weren't going to let her near Tanner without being family. If she had her computer, she could've changed files and made herself such an ironclad member of his family—at least on the screen—that nobody in this hospital would dare keep her away from him.

It would've been illegal, but so worth it.

She didn't have to break any laws. When a nurse tried to tell Bree that this particular waiting area was for family only, Mrs. Dempsey, who was already there, stepped up and very clearly stated that Bree *was* family.

Noah and Cassandra echoing the sentiment brought tears to her eyes. She was saved from saying what would no doubt be the wrong thing by the fact that she couldn't talk anyway. All she could do was collapse into Mrs. Dempsey's arms as the older woman pulled her close.

"He's going to be just fine," Mrs. Dempsey whispered. "Just you watch. My boy has everything to live for now. He's not going to give that up."

Ended up she was right, although it didn't look like it for the first forty-eight hours.

After the first few hours of sitting in the waiting room, Bree's body was shaking with pain and fatigue. It was Noah who recognized it and came and squatted right in front of her, looking so much like Tanner it was a little painful.

"It's time for you to get checked into your own room and deal with your own injuries. I give you my word that if something happens with Tanner, for better or worse, I will personally carry you to him. Even if I have to knock some doctors and orderlies unconscious to do it. He's going to need you. This isn't going to be something he bounces back from right away. The best thing you can do to help him is to regather your strength while he's out."

Bree finally nodded. She was in a hospital room and pumped full of medications less than an hour later.

When she woke up the next morning, Dan and Cheryl were sitting in the room with her. She couldn't talk to them, but her eyes filled with tears once again when they explained that nobody in Risk Peak wanted her to be alone. A member of the Dempsey family came by and reported in once an hour, to let her know how Tanner was doing.

Stable, but not awake. Always stable, but not awake.

She borrowed Whitaker's phone when he came by again and backdoored her way into the hospital system. It wasn't that she didn't trust the Dempseys; she just had to see the information about Tanner for herself. Tanner's patient file basically said the same thing the Dempseys had been reporting, but in medical jargon: stable, but not awake.

On the second day, when Tanner started to stir but not quite wake, he mumbled Bree's name. True to his word, Noah was back in her room to get her and bring her to Tanner. Fortunately, he didn't have to knock anyone unconscious, since she was doing so much better.

She rushed to Tanner's bed. "I'm here," she whispered.

She wrapped her fingers in his, and he immediately fell back into a more restful state.

He was in and out for two days after that. It was so obvious that he did better when Bree was around him—slept more deeply, had a more even heart rate and blood pressure—that the doctors didn't try to insist she not stay.

Every medical professional who had come in contact with him, from the paramedics to the surgeons, had stated that it was a miracle Tanner was even alive anyway. So the fact that his unconscious mind could seem to sense her presence, and his body rest and heal itself better with her near, seemed much less impressive, all things considered.

Bree was officially released from the hospital after two days. She'd stayed by Tanner's side the entire time except for when Cassandra, with the muscle of Noah, had forced Bree to go home to her apartment, take a shower and grab some clothes.

Bree and Cassandra had had plenty of hours to talk— well, mostly Cassandra talked and Bree listened since she couldn't say more than a few sentences at a time—

about plans for the shelter and the computer classes Bree could offer.

Cassandra wanted to start the classes as soon as possible. Bree, not even counting her voice, wasn't quite so gung ho. But like Cassandra said, the skills and hope they were providing these women couldn't wait. Bree's discomfort wasn't what was important.

"Of course, we'll wait until you can speak louder than a whisper," Cassandra said with a smile from across Tanner's hospital room. "You're probably a more effective instructor if people can actually hear you."

"Don't rush her," Mrs. Dempsey said. She'd been a constant in Tanner's room every day. "Your brother is going to need someone to take care of him for a while. Let them get themselves situated and then you can drag her into all your grand schemes."

"I know, Mom, and I don't expect her to do it until she's ready and healed." Cassandra winked at her. "So what is that, like two or three days?"

Bree just smiled.

"Bree, speaking of Tanner getting out of here… I don't want you to feel like you have to take him on all by yourself if you don't want to. I can assure you that my son is not a good patient. He doesn't like to stay in bed."

"I'll bet Bree will be a little better at keeping him in bed," Cassandra muttered under her breath with a grin.

Bree could feel heat rising through her whole face.

Mrs. Dempsey didn't look offended, thank goodness. "My obnoxious daughter may be right, but I still don't want you to feel like you have to be responsible for him. We can certainly all take turns."

Bree stared at Mrs. Dempsey, her heart feeling a little too big for her chest. Had she just been given first dibs on Tanner's care by his mother?

"I want to do it," she croaked out.

"Thank God," Cassandra muttered again. "He would've thrown a fit."

Bree wasn't exactly sure that was the truth. "Let Tanner decide," she whispered.

Mrs. Dempsey and Cassandra looked at each other before looking back at Bree. "Believe me, if it was up to my son, he would've moved you in to the ranch the day he returned to Risk Peak. He wants you there. He wanted you there back when he thought you might be a package deal with two sweet babies."

"Oh." Bree's lips formed the word, but no sound came out.

"So before you say yes, that you'll move in and take care of him, I want to make sure you understand exactly what you're getting yourself into. Once you move your stuff and yourself onto that ranch, it will be for good. Tanner's never going to let you go."

"Oh." Again, no sound. Bree wanted to believe Mrs. Dempsey's words more than anything she'd ever known.

Mrs. Dempsey got up from her chair near the window and came to stand next to Bree, who was sitting near the sleeping Tanner, holding his hand. "You have some doubts left about how he feels, and that's okay. He'll clear them up for you."

"I just want to make sure it's what he really wants. I don't want him to feel pressured into anything."

She squeezed Bree's shoulder. "Is it what *you* want?"

Hiding her feelings wasn't even an option. She wasn't sure if sharing them with Tanner's mother was appropriate or not, but she couldn't hold back the words. "Yes. It's what I want. *He* is what I want. In every possible way."

Her words didn't need to be loud to be forceful.

Cassandra's low whistle and muttered "damn" had Bree assuming her comment had been too much.

"I'm sorry," she whispered. Her voice would've been a whisper even if her throat was at full strength. "That wasn't appropriate."

"No. Don't ever apologize for loving my son with so much fervor. It's the most any mother could ever want for her child. And knowing he feels the same way about you just makes it that much more perfect." She reached down and squeezed Bree's hand where it rested over Tanner's.

"It's still his choice," Bree said. She wanted to make sure he knew he had options.

Mrs. Dempsey nodded. "And we'll make sure he understands that. Tanner always knows his own mind. He knows what he wants. You'll see."

SHE WAS RIGHT there next to him when Tanner opened his eyes the next day.

The doctors assured them it would happen, that he was showing more and more signs of alertness, but until she actually saw those brown eyes looking at her, Bree had not been able to escape the weight that had seemed riveted to her chest.

"Hey, freckles."

And with those two words the weight was gone.

"Hey, hot lips." She reached over and kissed him on them.

He barely made it through talking to his family before falling back asleep, but he was awake again just a couple of hours later. By the next day, he was complaining about the food, and they all knew he was back for good.

Whitaker came by to take Tanner's statement. He

was working with the Larimer County Sheriff's Department since so many of the crimes were tied in together. Whitaker asked Bree if she'd be willing to wait outside the hospital room so her testimony wouldn't become tainted by Tanner's version and vice versa. She'd already given her written statement but might have to give one verbally in the future.

Tanner hadn't wanted her to go, but Bree hadn't wanted to relive those details right then anyway. She'd just gotten Tanner back and awake. She didn't want to think of his still form lying so bloody in her arms again.

She told him she would head to her apartment to take a shower and be back.

While she was there, she looked around. Moving in with Tanner would be such a huge step emotionally, but such a small step physically. It wouldn't take her long to gather up her belongings—after years on the run, she was never going to be a pack rat.

She hadn't been lying to Mrs. Dempsey. There was nothing she wanted more than to be with Tanner. But she only wanted to move in with him if that was what he really wanted, too.

When she got back to the hospital, Whitaker had left, and Cassandra and Mrs. Dempsey were back.

And Tanner was angry.

"What happened?" she croaked, rushing to Tanner's side.

His arms snaked around her hip and pulled her down onto the bed next to him.

Cassandra rolled her eyes. "The big baby is mad because the doctor said he couldn't leave tomorrow. He has to be here at least another day."

"And I told Tanner that I've already got his old room at the house ready for him. I've got my schedule cleared, and I'm ready to wait on him hand and foot as long as he needs me to." Mrs. Dempsey looked pointedly at Bree. "I wanted him to know he has options and can stay wherever he wants."

Bree swallowed the ball of worry in her chest. This was what she'd asked Mrs. Dempsey to do. To make sure he knew he could do what he wanted.

She looked at Tanner. "That all sounds good to me."

His face was scrunched into the most adorable pout she'd ever seen. "First, I don't want to stay in the hospital anymore. The food has not gotten any better since I was here the last time. You would think with all the technological advances our society has made, they could make hospital food more palatable."

She fought not to smile, which was even harder when Cassandra let out a dramatic sigh.

"Just one more day," she whispered to him. "I'll sneak you in food."

"Fine," he said. "But here's the rest. I know it's not fair arguing this with you when your voice doesn't work, but it's the only chance I have against that big brain of yours anyway."

"What are we going to argue about?"

His hand tightened on her hip. "I want you to move in with me."

"Okay," she said instantly. "To help you."

He shook his head. "No, hear me out. I want you to move in with me, not as some sort of nursemaid, although I'm sure I'll need a little help for a couple weeks. I want you to move in with me and stay there. Long after the doctor clears me, I still want you there, waking up with me every morning and going to bed with me every night. This isn't about you being my caregiver or me being your bodyguard. I want you with me, freckles. I love you, and I've wanted you with me from the moment I first saw you shoplifting in that drugstore. If you're not ready, I'll wait. But if you are, there's nothing I want more than having you with me every single day."

She stared at him, heart swelling, not sure she could say anything even if her voice wasn't damaged.

Mrs. Dempsey cleared her throat. When Bree looked over at the older woman, she was grinning. "Looks like he's made his choice."

She nodded and then looked back at Tanner.

"I have made my choice, freckles. And it's you."

"I love you, too," Bree whispered. "And yes, I'll come with you to the ranch."

Tanner's hand slid up her back, pushing her down toward him. His lips pressed against hers gently, mindful of the wounds both of them were recovering from.

Just like the kiss he'd given her at her apartment in Kansas City all those weeks ago, this one was once again full of promise.

Neither of them broke away, even when Cassandra snickered. "I got all of that on camera, and I'm so posting it on YouTube."

Chapter Twenty-Seven

Tanner had honestly never thought he'd wake up again. When he and Bree had fallen to the ground in that bungalow, his last thought was that at least he'd saved her before he'd died.

Nothing had made sense to him as he'd heard her soft voice whispering in his ear while he lay on the floor. No words had penetrated his consciousness, just the knowledge that Bree was there. She was alive. That was enough.

So seeing those green eyes of her staring at him when he'd woken up in the hospital had been a very pleasant surprise. His entire body felt like he'd gone a few rounds with a steamroller, but the look of relief—of love—in Bree's eyes had been worth it.

Talking her into coming here to the ranch? His mother hadn't raised no dummy. And she hadn't tried to hide her approval of Bree coming here to take care of him.

Or her approval of Bree altogether.

And that was a good thing, because he planned to keep Bree around as long as he could talk her into it. Hopefully forever.

They'd been here three weeks already, and the days hadn't been easy—physically, at least. The road to recovery had taken a lot longer than Tanner had planned. The limitations of his own body as it healed was frustrating. Bed rest was not for him.

That was, until a few days ago, when he'd finally convinced Bree that he was definitely healed enough for her to be in bed with him for more than just sleeping.

After that, *bed rest* hadn't exactly included much *resting*.

Ended up he hadn't needed to take Bree to some fancy resort for their first time making love to be special. The most perfect place on earth had been in his bed at the ranch they both cared so much about.

Maybe their wounds had slowed them down a bit. But that just gave them more of an opportunity to learn everything about each other's bodies.

Not the bed rest the doctor had ordered, but definitely what they'd both needed after coming so close to losing each other.

He watched her now from the rocker on his front porch, coffee cup in hand, as she came walking from the barn. She'd been checking on Star again, as she did at least three times a day. He didn't mind. Like he'd known from the beginning, that pup was helping fill a void in her heart the twins had left.

"Everybody okay in there?"

"Two more weeks until Corfu can start weaning her." Her voice was still a little hoarse but had gotten much better since the attack. And thank God she was finally able to eat solid food. Neither of them wanted to see a smoothie again for the rest of their lives. "I measured Star, and she's definitely right where she should be in terms of size and weight."

Bree had researched enough about dogs over the past three weeks to know more than most vets. Tanner had no doubt that if she said the puppy was developmentally sound, it was true.

Tomorrow was a big day for both of them. Tanner would be back in the office, although he'd be on desk duty for another couple of months until everything healed up more, but still back at the job he loved.

Ryan Fletcher was sitting in a cell, still awaiting indictment. The crimes were complex and closely linked. Definitely three counts of murder—Newkirk, Anders and Duquette—and two counts of attempted murder for him and Bree.

It looked like he would be charged with Glen Carrico's murder, too. Ryan might have saved Bree's life by shooting Glen, but now it looked more like he'd done it to make sure Carrico couldn't tell the truth about what had happened than because of any altruistic impulse on his part to save Bree.

Fletcher had made a deal with Glen. He had agreed to help keep Darin from being transferred to maximum security if Glen took the fall for the murders if anyone came looking. Glen, dying anyway, had agreed.

Fletcher thought he was getting a desperate, witless patsy in Glen. But Glen had been smarter than Fletcher had realized. He'd left a package in a safety-deposit box a day before he died with a letter describing in detail the entire exchange between him and Fletcher. He'd provided plenty of recorded conversations to back up his claim. He'd sent a letter to his brother, explaining that the information was only to be used if Fletcher didn't come through on his promise to keep Darin out of maximum security.

Glen hadn't trusted Fletcher to keep his end of the bargain after he was gone. Smart man.

It was safe to say Fletcher would be spending the

rest of his life in prison. The thought didn't bring Tanner any comfort beyond knowing that he and Bree were now safe. Maybe if Tanner had shared his guilt about what had really happened with Nate—all the things he'd wished he'd done differently—instead of keeping his mistakes hidden from Ryan, everything could've turned out differently.

It would never have brought Nate back, but maybe Ryan wouldn't be lost, too.

But one thing bleeding out all over the floor and watching Bree swing from that noose had taught him: every day was a gift. You learn from your mistakes, and you move on—you don't let the past hold you captive.

Bree was learning that, too, in her own way. She was starting her first computer class for the shelter tomorrow. She'd dropped down to just one or two shifts per week at the Sunrise Diner, Dan and Cheryl more than happy to let her do that, especially once they understood the plan. They were helping at the shelter, too, offering short-order cooking classes and training for anyone who might be interested.

Cassandra and Bree had become fast friends; the two of them already had plans to expand the shelter. He had no doubt it would become a big part of the community.

She walked up the stairs of the porch and wrapped her arms around his waist.

He slipped an arm around her shoulders. "You ready for tomorrow?"

"Yep. Although I'm glad this first class is only for two women. I've already been thinking about some ways I could streamline it and make it more applicable to their lives."

Of course she had been. That didn't surprise him at all. "Oh yeah?"

"I've been doing some research, and I want to make this as effective as possible. These women deserve it."

He kissed the top of her head. "I have no doubt it's going to be the most useful class anyone's ever been a part of, by the time you're done with it."

"How about you? You ready for tomorrow? Ready to go back to being Captain Hot Lips?"

He smiled at the nickname and nodded. He was more than ready. Ready to be back on the job and doing his part to keep Risk Peak safe.

"Hopefully nobody but you will call me that, but yes, definitely ready. Although being here with you is nothing to scoff at, either."

"I know. It's been nice having some time just the two of us. But the real world will be good, too. What we do is important."

He hugged her more tightly against him. "It is—you're right."

She nodded against his chest and was quiet for a moment. "I've been researching some other important stuff, too."

"Like what?" He took a sip of his coffee and prepared himself for a fifteen-minute one-sided conversation about computer programming in which he would only understand about eight percent of the terms. But he never wanted to make Bree feel like he wasn't interested in what was going on in that giant brain of hers, even if he didn't always understand it.

"Reverse cowgirl," she said.

He spewed the coffee out over her head. "What?" he croaked.

"Reverse cowgirl." She leaned back so she could look in his eyes. "It's a sexual position where—"

"I know what it is." His voice was still choked. He

could not even imagine what she meant when she said she'd been *researching* it.

She nodded solemnly. "I think I would like to try it."

He swallowed a laugh and kissed her. *This woman.* She was going to keep him on his toes for the next sixty years or so.

And he couldn't wait.

* * * * *

ADIRONDACK ATTACK

JENNA KERNAN

This story is dedicated, with love and admiration, to my mother, Margaret C. Hathaway, who drove me to school, swim lessons, summer camp, dance lessons, art lessons, the Adirondack Mountains and the American West. Who could have imagined the world was so big?

Chapter One

On his first day off in three months, Detective Dalton Stevens shouldered his backpack and set out after his wife. He knew she'd be surprised to see him and possibly furious. She'd tell him that trial separations meant the couple separated. Well, the hell with that.

His wife, outdoor adventure specialist Erin Stevens, was up here in the Adirondacks somewhere. He had arrived last night, but as it was dark and he didn't know the location of her guided excursion, he'd had to wait until this morning. That meant she was well ahead of him. It seemed like he'd been chasing after Erin ever since he met her, and the woman knew how to play hard to get. But this time was different. This time he really didn't think she wanted to be caught. She wanted a separation. In his mind, *separation* was just code for *impending divorce*. Well, the hell with that, too.

Dalton adjusted the straps on his shoulders. He couldn't use the padded hip strap because it rubbed against his healing stomach wound.

The group she was leading had already been at it a full day. Normally he could have caught them by now. But nothing was normal since he'd told her he'd been cleared by the department physician to return to active duty.

"Did you hear anything I said?" she'd asked.

"I heard you, Erin," Dalton said to the endless uphill trail. Roots crisscrossed the path, and moss grew on the damp rocks that littered the way. He'd lost his footing twice, and the twisting caused a pain in his middle that made him double over in agony.

Cleared for duty did not mean cleared for hiking with a fifty-pound pack. It would have been lighter if he'd left the tent, but he knew his wife's tent was a single. He'd packed one that suited two. Ever hopeful, he thought. Now if he could just get her in there, he was certain the starlight and the fresh air would clear her mind.

She was always happiest in the outdoors. Erin seemed to glow with health and contentment in this bug-infested, snake-ridden, root-laden wilderness. Meanwhile, he couldn't tell poison ivy from fern, and the last time he'd carried a pack was in Afghanistan.

He stopped again to catch his breath, drawing out his mobile phone and finding he still had no service.

"Nature," he scoffed. He'd take a neighborhood with a quality pizza joint any day.

Erin's boss, and the director of the adult adventure camp, had given him a directions to the trailhead by phone and Dalton had picked up a topographical map. If he was reading this correctly, he should reach their second camping site shortly after they did. Yesterday they had used the kayaks to paddle the Hudson River before stopping for their first camp. This morning they should arrive here to await the scheduled release of water from Lake Abanakee this evening. This area of the Hudson was above the family rafting sites and would be wild running tomorrow, according to the director. The director said he would alert one of the rafting outfits to keep an eye out for him tomorrow, in case he needed a lift downriver.

Meanwhile, this trail from O-K Slip Road was all rocks and roots, and he seemed to catch his feet on each one. Recovery time from abdominal surgery certainly wasn't easy, he thought.

He reached the Hudson Gorge and realized it would be a miracle to find them, even knowing their general stopping point. If they changed the plan and camped on the opposite side, he was out of luck and up the river without a paddle or raft.

Gradually he left the pine forest and moved through birch and maple as he approached the river. He was relieved to finally come upon their camping site knowing she and her group would not be far.

Erin had chosen a rocky outcropping, away from the tall trees and on a covering of moss and grass that spread across the gray rock above the river.

The brightly colored tents were scattered in a rough circle. The trees below the outcropping made it impossible to see them, but he could hear their laughter and raised voices plainly enough.

He didn't see Erin's little single tent because she wouldn't camp very close to her charges. He was certain of that much, because his wife liked her privacy. Perhaps too damn much.

He found her camp in short order and dropped his pack beside her gray-and-white tent.

Erin's pack rested inside the tent, and her food was properly hung in the trees to prevent attracting animals.

The peals of laughter and howls of delight guided him to the trail to the river.

A young man and an older woman headed in his direction, winding up the steep path from the water. The route inclined so sharply that the pair clung to saplings as they climbed. The skinny youth wore wet swim trunks and gripped a towel around his neck. His legs were pearly pale, but his face and arms showed a definite sunburn. The woman wore a one-piece bathing suit with jean shorts plastered to her legs and rivulets of water running down her tanned skin.

"Having fun?" Dalton asked.

The youth pointed a toned arm back the way they had come. "There's a rock like a diving board down there. Water's deep and still. It's awesome!"

The woman held her smile as her brows lifted in surprise. "Well, hey there. Didn't see another paddler."

He thumbed over his shoulder. "Came overland. The trail from O-K Slip Road."

She passed him going in the opposite direction. "Well, that's no fun."

He stepped off the trail to let them pass and continued, landing on his backside with a jolt of pain more than once.

"No fun is right," he muttered.

At the bank of the river, he saw the three remaining adult campers and their leader. He'd recognize those legs anywhere. Firm tanned legs pushing off the gray rock as she climbed, leaving wet footprints from her water shoes as she easily scaled the boulder that was shaped like the fin of a shark, using a climbing rope. It was his wife.

On the pinnacle of the sloping boulder she waited

for a young woman in a pink bathing suit, which was an unfortunate match to her ruddy skin tone, to jump off and then followed behind, giving a howl of delight that made Dalton frown. He'd never heard her make such a sound of pure exhilaration.

The single male waded out of the water and came up short at the sight of him. Dalton judged the man to be early twenties and carrying extra pounds around his middle.

"Hiya," he said.

Dalton nodded and the young man crept past him on the uneven bank. The woman in pink swam and then waded after the man, followed by a lanky female with wet hair so short it stood up like a hedgehog's spines. Erin emerged from her underwater swim at the base of the rock, scaling the slope to retrieve her climbing rope before making a final leap with the coiled rope over one shoulder.

Dalton smiled as the pinkish woman, her face red from exertion, reached the muddy shore, her cheeks puffing out with each breath.

"Where'd you…come…from?" she wheezed.

"Your camp."

She gave him a skeptical look and paused, one hand on her knee.

"You don't look like an adventure camper."

"No?" He grinned. "What do I look like?"

She cocked her head and her eyes narrowed. "A soldier."

That surprised him as he had once been just that. But he'd left Special Forces at Erin's request.

"Why's that?"

She pointed at the hunting knife that he'd strapped

to his belt and then to his boots, military issue and which still fit. Finally, she lifted her finger to the tattoos staining his left forearm from wrist to elbow. The overall pattern spoke of lost comrades, blood, war dead and the corps.

"You sure you're with us?"

"Erin's my wife."

Her entire demeanor changed. Her face brightened and the look of suspicion vanished.

"Oh, hi! I'm Alice. Your wife, she's wonderful. So encouraging and warm." Her smile faltered. "You're her husband?"

He didn't like the incredulity in her voice.

"Yeah." For now. His stomach gave a twist that had nothing to do with healing tissue.

"Hmm. Can't see it."

"Why?"

"She's fun and you're, well, you seem kinda…serious, you know?"

His brows sank deeper over his eyes. He was fun.

The woman glanced back down the trail where all but one hiker had vanished. "She didn't mention you."

"Feel free to ask her."

Alice waved. "See you at camp."

She moved past him and continued up the trail with her comrade on her heels. This other woman said nothing, just gave him a sullen look and glanced away the minute they made eye contact.

Erin reached the spot where she changed from swimming in the calm stretch to wading. He waited beside the kayaks.

Her tank top clung to her skin, and he could see the two-piece suit she wore beneath, along with much of her toned, athletic build. Her wet light brown hair, cut bluntly at her jawline, had lost its natural wave in the water. Her whiskey-brown eyes sparkled above her full mouth, now stretched wide in a playful grin. He took a moment to admire the view of his wife, wet and smiling.

He had the sudden impulse to hide before she spotted him.

Dalton didn't know how Erin knew he was there, but she straightened, giving him a moment to study her standing alert and relaxed as if listening to the birds that flitted across the water. Then she turned and her eyes shifted to her husband. The set of her jaw told him that she was not pleased.

Dalton was six-three and weighed 245 pounds, but Erin's scowl made him feel about two feet tall.

"Surprise?" he said, stretching his arms out from his sides in a ta-da posture.

Her gaze flicked to his middle, where she knew he still wore a bandage though the stitches were out now. She didn't manage to keep from uttering a profanity. He knew this because he read it on her lips. The Lord's name…in vain. Definitely. Then she tucked in her chin and started marching toward him in a way that would have made a lesser man run. Instead, he slid his hands into the rear pockets of his cargo pants and forced a smile that felt as awkward as a middle school slow dance.

"Dalton, if that's you, you had better run."

He did, running toward her, meeting her as she reached the bank.

He stopped before her, then reached, preparing to swing her in a circle, as he did after separations of more than a day.

She pressed her palm against the center of his chest and extended her arm, blocking him. "Don't you dare lift me. You shouldn't be lifting anything."

He was suddenly glad he'd dumped his pack.

She hoisted the coiled rope farther up on her shoulder and aimed her extended finger at him. Her scowl deepened and her gaze shot back to him. "How long have you been tracking me?"

"Just today. I signed up for your group."

Her fists went to her hips. "So I couldn't send you home, right?"

Her two female adults had not climbed up to camp, opting to linger and watch the awkward reunion. Dalton glared, but they held their position, their heads swiveling from her to him as they awaited his reply, reminding him of spectators at a tennis match. Dalton pinned his eyes on his wife, an opponent, wishing they were alone but knowing that the women bearing witness might just play in his favor. Erin's tone was icy, but she had not raised it…yet.

He grinned, leaned in for a kiss and caught only her cheek as she stepped back, scowling.

"I can't believe this," she muttered, pushing past him and heading up the trail. Her campers scuttled ahead of them and out of sight.

He trotted after her, ignoring the tug of pain that accompanied each stride.

"Did you bring a kayak?" she asked.

"No."

"You planning on swimming the rapids tomorrow?"

"I thought you'd be happy."

She kept walking, leaning against the slope. Her calf

muscles were tight, and he pictured those ankles locked about his lower back. It had been too long.

"I'm taking a vacation. Just like you wanted," he added.

She spun and stormed a few steps away, and then she rounded on him.

"You didn't hear a word I said back there." She pointed toward a tree that he assumed was in the direction of Yonkers, New York, and their pretty little split ranch house with the yard facing woods owned by the power company and a grill on the patio that he had planned to use over the July Fourth weekend. Instead, he was adventure camping without a kayak.

She continued, voice raised. "A vacation? Is that what you got from our last conversation?"

"I missed you." He held his grin, but felt it dying at the edges. Drying up like a dead lizard in the sun. She didn't look back.

"You told me you understood. That you'd take this time to think…" She turned and tapped a finger on his forehead as if to check that there was anyone home. "Really think, about my concerns."

"You said a break."

"You knew exactly what kind of a break I wanted. But, instead, you went for the grand gesture. Like always."

He reached to cup her cheek, but she dodged and his arm dropped to his side. "Honey, listen…"

She looked up at him with disappointment, the hill not quite evening their heights. Then she placed a hand over his, and for a minute he thought it would be all right. Her eyes squeezed shut and a tear dribbled down her cheek.

Dalton gasped. He was making her cry. Erin didn't cry unless she was furious.

The pinkish woman appeared at the edge of the meadow, stepping beside them as her eyes shifted back and forth between them. She tugged on her thick rope of a braid as if trying to decide whether she should proceed or speak.

Dalton looked at his wife. She hadn't kissed him. When was the last time that she had greeted him without a kiss?

When she'd left for adventure camp yesterday, he recalled.

An icy dread crystallized around his heart. He would not lose her. Everything was changing. He had to figure out how to change it back. Change her back.

"Erin, come on," he coaxed.

She was listening, and so was the interloper. He turned to the camper.

"Seriously?" he said, and she scuttled away toward the others, who all stood together facing him and their camp leader, his wife.

Erin faced her group. "This man is my husband, Dalton," she said. "I wasn't expecting him."

The assemble stood motionless, only their eyes flicking from him to her.

Erin growled and strode away. She reached her tent, paused at the sight of his pack and dropped the rope. Her hands went to her hips. She turned to glare at him. He swallowed.

When he gave her his best smile, she closed her eyes and turned away. Then she stripped out of her tank top and into a dry sweatshirt, leaving her wet suit on underneath. He tried to hide his disappointment as she dragged on dry shorts. She spoke, it seemed, to her pack.

"If you were listening, you would have respected my wishes."

"I heard everything you said. I did. I just…" *Ignored you*, he thought, but wisely stopped speaking.

"I don't think listening is enough."

"What does that even mean?"

"You always listen to me, Dalton. And then you do as you darn well please. My feelings don't change your decisions. They don't even seem to weigh into your thought process anymore. You want to go on living like you always have, and that's your right. And it's my right to step off the roller coaster."

"Is *stepping off the roller coaster* punishment, Erin? Is that what you're trying to do? Is that why you left?"

"I can't talk to you here. I'm working."

"I'll wait."

"It won't matter how long you wait, Dalton. You don't want to change."

"Because everything is fine just the way it is."

"No, Dalton. It isn't."

The way she said "it isn't" froze his blood. The flat, defeated tone left no doubt that she was ready to cut him loose.

Erin opened her mouth to speak, but instead cocked her head. A moment later she had her hand shielding her eyes as she glanced up toward the sky. Her hearing was better than his.

He'd fired too many shots with his M4 rifle without ear protection over in Afghanistan. So he followed the direction of Erin's attention and, a moment later, made out the familiar thumping drone of the blades of a helicopter.

"That's funny," Erin said.

The chopper broke the ridgeline across the river, wobbling dangerously and issuing black smoke from the tail section.

Dalton judged the angle of descent and the length of the meadow. The pilot was aiming for this flat stretch of ground beyond the tents that ringed the clearing. Dalton knew it would be a hard landing.

He grabbed Erin, capturing her hand, and yanked her toward the trees. In the meadow, standing like startled deer amid their colorful tents, her charges watched the approaching disaster in petrified stillness.

"Take cover!" he shouted, still running with his wife. "Get down!"

Chapter Two

Erin cried out in horror as the rails below the chopper snapped the treetops above them. Branches rained down from the sky, and Dalton dragged her against him as the roar of the engine seemed to pass directly over her head. She squeezed her eyes shut as her rib cage shuddered with the terrible vibrations of the whirling blades.

She opened her eyes as the chopper tipped in the air, the blades now on their side rotating toward her and churning upright like a window fan gone mad. It was going to hit the ground, blades first, right there before her.

In the meadow, Brian Peters, the skinny seventeen-year-old who was here because his father wanted him away from his computers for a week, was now running for his life. She judged he'd clear the descending blade but feared the fuselage would crush him. Brian's acne-scarred cheeks puffed as he bolted, lanky and loose limbed. Behind him Merle Levine, the oldest of her group, a square and solidly built woman in her late fifties, lay prone beside her cheery red tent with her arms folded over her head. Merle was a single biology teacher on summer vacation and directly in the path Erin feared the chopper would take as it hit the ground.

Erin squeezed her face between open palms as the propeller caught. Instead of plowing into the earth, the helicopter cartwheeled as the blades sheered and folded under the momentum of the crash.

Erin saw Carol Walton lift her arms and then fall as debris swept her off her feet. The timid woman had reminded Erin of a porcupine, with small close-set eyes and spiky bleached hair tufted with black. Erin's scream mingled with Carol's as the woman vanished from sight.

The chopper careened toward the escarpment, some twenty feet above the river just beyond the meadow. The entire craft slowed and then tipped before scraping across the rock with exquisite slowness.

Richard Franklin, a twentysomething craft beer brewer from Oklahoma, was already close to the edge and he stood, watching the chopper as it teetered. He reached out toward the ruined aircraft and Erin realized he could see whoever was aboard. Then he ran as if to catch the two-ton machine in his pale outstretched arms. The chopper fell over the cliff and Richard dropped to his posterior.

Erin scanned the ground for the flash of a pink bathing suit. "Where's Alice?"

Not a bird chirped or squirrel scuttled. The wind had ceased and all insects stilled. The group rose, as one, staring and bug-eyed. The sudden quiet was deafening. They began to walk in slow zombie-like synchronicity toward the spot where the helicopter had vanished. All except for Dalton.

Dalton released Erin and charged toward the spot where Carol Walton knelt, folded in the middle and clutching her belly like an opera soprano in the final act. Only Erin knew the blood was real.

Alice Afton appeared beside her, having obviously been hiding in the woods.

"Alice, get my pack. There's a med kit in there," Erin said.

Alice trotted off and Erin moved on wooden legs toward Carol Walton, knowing from the amount of blood spilling from her wounds that she could not survive.

Dalton cradled Carol in his lap, and her head lay in the crook of his elbow. In different circumstances the hold would seem that of a lover. His short, dark brown hair, longer on top, fell forward over his broad forehead, covering his heavy brows and shielding the green eyes that she knew turned amber near the iris. She could see the nostrils of his broad nose flare as he spoke.

"I got you," said Dalton. "Don't you worry."

"Tell my mom, I love her," said Carol.

Erin realized then that Carol knew she was dying. But there was none of the wild panic she had expected. Carol stared up at Dalton as if knowing he would guide her to where she needed to go. The confidence he projected, the experience. How many of his fellow marines had he held just like this?

Army never leaves their wounded. Marines never leave their dead.

"Can I do anything?" asked Erin. She couldn't. Nothing that would keep Carol with them.

"Take her hand," he said in a voice that was part exasperation, part anguish. She knew he'd lost comrades in war and it bothered him deeply.

Erin did, and warm blood coated her palm.

Alice arrived, panting, and extended the pack.

"Just put it down for now," said Dalton, his voice calm.

"Why doesn't it hurt?" asked Carol, lowering her

chin as if to look at the slicing belly wound. Something had torn her from one side to the other and the smell of her compromised bowels made Erin gag.

But not Dalton. He lifted Carol's chin with two fingers and said. "Hey, look at me. Okay?"

Carol blinked up at him. "She's a lucky woman, your wife. Does she know that?"

Dalton smiled, stroking her head. "Sometimes."

Carol's color changed from ashen to blue. She shivered and her eyes went out of focus. Then her breathing changed. She gasped and her body went slack.

Dalton checked the pulse at her throat as Erin's vision blurred. He shook his head and whispered, "Gone."

From the lip of the cliff, Brian Peters called. "I can see someone moving down there."

Dalton slipped out from under Carol's slack body and rose. He glanced down at Erin, and she pressed her lips together to keep from crying.

"Come on," he said, and headed toward the rocky outcropping.

He tugged her to her feet and she hesitated, eyes still pinned on the savaged corpse that was Carol Walton just a few minutes ago.

"Erin. We have to see about the crew." His voice held authority.

How was he so calm? she wondered, but merely nodded her head and allowed him to hurry her along, like an unwilling dog on a leash.

And then, there they were on the lip of rock that jutted out over the Hudson. Twenty feet below them the ruined helicopter lay, minus its blades. One of the runners was snagged over a logjam that held the ruined chopper as the bubble of clear plastic slowly filled with river water. Inside the pilot slumped in his seat, tethered in place by the shoulder restraints.

"Is he alone?" asked Merle, coming to stand beside Dalton, asking him the questions as he emerged as the clear leader of their party.

"Seems so," said Dalton as he released Erin's hand.

"He's moving!" said Richard, pointing a finger at the river.

Erin craned her neck and saw the pilot's head turn to one side. Alive, she realized.

"He's sinking," said Brian. "It's at his feet now."

"We have to get him out of there," said Alice.

"He'll drown," added Richard.

"You have rope?" asked Dalton.

Erin roused from her waking nightmare, knowing exactly what her husband planned. He'd string some rope up and swing down there like Tarzan in a daring rescue attempt.

Except she was the better swimmer. Dalton was only an average swimmer at best and today he was four weeks post-surgery. His abdominal muscles could not handle this. He'd tear something loose, probably the artery that the surgeon had somehow managed to close. She squared her shoulders and faced him.

Erin regained control of her party.

"You are not going down there!" she said.

He ignored her and lifted a hand to snap his fingers before Richard's face. "Rope?"

Richard startled, tore his gaze from the drama unfolding in the river and then hurried off.

"Dalton, I'm the party leader. I'm going," she said.

He smiled at her. "Honey…"

Her eyes narrowed at the placating tone as she interrupted. "You might get down there, but you can't climb back up. Who's going to haul you back?"

He glanced at the drop and the chopper. The water now reached the pilot's knees.

When Richard returned with the gear bag, Erin dropped to the ground and unzipped the duffel. As she removed the throw line and sash cord, she kept talking.

"I'm a better climber. More experienced." She reached in the bag, removed a rope and dropped it at his feet. "Tie a bowline," she said, requesting a simple beginner knot.

His eyes narrowed.

She held up an ascender used to make climbing up a single belay rope as easy as using a StairMaster. "What's this for?" she asked, testing his knowledge of climbing.

His jaw tightened.

"Exactly. I'm going. That's all."

Erin showed Dalton the throw ball, a sand-filled pouch that looked like a cross between a hacky sack and a leather beanbag filled with lead shot. Its purpose was to carry the lighter sash cord up and over tree branches, or in this case, down and around the top of the chopper's damaged rotor. Finished, she rose and offered the throw ball and towline to Dalton because he was better at throwing and because she needed him to leave her alone so she could work.

"Knock yourself out," she said, leaving him to try to snag the helicopter as she slipped into her climbing harness and fastened the chin strap on her helmet.

"How deep is the river here?" asked Dalton.

"Twenty feet, maybe. The river is deeper and wider here, which is why there's no white water. The gorges close back in farther down and the water gets interesting again."

Twenty feet was deep enough to sink that fuselage, she thought.

Erin selected a gap in the top of the rocky outcropping for her chock. This was an aluminum wedge that would hold her climbing rope. The climbing rope, on which she would belay, or use to descend and then return, was strong and much thicker than the towrope, which was no wider than a clothesline. Belaying to the pilot meant using this stronger rope and the cliff wall to drop to his position and then return using two ascenders. The ascenders fixed to the rope and would move only in one direction—up. The ascenders included feet loops, so she could rest on one as she moved the other upward.

She set the wedge in place and then set up her belay system. Finally, she attached her harness to the rope with a carabiner and figure eight belay device. She liked old-school equipment. Simple was best.

By the time she finished collecting all her gear, a second harness and the pack with the first aid kit, Dalton had succeeded in snagging the chopper with the throw ball and pulled the cord tight.

"Got it." He turned to her and grinned, showing her the tight towline.

"Fantastic," she said, squatting at the lip of the cliff. Then she fell backward. She had the satisfaction of seeing the shock on Dalton's face before he disappeared from her sight. Only momentarily, unfortunately. When she glanced up he was scowling down at her. Holding the towrope aloft.

"What's this even for?" he shouted.

"It's like those spinner things, only for grown men."

She continued her descent, smoothly releasing the rope and slowing as she reached the river's uneasy surface. As she approached the chopper, she realized the wreckage was moving, inching back as the rotor dragged along the branch anchoring it in place.

The pressure of the water splashed over the dome in front of the pilot, who turned his head to look up at her. She could see little of the man except that his headphones had fallen over his nose and there was blood, obscured from above by his dark clothing.

Her feet bumped the Plexiglas dome and she held herself in place, dancing sideways on her line to reach the door on the downriver side. It was partially submerged, but the other one took the full force of the current. She'd never be able to open it.

The pilot clutched his middle and turned to the empty seat beside him. He grabbed a red nylon cooler and laboriously moved it to his lap.

"I'm going to get you out," said Erin, doubting that she really could.

Chapter Three

Dalton watched in horror as his wife opened the side compartment door and gave herself enough slack to enter the ruptured compartment of the wrecked chopper.

The pilot lifted his head toward her as she perched on the passenger's seat, now pitched at an odd angle. Her added weight had caused the chopper's runner to farther slip along the anchoring branch. When the chopper tore loose, it would sink and she might be snagged. Cold dread constricted Dalton's chest as he watched helplessly from above.

If he had been the one down there, he was certain the chopper would already have broken loose. She'd been right to go, though he'd still rather switch places with her. She'd been so darn quick with those ropes. Erin knew he was capable of belaying down a rope. And he could climb back up on a good day, but he didn't know how to use the gizmos she had in that pack on her back and jangling from her harness. And today was not a good day.

Beside him, the four surviving campers lay on their bellies and knelt on the rock, all eyes fixed on the drama unfolding below.

The pilot was pushing something toward Erin; it

looked like a small red bag. Erin was unbuckling his restraints and shoving the harness behind his back.

The water foaming around the wreckage drowned out their words.

Erin succeeded in getting the waist buckle of the climbing harness clipped about him and was working on tugging the nylon straps of his harness under his legs as the pilot's head lolled back. Erin glanced up at Dalton, a frown on her lips as she exited the compartment and retrieved the towline he had thrown. She was signaling to him with the rope. Pantomiming a knot.

"She wants you to tie a climbing rope to the line," said the older woman. "I'm Merle, by the way. I used to do a lot of rock climbing before I got pins in my ankle."

She lifted the coiled climbing rope, expertly connected it through an anchored pulley that she tied to a tree some five feet from the edge, and then tied the larger belay line to the towline. Finally, she signaled to Erin. A moment later Erin was hauling the towline back down, dragging the connected larger rope through the pulley. She continued this until she grasped the belay rope, at which point she quickly tied a loop through which she connected the belay rope to the pilot's harness with a carabiner. Erin removed the pilot's headphones and fitted her own helmet to his head.

Merle lifted the other end of the line, which ran through the pulley secured to the tree trunk, and returned to the rock ledge.

"Take this a minute." Merle offered Dalton the rope. "I know I can't haul that guy up." She then motioned to the others. "Brian, Alice, Richard, come take hold. We'll act like a mule team. Walk that way when I tell you. Slowly." She folded the rope back on itself and tied a series of loops every few feet. Then the others took hold.

Dalton dragged his hand across his throat while simultaneously shaking his head. This, of course, had no effect on his wife who offered a thumbs-up and then used her strong legs to haul the pilot toward the open side door. For a moment the pilot tried again to get Erin to take the red squarish nylon bag. When Erin rejected his attempts to make her take it from him, he gripped the seat, foiling her attempts to remove him from the compartment. Finally, Erin looped the small container over her arm using the black nylon strap. Only then did the pilot assist in his extraction.

Merle extended an arm and pointed at the struggling pair.

"It's moving!"

Dalton shifted his attention from his wife to the helicopter runner. He watched in horror as the twisted remains of one blade slipped free from the branch. In a single heartbeat, the compartment vanished beneath the surface, leaving the pilot, in Erin's helmet, dangling from the rope, half in and half out of the water. With his legs submerged, the pilot was dragged downriver.

Erin's rope went taut. Dalton's breathing stopped as he gripped his wife's rope from the surface of the rock before him and wrapped it behind his legs. He hadn't done this since he was in active duty. He remembered how to anchor a climber, but he had never had to anchor a climber who was below him. Dalton sat into the rope and pulled.

Merle shouted from behind him. "Pull!"

The pilot began to rise, his legs clearing the churning torrent.

Dalton ignored the pain of his healing abdominal muscles as he succeeded in inching back from the edge. How long could Erin hold her breath? What if she was snagged on something in that compartment? The rope stretched tight as if tied down at the other end. He scanned the water for some sight of her, fearing the chopper had rolled onto her line or, worse, onto Erin.

The rope vibrated. Was the fuselage settling or was that his wife moving? Dalton smelled the fear on his perspiration. If the compartment tipped to that side, she would have no escape. She'd be pinned between the compartment and the bottom. Dalton considered his chances of moving upriver and jumping into the water. He made the calculation and came back with the answer. He had zero chance of succeeding. The river would whisk him past the wreck before he could reach her.

Just then he saw movement on the line. He stepped closer to the edge and a hand submerged again as the pilot rose closer to the lip of rock where he stood.

Dalton tugged and Erin's hand appeared again. She clutched something; it looked like a metallic gold coffee mug handle. She slid the handle up the rope and her head emerged.

"She's using an ascender," called Merle. "Two! Holy cow, she set that up underwater? Your wife is magnificent. If I was ten years younger I'd steal that woman."

He saw her then, first her arms, sliding the ascenders along the taut rope. One ascender slid upward and her head cleared the water. Wet hair clung to her red face as she gasped. Her opposite hand appeared, moving upward while gripping the second ascender. The device fixed to a carabiner and then to a sling that she had somehow clipped to her harness. In other words,

Erin had released her original attachment to the line and then succeeded in attaching two ascenders and slings to the free portion of the rope all while underwater.

Magnificent was an understatement.

Her torso cleared the water and he saw that the red nylon bag still hung from her shoulder, clamped between her upper arm and side.

"Keep going," called Merle to the pull team as the pilot appeared beside her and was dragged up onto the flat expanse of rock.

Fifteen feet below him, Erin made progress ascending as he leaned over the edge for a better look at her. This caused the rope to slacken and for Erin to drop several inches. Dalton straightened and sat into the rope. He lost his view of his wife, but Merle called the remaining distance to the top as the pilot's pull team, having finished their job, abandoned their posts to run to the pilot who was struggling to move.

"Five feet," called Merle, motioning him to hold position. Merle extended her hand and Erin gripped it, sliding the opposite ascender into Dalton's line of sight. Then she scrambled up onto the rock, rising to stand before them.

She didn't even look out of breath. He, on the other hand, had lost his wind. Seeing her disappear had broken something loose inside him, and his legs gave way. He collapsed onto the moss-covered rock as he struggled to keep down the contents of his stomach. The climbing rope fell about Erin's feet, and she released the ascenders that clattered to the stone cliff top.

How had she escaped?

Merle was hugging his wife as Erin laughed. The

men patted her on the back, and Alice got a hug as well, weeping loudly so that Erin had to comfort *her*.

"I'm getting you all wet," said Erin, extracting herself from Alice's embrace. She ignored Dalton as she turned to the pilot. "How is he?"

Dalton had a rudimentary field experience with triage and rallied to meet her beside the pilot.

"You okay?" he asked.

She nodded, still not looking at him. "Thanks for your help."

But she hadn't needed it or him. All he had done was dunk her as she emerged and possibly speed her arrival slightly by keeping the rope tight.

"Did you get pinned?" he asked.

"Just the rope."

"How did you get out?" he asked.

"Later," she said, and set aside the bag that he now saw was a red nylon lunch cooler. Why had the pilot been so insistent that she retrieve it?

Illegal possibilities rose in his law-enforcement mind, but he turned his attention to the injured man, checking his pupils and pulse.

"Where's your pack?" he asked her.

"Dumped it. Couldn't fit out the side window."

Erin dropped to her knees beside the pilot.

"Shock," he said. At the very least. If he had to guess, and he did have to, because there was no medical help for miles, he'd say the man was bleeding internally. He took a knee beside her and pressed on the pilot's stomach with his fingertips and found the man's skin over the abdominal cavity was tight and the cavity rigid.

"His leg is broken," said Merle, pointing at the pilot's foot, which was facing in the wrong direction for a man lying on his back.

So is his spleen, thought Dalton.

Chapter Four

"I don't like the sound of his breathing," said Erin, her brow as wrinkled as her wet tank top.

The pilot wheezed now, struggling for breath. His eyes fluttered open.

"Captain Lewis, this is my husband. He's a New York City detective. You wanted to speak to him?" The pilot had given them his name but little else.

The captain nodded. "Just you two," he said, lifting his chin toward the curious faces surrounding him.

Erin pointed at Merle. "Please go find my pack and get my phone. Then call for help. Brian, go find something to cover Carol up with and, Alice and Richard, can you gather my climbing gear?"

The campers scurried away.

"Now, Captain Lewis," said Erin. "What in this cooler is so important that you were willing to kill us both?"

Lewis turned to Dalton and spoke in a guttural whisper. "I work for the Department of Homeland Security. Orders to collect this and transfer same to a plane bound for the CDC in Virginia."

Dalton felt the hairs on his neck lifting, as if his skin

were electrified. The mention of the CDC or Centers for Disease Control indicated to him that whatever was inside was related to infection or disease.

"What's in there?" he asked, aiming an index finger at the bag.

"Flash drive with intel on terrorist cells within the state. Siming's Army, and those vials hold one of the three Deathbringers."

"The what?" asked Dalton.

"I don't know, exactly. Mission objective was to pick up a package, which contains an active virus—a deadly one—and the vaccine."

Erin moved farther from the cooler that had been dangling recently from her arm.

"So it's dangerous?" she asked.

"Yes, ma'am. Deadly. You have to get it to DHS or the FBI. Don't trust anyone else."

"Who shot you down?" Dalton had seen the bullet holes in the fuselage.

"Foreign agents. Mercenaries. Don't know. Whoever they are, they work for Siming's Army. And more will be coming to recover that." He pointed at the cooler.

"Where'd you get it?" asked Dalton.

"An operative. Agent Ryan Carr. Use his name. Get as far from here as possible."

"But you're injured," said Erin.

"No, ma'am. I'm dying." He glanced to Dalton, who nodded his agreement.

"Internal injuries," said Dalton through gritted teeth. Two deaths, and he'd been unable to do a damned thing to save them.

"I thank you for pulling me out. You two have to complete my mission."

"No," said Erin at the same time Dalton said, "Yes."

She stared at him. "I can't leave these people out here and I'm not taking charge of a deadly anything."

The captain spoke to her, slipping his hand into hers. "It's a dying man's last request."

She tried to pull back. "That's not fair."

He grinned and then wheezed. His breath smelled of blood. "All's fair in love and war."

He used the other hand to push the cooler toward Dalton, who accepted the package.

She pointed at the red nylon travel cooler. "Dalton, do not take that."

But he already had.

"Get him a blanket, Erin. He's shivering."

She stood and glared at him, then hurried off.

Dalton stayed with the captain as he grew paler and his eyes went out of focus. He'd seen this before. Too many times, but this time the blood stayed politely inside his dying body. The pilot's belly swelled with it and so did his thigh. The broken femur had cut some blood supply, Dalton was certain, from the lack of pulse at the pilot's ankle and the way his left pant leg was now so tight.

"Tell my girlfriend, Sally, that I was fixing to ask for her hand. Tell her I love her and I'm sorry."

"I'll tell her." If he lived to see this through. Judging from the number of bullet holes in that chopper and the size of the caliber, staying alive was going to be a challenge.

Erin returned with her down sleeping bag and draped it over the shivering captain. Before the sun reached the treetops as it dipped into the west, the captain joined Carol Walton in death.

Dalton stood. "We have to go."

"Go? Go where? I've got two dead bodies and re-sponsibility for the welfare of my group. I can't just leave them."

No, they couldn't just leave them. But there were few safe choices. Traveling as a group would be slow. "Get the kayaks ready. We're going."

"I am not taking this group into river rapids ninety minutes before sunset. Are you crazy?"

"Not as crazy as meeting them here." He motioned to the open field.

"Meeting who?" she asked.

"Siming's Army."

Twenty minutes later Erin, now in dry clothing, gathered the surviving campers and explained that the captain's helicopter was shot down, he claimed, by ter-rorists who would be coming for whatever was in that bag. She explained that leaving this evening was haz-ardous because of the volume of water at the forefront of the scheduled release from Lake Abanakee. Finally, she relayed that it was her husband's belief that they needed to leave this site immediately.

"I'm for that. Staying the night with two dead bod-ies gives me the creeps," said Brian.

"You can't just leave them out here for the preda-tors," said Richard.

"You rather be here when the predators show up?" asked Merle.

"We called for help. They are sending an air rescue team for them," Brian said. "We should at least wait until they pick up the dead."

"We wait, there will be more dead," said Dalton.

"What do you think, Erin?" asked Brian.

"I would prefer to stay put and wait for help."

"What's coming isn't help," said Dalton.

ON EMPTY STOMACHS, the campers packed up their tents and gear, while Erin and Dalton headed down the rocky outcropping to ready the kayaks that had been stowed for their excursion the following morning. Dalton took Carol's gear and kayak.

"You really sure about this?" asked Erin, her gaze flicking from Dalton, who carried one end of Carol's kayak, and then to the frothing river behind him.

"Sure about our responsibility to deliver this? Yes."

"Sure about taking inexperienced kayakers into the roughest stretch of white water one hour before sunset. What if someone upends?"

He lowered the kayak onto the grassy bank. "What would you normally do?"

"Pick them up from the river and guide them to shore."

"We'll do that."

"In the dark?"

"You're right. We can't do that."

"So your plan is to leave anyone who gets into trouble. And here I thought you were the hero type."

That stung. He wouldn't leave anyone behind. She had to know that. "Erin, he said they're coming. Mercenaries. You understand? That means hired killers, and I know they are using high-caliber rounds from the size of the holes in the tail section of the chopper. We can argue later about specific logistics. Right now we need to…"

She was cocking her head again. Looking toward the

sky. He didn't hear it yet, not over the roar of the river. But he knew what was coming.

Dalton looked at the three kayaks they had retrieved from cover. Her gear lay beside her craft, neatly stowed in her pack. Dalton slipped her gear into the hollow forward compartment of her craft and added her paddle so that it rested half in and half out of the opening.

Erin arched backward, staring up at the pink sky with her hand acting as visor. Dalton packed his gear into the bow of Carol Walton's craft and added the red nylon cooler, which now contained nothing but a river rock. The black case, recently within, held two small vials in a padded black compartment with a thumb drive. This precious parcel now rested safely in the side pocket of his cargo pants.

"They're here," she said, pointing at the red-and-white helicopter with Rescue emblazoned on the side.

The chopper hovered over the meadow, then began a measured descent. Erin stepped back toward the tree-lined trail that led to the meadow. Dalton glanced at the kayaks, packed and ready, and just knew he'd never get her to go without her group.

So he abandoned their escape plan and followed her. He could at least see that she wasn't one of the welcome party.

Dalton made sure he was beside her when they reached the sharply ascending trailhead at the edge of the open field. Before them, the chopper had landed. The pilot cut the engine and the copilot stepped down. Dalton studied the man. He wore aviator glasses, slacks and a button-up shirt. Nothing identified him as mountain rescue and his smile seemed out of place. As he crouched and trotted beneath the slowing blades that whirled above him, Dalton spotted the grip of a pistol tucked in the back of his slacks.

Erin moved to step from cover and he dragged her back.

"What are you doing?" she said.

He held a finger to his lips. "Wait."

Merle was first to greet the copilot. Their raised voices carried across the meadow.

"How many in your party?" asked the new arrival, straightening now. He was a small man, easy to underestimate, Dalton thought. The relaxed posture seemed crafted, just like his casual attire.

"There are six of us," answered Merle, omitting the two dead.

"Where's the crashed chopper?"

Merle pointed, half-turning to face the river. "Went into the Hudson and sank."

The copilot glanced back to the chopper and the side door slid open. The man within crouched in the opening. There was a familiar metal cylinder over his shoulder and a strap across the checked cotton shirt he wore. Dalton had carried a rifle just like it on many missions while in Special Ops. It was an M4.

"What about the pilot?" asked the newcomer. "He go down with his chopper?"

Brian answered that one, coming to stand beside Merle. "We got him out. But he died."

Dalton groaned.

"Too bad," said the copilot.

Alice smiled brightly, standing in a line beside Brian. The only thing missing was the wall to make this a perfect setup for a firing squad. Dalton had a pistol but it would hardly be a match for three armed mercenaries. They'd kill him and, more importantly, they'd kill Erin. So he waited, backing her up with a firm pull on her arm. They now watched through the cover of pine boughs.

Dalton knew what would happen next. He ran through possibilities of what he could do, if anything, to prevent it.

"Do something," whispered Erin.

"If I do something, they'll know our position."

"They're going to kill them."

"I think so."

"So save them."

"It will endanger you."

"What would you do if I wasn't here?"

He glanced at her. "You *are* here."

Dalton watched from his position. "Get behind that tree." He pointed. "Stay there and when I say run, you run for the kayaks."

"Dalton?"

"Promise me."

She met his gaze and nodded, then stepped behind the thick trunk of the pine tree. He moved beside her.

In the clearing, one of the new arrivals glanced in his direction and then back to Alice.

"You retrieve anything from the craft before it went down?"

"Yeah," said Alice,

Dalton aimed at the one with the rifle.

"What exactly?"

"A red cooler. We have to take it to the FBI," said Brian.

"That so? Where is it now, exactly?"

Brian seemed to have realized that he faced a wolf in

sheep's clothing because he rested a hand on his neck and rubbed before speaking.

"Back by our tents," he lied. "I'll get it for you." He turned to go.

The man with the aviator glasses motioned for the pilot to follow. The copilot lifted his hand to signal the shooter. The rifleman raised his weapon and Dalton took his shot, dropping him like a sack of rags.

By the time Dalton swung his pistol away from the dead man, the copilot had Alice in front of him, using her as a human shield.

"Come out or she dies," said their leader.

He didn't, and the man shot Merle and Richard in rapid succession. They fell like wheat before the scythe.

From the brush where Brian had disappeared came the sound of thrashing. Dalton suspected the teen had made a run for it.

The copilot dragged Alice back toward the chopper, using the nose cone as cover, as he shouted to the pilot. Another shot sounded and Alice fell forward to the ground, shot through the head.

"Kill whoever is shooting. Then find the sample," said the copilot.

"The boy?"

"No witnesses."

Dalton leaned toward Erin and whispered, "When they find that cooler, they'll kill us. You understand?"

She nodded.

"Run!"

Erin didn't look back at the carnage. Instead, she fled down the trail toward the river. Dalton had a time trying to keep up.

At the bank of the Hudson, Erin finally came to a

halt. She folded at the waist and gripped her knees with both hands, panting.

"They killed them. Just shot them down," she said.

Dalton thought he'd heard his wife express every emotion possible from elation to fury. But this voice, this high reedy thread of a voice, didn't seem to belong to Erin.

"Where's Brian?"

He wouldn't get far with two trained killers on his trail.

Erin, who had just belayed into a river and rescued a wounded man. Who had led this group here to disaster. Who had just watched three more people die. The first deaths she'd ever witnessed.

A sharp threat of worry stitched his insides.

She straightened, and he took in her pale face and bloodless lips. He felt a second jolt of panic. She was going into shock.

"Erin." He took a firm hold of both her elbows and gave a little shake. "We have to go now." Her eyes snapped into focus and she met his gaze. There she was, pale, panting and scared. But she was back.

"Brian," she whispered and then shouted. "Brian!" He appeared like a lost puppy, crashing through the brush, holding one bleeding arm with his opposite hand.

Behind him came the pilot. Dalton squeezed off two shots, sending his pursuer back into cover.

Erin and Brian crouched on the bank as Erin removed a red bandanna from her pocket and tied it around the bullet wound in the boy's arm.

She closed her mouth and scowled as a familiar fierce expression emerged on her face.

"Those animals are not getting away with this."

She glanced toward the trail. His wife was preparing to fight.

"Erin, get into your kayak. Now." He tugged her toward the watercrafts.

She paused and looked at her pack and the paddle already in place for departure. Then she glanced at him.

"You knew?"

"Suspected."

She clutched Brian's good arm. "He can't paddle with one arm." She wiped her hand over her mouth. "And you don't know how to navigate in white water."

True enough.

The kayaks each held only one person. Dalton took another shot to send their attacker back behind the tree.

"He'll have to try," said Dalton.

"Get in, Brian. I'll launch you."

Tears stained the boy's pink, hairless cheeks, and blood stained his forearm, but he climbed into a kayak. Erin handed him a paddle and shoved his craft into the river.

"Now you," she called to him.

He knew what would happen when he stopped shooting. They'd be sitting ducks on the river.

"I'll be right behind you."

"Dalton. No."

"You promised," he said.

Brian was already in the current, struggling to paddle.

"Go," he coaxed, wondering if this was the last time that he'd ever see her.

She went with a backward glance, calling directions as she pushed the kayak into the Hudson.

"Get to the center of the river and avoid the logs. Hug

the right shore going into the first turn and the left on the second. How far are we going?"

"Get under cover." They would be sitting ducks on the river once the chopper was airborne. He needed to kill that pilot.

"Got it."

He moved his position as the pilot left cover to fire at what he assumed was three kayakers.

Never assume. Dalton took the shot and the man staggered back to cover.

Body armor, Dalton realized.

He caught a glimpse of the man darting between the trees in retreat. He took another shot, aiming for his head, and missed. Then he climbed into the kayak. Erin's graceful departure had made the launch look easy. His efforts included using the paddle to shove himself forward, nearly upending in the process.

He moved by inches, shocked at how much his abdomen ached as he felt the grass and earth dragging under him. The river snatched him from the shore. He retrieved his double-bladed paddle, glancing forward to catch a glimpse of Erin before she vanished from his view. The pitch and buck of the river seemed a living thing beneath him, and this was the wide, quiet part.

He used his paddle to steer but did not propel himself forward. The river began to churn with the first set of rapids. He rocketed along, propelled by the hydrodynamics of the surging water.

Above him, the sky blazed scarlet, reflecting on the dark water like blood. Erin had never seen a dead body. Today she had seen six.

As if summoned from the twilight by his thoughts,

he glimpsed Erin on the far bank, towing Brian's kayak to shore. He tried and failed to redirect her.

Erin reached the rocky shore and leaped out, holding both crafts as Brian struggled from his vessel. He didn't look back as he ran into the woods and vanished.

Dalton shouted as he slipped past her, using his paddle in an ineffective effort to reverse against the current.

He still splashed and shouted when Erin appeared again, towing an empty kayak. She darted past him, her paddle flashing silver in the fading light. She took point and he fell in behind her, mirroring her strokes and ignoring the painful tug in his middle that accompanied each pull of the blade through the surging water. She hugged the first turn just as she'd instructed him and he tried to follow, but swept wider and nearly hit the boulder cutting the water like the fin of a tiger shark.

She glanced back and shouted something inaudible, and they sped through a churning descent that made his stomach pitch as river water splashed into his vessel's compartment. He could hear nothing past the roar of the white water, and neither could Erin. He knew this because he spotted the second turn in the river at the same moment he caught the flash of the red underbelly of the helicopter.

Erin's head lifted as the chopper swept over them and took a position downriver, hovering low and then dropping out of sight. It would be waiting, he knew, low over the water to pick them off when they made the next turn.

Hug the right shore on the first turn and the left on the second. That was what she had told him, but his wife was very clearly making a path to the right on this second turn.

Dalton struggled to follow against the pull of the river that tried to drag him left. On the turn he saw the reason for her warning. There before him loomed the largest logjam of downed trees he'd ever seen, and it rushed right at them. Waves hit the barrier and soared ten feet in the air, soaking the logs that choked the right bank of the turn. The pile of debris seemed injected with towering pillars of rock.

It occurred to him then why most groups did not run this section of the river and never after a release from the dam.

Erin performed a neat half turn, riding a wave partially up the natural dam as the second kayak flipped. The river dropped her back and she pulled until she grasped a branch near the shore. She held on as the river tore the empty craft from hers. The empty vessel bobbed up beyond the logs and sped downriver as Erin struggled to keep hers from being dragged under the web of branches.

He tried to mimic her maneuver but instead rammed bow-first into the nest of branches. The water lifted the back of his kayak while forcing the bow down and under the debris.

"Grab hold," Erin yelled.

He did, managing to grip the slimy, lichen-covered limb as the kayak continued its path downward and into the debris. He used both feet to snag the shoulder straps of his pack as his watercraft vanished beneath him. His stomach burned and he knew he could hold his pack or the limb, but not both. His current physical weakness infuriated him, but he dropped his pack. It fell to his seat in front of the red cooler decoy. Both his gear and the kayak were pulled under.

He hauled himself farther up on the debris as his kayak resurfaced beyond the fallen tree limb where he clung and his craft was whisked away.

He sighed at the loss, but with his feet free he could now climb to a spot above where Erin was snagged. He help move the nose of her craft back and clear of a branch. Then she dragged and pulled herself toward the shore. Just a little farther and the current calmed. Erin shoved with her paddle and reached the shallows as he scrambled beside the log dam.

How many seconds until the chopper realized they were no longer on the river?

Chapter Five

Erin clambered onto shore, pausing only to tug her backpack from the inner compartment. Dalton dropped from the brush pile to land in the shallows beside her and dragged her kayak off the shore and well into the cover of the pines before halting to look back at the river.

No one ran that portion of the river on the day of a planned release. The water was too deep and too fast. She was shocked she hadn't rolled under the mass of twisted branches. Even experienced paddlers could be pinned by rolling water or submerged obstacles.

She looked back at the river now thirty feet behind them. The sound of rushing water abated. The roar lessened to a churning tumble, like a waterfall.

By slow degrees, the sound changed to something mechanical. The whirling of the chopper blades, she realized.

The killers had waited long enough. They were coming upriver.

Erin shouldered the second strap of her pack and crouched down as the helicopter swept low over the water, heading upriver. Dalton paused for its passing, then grabbed the towrope and hauled the kayak farther back into the woods until he and her vessel disappeared.

The helicopter raced past again and then hovered over the brush pile. Could they see Dalton's pack or his kayak? They definitely saw something.

How was this even happening?

Was Brian all right? He couldn't paddle with his wounded arm and she knew she'd never navigate the rapids towing him. The choice was hard, but leaving him gave him his best chance. They wouldn't know where or on which side of the river to find him. His wound was serious but he could walk, run actually.

Run and hide. When they're gone, when you're certain, you can find the river trail. The blue trail. Follow it upriver to the road.

He'd understood, she was sure, but with his pale cheeks and the shock, she didn't know if he could make it to safety.

"Please let him be all right," she whispered.

If her muscles didn't ache and her teeth weren't chattering, she'd try to chalk this up as some bad dream. Instead, it was a full-fledged nightmare. A waking one.

Her mind flashed on an image of Carol Walton, her stomach torn open by a soulless piece of debris that could have struck any one of them. Erin covered her eyes, but the image remained, emblazoned in her mind. That flying metal could have killed Dalton just as easily as Carol. And then she'd be dead in that meadow with her entire outdoor adventure group. Erin's shoulders shook.

Something warm touched her arm and she jumped. Dalton squeezed and she rolled into the familiar comfort of his embrace. She forgot the imminent doom of the men on the helicopter lurking just a few yards from where she wept in her husband's arms. He let her go after a few minutes, rubbed her shoulders briskly and drew back.

"We have to go," he said.

She nodded and sniffed. "Will they think we're dead?"

"Here's hoping. Will your kayak hold two?"

"No. We'd swamp in rough water."

"Then we go on foot."

"Where?"

"As far from here as possible."

She nodded and then looked around.

"They're gone?" she asked.

"For now."

Under the cover of the trees it seemed that night had already fallen, until you glanced at the purple sky visible through the gaps in the foliage.

Where was Brian?

"Do you think they'll catch him?" Erin could not keep the tears from coming as she spoke. "I had to get him to shore. I couldn't…he couldn't…"

Dalton gathered her in.

"It was the right choice. The boy has a better chance away from us."

"I was afraid he'd upend and drown. I told him to hide and then how to walk out, but he's bleeding and scared."

"He's young and strong." Dalton released her. "He'll make it."

Was he just telling her what she needed to hear? She didn't know, but if Brian survived, it was because Dalton did as she asked. His remaining at her request had saved the boy, at least. Or it might have.

"Which way?" he asked.

"Well," she said, adjusting her pack. "We should head downriver. That's the closest place to find help."

"Then they'll expect us to head that way." Dalton looked in the opposite direction. "What's upriver?"

"Brian, I hope, and the dead."

He turned back to her, and she knew that the tears still rolled down her damp cheeks.

"I'm sorry about them, Erin. If we are lucky and smart, you'll have time to process this and grieve. But right now we must get clear of this spot. We need full cover, and the more difficult it is to follow us the better."

"Maybe we should head west awhile. There isn't much in that direction. Not a destination. Then we can turn either to Indian Lake or Lake Abanakee. There are vacation cottages on both. Golf courses, some camping." She turned in a full circle tapping her index finger on the small indentation between her upper lip and nose.

"What?" he asked.

"You know, they'll expect us on this shore."

"Because they saw my gear on the jam."

"Yes, so what if we cross the river?"

He frowned, really not wanting to get back into that sucking vortex of death.

"How?" he asked.

"I'll cross with the towrope tied to my kayak. You keep hold of the throw ball until I'm ashore. Then, you can haul back my kayak and use it to follow me."

"What if it tips on the way back? Then you're over there and I'm over here."

"Won't matter if it tips. It won't sink."

"Then we go together."

"The kayak won't sink, but it will be floating beneath the surface. We'll be swept out."

He nodded. "All right. One at a time. You first."

She gave him an impatient smirk for repeating her plan back to her, only this time taking credit, and then gave him a thumbs-up.

"Good plan. Let's do it your way."

He flushed as she sat to wait out their pursuers. The chopper continued to circle them like a shark smelling blood. Finally, their pursuers flew up and out of sight. Erin and Dalton waited for full dark so their crossing would not be noted.

Then she tumped the kayak, carrying it upside down on her head over the stretch they could not paddle. Dalton tried to take it, but the pain of stretching his arms too far above his head made it impossible. Erin carried the craft a quarter mile downriver to a spot beyond the turn. After that, he helped load her pack and held on to the thin cordage as she pushed off and flew out of his sight. He marked her progress by the line that slipped over his palms. He eyed the diminishing line, worrying that she would not reach the opposite shore before he reached the end of the towline. He wasn't sure that she'd calculated how far downriver the current would carry her before she could reach the opposite bank.

Abruptly, the towline stilled, then shuddered and moved two measured feet along. She was snagged or across. He counted the time in the rapid rasp of his breath and the sweat that rolled periodically down his back. Finally, he felt the four short tugs that signaled him to retrieve the kayak.

Dragging the craft back to him was not as easy as

he had anticipated, and he was sweating and cursing by the time he sighted her kayak.

He took a moment to catch his breath and check the two vials he carried in their custom pack. Both they and the thumb drive were intact and dry. He zipped closed the case, returning it to his side pocket. Then he checked his personal weapon.

"Ready or not," he said, and climbed into the kayak, where he shimmied until the bottom cleared the bank and the river took him. Moving fast and paddling hard. The water seemed a glittering deadly ribbon. He could not see the rocks that jutted from the churning surface until they flashed past him. One pounded the underside of the kayak, making it buck like a bronco. He continued on, realizing that he was riding lower and lower in the water with each passing second. The kayak's bottom was compromised. He was certain.

The hollow core of the craft was filling with water. In other words, he was sinking.

Chapter Six

Erin's damp skin turned icy as she watched the dark shape of her kayak sinking below the surface. She caught a glimpse of the paddle sweeping before the craft and held her breath. Her husband was in the river, swimming for his life.

She grabbed her pack and cursed. It was a stupid dangerous idea to have him try to cross the river alone and at night. She knew this section and the location of the rocks that loomed from the water. Dalton did not and, as far as she knew, he had never kayaked before.

Brush and brambles lined the bank, but she raced along, searching for his head bobbing in the dark water.

"He's a strong swimmer," she told the night, but he wasn't. He was only average, his muscle mass making him what she called "a sinker."

And he should be at home on medical leave recovering from the abdominal surgery that followed the bullet wound.

She tripped, sprawled and righted herself.

"Dalton!" she shouted.

Where was he? The kayak had vanished and her paddle had been carried off. She judged the river's flow and imagined a line from where he went into the Hudson to where he might be.

He'd had loads of time in the pool and the ocean practicing escapes from crafts. He had jumped out of helicopters in to the ocean. So he'd know not to fight the river. The only thing to do was to use the forward momentum and patiently angle your stroke toward the shore.

How far would the river take him?

Her heart walloped against her ribs as she raced around tree trunks and scrambled over rocks.

What if he hit his head? What if he were unconscious?

She'd wanted a break, a time to think and a time for him to hear her fears. She didn't want him dead. That was why she'd called for a separation. He didn't see what he was doing, how dangerously he lived. And he didn't understand how his decisions affected her. If he died, oh, what if he was drowning right now?

He could be pinned against a rock or held down under a snag that wasn't even visible from above. Had he left her, finally, once and for all?

Something was moving up ahead.

Erin ran, howling like a wolf who had lost her pack, crying his name and wailing like a banshee. Her legs pumped. When had she dropped her pack?

Was it him? Had the Fates brought him back to her once more?

I swear, I'll never leave him again. Just don't let him die. Please, please, dear Lord.

It was big, crawling up the bank. A man. Sweet Lord, it was her man.

"Dalton!"

He turned his head—lifted a hand in greeting—and collapsed on the bank.

The roar of the river blocked any reply, but he'd seen her. She fell on her hands and knees before him. Gathering him up in her arms. Rocking and weeping and babbling.

He patted her upper arm, gasping but reassuring her with his action. It only made her weep harder. He shouldn't even be here. He could have died.

It would have been her fault. He was here because of her. He'd tried the river because of her, and he'd nearly drowned…because of her.

Dalton struggled to a seat on the muddy bank. His skin was as cool as river water and his clothing drenched. It didn't have to be that cold for someone to die from exposure. Being wet upped the chances. And being weakened from exertion and the healing wounds all made him more susceptible.

She needed her pack.

"Can you stand?" she asked.

He struggled to his knees and then to his feet, leaning heavily on her. The amount of weight that pressed down upon her nearly buckled her knees and terrified her further because he wouldn't lean so heavily if he didn't have to.

The sound of the river changed. There was a rhythmic quality that lifted to her consciousness and caused her to look skyward. A field of stars littered the velvety black and then, from upriver, came a cone of light.

"Helicopter," she said.

Dalton straightened and glanced up. "Cover," he said, and struggled up the bank. The tree line loomed like a dark curtain, impossibly far. They lumbered along, he the bear, she the fox. Nearly there when the helicopter shot past them.

The searchlight swept back and forth across the river's surface.

"They're on the logjam," he said, his voice shaking with the rest of him.

The chopper hovered, the beam shining on something beyond their line of sight.

"My kayak or my pack," he guessed.

"They'll think we drowned."

"Maybe."

"I don't understand. Why would they come after us? They must have found what they were looking for by now."

Dalton said nothing, just sank to his knees on the cushiony loam of pine needles.

"Where is your pack?" he asked.

"I dropped it."

He lifted his head and stared at her, his eyes glittering.

"In the open?"

"I'm not sure."

"Go get it, Erin. Hurry. Take cover if they go over again. Find it if you can."

"What about you?"

"I'll be here."

She stood, indecision fixing her to the spot. Go? Stay?

"We need that gear," he said.

They did.

"And if they spot it…"

Erin set off again as the helicopter continued to hover. She didn't look back as she returned to the shore and hurried upriver. She couldn't see more than a few feet before her. It would be easy to miss a green pack, but the frame, it was aluminum. She'd come too far, she thought. Must have missed it. She must have been carrying it here.

And then, finally and at last, she caught the glint of her silver water bottle.

She dashed the remaining distance and scooped up her pack. Then she turned to see the helicopter descending low on the river. Was it in the same place?

No, it was moving, shining its light on the opposite bank. The ruse was working. Still she hurried under cover and waited as it surged past her position. Then she retraced her steps.

"Dalton?"

She wasn't sure how far she needed to go, but this seemed the right distance.

"Dalton?"

"Here!"

She followed the direction of his call and found him sitting against a large tree trunk, arms wrapped about his middle. He wasn't shivering. Instead of taking that as a positive change, she saw it for what it was. When the body was cold and stopped shivering, it was dying.

Erin tore the lower boughs from the pines and set them beside the log. Then she unrolled her black foam mat and shook out her sleeping bag because the down filling needed to trap dead air within the baffles in order to insulate and help hold body heat.

When she finished, she helped him rise. He staggered and fell and then crawled as she urged him on, whispering commands like a hoarse drill sergeant. She stripped him out of his jacket, shoulder holster and personal weapon, then she tugged off the wet T-shirt and cargo pants that were predictably heavy and likely carrying his service weapon and extra clips for his pistol. All were wet, but that was a problem for another time.

"I'm not cold," he whispered, his words slurring.

He stretched out in the open sleeping bag and lay on both the mat and pine boughs. She zipped him in.

Erin thought about calling the emergency number of the Department of Environmental Conservation. The rangers could call the New York State Police Aviation Unit or the Eagle Valley Search Dogs, but she very much feared that rescue would be hours away. So she left her phone off and stowed for the time being. Right now she needed shelter and to get Dalton warm.

She was a survival expert and knew the rule of threes. The body could survive three minutes without air, three hours without shelter, less depending on the weather and their physical condition, three days without water and three weeks without food.

She fitted her pack half under the log at his head and then set to work on the shelter. Fallen sticks and branches littered the forest floor and she gathered them by the armful, making a great pile. Then she constructed a brush shelter around him using the log beside which he lay as the center beam and leaning the larger sticks against it. It was low to the ground, easy to miss if you were not looking. She did not know if the men who had killed her party would follow them into the woods, but she was taking no chances.

Her tent was too geometrical and too light to make good cover. But her camo tarp could work if she used it correctly. Erin laid the ten-by-ten tarp over the logs and sticks, then staked it down on the opposite side of the downed trunk. The remaining four feet she stretched out away from the log before securing it to the ground. Then she added evergreen boughs to further disguise their burrow.

Erin stepped back to study the structure she had built. The resulting shelter was roughly the shape of a lean-to and stood only two feet tall at the highest point, tapering to the ground from there and was no taller than the fallen tree trunk. The tarp would break the cold wind that was rising carrying the scent of rain.

As the helicopter searched the far bank, she finished all but the small gap needed to crawl inside. This she would close once she was beside her husband. The fact that Dalton did not move to help her frightened her greatly.

Shivering herself, exhausted and sick at heart, Erin crawled in next to Dalton. Before she closed the opening, she watched as the helicopter hovered beyond the barrier of tree trunks and crossed the glistening water. That too was a problem for another time. They could no longer run. So, it was time to hide.

Erin wiggled in beside her husband. His skin was cold as marble. She managed to get the zipper up and around them. The bag was designed for one, but accommodated them both with Dalton on his back and her tucked against him on her side. She knew how much body heat was lost from the top of a person's head so she tugged at the drawstring, bringing the top of the bag down around Dalton's head like the hood of a parka.

Still at last, she pressed her warm body to his icy one. Gradually, her temperature dropped and she shivered. Dalton lay unmoving except for the shallow rise and fall of his chest.

What if he was bleeding inside again?

She could do nothing if he was, and that was why her mind fixed upon it. Why was that?

When one shoulder began to ache, she pushed herself on top of Dalton. She inhaled fresh pine, damp earth and the aftershave that still lingered faintly on Dalton's skin. He lifted an arm across her back, holding her in his sleep. His movement made her tear up. By the time she shifted to his opposite side, he was shivering.

The helicopter rotors continued to spin and the beam of light crossed over them twice. She wasn't sure when the chopper finally moved off. Sometime after Dalton had stopped shivering.

She fell asleep with the uneasy feeling that the men who had murdered her party had not given up. A cold wind rushed through the shelter, cooling her face. She tasted rain.

Sometime later, the storm struck, hitting the tree canopy first, rousing Erin from uneasy slumber. Dalton's breathing had changed to a slow, steady draw and his heart beat in a normal rhythm. Eventually the rain penetrated the interlocking branches of the trees and the droplets pattered on the dry leaves. The torrent of water grew in volume until she could no longer hear the river rush.

The sky lit in a brilliant flash of white and Erin began her counting as she waited for the thunder. She didn't like being under the trees in such a storm. Tall trees were natural lightning rods, and the wind could bring down limbs and dead trees on hapless campers. It was why she had selected the fateful rocky outcropping.

She imagined the rain merging with the drying blood

on the bodies of the ones she had left behind, and her chest constricted.

"Erin?" Dalton whispered.

"Yes?"

"You okay?"

"I don't think so."

"The chopper gone?"

"Yes."

"I thought I just saw the spotlight."

The thunder rolled over and through them.

"It's the storm."

He relaxed back into their nest. "Good. Make it harder to track us."

"Why would they want to track us?" she asked, and in answer heard his gentle snore.

Erin rolled to her side, pressing her back against him and curling her arms before herself. The thunder was still a mile off, but over the next quarter hour it passed overhead.

The cascade of water finally penetrated their burrow, soaking the evergreen and running down the needles and tarp away from where they rested.

Gradually the rainfall diminished, and the sound of the river returned, rushing endlessly. When she next roused it was to some unfamiliar sound. She stiffened, listening. The gray gloom inside their nest told her that morning approached. She could now see the sides of the shelter above her.

The sound came again, this time recognizable. It was the snapping of a stick underneath the foot of something moving close at hand.

Chapter Seven

Erin strained to listen to the creature moving close to their shelter. Squirrel or possum, maybe. Or a deer, perhaps. When animals moved, they sounded much larger than they actually were. She'd seen grown men startle in terror from the crackle of dried leaves under the paws of a scurrying chipmunk.

The sound came again. That was no chipmunk.

Now there was another snap of a branch, this time coming from a slightly different direction. Dalton's eyes popped open and she pressed a hand over his mouth. Whatever was out there, she did not want to reveal their position.

DALTON WOKE WITH a jolt to feel Erin's warm hand pressed across his mouth. He shifted only his eyes to look at her. In the gray predawn gloom, he could see little. But his body was on high alert.

She had heard it, too. He was certain from the stiffness of her body and the way she cocked her head to one side, listening. Something was coming. To him it sounded like the even tread of boots. He had been on enough covert ops to recognize the sound of a line of men moving in sequence.

He lifted his head from the sleeping bag. Listening.

Where was his gun?

The sound came from the right and left. He counted the footfalls. He heard three distinct individuals moving together, searching, he guessed, the forest on this side of the river.

Had they already finished their sweep of the opposite bank?

Where the hell was his gun?

The group continued forward and then passed them. Why hadn't they seen them?

Dalton gazed up at the unfamiliar roof some eight inches above his head. They were in some sort of shelter constructed of broken sticks leaning on a large fallen log and then covered with a camo tarp. More branches on the outside, judging from the way the light cut through the tarp. His gaze swept above his head and down to his toes. Then he turned his face so that his lips pressed to his wife's ear.

"They missed us."

Now she turned her head to whisper into his ear.

"What if they come back?"

He did not answer. But he knew exactly. It was not to tie up loose ends or to silence them forever. It was to retrieve what had been stolen from them or from their employers. They were acting on orders to retrieve the contents of the red nylon cooler. Just as the pilot had told them. These men would keep coming until they recovered what he carried. And he would stop at nothing to get it into the hands of his own government.

But first he had to empty his bladder.

Erin was still for a very long time. Finally, she

shifted beside him, lifting her knee across his thigh, rising up to one elbow to stare down at him.

"They were searching along this side of the river."

"Yes."

"Should we stay here or make a run for it?"

"I've got to get up. Let me do a little recon."

"Good plan, except you're naked, your clothes are wet, your gun is wet and recon means leaving me alone. Let me rephrase that. Bad plan. Really, really bad."

"I still have to get up."

"Me, too."

"After you then. I haven't climbed out of a foxhole in some time."

"It's a brush shelter."

Erin removed the sticks that obscured the opening. Then she wiggled out of the bag to crouch beside the tree. She saw immediately why they were invisible to their pursuers. Several more pine boughs had fallen during the storm. Her shelter seemed just more debris.

Not only that, the warm ground in the cool air had resulted in a low mist that crept around the tree trunks and hugged the earth. To disappear, one only had to lie flat.

She took her time listening and looking for the men. Seeing nothing, she called back to Dalton and then moved away to relieve herself. When she returned to him, he was crouching naked beside the shelter.

"It's freezing out here."

"The mornings can be chilly."

"I'm shriveled up like the… Do you have anything that I can wear?"

Erin moved to the shelter to slide her pack out of the gap. She sorted through her gear and retrieved the plastic rain poncho.

"Maybe this?" She offered the poncho and then added one of his olive green T-shirts.

He held the familiar garment aloft. "Why did you bring this?"

"Hey, don't read more into it than there is. It's soft and I like to sleep in it." She did not like his self-satisfied smile.

A moment later he had slipped into the T-shirt. As his head vanished into the fabric she glanced to his stomach. She always admired the heavy musculature of his chest and stomach, especially in motion. But this time her gaze tracked to the swollen red suture line at the flesh just above his hip bone. The man should be home, resting and not lifting anything over forty pounds.

Dalton tugged down on the hem of the cotton T-shirt and then donned the poncho. He chose to wear his damp cargo pants commando style. Then he spent the next twenty minutes disassembling, cleaning and drying his pistol. He dried every bullet in the four clips that he had stowed in the pockets of his pants.

Erin occupied herself scattering the branches used for her shelter. Then she stuffed the sleeping bag back into its nylon bag, rolled her foam pad and collected the tarp. She stowed all of these but the high density foam bedroll into her pack. That she tied on the top.

"Ready?" he asked.

"Which way?" she asked.

"Away from our company. When they don't find us, they'll backtrack"

"You want me to call the forest rangers?"

"Is your phone still off?"

"How did you know it was off?"

His mouth tipped down. "I tried calling you yesterday. Kept flipping to voice mail."

"I told you I wouldn't be calling."

"You did."

Now she was scowling. "I'll keep it off for now."

Dalton removed the strap from her shoulder and took her pack.

"You shouldn't carry that," she said, staring pointedly at his middle and the healing surgical scars that she knew were there.

"Circumstances being as they are, I am."

"We still have to talk about this."

He nodded and set off. Erin knew he'd likely rather face those mercenaries than have a talk with her, and that was exactly the problem, wasn't it? But they were going to talk, and even commandos were not going to keep her from saying her piece.

If he didn't like it, that was just too darn bad. Next time maybe he'd stay home when she asked him.

By the time Dalton finally stopped, the gray dawn had morphed into a fine drizzle that coated the leaves and dripped down upon them. It saturated her hair and dampened her clothing. Erin could see from his pallor that Dalton had pushed too hard and traveled too many miles.

"Where do you think we are?" he asked.

They'd been traveling in roughly a northerly direction according to her compass, paralleling the river, and she could guess the distance at three miles of scrambling down bramble-covered ravines and up lichen-covered rock faces. The topography on this side of the river was challenging, and the closer they got to the gorges the steeper the climb would become.

"Don't you know?" she asked.

He shook his head.

"Then just maybe you should let the one with the compass and maps lead."

He pressed his lips together in that suffering look, and her internal temperature rose to a near boil. She reminded herself that he'd nearly died last month and again last night. It seemed he was determined to leave her. Her leaving was intended to keep that from happening, but somehow it had just made everything worse.

She removed the bottle from the pack she carried and offered it to him.

"Almost empty," he said, refusing.

"I can fill it anywhere. I have a filtration system on this bottle."

"You mean I've been conserving all morning for no reason?"

"No, there was a reason. You didn't ask me."

His eyes lifted skyward as if praying for patience, and then he drank all that was left in the bottle.

"Why don't we just call DEC?"

"DEC?" he asked.

"Department of Environmental Conservation. The forest rangers. They can dispatch a helicopter and lift us out of here."

"No."

"Why not?"

He shook his head and looked skyward as if expecting a phantom helicopter. Honestly, the man seemed to want to do everything the hard way.

"Dalton, why?"

"The call for air evac would be via radio, and that transmission is being monitored by our pursuers."

"You don't know that."

"It's what I would do."

"Well, then, let me at least send search and rescue after Brian Peters and to my group." Her voice broke on the last word and she clamped her mouth closed to keep from crying.

"Your mobile is still off?"

"Yes. Why?"

"If the kid made it out, then they already know what happened and where."

She thought of the teen alone on the trail and the worry squeezed at her heart. "Do you think he's safe?"

Her husband offered no assurances and his expression remained grim. "He's a wounded kid and they're trained mercenaries. He went the way you told me that they'd expect us to go."

She had sent him straight into more trouble. Erin scowled. "I never should have left him."

"If you hadn't, we'd all be dead. His only chance was away from us. You made the right call. In any case, you are overdue to check in. When DEC finds your party, they'll know you are missing with three kayaks. But if you switch on that phone our pursuers will find us."

"How?"

"Forest Rangers will request GPS coordinates from the county 911."

Erin said no more as she studied the map for several minutes. "You want to backtrack to Lake Abanakee or continue downriver to the community of North River?"

"Neither. Those are the two directions they will expect us to travel. What else have you got?"

"Why are they even following us? Is it because we are witnesses?"

Dalton's gaze shifted away. Erin scowled as she remembered something.

"You took that cooler. The one from the helicopter. I saw it in your kayak."

"The pilot entrusted the information—"

"To me! And I left it behind. I left it because our lives are more valuable to me than some flash drive and a pair of glass vials."

He saw the look in her eyes, registering what he had done. He didn't deny it. But neither did he offer reassurance. She was right. He'd put them in danger.

"But you lost all your gear with your kayak. If they were searching, they should have found both. Even if the cooler popped out of your kayak…"

"It didn't. I tied it down."

Dalton's eyes shifted back to meet hers and she saw the guilty look on his face.

"Where is it?" she demanded.

Dalton lifted his hands in a gesture meant to placate. "Now, honey. Listen to me."

"Where?"

His right hand moved to the side pocket on his cargo pants. He gave the full pocket a little pat.

"Why in the name of heaven would you risk our lives for whatever trouble that pilot was carrying?"

Dalton reached for her shoulders and she stepped away. Then she released the waist buckle at her middle and dropped her pack. She spent the next several moments stalking back and forth like a caged animal, gathering her fury about her like a cloak. Finally, she came to a complete stop, pivoting to face him.

"You just don't get it. This is why I wanted a break. This…" She waved her hand in a circular motion and continued speaking. "This obsession with playing the hero. It's not our job to deliver that nonsense. It was his."

"This is bigger than that," said Dalton. "This could save thousands of lives. Maybe our own."

"If we don't get killed in the process." She turned her back on him and covered her face with her hands.

Tentatively, he wrapped an arm around her shoulders and turned her to face him.

"Erin, I'm sorry. But I didn't see a choice."

She shook her head. "And that's where you're wrong. There's always a choice. The choice to reenlist in the most dangerous arm of the Marines."

"I left them because you were unhappy."

"I wasn't unhappy being married to a marine. I was unhappy being married to a marine who insisted on being on the front line of every assignment."

"I quit because of you."

"You didn't quit. You just shifted from one dangerous assignment to the next. New York City Real Time Crime Center? Come on, Dalton. What is the difference between that and Vice?"

"It's not undercover work."

"You're a cop. You're a target."

"Is that what you think I am?"

"They shot you! They killed your partner."

"Not while I was on a call."

"What difference does that make? You were in a coma, Dalton. You didn't have to attend your partner's funeral. You didn't have to see them give a flag to his widow. You didn't have to comfort his children. I did that. I did that alone while you were recovering from internal injuries."

"I understand how you must feel."

"Clearly you don't or you would have stayed home as I asked. You would have considered that my fears are justified."

"And you'd be dead now."

"As opposed to in a day from now? If you really believe that those guys are after us, trained killers, what chance do we have? They have helicopters and guns. All we have is each other."

"Maybe that's enough."

She rolled her eyes. "Oh, Dalton. Just leave it. Put it on a rock on a bright red T-shirt with a note that says, 'Enjoy!' and let's get out of here with our lives."

"That's why I love you, Erin. You are a survivor."

She pressed her lips tight and glared. "The way you are headed, I'll have to be."

"Don't be like that."

"Like what? I'm trying to keep you alive. To save you from yourself because if I don't, one way or another, you're leaving me. Getting shot at, blown up in Afghanistan, coming home with knife wounds and now carrying a vial of something that, if it breaks open in your pocket, will kill us both."

She loved him, but she was not going to stand over his coffin and accept a flag from a grateful city or nation. If you couldn't stop the oncoming train, sometimes all you could do was step out of its way.

He stared down at her with that hangdog look, and she tried and failed not to feel his sorrow.

"How do you see this ending?" she asked.

"We make it out and get this to the FBI in Albany."

"Fine." She shouldered her pack and stared up at the victorious smile on his handsome face, and she ignored the jolt of awareness that he stirred in her. "And then I want a divorce."

Chapter Eight

Erin studied the topographical map. "If we walk along the gorge beside the Boreas River, we'll run into North Woods Club Road."

"How far?"

"Roughly three miles east to the confluence of the Boreas River and Hudson, bushwhacking because there is no trail. Then it's a two-mile uphill hike, steep for the first mile or so, on a marked trail to the gravel road. From there we can head west to a small community at the terminus of the road or east to Minerva. The community looks like about five houses. Either one is somewhere around five more miles."

"Ten miles."

"Only six to the road. We can get help there."

"Or get intercepted."

"The rain will fill the rivers and make the going slippery, but we should reach the road in a couple of hours. We can call the rangers."

He looked unconvinced.

"They can search for Brian, send help, and I'll tell them not to use radio communication."

"You can't guarantee it. With so many rangers, someone will pick up a radio."

"Who do you want to call, your detective bureau?"

"Too far. But I could have them call for help once we get out of the woods."

"What about my camp director? He can drive to the station. By now they've found—" she struggled to swallow "—my group. He'll believe me when I tell him we are on the run, being stalked. And if Brian got through, they'll know our situation. We know there's help out there. We just have to get to them or help them find us."

"When we get closer to the road."

"Fine." She kept hold of her pack and the map, leading the way back. "You know, there will be rafting groups on the river all day. We might get one of them to pick us up."

"No. They'll be at the terminus of every rafting trip."

"How many of these people do you really think there are?"

"Three in the chopper last night and three in the woods beside our shelter. Plus, the ones who shot the chopper down."

"They might be the same group."

"I don't know how many. Neither do you. So assume everyone we meet is one of them."

She'd seen what they could do, and she did not question her husband's assessment of their situation.

Erin led the way, using her compass only and staying well away from the Hudson. She stopped to fill the water bottle at a spring. All she had were several power bars she kept for emergencies, which this surely was. She handed Dalton the lemon zest bar and kept the chocolate chip for herself. She peeled back the wrapping and glanced up to see the second and last bite of the lemon zest disappear into Dalton's mouth.

"When did you last eat?" she asked.

"Yesterday morning."

He was a big man and burned a lot more calories than she did. She rummaged in her pack and offered a second bar.

"You have more?" His brows lifted in that adorable way that made her want to kiss his face.

"Yes, plenty." Plenty being one.

Midmorning, they paused at a stream and Dalton returned her poncho. He did fill out the shirt she slept in, and she surreptitiously enjoyed the view of his biceps bulging as he lifted the bottle to his lips and drank. The sight made her own mouth go dry.

Erin glanced away, but too late. She was already remembering him naked beneath her last night. Dalton's large, strong body never failed to arouse her. It was just his attitude that pushed her aside. Just once she'd like to have him choose them above protecting the city or the nation or whatever it was he thought he was doing. If he was right, the men hunting them were still out there.

Despite her reservations, her mind swept back to the last time they'd made love. Before the shooter had walked up to her husband's unmarked police unit and shot his partner, Chris Wirimer, in the head before turning the pistol on Dalton. The shooter had targeted the pair solely because they wore police dress uniforms. They were en route to attend the annual medal day ceremony in Lower Manhattan. The gunman had managed to get a bullet between the front and back of Dylan's body armor. It had taken six hours to patch all the bleeders from the bullet, which had traveled between his body armor and his hip bone from front to back stopping only when it had reached the back panel of his flak jacket. A through and through with no internal organ damage, but Dalton had nearly bled out, nearly left her in the way she always feared he would.

From beneath the cover of the canopy of hardwood and pine, Erin again heard the rush of running water. A short time later they reached the Boreas River, flowing fast and swollen from the heavy rains. Here at the river's terminus, the water stretched forty feet from side to side. Erin knew that farther up, the river ran through narrow gorges on the stretch of white water known as Guts and Glory. Here, it tumbled and frothed, making for an excellent run.

She found the trail easily and turned north. Looking back, she could see where the two rivers met. She did not linger as she led them up the steep, muddy trail. Dalton's breathing was labored, and she paused to let him rest. She didn't like his grayish color and was angry again that he'd decided to ambush her instead of giving himself time to heal and her time to think.

She turned her head at the jangle of a dog's collar. A few moments later a young black Labrador retriever appeared wearing a red nylon collar and no leash. Its pink tongue lolled and it paused for just a moment upon sighting Erin, then dashed forward in jubilant excitement.

Erin laughed and offered her hand. The dog wore a harness and was likely carrying her own food and water. Erin stooped to give the dog a scratch behind the ears. She glanced at her collar, fingering the vaccination tag and the ID.

"Jet, huh?" she asked.

The dog half closed her eyes and sat at her feet.

Erin glanced up the trail, waiting for the dog's owner

to appear. She did, a few moments later—a fit older woman with braided graying hair who wore a slouch hat that covered most of her face, hiking shorts and a T-shirt, cotton button-up shirt, wool socks and worn hiking boots. In her hands she carried a hiking stick, and there was a day pack upon her back.

"Oh, hello," said the woman, drawing to a halt. "He's friendly."

Erin wrinkled her nose because the dog was clearly female. That was odd. There was something not right about that woman. Erin took a reflexive step back, trying to determine why her skin was tingling a warning.

"You been to the Hudson?" asked the woman.

The dog did not dart back to her master but instead sat beside Erin. A chill crept over her. She took another step away.

"Yes, it's only a mile and a half down this trail."

"You camping along here?" asked the woman.

"Yes."

"You alone?" the woman asked.

Alone?

Erin turned back in the direction they had come and was surprised to see only the dog at her side. Where was Dalton? Erin's skin prickled as if she had rolled in a patch of nettles. She turned back to face this new threat.

"Yes, why?" Erin thought the woman's smile looked forced and she realized the hiker was younger than she appeared. She wondered vaguely if the gray braided hair was actually attached to this woman's head.

"Where's your partner?"

"What partner?" Erin asked.

"Detective Dalton Stevens." The female drew a small handgun from her pocket and pointed it at Erin's belly.

Erin's mouth dropped open and her heart seemed to pulse in the center of her throat. She could not have spoken if she had tried.

"Does he have it? Or do you?"

"I don't know what you're talking about."

The woman snorted. "Yes, you do. Drop the pack."

Erin did as she was told.

The woman waved Erin back with the barrel of the pistol. Then she moved forward, keeping her gun on Erin as she swept the surroundings with a gaze.

"Come out, Detective, or I shoot your wife."

Chapter Nine

Erin faced the female pointing a pistol at her belly, clearing her throat before she spoke.

"Is this your dog?" Erin asked.

The woman's mouth quirked. "Took it off a pair that were camping back a ways. Unfortunately for them, I'm not so good with faces and I thought they were you. Should have checked before I shot them in their sleeping bags. Lesson learned."

Erin couldn't keep from covering her mouth with one hand.

"Don't figure they need a dog anymore and I thought it added to the whole look." She glanced at the trees on either side of the path. Then she raised her voice. "Detective? I'm counting to three. One…"

Erin jumped at the report of the pistol. Her hands went to her middle, but she felt no pain. Before her, her attacker sank to her knees. Dalton stepped from cover. Pistol aimed and cradled between his two hands as he moved forward with feline grace.

Her canine companion moved forward to greet him, but Dalton ignored the dog, focusing all his attention on the woman, who had released her pistol and sunk to her side. Blood bloomed on the front of her T-shirt and frothed from her mouth.

"How many are you?" asked Dalton.

She laughed, sending frothy pink droplets of blood dribbling down her chin.

"We're like ants at a picnic."

Dalton knelt beside her, transferring the gun to one hand; with the other he patted her down. His search yielded a second pistol, car keys, phone and several strips of plastic zip ties. Erin's stomach twisted at the thought of what she had intended to do with these.

She crept forward and removed the floppy blue hat. The gray braid fell away with the headgear. The end of the braid was secured with a hair tie to the hat's interior tag and looked to have been sliced from someone's head.

Had she stolen a woman's dog, hair and walking stick along with her life? Erin glanced at the plaid shirt and noted it was miles too big. Somewhere up ahead were the victims of this woman's attack. Erin feared she might be sick.

Dalton pocketed the key, one of the pistols, radio, phone and a folding knife. He extended the second gun to Erin.

"Take it."

She did, hoping it would not go off in her pocket.

"Who are you?" Dalton asked the downed woman.

"One of Siming's Army."

"Who?"

"You'll find out." Her smile was a ghastly sight with her lips painted red with her own blood. "The first Deathbringer. You have it. We'll get it back."

"Deathbringer," whispered Erin remembering the name.

The woman turned to look at her. "Oh! So you know

them. Very good. One. Two. Three. Each body to his own fate."

The woman began to choke on her blood, struggling to draw air into her damaged lungs. Erin glanced at Dalton, who shook his head. She didn't need him to tell her that the woman was dying.

"Why are you doing this?" asked Erin, her voice angry now.

"A corrupt system must fall."

"You murdered hikers because of a corrupt system? That's insane."

"Acceptable—" she gasped and gurgled "—losses."

"We need to get off the trail," said Dalton.

He stood and Erin followed, hesitating.

"We just leave her?"

He nodded and offered his hand. "Come on. Off the trail."

The dog danced along beside them, and no amount of shooing would send her away.

"We'll have to take her," said Erin.

Dalton shook his head, adjusting the grip on the gun still in his hand.

"You will not shoot a dog!" she said, stepping between him and the black Lab.

Dalton smiled. "I was just going to tie her up on the trail."

"I'll do it." Which she did, but she also filled the water dish she carried in her pack and fed her dry food. When she left Jet, tied with a bit of her sash cord in plain view of anyone who came along here, she imagined the reaction of the poor next hiker who would stumble on this turn in the trail.

Then she petted the dog's soft, warm head and said goodbye.

When she returned, it was to find Dalton watching her.

"We should get a dog," he said.

Erin sighed and lifted her pack. "I don't like leaving her."

"We'll send somebody for her when we're safe. She'll be okay until then."

They bushwhacked uphill, staying well away from the trail and stopping when they heard people moving in their direction.

Dalton squatted beside her as they waited for the group to pass.

When he spoke, his voice was a whisper. "Once they report that death, Siming's Army will know our position. We need to move faster."

"Well, I lost my kayak."

They hurried up the rest of the slope, pausing only when they heard something tearing uphill in their direction.

Dalton motioned her to take cover and ducked behind a tree trunk. Then he drew his handgun, aiming it toward the disturbance. Something was running full out right at them.

She watched Dalton sight down the barrel of his gun, gaze focused and expression intent. She knew he would protect her and she knew he loved her. It should be enough. But who was protecting him?

The barrel of his pistol dropped and he relaxed his arms, his aim shifting to the ground. She saw him slide the safety home as he straightened.

"I don't believe this." Dalton stepped from cover.

Erin glanced around the tree trunk to see a streak of black fur barreling toward them.

"Jet!" she said.

The Lab leaped to her thighs, tail wagging merrily. Then the canine greeted Dalton by racing the few steps that separated them before throwing herself to the ground to twist back and forth in the dead leaves, paws waving and tail thumping.

Dalton holstered his pistol in the waistband of his pants and stooped to pet the dog's ribs. This caused Jet to spring to her feet to explore the area.

"She doesn't seem very broken up by the death of her owners," said Erin.

"Because she's decided we're her owners."

Erin grabbed Jet when she made her next pass. She sat before Erin, gazing up adoringly, her pink tongue lolling.

"She chewed through the sash cord." Erin held up the frayed evidence of her deduction. "She'll have to come with us."

"Not a great idea."

"I'm not leaving her again."

"She could give away our position."

She placed a fist on one hip. "If you can carry a deadly virus, I'm allowed a dog."

He twisted his mouth in frustration and then blew out of his nostrils.

"Fine. But let's go."

They scrambled over roots and waded through ferns that brushed her knees. She walked parallel to the trail that led to the gravel road, far enough away so as not to be seen. This made for slow going, and there were two places where they had to scramble up large sections of gray rock.

Mercifully, they did not see the couple that their attacker had mentioned before they finally reached the road. Dalton grasped her arm before she left the cover of the woods. Erin hunched down as he glanced right and left.

"Now we need to find the parking area for that trail. Good chance they might be there."

"We could call 911 with that woman's phone. If they're tracking her GPS signal, it'll just confirm she's where she's supposed to be—looking for us."

"Maybe. You know where the parking area is?"

"Usually right beside the trailhead. Sometimes across the road. That would be that way." She pointed to her right.

"Stay in the woods."

They picked their way over downed trees and through last year's fallen leaves, making a racket that Erin feared could be heard for miles. Under the cover of the pines, the ground was soft and their tread quiet. Jet found a stick which she tried unsuccessfully to get Dalton to throw.

Erin was willing and Jet dashed back and forth joyfully engaged in the game of fetch. Dalton came to a halt and Erin pulled up beside him. Through the maze of pine trunks she caught the glint of sunlight on metal. Automobiles. They had reached the lot.

She took hold of the dog's collar as Dalton scouted ahead. In a few minutes he returned, holding the key fob.

"This doesn't unlock either of the cars in that lot."

"What does that mean?"

"It means she was dropped at the trailhead, which means they are close."

Erin absently stroked the dog as she stared out at the lot. "What do you recommend?"

"Use her phone. Call the state police and wait for them behind cover."

They crossed into the open and then jogged across the mowed grass and over the gravel road to the opposite side. From a place in deep cover that still afforded a glimpse of the road, Dalton made his 911 call and was connected to NY State Police dispatch.

"I'm calling because my wife is on a kayaking expedition." Dalton gave the name of her camp and said that he had not heard from her. He flipped the phone to speaker so Erin could also hear the dispatcher.

"Yes, we have them listed as overdue. DEC rangers are searching."

"Should I be worried?"

"I can report that they located their camp from last night. No signs of trouble."

Erin scowled and opened her mouth to speak. Dalton held her gaze and shook his head.

"Whereabouts was that?"

There was a pause, and then the dispatcher correctly mentioned the bluff over the Hudson where her group had been murdered.

"I'll check back. Thank you." Dalton disconnected.

"What about the bodies? The helicopter piece that killed Carol? The tents, kayaks? What about the blood, Dalton?"

He gripped the phone in his hand. "The storm would have washed away the blood. Most of the helicopter sank in the Hudson, and as for the rest, someone had to remove all the evidence of the massacre."

"Just how darn big is Siming's Army?" she asked.

Chapter Ten

"Call your camp director," said Dalton.

He passed her the phone and she placed the call. Erin gripped the phone in both hands as she held it out and on Speaker. The call was answered on the first ring. Her director, Oscar Boyle, a sweet, fortyish guy with tons of canoeing experience and a sunny disposition, picked up the call. Today, however, his voice relayed an unfamiliar note of anxiety.

"Erin! Oh, thank goodness. We've been going crazy. Your husband is here. He wants to speak to you."

"My husband?" She glanced at Dalton.

"Yes. He showed up yesterday to surprise you but couldn't locate your camp, so he… Do you want to speak to him? Wait, tell me where you guys are. Did you move camp because of the storm?"

Dalton gave her the cut sign and she ended the call. Then she handed back the phone.

"Do you think they'll have our coordinates?"

"Not yet. Your director will have to ask 911 to check this call and the coordinates. But they'll get around to it and they'll have this phone number, the registered owner, that is *if* it's not a burner, and after that, our position. We have to move." Dalton retrieved the phone and flicked it off.

"Which way?"

"They'll expect us to use the road and head toward Minerva. So either we go back into the woods in a direction they can't predict, or we walk on the road toward the fish and game club."

"Why there?"

"Food, shelter and possibly weapons."

"We need to get rid of that package. Just leave it on top of a car with the thumb drive. They find it and they'll stop chasing us."

He gave her a long look and she set her jaw.

"Is that really what you want me to do?"

She paced back and forth, and Jet crouched and leaped, trying to get Erin to throw the stick that the dog had carried across the road with her.

Erin stooped and took possession of the stick. Then she threw it with all her might. Jet tore off after it, of course. Erin turned to face Dalton.

"No, damn it, I don't."

He smiled. "That's my girl."

She rubbed her forehead. "We could hike over that mountain and come down at the town of Minerva. Or we could head west, past the gun club toward Lake Abanakee. Or we could backtrack to the Hudson."

"Distances?"

"Maybe twenty miles to the lake. Five up and over the mountain to Minerva, and that's if we use the trail system."

"Maybe Minerva," he said, but his face was grim and she could feel the tension in him.

He didn't like their chances. She knew that frown, the deep lines that cut across his brow.

"They're getting closer, aren't they?" she asked.

He met her gaze and told her the truth. "Yes."

"And you think this is worth the risk of our lives?" she asked.

He glanced away. "It's worth the risk to my life." His gaze flashed back to her. "But not the risk to yours."

She swallowed down the lump, her throat emitting a squeaking sound.

"I have another idea," she said, and explained it to him. She knew there was an old trestle bridge that could take them safely across the Hudson and, from there, it was an easy eight-mile hike to the community of North River. "I don't think they'll be expecting us in the river now."

He nodded. "Yeah, that might work."

Was it the best plan? She didn't know. Dalton used their attacker's phone once more to call one of his comrades. Henry Larson had been in Dalton's unit for five years and they had come up through the academy together. He gave Henry, now in Queens, NY, their basic location and where they expected to be this evening. Henry would be calling the FBI the minute Dalton hung up. With luck they'd have help they could trust in about seven hours.

Dalton left the phone behind.

The walk downhill, off the trail, took most of the afternoon. She hoped they could reach the trestle bridge after the last group passed by. The rafters on this section were not looking for the kind of jarring thrills of the paddlers who shot the canyon. This trip was more family friendly. She had to be certain they crossed the bridge without any raft expedition or kayakers spotting them.

They paused just off the abandoned railroad bridge, behind cover and looked upriver. Erin had never crossed such a bridge and worried about the wide gaps between the horizontal wooden slats beneath the twin rails.

"What about the dog?" she asked. "Will she be able to cross the trestle bridge?"

"We'll see."

Erin heard the group before seeing them, their shouts as they descended one of the gentler falls. Dalton and Erin held Jet, remaining in hiding as the rafters floated by one after another. Only when they were out of sight did they stand.

"How deep is it here?" he asked.

"Deep enough to jump. I've seen teenagers do it."

Dalton looked over and down to the river some forty feet below. "Seems a great way to win a Darwin Award."

He spoke of the online list of folks who had, through acts of extreme stupidity, removed themselves from the gene pool by accidentally killing themselves.

He looked to her. "You ever try it?"

"I only like heights when I'm strapped into a belay system."

Dalton studied the river. "There might be lookouts."

"It's the only way across without swimming."

"Yes, that's what worries me. Ready?"

She nodded and started across. Jet whined and danced back and forth, anxious about following.

Erin turned back and called to the dog. Jet took a tentative step. Then another. The dog leaped from one slat to the next, jumping the eighteen-inch gaps. Dalton continued along, ignoring their four-legged companion and passing Erin.

Erin followed but then turned back in time to see Jet miss landing with her back feet, scrabble with her front and vanish between the slats. The splash came a moment later.

She glanced at Dalton, who was already kneeling, hands on the rail, as he judged his target and the distance down.

Erin ditched her pack, acting faster than Dalton.

"What are you doing?" he asked, standing now, reaching. She returned his frown and then jumped into the river after Jet. She heard his shout on the way down.

"Erin!"

The current was swift, even here on the wide-open section of the Hudson. She pulled and kicked, lifting her head only to mark the location of her new best friend. Jet paddled toward her, of course, instead of using the current, but the river swept her away. Erin swam harder, grabbing the dog's collar before turning toward the opposite bank.

Above, Dalton jogged along, carrying her pack, following her with an intent frown on his face.

She struggled against the current, using a scissor kick and one arm. Jet thrashed at the water, managing to keep her head up as they inched toward the southern bank. They made land at the same time as Dalton disappeared into the tree line above.

Racing, he reached her in record time.

"That was stupid," said Dalton.

She wiggled her brows.

Jet shook off the water, tail wagging as the dog immediately began sniffing the ground about them. Then she waded back into the river.

"Jet, come!" she shouted.

"You are not diving in after her again," said Dalton.

"No need."

Jet dashed back to her, tongue lolling and eyes half-closed.

"Someone will sleep well tonight," she said. When she turned her attention from Jet to Dalton, it was to see him scowling at her with both hands on his hips.

"You could have died," he said.

"Yes? How does that make you feel?" she asked.

"Mad as hell."

"Well, now you know how I feel every darn day."

His scowl deepened, sending wide furrows across his forehead.

"So it's all right to risk your neck for a dog but not for the safety of a nation?"

She lifted her chin, ready for the fight he obviously wanted. "I jumped to keep *you* from jumping."

"I wasn't…" He stopped just short of lying.

Erin shouldered her pack and turned to go and Jet followed. Dalton had caught up before they reached the highway.

"Do you think anyone saw us cross?" she asked.

"I don't know, but if there was anyone spotting, they couldn't have missed you and that darn dog."

Chapter Eleven

Erin changed into dry clothing and they ate the last of her food stores. Then they endured another four-mile hike over relatively flat terrain on the railroad tracks that flanked the river. Their trip was stalled twice by hikers and once by horseback riders. Thankfully, most travel in this area was by river rather than by land. Still, Erin was wistful as she watched the young women riding slowly past on a buckskin and a small chestnut mare. Her tired legs made it especially hard not to bum a lift.

She got her bearings when they reached the garnet processing plant, where abrasives were produced from the crushed red garnets mined nearby. She'd been on the mine tour more than once and knew the working mine was south of North Creek.

When they reached Route 28, Erin's ankles and knees pulsed with her heart, and her pack seemed exponentially heavier. Dalton drew to a halt and Jet groaned, then lay down, panting.

"You have anything we can pawn or trade for a hotel room?" Dalton asked, studying the mine plant from behind cover. "And maybe dinner?"

"No, but I do have three hundred dollars in my wallet. You lose your wallet?"

"I only have fifty bucks left," he admitted.

"Always prepared, except for things you have to pay for," she joked, and they shared a smile.

"How well do you know the area?"

"Drove through it, passed all the rafting outfits along the highway. Post office, roadhouse and bed-and-breakfast."

"Fancy. What about a motel?"

"I'm sure we could ask."

"I could. I'm traveling alone with my dog. You need to stay out of sight," he said.

"I can do that. I'll wait right here." The prospect of stopping and resting appealed.

"Let's get closer to town. That way?" he asked.

"Yes. A little farther past the garnet plant. We should see the highway and the river takes a turn. This is a really small community."

"Good and bad. Let's go."

They continued on the tracks until it reached the road. Erin suggested a state park that included cabin rentals, and they walked the remaining mile and a half on tired legs, reaching the ranger station after closing.

"Better off," Dalton said. "No paper trail. Should be easy to see if any of the cabins are empty."

They walked the looped trail past occupied cabins, waving at other campers.

"I could set up my tent," said Erin.

"I need a shower," he said.

She agreed that he did. So did she, for that matter.

"Bathhouse?" he suggested.

"Let's finish the loop."

As it happened, the ranger was making rounds to invite guests to a talk on the reintroduction of wolves to the Adirondacks that started at nine. Erin asked the tanned ranger in his truck if any of the cabins were still unoccupied.

"You two hiking?"

"Yeah. Going into the Hudson Gorge Wilderness and up Vanderwhacker Mountain."

"We should be able to set you up."

"Cash okay?" asked Erin.

"That'll work."

They accepted a ride back down to the station. When the ranger asked for ID, Erin held her smile but her gaze flashed to Dalton.

"I have your wallet still, I think," he said, and offered the Vermont license of the woman who had killed the pair of campers, stolen their dog and then tried to kill them.

Erin remembered the hair the woman had commandeered and shuddered. The ranger listed them in his book but never ventured near a computer. They were Mrs. Kelly Ryder and her husband, Bob.

The ranger handed over a key on a lanyard and Erin gave him seventy bucks. Transaction complete, Erin headed back out. Jet rose and stretched at their appearance. The ranger called from behind the counter.

"You'll need to put your dog on a leash."

Dalton waved his understanding as they left.

Cabin number eleven was a log structure with two bedrooms. Once inside, Erin removed her pack and groaned as she lowered her burden to the floor. Dalton flicked on the overhead light and glanced around at the living area, which included a full kitchen with a four-burner stove, refrigerator and small dinette. The living room had a saggy sleeper couch and a wooden rocker. A pair of crossed canoe paddles decorated the wall above the hearth made of river rock.

DALTON HEADED DOWN the hall past the living area and found a bathroom with toilet, sink and small shower. The first bedroom was equipped with bunks and the second with a full-size bed, dresser and side tables holding lamps with decoy bases that resembled wood ducks. He really hoped he wouldn't be sleeping alone in one of the bunks.

When he returned, Erin was staring at the stove with folded arms and a contemplative expression.

"Kinda makes me wish I had some food," she said as she looked at the stove.

"We have to eat," Dalton said. A glance out the window showed that the night was creeping in.

"How are you going to pull that off?" She sank to the hard, wooden chair at the dinette and stared wearily at the knotty pine cupboards. Jet sat at her side and the dog rested her head in her new mistress's lap.

Erin stroked her dark head and said, "'Old Mother Hubbard went to the cupboard…'"

Dalton glanced out at the night. "I'll be right back."

He wasn't, but it didn't take him long. The ranger giving the talk was one of two, as he discovered upon knocking at the door to the rangers' quarters.

"I hate to bother you but those folks in cabin sixteen are shooting off bottle rockets. Guess the Fourth is coming early?"

The ranger cursed under her breath and headed out. Dalton waved her away and started off the porch, then retraced his steps after she drove off.

The door was unlocked and there were steaks in the

freezer. He collected a paper bag full of groceries, left two twenty-dollar bills on the top of the drip coffee maker and headed out, returning to find Erin asleep on the sofa with her hiking boots unlaced but still on.

He didn't wake her. He let the smell of the steaks do that.

A few minutes later she opened one eye and then another. Her feet hit the floor and she rose stiffly to set the table.

"What have you got?"

He rattled off the menu. Fries and steaks, navel oranges and a box of chocolate-chip cookies. She started on those, offering Jet a one-to-three ratio on distribution, as Dalton tended the steaks.

"Where did you…never mind," she said. "I don't want to know."

He turned back to the steaks.

"Are these marshmallows?" She hefted the bag. "I love these!"

She had one toasting on a fork over the unoccupied burner of the gas stove as he used the salt and pepper before turning the meat. The only item of food in the cupboard other than salt and pepper was a ziplock baggie full of little packages of ketchup and mustard.

Dalton fed Jet from a box of breakfast cereal mixed with pan drippings and the gristle from the steaks. Then he put the dog outside without a leash.

They ate at the kitchen dinette.

Erin smiled across the table at him, and he realized he could not remember the last time he had cooked for her or even the last time they had shared supper together. His job kept him gone for long hours and took him away unexpectedly and often—far too often, he realized.

"This is nice," she said.

"I've missed this," he admitted.

Her smile turned sad. "Me, too."

"Erin, I never meant for my work to take over. I don't even know when that happened." He was never home before nine anymore. By the time he got on the train and made it back to the suburbs, Erin was often asleep on the couch. Her days began early at the sports club where she taught rock climbing with frequent weekend jaunts up to New Paltz, NY, to head rock climbing outings.

"Your partner will be here tomorrow?" she asked, finishing her last fry.

"He should be here already with the cavalry."

"Great. How far do we have to go to get to him?"

"North Creek."

"A couple of miles."

He nodded and then reached across the table to take her hand, but at the last second, he panicked and instead retrieved her plate. He stood to clear the table and she followed.

"Boy, am I stiff," she muttered, rolling her shoulders. The action forced her very lovely bosom out and he took that moment to stare. She caught him of course and laughed. "I'm surprised you have enough energy for that."

"Looking doesn't cost energy."

He recalled the last time he'd loved her, the evening before the shooting. He had hoped that she'd attend the ceremony, but he'd been too preoccupied with loving her before bed to remind her and she'd been up and out before he rose. He never did find out if she had planned to be at the presentation. He and his partner were both being honored at the annual medal day ceremony, so he had been in full dress uniform. That uniform now had a small hole in the front above his right hip. That was nothing compared to the holes in his body.

Erin called his uniform a target. That day, she'd been right. Targeted for no reason other than the uniforms they wore, and the shooter in custody after clearing his psych exam. Not crazy, just murderous over old grudges stretching back through his childhood.

"Why don't you go shower?" he said. "I'll clean up."

She regarded him with mock surprise. "That's the sexiest thing you've said to me all day."

"The shower?" He couldn't help feeling hopeful.

"The cleanup." She dropped a quick kiss on his mouth and then spun away before he could reel her in. But she'd left him with something else.

Hope.

Hope for the night. Hope for their marriage.

He found himself humming as he went about clearing the table. The scratch at the door told him the canine had returned. He held the door open, but Jet danced off the porch and then paused on the spongy loam of pine needles, beyond the steps. She turned back, waiting.

The young female made a complete circle of the cabin, encouraging Dalton to do the same. He stepped out of the doorway, his instincts making him uncomfortable being backlit in the gap. He headed after Jet and discovered that the rear of the cabin stood on stout logs and, behind them, the hillside sloped steeply toward the ranger station. Usually he would have done a quick recon at a new place, but his fatigue and hunger had taken precedence.

The stars seemed bigger here and he took a moment to gaze up and enjoy their brilliance. It had been a long stretch between now and the last time he'd noticed them, but they'd been there waiting. On the side of the cabin, making his return route, he paused at the light streaming from the cozy structure and at the sound of the shower running. Water was gliding over his wife's beautiful naked body. And he was out here with the dog.

"Idiot," he muttered, and continued back to the porch.

He still didn't understand how getting ambushed while in uniform, and nearly dying, had split them up. He'd explained it was just one of those things, and that just made her madder.

He hadn't really thought of her having to attend Chris's funeral alone. Of having to speak to the widow, see his partner's children's faces as they lowered their father's coffin into the ground.

It scared her. He got that.

"Come on, Jet," he said, opening the door.

The dog streaked past him, so fast she was a moving shadow. Back inside, Jet was already on the couch.

"Better you than me, girl," he said, and left her there, hoping he could hold the towel for Erin.

She met him at the door, her hair a wet tangle and her skin flushed pink. Steam billowed out behind her and she wore a clean white tank top and pink underwear. Both skimpy garments clung to her damp skin in a way that made his mouth go dry.

"It's all yours," she said, and slipped past him.

He caught her arm and she turned; her smile flickered and dropped away.

"Did you pick a room?" he asked.

"Yes?"

"Where do you want me?"

She lifted her chin, holding the power he'd given her.

"In my bed," she said.

He exhaled in relief. But she lifted a finger.

"We are still not okay, Dalton. You know that."

All he knew was that Erin would have him in her bed, and that seemed enough for now.

She regarded him with a serious expression that he could not read. He nodded and she left him the bathroom. He stripped and was in the narrow plastic compartment a moment later, leaving his clothing strewn across the floor. The water felt so good running over his sore muscles that he groaned. Then he washed away the sweat and grime. It seemed an eternity ago that he had showered in their small ranch-style home on a hill in Yonkers. Erin had left him a small liquid soap that was biodegradable for use on her hike. It barely foamed but did the job, leaving his skin with a tingle and the unfortunate scent of peppermint.

He scrubbed his scalp and the beard that had turned from a light stubble to the beginnings of something serious, and banged his elbows on the sides of the shower casing. The capsule had not been designed for a man who was over six feet and 245 pounds.

When he exited the shower, he found she'd left him only the tiny towel she used when hiking. It was the size of a gym towel, but he used it to dry off. Then he used her deodorant, toothbrush and toothpaste—one of the advantages of marriage, he thought, working out the tangles in his hair with a pink plastic comb the size of his index finger.

Dalton touched the three punctures in his abdomen left by the arthroscopy. Blood loss had been the biggest threat. The scars from the bullet were pink and puckered, but his stomach was flat and showed no bruising from the recent ordeal.

He glanced at his cargo pants, underwear and the shirt she had commandeered. All of it was filthy and he was not wearing any of it to bed. He did rinse out his T-shirt and boxers, hanging them on the empty towel rack to dry.

Erin knew he preferred to sleep in the nude. He retrieved only the firearms and the black zippered case containing the thumb drive and vial case. He used the minuscule towel to hide them in one broad hand as he glanced at himself in the mirror over the sink.

"Wish me luck," he said to himself.

He'd never needed it before with Erin. She'd always welcomed him, but that was before the shooting and all the fury it had kindled in her.

Dalton stepped into the room to find the light already switched off and Erin sitting up against the pillows. The room was cast in shadows. He navigated to her by the faint bluish light from the night sky. He sat on the opposite side of the bed from where she lay stretched out and seemingly naked beneath white sheets. He set the weapons and case on the bedside table. A glance told him that the weapon he'd given her sat on the table beside her.

"There was a packet of sheets and a woolen blanket on the bed," she said, explaining the bedding.

"Nice," he said, slipping in beside her.

She nestled against him and inhaled. "You smell like my soap," she said.

He wrapped an arm around her and drew her close, resting his cheek on the top of her head. Then he closed his eyes and thanked God that she was safe and here with him.

"We're lucky to be alive, you know?" she said.

"Same thought occurred to me. People were shooting at you and you weren't even wearing a uniform."

This comment was met with silence and he wondered what was wrong with him. Reminding her of why she was furious with him was not a great way to slip back into her good graces.

"Will you call your friend and tell him our location?"

"Yes. I'll head down to the ranger station and give a call."

"They have a phone?"

"An actual pay phone. Hard to believe."

"Can you even reverse the charges to a mobile phone?" she asked.

"I guess I'll find out."

"Wait here or come with you?" she asked.

"I'll only be a few minutes."

He kissed her forehead and was surprised when she looped her arms about his neck and kissed him the way she used to. Now he didn't want to leave, and he was certainly coming back as fast as humanly possible.

"I'll be quick."

She released him and he waited until he was outside before jogging to the station to make his call. Henry sounded relieved to hear his voice. He promised to be there in thirty minutes. Dalton wondered if that would be enough.

When he got back, he was greeted by Jet. Alarm bells sounded as he drew his weapon and searched, room by room for Erin. He found her in the bedroom, curled on the blanket. She opened her eyes at his appearance.

"Everything all right?"

"Yes. They'll be here within the hour."

He sank down beside her. His shoulders definitely drooped with the rest of him as the fatigue he had pushed aside finally caught up with him. And then he felt her hand on his thigh, sliding north with a sure path in mind. His shoulders lifted with the rest of him, and he rolled to his side.

"Erin, I've missed this."

"Doctor said you needed time to heal."

"I think we've established that I am healthy enough for sex."

"I'll be the judge of that," she said, and kissed him.

Her mouth demanded as her tongue sought access. Erin's kisses were so greedy and wild that they scared him a little. Her fervor pointed him toward fear.

Did she believe they would not get out of this?

The desperation of her fingers gripping his shoulders and her nails scoring his back told him that something had changed.

Early in their relationship, he and Erin had giggled and wrestled and enjoyed the fun and play of intimacy.

Now, after three years of marriage, they had fallen into a general pattern. He knew what she liked and gave it to her. He liked everything and was always happy when Erin wanted to try something new. But this wasn't new. It bordered on manic.

Her hands flew over his shoulders and then down the long muscles that flanked his spine. Nails raked his skin as her kisses changed from passion to something that lifted the hairs on his neck.

He drew back, extending his arms on either side of her head and stared down at his wife.

"Erin? You all right?"

"I don't know. I just want... I want..." Erin then did something she never did. She burst into tears. All the horror and the fear and the fight drained out of her, and she wept.

Dalton rolled to his side and gathered her up, stroking her back as she sobbed against his broad bare chest. She sprawled over him, limp and still except for her labored breathing and the cries that racked her body.

Jet arrived and poked Dalton's bare leg with her wet nose. That made him jump and caused Erin to lift her head.

"Dog scared me," he said, in explanation.

She turned her head and reached, patting the mattress. Jet did not hesitate. She leaped up beside her new mistress and licked her wet face.

Erin laughed, hugging the dog with one arm and him with the other. Then she released them both, nestling in beside him. Jet, seeming to feel the crisis averted, hopped from the bed and left the room.

"Erin, I'm going to get us out of this."

She said nothing.

"You don't think we're going to make it. Do you?"

"I've lost count of the times I thought we were both going to die. Whatever that thing is in that case you are hiding beside the bed, people are willing to kill for it."

"You still want me to leave it behind?"

He held his breath, waiting.

"No. My party died because of that thing, whatever it is. I've decided to see this through."

"For a minute I thought you were only willing to jump off trestle bridges after stray dogs."

"Jet isn't a stray. Her owners were murdered, just

like my party." She lifted up on an elbow and stared down at him. Her hair fell across her face, shielding her expression from his view. She stroked his forehead with a thumb.

"I just want you to stay with me. You know?"

"Planning on it." He cradled her jaw in his hand, and she turned to press a kiss against his palm. "I've even signed up to take the civil service exam."

"You're going to be a supervisor?" Her voice held a squeak of elation that made him smile.

"Well, I can't run down crooks all my life."

She rested her head on his chest. "Oh, Dalton. That makes me so happy."

He didn't remind her that he still could be shot for just wearing his uniform, as was the case when he'd actually taken the bullet. Ironic that, when he had faced armed gunmen on the job, he'd never fired a round and that he'd escaped Afghanistan without catching lead, only to be shot at a red light.

And Erin wasn't immune from danger. She'd happened onto the worst of all situations, being the rabbit in a deadly game of chase.

He stroked his wife's drying hair as he calculated how far away Larson might be. The backup should be here anytime, and his friend was bringing the FBI, DHS and the New York State Police.

Odds were about to even up, he thought.

Dalton shut his eyes, determined to rest a few minutes before help arrived. But his eyes popped open when Erin slid up and over his body, straddling his hips as she indulged in a leisurely kiss that curled his toes.

Chapter Twelve

It had been too long, Erin thought as she deepened the kiss. Dalton's big body warmed her and she slid across him. His fingertips grazed her back and down over one hip, leaving a trail of tingling awareness.

His breathing rate increased, and she turned her head to allow them to snatch at the cool night air. Moonlight filtered through the glass window to splash across their naked bodies, revealing the tempting cording of his muscles as he caressed her.

Erin moved over him, showing him without words that she was ready for him, near desperate. He made a sound of surprise at her boldness as she took him, gliding over him to claim what was hers and remind him what he had missed.

The next sound he made was a strangled groan as his head fell back as he captured her hips in his broad, familiar hands. They rocked together in the night, savoring the perfect fit and rising desire. How had she ever thought that leaving this man would solve their problems?

She'd only increased them. Now she didn't know what to do. Except she knew she needed this, him, inside her and holding her and bringing her pleasure as he took his own.

He pulled her down against his chest, his hold becoming greedy as she reached her release, letting her cry tear from her throat and mingle with the sounds of the night.

Dalton arched, lifting her as she savored the receding echoes of pleasure and felt him reach his own. Together they fell, replete and panting, to the tangled bedsheets. Their slick bodies dried in the cool air. Their breathing slowed and Erin shivered. Dalton had reached for the blanket when something cold touched Erin's thigh.

She jumped. Dalton stilled, and a moment later the wet nose of their new addition poked him in the hip. Jet sat beside the bed, gazing up at the two of them as if asking if they needed anything.

"Jet," growled Dalton. "Git."

The dog stood, stretched and sauntered out the door.

Erin giggled. "How long was she there, do you think?"

Dalton threw an arm across his eyes. "I don't want to know."

Erin cuddled next to him and he dragged her close.

"I've missed you," he whispered. "Missed us."

"Me, too."

"I was so scared," he said.

She lifted up to see his face. Her husband was not scared of anything or anyone. It was one of the things she both loved and hated about him.

"Of what?"

"Losing you. Losing us."

She tried for a smile, but it felt sad right down to her belly, which was tightening in knots.

"I was scared, too. You were unconscious for so long and they said there might be brain damage. I thought you'd already left me."

He threaded his fingers in her hair. "I'm right here."

"This time."

They lay side by side on the sheets as the cool night air chilled their damp skin. Her husband was not only able to keep up with her on a cross-country hike and kayak rapids—he was able to keep up with her in bed.

His recovery was complete, and she smiled at the proof that all systems were up and running. Dalton had always made her see stars, but tonight he'd given her something more—hope for the future.

"So, we have a house and a dog," said Dalton. He left the rest unsaid. He'd been after her to get a dog, seeming to think that would fix his late-night absences and ease her loneliness. But it wasn't loneliness that kept her awake at night. It was fear of the day he couldn't come home.

And it had happened. And, somehow, they had both survived.

This time.

She was with him again and he was with her. They were a team, and together they would deliver this devil's package and hopefully help the authorities catch these dangerous maniacs of Siming's Army.

Only a few more minutes and they would be safe.

"We should get dressed," she muttered, her voice slow with the lethargy that gripped her.

"Yeah. We should."

They could head home with Jet, who she already considered an important part of her family. Dalton would pass the promotional exams and become a supervisor.

Then she could stop looking at her phone as if it were the enemy and treating every knock on her door as if she were under attack.

Erin slipped from bed to use the bathroom and on her return, she cracked open the window in the bedroom. She liked to hear the wind blow through the big pines all about them and hear the peepers chorus. She lay back beside Dalton and closed her eyes, feeling happy and satisfied.

He'd finally heard her and was taking steps to do as she asked. She didn't want him to quit the force. She just wanted him around to collect his pension. And in the meantime, maybe they could talk about kids again. She knew Dalton wanted them. She just never felt safe enough to try.

Widows and orphans were seen to by the NYPD, and that was only right. But she did not savor the prospect of joining their ranks. If Dalton wanted kids, he could darn well be there to raise them.

She had meant to get up and dressed, but instead she closed her eyes and drifted into a sleep like a feather falling to earth. She was in that deep sleep, the one that paralyzed you so that rousing felt like swimming up to the surface from deep water.

Someone was shaking her. She opened her eyes and looked around the dark room, struggling to get her bearings. From the hallway came the feral growl of a large animal.

"Dalton?" she whispered.

He pressed a pistol into her hand. "Get dressed."

"What's happening?" she said.

"Not sure. Jet hears something."

"Larson?"

"I don't think so."

She was about to ask who Jet was and where they were when the entire thing dropped into place. Her hairs lifted and the lethargy of sleep flew off. Her heart pummeled her ribs, and she sat up so fast her head spun.

The breeze from the window had turned cold and she was suddenly regretting opening it. The cabin was perched on a slope, so crawling in the window would be difficult—but not impossible.

"Have they found us?" she asked.

"Not sure. Might be a raccoon. Porcupine."

Or a man, she realized.

Dalton disappeared and returned carrying her pack and wearing his cargo pants and shirt. He sat on the bed for the few seconds it took to tug on his boots.

She set aside the gun to scramble into jeans, shirt, jacket and socks, and then realized her boots were in the living room.

"My boots are out there." She pointed.

"Come on," he said, offering his hand.

"Take the pack?"

"For now."

They reached the hallway and Erin called Jet's name just above a whisper. The dog came immediately and Erin grabbed her collar. Her hand at Jet's neck relayed that every hair on the dog's neck was standing straight up.

"Her hackles," she whispered.

"Yeah. Mine, too," he said.

Something large flew through the front window. Dalton lifted his pistol and aimed as the log rolled across the living room floor.

"They're trying to force us to go out the back," he said. "Safer than coming in here."

"They? Just how many are there?" Erin snatched up her boots. Quickly, she tugged them on.

He crept toward the door and the automatic gunfire exploded in the night.

"Down!" roared Dalton, and she fell to her stomach, sprawling as bullets tore through the frame and door.

Jet tugged against her, trying to break free.

"Two shooters, at least," said Dalton. "Get to the bedroom."

The gunfire came again as she scrambled down the hall, dragging her pack in one hand and Jet by the collar in the other. Then something else flew through the open window. She heard the object hit the wood floor and shatter, and the acrid tang of gasoline reached her.

"Molotov cocktail," he said.

She glanced back. Fire erupted in the living room. A log cabin, with wooden walls and wooden floors. How long until the entire place was ablaze?

"Forcing us back," he said, following her into the bedroom and closing the door against the wall of fire.

"What do we do?" she said.

Dalton moved to the window, keeping low, but the moment he lifted his head someone started shooting. He ducked back down.

"Are you hit?" she said, unable to keep the panic from her voice as she crawled to him, dragging Jet along.

Smoke now billowed under the closed door. Dalton dragged the wool blanket off the bed and stuffed it against the base of the door.

"They've got infrared," he said.

"How do you know that?"

"Because he just missed my head and I can't see a thing."

Smoke continued to creep around the door.

"We have to use the window."

Footsteps sounded in the hall. The second shooter was out there. Bullet holes riddled the bedroom door and Dalton rolled clear of the opening, crouching beside her near the bed.

"When he opens the door, let go of the dog."

The shooter kicked the door open and Erin released her hold on Jet's collar. The dog moved like a streak of black lightning. The shooter fired as Jet jumped, knocking the intruder back. Erin held her breath as both intruder and canine vanished in the smoke.

Dalton charged after the dog with his pistol raised. She lost them in the smoke but clearly heard two shots. A moment later, Dalton emerged from the billowing smoke with Jet at his heels and kicked the door shut. In his hands was a semiautomatic rifle.

The shooter outside opened fire as Jet reached Erin. She swept a hand over the dog's coat, searching for the sticky wetness that would tell her that Jet had been shot. But her hands came away dry.

Dalton reached her. "I'm going to knock out that window. Then I want you to let the dog go again."

"He'll kill her."

Dalton said nothing for a moment. "She's fast. She's black and the shooter won't be expecting it. Jet's our only chance."

Erin did not want to die in this cabin.

"All right."

Dalton threw her pack outside. Gunfire erupted and then ceased.

"Now!"

She released Jet, who jumped out the window and vanished. Dalton went next. She heard him land. Then came the sound of someone screaming and shots firing.

Afterward there was only the crackling sound of burning wood.

"Erin! Clear! Come out the window."

She choked on tears and on smoke as she groped for the opening, grabbed hold of the sill and dropped to the ground some seven feet below. The slope sent her into an unanticipated roll that ended with her flat on her back against the roots of a tree.

Jet reached her first. Her dog licked her face until she sat up and then the dog charged away, likely back to Dalton.

"Where are you?" she called.

Dalton called back. She stood then and fell over her backpack. She groaned as every muscle in her back seemed to seize, but she righted herself and headed toward her husband's voice, carrying the pack over one shoulder.

Jet raced to her and then away. Behind her, the light from the blazing cabin illuminated the hillside. Sparks flew up into the sky, and she prayed that the ground was still wet enough to keep this fire from spreading to the forest surrounding them.

"Did you get him?" she asked.

"Yes."

Dalton returned up the hill for her and took hold of the pack, then dashed down the slope away from the fire.

"Shouldn't we wait for fire and police?"

"I'm not certain there aren't more of them." He tugged her along.

The ground was dark, and she stumbled over roots and through shrubs.

"If there are more, they can just pick us off from the woods."

"But if we get to the police."

Dalton didn't slow. "I don't know them. I know my people. We need to get to them."

They reached the other side of the roundabout on the cabin road and he paused, waiting. She heard the engine sound a moment later. Jet sat beside her and she grabbed her collar.

"She saved our lives," she said, and stroked Jet's soft head with her free hand.

"Yesterday she nearly cost you yours, so we're even."

She recalled her jump from the bridge.

"She fell."

Dalton said nothing as he watched the ranger's truck sweep past.

"How are you planning to get out of here?"

Chapter Thirteen

Dalton doubled back and waited as other cabin dwellers gathered at a distance from the fire. He watched them, looking for some sign that one or more were armed. The first to arrive were the rangers, who quickly disconnected the propane tank outside the kitchen window and dragged it away.

They told everyone to keep back and asked if the two in the cabin had made it out. He waited with Erin outside the circle of light cast by the flames until the fire department and state police arrived. Only then did Dalton leave cover. He made straight for the police. Erin followed, despite his order for her to wait. She left her pack and the automatic weapon behind.

Dalton scanned the crowd. Everyone seemed intent on watching the cabin blaze. He worried about the surrounding dark. A sniper could pick them off with ease.

"What happened?" asked a park ranger. "Stove blow?"

Dalton pulled Erin down so that the ranger's pickup truck was between them and the woods above the cabin. Before them, flames shot out of the windows and smoke curled onto the roof of their cabin.

"I heard gunfire," said a woman in pink yoga pants and an oversize T-shirt.

"Automatic gunfire," added the tall, balding guy holding a half-finished cigarette.

The group clustered together, arms folded as they watched the firefighters set up. Erin held Jet and squatted beside a rear tire.

"Can you wait here just a minute?" Dalton asked.

She hesitated, chewing a thumbnail. "Where are you going?"

He pointed to the well-built trooper, his hat sloped forward revealing the bristle on the back of his head. He was tall and broad shouldered, wearing a crisp uniform with a black utility belt complete with all appropriate gear.

"That guy is the real deal. I'd bet my life on it," he said.

"Good, because you're about to."

"I'll be right back," he said.

"You said there might be more of them out here."

"We need help, Erin."

She stood and shouted, "Mr. State Trooper. I need help."

The trooper turned and looked their way. Erin waved.

"Over here."

The officer strode toward them. Dalton had to smile. Erin had gotten help without leaving cover.

"Yes, ma'am?" said the trooper. He was young, Dalton realized, without a line on his baby face. Still, he stood with one hand casually near his weapon and eyes alert.

Dalton identified himself to the trooper as an NYC

detective and showed the officer his gold shield. Then he quickly described the situation.

"Two dead. One in the cabin and one behind the cabin."

The trooper lifted his radio. "Wait here."

"If you use that radio, anyone listening will know our position. Call it in with your phone."

The trooper hesitated, then nodded. "That your dog?" His gaze went to Jet, who sat calm and alert beside Erin.

Erin slipped an arm about Jet, suddenly protective.

"Is now," said Dalton. "Why?"

"Do you know anything about a couple murdered in the Hudson Gorge Wilderness? They were camping with a black dog."

"Plenty," said Dalton.

Erin interrupted. "Did you find a teenage boy, Brian Peters. He was in my party."

"Not that I'm aware of. But we do have a missing party of adult kayakers."

"That's my party," said Erin, pressing her palm flat to her chest. "I was the expedition leader."

"Erin Stevens?" asked the trooper.

"Yes. That's me."

"Where is the rest of your party?" asked the trooper.

Erin burst into tears.

Dalton took over. "I was with them when their camp was attacked. We escaped with the boy, Peters. He suffered a gunshot wound to his upper arm, couldn't hold a paddle. My wife towed him to the opposite bank from her camp and gave him instructions on how to walk out, then she and I proceeded downriver. The rest of her party aren't missing. They're dead."

"No evidence of that."

"There is. And there is a downed chopper in the river below the cliff."

"I'm going to need to bring you both in."

"Sounds good to me. Can you get some backup? I'm not sure that there aren't more out here."

"Who's after you?"

"Long story. You need to send help after Peters. Also, I need you to call New York City detective Henry Larson. He's here in North Creek. That was our destination."

"You can call from the station." He aimed a finger at them. "Wait here."

Dalton watched him stride away. It seemed to take hours, but he suspected it was less than forty-five minutes before they were transported to Trooper Barracks G in Queensbury. Another thirty minutes and four FBI agents arrived with two beefy guys from DHS.

It was five in the morning and the knot in Dalton's shoulders finally began to ease. They had made it. They were safe, though he still had the package.

Erin and he were separated, something that rankled and made him anxious. He felt the need to keep looking out for her, regardless of how many times she'd proved her own capabilities. He went over the events with the FBI agents Nolen Bersen and Peter Heller. Bersen took lead. He was tall, fit and had hair that was cut so brutally short it seemed only a shadow on his head. Heller stood back, arms folded, his freckled forehead furrowed beneath a shock of hair so red that it appeared to be illuminated from within.

By six thirty in the morning Dalton needed the bathroom and some food. He was informed that Henry Larson had been notified that they were now safe and had arrived, but Dalton could not see him. In the bathroom he discovered he was not to have a moment's privacy when a Homeland Security agent, Lawrence Foster, flashed his ID. He wanted a word. Dalton told him to get in line.

"Do you still have the package?" asked Foster.

This was the first person who seemed to know anything about the intelligence he and Erin had rescued. Dalton used the urinal and ignored him until he was finished. Then he faced the guy, who was heavyset with close-cropped hair, brown skin and dressed like an attorney in a well-fitting suit.

Dalton narrowed his eyes on the man. He knew all about interagency competition. His office hated it when the FBI came and took over an operation or, worse, took their collar. So he understood Foster's attempt to get something but still resented his choice of time and place.

"This is my first time being interviewed in a toilet," said Dalton. "You want to join us in interrogation room three, come on along."

Foster smiled and stepped away from the door he had been blocking. "I'll see you there."

Dalton headed back to the interrogation room. It was nearly eight when the room was cleared of everyone but two men in plain clothes. The elder one stepped forward. Dalton guessed him to be just shy of forty, with close-cropped salt-and-pepper hair, going gray early. He wore a slouch hat, fisherman's-style shirt, worn jeans and muddy sneakers. At first glance, he looked as if he'd been hauled off an angling excursion. Second glance made Dalton's skin crawl. He'd worked with CIA, and this guy had that look.

His gaze flicked to the younger man. This one would

fit in almost anywhere. He was slim, with a thick beard, glasses and hair that brushed his collar. His clothing was banal, jean shorts and a white tee worn under a forest green plaid cotton shirt. He could be pumping gas or passing you at the horse race track. The point was you wouldn't notice him. The guy's gaze finally flicked to Dalton, and those intent gray eyes gave a whole other picture. A chill danced along the ridge of his spine.

"What agency?" asked Dalton.

"Federal," replied the older guy. His cap said he'd fought in Operation Iraqi Freedom, but somehow Dalton thought he was still active. "You got something that you want to give to us?"

"I don't know what you mean."

The men exchanged a look.

"Let's start again. We were expecting the delivery of some sensitive material. Our courier delivered that information successfully to one of our operatives. The helicopter he was flying crashed into your wife's party, killing Carol Walton."

"You all clean up that scene?"

He nodded.

"Terrible tragedy. Surprised you made it out. Looked professional. Helicopter, according to reports."

"You CIA?"

The second man took that one. "We are here to see just how much you know. Clearly you know something because you ran, survived, and we have not recovered our package. Judging from the trail of bodies, neither have your pursuers. Though, close one tonight."

"You recovered the two that came after us?"

"Bagged and tagged," said the Iraqi vet. "How did you end up with our intelligence and do you still have it?"

Dalton ground his teeth together for a few seconds, opened his mouth. Closed it again and then wiped it.

His initial interviewer passed him something. He drew back, leaving a folded sheet of paper on the desk. Dalton looked from the page to the man across from him at the table. Then he lifted the paper and read the contents of the letter.

It was from his direct supervisor returning him to active duty and notifying him that he was on loan to a Jerome Shaffer. Dalton recognized the signature. His gaze flicked up to the Iraqi vet, who had removed his wallet from his back pocket and laid a laminated ID card before him.

This was Jerome Shaffer and he worked, according to the card, with the Central Intelligence Agency.

The two stared at each other from across the table.

"I need to hear it from my boss."

The call was made and a sleepy, familiar voice verified that Dalton was now on loan to the CIA until further notice. He handed back the phone.

"Okay," he said.

Agent Shaffer nodded. "So where is it?"

Dalton opened the side pocket of his cargo pants and laid the black leather case on the table.

Both men stiffened. Shaffer rose and they backed toward the door.

"Don't move," said Shaffer. A moment later the pair were in the hallway and the door between him and the agents closed firmly shut. The click told him he was locked in the interrogation room. He looked to the mirrored glass, knowing there were others out there, but as he could not see them, he still didn't know what was going on.

Fifteen minutes later the door swung open and in stepped a woman in a full hazmat suit.

Chapter Fourteen

They had separated Erin from Dalton shortly after their arrival at the troopers' headquarters. Dalton told her it would be all right, but as the minutes ticked by she became restless and had just given up pacing in the small interrogation room in favor of drinking from the water bottle they had furnished.

She looked up as the door clicked open, hoping to see Dalton. Instead, a trooper stepped in, preceding two men who were not in uniform.

Erin lowered the bottle to the table.

The trooper made introductions and Erin shook hands with each in turn. Agent Kane Tillman was first. He wore business casual, loafers and tan pants with a gray sports coat and a classic tie on a pale blue shirt. His face was cleanly shaven and his short hair had a distinctly military air.

Agent Tillman said he was a government investigator of some sort. She missed his title as the other man offered his hand. His associate was more unkempt with hair neither stylish nor unfashionable. His clothing was as drab as his features. She glanced away from him after the introduction and realized she'd only heard part of his name. Gabriel. Was that his first or last name?

She assumed that they were FBI agents, though Gabriel was not dressed like the other FBI agent, Jerome Shaffer, whom she had met on arrival. Her gaze slid to Gabriel. Was his hair dark blond or light brown? She wasn't sure, but Agent Tillman was speaking, so she turned her attention back to him.

They told her that they'd spoken to Dalton and that she'd be allowed to see him soon. The best news was that Brian Peters had been found alive.

"He was picked up by a ranger and driven to their station. We took charge of him from there."

"His wounds?"

"Superficial. He'll make a full recovery."

She sank back in her seat as relief washed through her, closing her eyes for a moment before the questions began again.

Her interviewer wanted to hear about the helicopter crash.

She relayed to Agent Tillman all she recalled of the attempted rescue of the pilot. They told her the pilot was a friend. Agent Tillman said that he'd known the man, and so Erin had been thorough. The other man, she could not recall his name now, only the letter *G*. The other one listened but rarely spoke.

"And he said to tell the authorities what exactly?"

"He said to tell you this was taken from Siming's Army."

"Right. And he gave you something?"

"Yes, a cooler."

"Which your husband carried."

"At first. Then he just carried the contents. We left the cooler to throw our pursuers off us."

"You believe they were after what you carried?"

She reported what they had overheard before running for their lives.

"Right," said Tillman. "We were looking for you, as well. Seems you outfoxed both pursuing parties. Even our dogs couldn't find you."

She shrugged. "Rain helped. We only left the river day before yesterday. I'm glad you didn't stop us. I'm afraid Dalton might have thought you were one of our attackers."

Tillman just smiled. "Well, this is better."

"Will we be able to go home?"

Tillman's smile grew tight. "I'm afraid not quite yet. You see, all the opponents you two faced are dead. But we believe there are several more in the region. We are very anxious to capture someone from this organization."

"I see." She didn't, and her face twisted in confusion. Why was he telling her this?

"Your husband has agreed to go back to the Hudson. He will be helping us catch the people who tracked you."

Her eyes narrowed. "Helping how?"

"He's a detective. He's worked undercover. We think it's our best option."

Erin straightened in her chair as her gaze flicked from one to the other.

"He said that?"

Tillman didn't answer directly. "He'll explain the details to you."

Something stank. Either he was lying or Dalton was ignoring every promise he'd made to her.

"What about his wife? He wasn't out there alone. Don't you think they'll notice that I'm no longer there?"

The other guy spoke and she jumped. She'd half forgotten he was even in the room and now he was right next to her, leaning against the wall beside the door.

"That's no problem."

What color were his eyes? she wondered, squinting. Green, gray, blue? It was hard to tell and he was only two feet from her.

He was smiling at her. It was an unpleasant smile that raised the hairs on her forearms.

"We have a substitute. Someone to play your part."

"The hell you say." She stood and faced them. "We just spent two days running for our lives and you want him to go back there without me? Phooey on that!"

"It's our best option."

"I want to speak to him now," she said, arms folding.

"Not possible," said Tillman.

"Now," she said, leaning across the table, looking for a fight.

Tillman backed toward the door. The other guy was already gone. She rushed the closing door.

"I want to see him!"

Tillman shut the door before she reached it, and the lock clicked behind him. Tugging on the handle only made her remember how sore her muscles were.

They allowed her to leave the vile little room to use the bathroom, escorted by a female trooper with umber skin and unusual height.

"I want to see my husband."

"I'll relay the message," she said.

"Where is my dog?"

"They are processing her for evidence."

"If you hurt one hair…"

The threat was cut short as the athletic woman lifted a thin eyebrow.

"She has bloodstains on her collar. They are taking samples."

Back in the interrogation room she found only the empty chairs and table. She walked to the one-way mirror and slapped it.

"I want my husband or my phone call now!" Who would she call? The camp director? She snorted and began her pacing again.

Tillman opened the door and motioned to someone in the hallway. In stepped a slim, athletic woman of a similar height to her.

Erin glared at the new arrival.

"Mrs. Stevens, this is DHS agent Rylee Hockings out of Glens Falls."

"My substitute," said Erin, standing to face her replacement. "She has blue eyes and she's blond."

"Contacts. Hair dye," said Tillman.

From the sidelong look Agent Hockings cast him, Erin guessed no one had told her about the dye job.

"It's a pleasure to meet you, Erin." Hockings extended her hand. Unlike Erin's hand, Hockings's was dirt-free, her nails trimmed into uniformed ovals and coated with a pale pink polish. She was clean and smelled wonderful.

"Look at her." She swept her hand at Hockings and then at herself. "Now look at me."

Erin wore damp, rumpled clothing and hair tugged into a messy ponytail. She knew she had circles under her eyes. She smelled of smoke and gasoline, and there were numerous scratches on her shins and forearms.

"I look like I spent the night in a bramble bush. But she looks like she just left a resort hotel."

Tillman's mouth went tight, but he said nothing.

Erin faced her replacement. "Have you been camping, Ms. Hockings? Do you know how to kayak in white water or set up a climbing rope?"

"I doubt that will be necessary."

"But it *was* necessary. Or I wouldn't be here."

Hockings glanced to Tillman, who offered no backup. So Hockings straightened her shoulders.

"I can fill this role, Erin."

"You are asking me to trust you to keep my husband alive. I don't think so."

"I'm an excellent shot."

"He's got that one covered all on his own."

Tillman stepped in. Erin had crept forward and was now right up in the agent's face. Funny, she didn't remember even moving closer.

"This isn't your call, Erin. She'll be in the field in less than one hour with or without your help. All you get to decide is if you help Hockings prepare or not?"

"Not," said Erin as she returned to her seat, folded her arms and scowled.

The two retreated out the door, leaving her alone again.

THE DOOR TO the interrogation room opened, and Dalton turned to see both the small blond DHS agent and the CIA operative. Both of them were flushed. He stood for introductions. The woman, Rylee Hockings, chewed her bottom lip, and Kane Tillman had both hands clamped to his hips.

Dalton narrowed his eyes on them, speculating. Who did he know that could rattle both DHS and CIA?

He smiled. "You spoke to my wife."

Tillman nodded, removing his hands from his hips to lock his fingers behind his neck and stretch. He dropped his arms back to his sides and faced Dalton.

"Can you point out to us your route and specifically your position yesterday when you encountered the female shooter?"

Dalton's smile broadened. "Nope."

"The general location?" asked Rylee, hope flickering weakly in her gaze.

"Out of sight of the Hudson River on a hill." Dalton chuckled at their dismay. "I told you. You need her."

Tillman said nothing.

"She agree to help?" Dalton asked.

He shook his head. "She wants to see you."

"I told you it wouldn't work."

"You need to convince her to cooperate with us," said Hockings.

"You know that she asked for a separation. Right?" he asked Tillman.

"Yes."

"Do you know why?"

Tillman shook his head.

"Because I go undercover and stay away for days. She wants me to ride a desk and collect my pension. What she doesn't want is for me to play secret agent with a younger model who—no offense, Miss Hockings—looks like she does most of her traveling first-class."

"Business class," corrected Hockings.

"But not in the woods carrying a fifty-pound pack on your back."

"I can fill this role." She was speaking to Tillman now.

Dalton had told them that lying to his wife about his cooperation was a bad idea and that he wouldn't go without her consent, but they'd thought to trick it out of her.

He smiled. Erin was many things—stubborn, driven, protective—but not stupid.

"My wife rescued that helicopter pilot. Not me. She swam through white water, rigged him so we could haul him out and then got out herself, even though the wreck rolled on her tether rope. She got us downriver, through rapids. It was her idea to leave the kayaks on the opposite side of the river, to throw them off our trail, in the pouring rain."

"All very admirable."

"I told you that she won't want me to go back."

"You don't need her permission."

"No. But I'm not going without it."

"I don't understand. You're a professional."

"I'm a man about to lose his wife. I came up here to fix my marriage. Now you want me to go right back to telling her to wait at home and that everything will be fine when the last time I told her that I caught a bullet."

Tillman's hands slid back to his hips.

"We all know that these people are crazy, armed and dangerous," said Dalton. "She knows, too, firsthand."

"You willing to risk her life?"

"Heck no. But we have both been convinced of the importance of this. I think she should have a choice. She's right. I've asked her to sit on the sidelines too

long. I wouldn't like it. Neither does she. I understand
now why she didn't like it. Why she's been so angry.
My thick head has been an asset in the past. But I don't
want it to end my marriage."

"So what are you suggesting?" asked Tillman.

"Get her to help or let us go home."

Tillman looked at Hockings. "Sorry for dragging you
up here. Seems we don't need you after all."

"This is bull," said Rylee. "I can do this job."

"We'll never know." He turned to Dalton. "That is
assuming you can convince your wife to help us."

"She'll do what she thinks is best."

"For you or for her country?"

"Let's go find out. Shall we?"

Chapter Fifteen

The door had barely closed behind DHS agent Lawrence Foster when it opened again, this time to admit Hockings, Shaffer, Tillman and her husband. Erin kept her face expressionless as she met Dalton's gaze but was relieved to see him. Something about DHS agent Foster had put her on edge. His questions were off, somehow, different from the others who had questioned her. Dalton winked at her and she could not keep the half smile from lifting her mouth.

"You going back there without me?" she asked.

Dalton turned to the three agents. "Give us a minute."

The two exchanged impatient looks.

"We don't have a lot of time," said Tillman.

"Understood," said Dalton. He wasn't looking at Tillman, and only Erin watched the others retreat and close the door behind them.

"I hear you've been less than cooperative with our federal friends," Dalton said, and drew up a chair beside her.

"I was cooperative with the DHS agent." She'd answered all his questions about the pilot's death, their escape and details about the woman who attacked them.

He asked what was in the package that Dalton carried, and she told him it was vials and a thumb drive. The agent then asked about Dalton's colleague, Henry Larson, or "the NYPD SWAT officer," as Foster had called him. Maybe that was the thing that bothered her. Why didn't he know Larson's name?

"You weren't cooperative with the CIA," said Dalton.

"Because Agent Foster wasn't trying to replace me."

Dalton made a growling sound in his throat by way of reply that showed both skepticism and some aggravation. Then he took her hand and entwined her fingers with his.

"What should we do, Erin?"

"Don't ask me to let you go back there," she said.

"I won't," he said.

That got her attention. She waited, but he said nothing else. Just stroked his thumb over the sensitive skin at the back of her hand at the web between her index finger and thumb.

"They want to send you out with that woman."

"Yeah. They do."

"So you're going back without me," she said.

"That what they told you?" he asked.

She nodded.

"And what have I told you about interrogation techniques?"

Her brow knit and then arched. "You don't have to tell a suspect the truth." She let out a breath and drew another. "They lied? To me?"

She smiled, but instead of returning her smile he was frowning.

"And you believed them."

"You've run off on dangerous business for years. Why wouldn't I believe them?"

"Because I told you that I wouldn't do that again."

Now she shifted, suddenly uncomfortable with the man she had once felt was an extension of herself. They'd moved apart now, like heavenly bodies changing their orbits. She wanted to align with him once more. Why was this so hard?

"What did you tell them?" she asked.

"I told them it's a bad idea to send our Ms. Hockings as your replacement."

She cocked her head. "You did? Why?"

"Because she can't fill your hiking boots. Because our pursuers are not stupid, and because I promised you that I wouldn't go out there."

"Without me."

Now he was off balance. She knew from the way he tilted his head as he narrowed his eyes. "What are you saying, Erin?"

"You think this is worth risking your life for?"

"I do."

"You ready to risk *my* life, too?" she asked.

"No," he said.

"Yet you think the information they could get from a living member of Siming's Army would be invaluable," she said.

"That information could save the lives of many innocent people. Might stop whatever is underway. But that is only if we manage not to get killed and they manage to capture someone alive."

"You believe they can keep us safe?"

"I believe they will try. But I don't think they can

keep us safe *and* allow the bad guys to get close. So…" He lifted his hands, palms up as if weighing his options.

"They'll put us in danger."

"I'd say so."

"Thank you," she said.

"For being honest?"

"For not going without me."

"I'm done with that," he said.

"And I'm sorry for believing them."

He nodded, but the hurt still shone in his troubled gaze.

"Are we still okay?" he asked.

She forced out a breath between closed lips. "Let's talk about this after. Assuming there is an after."

"Erin, I came up here to save our marriage."

She nodded. "I know it. But trouble just has a way of finding you."

"Seems this time it found you."

Erin looked at the ceiling, taking a moment to rein herself in. They did not have time to hash out their differences. He might have told her that he was done taking chances and willing to change. But all actions pointed to the contrary.

"Where are they taking us?"

"Heck if I know. You know I can't read a map as well as you."

She rose then, went to the door and knocked. When Tillman's face appeared in the window, she motioned him inside.

"We've agreed to go back." She glanced at Dalton. "Together."

Rylee Hockings pressed her lips flat, exhaled like a horse through her nostrils and then stormed away down the hall, back to wherever she had come from, Erin hoped. Erin would not be sad to see the backs of either of the DHS agents—Hockings or Foster. One made her angry and the other gave her the creeps.

Tillman pressed a phone to his ear. "Yeah. They're in."

THE STEVENSES WERE left just outside the Hudson Gorge Wilderness on North Woods Club Road between the Boreas River and the small community of Minerva. This was the same side of the river where they had left the body of their female attacker and a reasonable distance for them to have traveled after that encounter. The dog, Jet, had remained back with their handlers. So at least one of them was safe.

Erin hefted her pack, knowing it was lighter but still thinking it felt heavier than before. Dalton carried the case of vials and thumb drive in his side pocket just as he had before. Only now the new thumb drive was inoperable due to irreparable damage and the vials were full of water.

"So we just use the road, after spending all that time keeping in cover?" asked Erin.

"That's the best way to be spotted."

"It doesn't make sense. We wouldn't do that, not after being attacked."

"At some point you have to leave cover and get help," he said.

"They said they'd keep us in sight," said Erin. "But there is no one here."

"How do you know?" he asked.

"Insects still singing. Jays and red squirrels aren't giving any alarm."

"It's a drone and it's up high enough that we can't hear it. But it surely can see us."

They also wore trackers. She had several. The coolest by far were in the earring posts she now wore.

"They might just shoot us and then search our bodies," she said.

Dalton groaned. "You are such a drop of sunshine today."

"Well, we don't have vests or armor, whatever you call it."

"Car," he said.

"What?"

He pointed to the rooster tail of dust growing by the second. It turned out to be a silver pickup truck. The driver came from the opposite direction. He slowed at sighting them but merely lifted two fingers off the steering wheel in a lazy wave as he passed them.

"Well, that was anticlimactic," Erin said.

"Could be a spotter."

She hadn't thought of that.

"Did Tillman tell you anything that I didn't hear?" she asked.

"Don't think so."

"So, this guy, this Japanese agent."

"Yes. A Japanese operative working out of Hong Kong," he said.

"Right," she said. "Hong Kong, which is where he obtained this information and put it on our flash drive."

"And he had the samples."

"Which he put on a commercial jet with hundreds of people and flew all the way to Canada."

"Toronto."

"And then, instead of meeting our government's agent, he changes the meeting to Ticonderoga."

"Fort Ticonderoga," said Dalton.

"See, that's why I'm going over this. You're the detail guy."

Dalton took it from there. "But they are attacked during the drop. Our guy gets away. Their agent takes off and leaves the country. The foreign agents chase our guy all over the place, but he made the pickup anyway and they send a chopper."

"And he makes the drop. But the helicopter—our helicopter—takes gunfire and goes down on my camping site."

"And queue the chase music. Both parties have been after us ever since."

"This Siming's Army seems more like a foreign agency."

"Backed by one."

"Which one?" she asked.

"They didn't say."

"To me, either." Erin rubbed the back of her neck. "Did they say how many people they have?"

"Sleeper cells, so it's hard to know. But you just imagine that they have people downstate. NYC is a target and it's my city. Damned if I'll let that happen if I can prevent it."

"If *we* can prevent it."

He wrapped an arm around her and gave a squeeze. "We."

"Did you tell them about the pilot? I heard him mention his girl."

"Yes, Sally. I told them. They'll speak to her. Relay his last words."

"Good. But it's so sad."

She heard the engine, the same truck returning toward them. The driver slowed and lowered his window. Erin stared at the face of a man in his middle years. His hat advertised the sports club that lay at the terminus of this road, but she knew the distance and he had not had time to have reached it and returned. The niggling apprehension woke in her chest, squeezing tight as her skin crawled. She shifted from side to side, unable to keep still.

"So we just let them take us?" she asked.

"That's right."

"What if they just shoot us?"

"I won't let that happen."

"Still time to run," she said, edging off the shoulder, eyeing the distance to the trees.

The truck stopped and the dust caught up, drifting down on them in a haze.

"Hey there," called the driver, keeping his hands on the wheel. Between his arms was a small, overweight dog that seemed to be both smiling and preparing to steer the truck. Her gaze flicked up to the man to note that he was clean shaven, with salt-and-pepper hair that touched his shoulders, making a veil from under his cap. His glasses were thick and black rimmed.

"You two need a lift?"

Accent was right, Erin thought.

"Appreciate it," said Dalton. His voice was calm and even.

Erin doubted she was even capable of speech. She was good at the game of hide-and-seek, but less comfortable with the bravado required for confrontation.

She thought of Rylee Hockings and straightened her spine. Her feet stilled and her jaw tightened.

Dalton moved to the truck, opening the passenger-side door. He motioned to Erin.

She spoke to the driver, her voice a squeaky, unrecognizable thing. "Okay if I put the pack in the back?"

"Sure thing."

Dalton took the pack and placed it in the truck bed. When he turned around, he had his pistol in his hand. He slid that hand back into his pocket and motioned for her to get in.

Dalton slipped in beside her and pulled the door shut.

"This here is Lulu. She's my copilot," said the driver.

The small pug moved to sniff Erin and then used her as a boardwalk to sniff Dalton's extended hand. She wondered if the canine smelled gun oil.

"Where you two heading?" The driver flicked on his wipers to push away the settling dust from his windshield and then set them in motion.

"Minerva."

"Oh, that's right on my way."

Erin let Dalton do the small talk. He'd always been better at it. She focused on the driver's hands as she wondered what he had in the pockets of his denim jacket.

"Surprised to see you two out here."

"Why's that?" asked Dalton.

"Ain't ya heard about the trouble?"

"No."

"Where you been then, you ain't seen the helicopters and K-9 units. Yesterday this place looked like a TV movie set with all the cop cars. They all showed up like buzzards circling a dead woodchuck."

"Why? What happened?" Dalton asked.

"I don't know how to tell you this, but there's some maniac out here killing campers in their tents. Husband and wife. Right down that way on the trail to the trestle bridge."

Erin tried to look shocked but felt her face burning. This was why she had landed nothing more than chorus in the high school plays. Her acting left so much to be desired.

"That's terrible," she managed.

"That ain't all. There's a whole party of kayakers two days overdue. DEC's been out searching, but so far they're just gone."

She glanced out the window as they drove along at a break in the forest revealing a wide-open stretch of flat mossy land.

"What I heard is they ain't found hide nor hair of those tourists."

The mention of hides provided Erin with a perfect picture of Carol Walton's mangled body. The rest of the faces of her party flashed before her. Her stomach gave an unexpected and violent pitch, and she had to cover her mouth with her hand.

"That's odd," said Dalton as he gave Erin's arm a squeeze. She needed to get hold of herself before she gave them away.

Dalton frowned, his look concerned, before he shifted his attention back to the driver, the possible threat.

"It's all been in the papers." The driver frowned. "Course you wouldn't see them out here, I suppose."

Lulu settled back to the man's crowded lap, the wheel just missing the top of her tawny hide.

"That's why I picked you both up. Something terrible is going on up here. I'm Percy, by the way."

Dalton nodded and gave over their real names.

"A pleasure," said Percy. His smile dropped away as he saw something before them. "Oh, okay, they're still here."

Dalton's gaze flicked away, and Erin looked through the dusty windshield.

Before them was a roadblock consisting of two DEC vehicles. One was an SUV and the other a pickup truck parked at such an angle that approaching drivers would have to go around them. This was impossible on the northern side because of the bog. The open stretch might look like a meadow with brush and flowers and even clumps of tall cotton grass, but there were no meadows in these woods. Any cleared space was intentionally cleared by men, or it was clear because it was impossible for trees to grow there. That was the case here for, though the ground looked solid, it was in fact a thick well-adapted spongy mat of living sphagnum, a moss that knit together like raw wool. This bog was famous for both its size and proximity to the road. Hikers venturing onto the moss would quickly find the ground lower and themselves in water up to their ankles. Below was a secret lake.

She knew this because she was scheduled to take a canoeing trip on this very bog. Canoes carrying passengers were heavy enough to sink the moss below their keel so the party could glide along over the bog that sprang back in place after their passing.

Erin looked out at the tuffs where the thick brush was actually cranberry bushes whose blossoms had given way to tight green berries. There were orchids and carnivorous pitcher plants, as well.

"Erin?" She glanced to Dalton. "Percy says we need to show our ID."

"Oh." She turned to look out the back window. "Mine is still in my pack."

She wondered if these were really DEC rangers or CIA agents in disguise. She couldn't ask Dalton, of course, so she just watched as a ranger stepped out from the truck and held up a hand for them to halt.

Percy laughed. "Think the truck in the road is all the stop sign I need."

The ranger wore the correct uniform and utility belt that included a gun. Many of the rangers here were tasked with law enforcement, so that was not all that odd. But the sight made her uncomfortable.

"Where's the other driver?" asked Dalton.

The ranger approached Percy's side of the truck.

Dalton opened his door and had one leg out when the ranger reached Percy.

"Hello again," Percy said.

The ranger dipped to look into the vehicle and then drew his pistol and fired.

Chapter Sixteen

The pistol shot exploded so close to Erin's head that afterward she could hear only a high-pitched buzz. She gasped like a trout suddenly out of water. Percy slumped over the wheel. Her entire body went stiff with terror and sweat popped out all over her body.

Dalton wrenched her from the truck and down to the ground. His service weapon was out and he aimed forward toward the two vehicles, firing three quick shots.

Erin clamped her hands over her ears and squatted beside him, her back against the truck bed. The other ranger fell sideways in front of the truck.

Dalton rose, arms extended to quickly check through the open door to the place where the first man had been, ready to fire through the truck and past Percy. An instant later he dropped down beside her.

"He took the keys," he said.

Her ears still buzzed and his voice seemed distorted. Something moved in the truck and Dalton aimed.

"Wait!" she shouted.

Lulu leaped down from the cab, her coat spattered with Percy's blood. The dog disappeared beneath the truck.

"Where did he go?" she asked, referring to the shooter.

The road was now silent except for Lulu's labored, wheezing breath. Erin dropped to her belly to check the dog and saw the shooter's feet as he rounded the back of the truck.

She tugged at Dalton's sleeve and pointed. He nodded, motioning her under the vehicle. She rolled beneath the truck bed as Dalton dropped to his stomach and fired two shots.

There was a scream and the shooter collapsed to one knee as blood dripped from his foot. Dalton shot him again. Two shots. One in the knee. The other in his hand. The shooter dropped his gun and howled, scrambling back. Then he vanished from sight.

"No shot," said Dalton to himself as his target disappeared.

Erin remembered belatedly that she also had a pistol. She drew it now, holding the muzzle up and hoping she didn't shoot herself in the face. A pounding came from above her head.

Gunfire sent shafts of sunlight beaming through the new holes in the pickup's truck bed.

"We have to get to those vehicles," he said.

"My pack?"

"Leave it."

Dalton tugged her up and pushed her before him. She ran toward the SUV, dancing sideways to avoid the still body sprawled in the road. When she reached the SUV, she peered inside.

"No keys," she said.

Dalton had paused to check the corpse of the downed attacker, rummaging in his pants pockets. An engine revved.

Somehow the shooter had reached the cab with two

bullets in his legs and one in his hand. Percy's body lay crumpled in the road beside his truck, and the wounded shooter was throwing the truck into gear.

Dalton made it to her as the truck raced forward. They dove from the road as the driver plowed into the SUV where she had stood. The SUV spun off the road toward them as the truck raced by. She fell to her stomach and slid as the SUV bounced down the embankment in front of them and rolled to its side.

"Where the hell is our backup?" he growled.

The pickup sped past and then turned around.

"He's coming back," said Erin.

Dalton lifted his weapon and fired continuously, every few seconds, with well-timed intervals, as the ranger smashed into the second truck pushing it along the road before him. The driver used Percy's vehicle to sweep the last useful getaway truck into the opposite ditch, where it tipped, engine down and back wheels clear off the ground.

"They did a good job grading this road," said Erin. The high ground was dry and out of the bog, even after that heavy rain.

"We have zero cover," he said.

"But he lost his weapon," she reminded.

"That truck is two tons of weapon."

Lulu sat on Erin's right foot and glanced up at her. Something niggled in her mind. Two tons of weapon. The idea sprang up like a mushroom after a rain.

"Do you think he has another gun?" she asked, watching him back up.

"If he did, he'd be shooting at us." Dalton removed his empty clip and pushed the spare into place in the pistol's handle.

"You want to keep shooting at him?"

"Unless you have a better idea. We can use the culvert for cover."

"He'll just run us down."

He looked around. "We need to get to the SUV. Use it for cover."

"He can just hit that again."

He gave her an exasperated look. "What do you want to do?"

Their attacker spun Percy's truck back to the road and put it in Reverse.

"He's getting a running start," said Dalton, more to himself than to her.

"We could go out on the bog," she said, pointing.

He glanced at the open area broken only by tufts of grass and clumps of brush. "No cover."

"We won't need it. It's a bog."

He shook his head, not comprehending. "Here he comes."

"That moss is floating on a lake like a carpet or a giant lily pad. He can't drive on it because it's not solid ground."

Dalton turned his head, focusing on the bog now. "Can we run on it?"

"Yes, but we'll get wet. Sink a foot or so. It's spongy, like running on foam rubber and—"

He cut her off. "Okay. Okay. Go!"

She lifted Lulu off her foot and into her arms, then darted down the hill past the SUV. The tail section of the vehicle had already sunk into the moss, which accommodated the weight by moving out of the way.

Running out on the sweet-smelling, soggy sphagnum moss was like running on a field of wet loofah sponges, a rare experience that she would have enjoyed in other circumstances. The plant that most people only saw in wreaths and at the base of floral arrangements was a living sponge and just as easy to run upon.

Dalton swore as he stumbled and tipped forward. The bog absorbed his fall like a living crash pad, soaking his front in six inches of clear water. He scrambled to his feet, now standing in twelve inches of water as she raced ahead of him. She'd been on this bog before, looking for native orchids to show her expedition, and knew the best way was high steps and a little bounce. Her experience allowed her to get well out in front of him. Lulu whined in her arms and scrambled to reach her shoulder. Once there the little dog perched, looking back at the truck that was no doubt in pursuit.

"Erin?" Dalton paused, glancing behind him. They had made it some forty feet out on the bog.

Not far enough, she feared, seeing the pickup gaining speed in what she thought might be preparation for a jump from the road, some five feet above them, and onto the bog.

If he landed near them, the truck would sink down with the moss and take them with it. And the moss would tear… She had a dreadful premonition of what could happen to them. Stories told of early settlers rose in her memory. Entire mule teams vanishing with wagons and all. Swallowed up in an instant as the sphagnum moss rent like fabric, dropping men, animals and wagons through the spongy layer that instantly sprang back into place above them. Leaving them beneath the two feet of moss and as trapped as anyone who had ever been swept beneath ice by the water's current.

Her heart raced as she looked around for something

to anchor them should the moss tear, keep them on the right side of the sphagnum mat, even if they temporarily sank.

"Grab the cranberry bushes and don't let go!" she yelled to Dalton.

She dove, using her one arm to grip Lulu and the other to latch onto the wrist-sized trunk of a hearty bush covered in tight green berries.

Dalton did not ask questions or try to take control. He just followed suit, landing beside her. Their combined weight sank them in eighteen inches of cold clear water. She lifted her head to breathe and looked back.

The truck was airborne. Lulu struggled, her body underwater. Erin held on.

The impact of the truck rolled under them like a wave. The vehicle landed upright, several yards away. Instead of speeding along the open field, it stopped dead as the tires turned uselessly and the motor revved.

The driver's hand went straight up as the moss sank instantly to the windows under the two tons of weight. She heard the wail and saw the brilliant red blood streaming down his shooting arm from his wounded hand. The moss yielded without a sound, the gash tipping the truck engine down before the vehicle vanished. The scream cut short as the moss sprang back into position, grass, plants and bushes appearing just as they had been, leaving no sign of the horror that must be playing out beneath them.

Erin rolled to her back and Lulu dog-paddled away, her stumpy front legs thrashing until she reached a clump of grass that barely moved under her slight weight. There Lulu sat on a pitcher plant, panting.

Dalton lifted a hand to his forehead.

"Remind me to never cross you," he said. He sat up in the water that reached his hips, staring back at the empty bog. "It's like it never happened."

He was soaking wet, with bits of pale yellow-green moss sticking to his clothing.

"Why aren't there any helicopters or CIA agents charging from the trees?" Erin asked.

He glanced around. "Great question."

"You know what I think?"

"What?" He had one hand pressed to his forehead as he continued to look back at the tranquil expanse, disbelieving.

"They're dangling us like a worm on a hook," she said. "Doesn't matter what happens to the worm as long as you catch the fish."

"Only both our fish are gone."

She nodded. "We should get off this bog."

"I'll say."

"It's a protected habitat. I don't want to damage it any more than necessary."

"You're worried about the swamp?"

"Bog. It's a completely different ecosystem from a wetland. I'm scheduled to lead expeditions on this very site later in the week."

"Well, if I'd known that, I wouldn't have let you come up here." He tucked his gun into a pocket that was still underwater and shook his head in bewilderment. "And you think *my* job is dangerous?"

Chapter Seventeen

"They wanted one alive," said Erin to Dalton as they stood on the road staring out at the bog. They were soaking wet and the breeze chilled him, but not as much as that sphagnum moss.

"You can't even see the tear. Nothing." Dalton shook his head. "It's the most terrifying thing I've ever seen." He glanced her way. "You canoe on that?"

"Walk, too. It's safe."

"Yeah, right. You'll never convince me of that."

She hiked Lulu up higher on her chest and scratched behind the dog's ear. "Now what?"

"The way I see it," Dalton said, "we can wait for the Feds to come and perform their catch and release. Try to capture another member of this terrorist outfit, preferably without getting killed, or we can get out of here and try to make it to someplace safe."

"Nowhere is safe as long as they think we have the vials."

"You're right, and I have a feeling Siming's Army will not take our word for it that it's gone."

"And we have no proof that the CIA took it from us."

"Or that we even met with them." He turned to her. "What do you think?"

Her brows lifted, and she stopped stroking the trembling dog. He wanted to take her in his arms and hold her, tell her that they'd get out of this. But he was no longer sure. Bringing her back out here now seemed the stupidest play imaginable. The CIA didn't have their back. His fanny was swinging out here in the breeze, and he'd dragged her with him.

The uncomfortable distance that had yawned between them, the one he had hoped to close, seemed to have torn open again.

"You're asking me what I think?" She didn't have to look so astonished.

"Yeah," he said, unable to keep the terseness from his tone. "I'm asking."

"I think we shouldn't have trusted those agents. I think we now have nothing to bargain with."

"Easy to catch us whichever way we go," he said. "And it's anyone's guess who will show up first."

"I hope it's not someone like Percy. That poor man."

Lulu licked under Erin's chin, the pink tongue curling up his wife's jaw.

"Oh, you poor thing."

"You keeping her, too?" asked Dalton, already knowing the answer.

"I'm not leaving her on a bog."

"Those pitcher plants might eat her," he said, referring to the cylindrical plants that held a sweet water designed to lure and drown insects. She'd told him about them once before. Not as flashy as the Venus flytrap, but just as deadly.

She didn't laugh at his joke. Lulu was tiny but not small enough to succumb to carnivorous plants. And not big enough to keep up on a hike, either.

Erin scratched under Lulu's chin. "Not a chance. Right, Lulu?"

The soft and sympathetic voice caused a sharp pang of regret. Not that he wanted her to speak to him this way; still he could imagine her, cooing and fussing over a baby. Their baby. But first they had to get out of this mess alive.

"I'm going to check the other one for keys." He thumbed back at the corpse sprawled in the road. Erin followed him and then turned to look at the sky.

"You think they're up there watching?" she asked, using her hand as a visor.

"Definitely."

Erin lifted her hand from her eyes and presented her middle finger to the sky.

Dalton laughed. "Feel better?"

She gave him a half smile as if that were all she could spare. He went back to searching the pockets of the dead man. His diligence was rewarded. The guy kept his keys in his front shirt pocket, which was why he'd missed them before.

He stood and tossed the keys a few inches, catching them again. Then he looked at the pickup truck, engine down and back wheels off the ground. The vehicle was diagonally across from the SUV, which lay on its side at the bottom of the opposite incline. Neither one of them was getting them out of here.

Lulu stood at the road alone. Erin had disappeared. His heart gave a jolt as he glanced to the bog. But Lulu was on the opposite side of the road, panting.

He headed that way at a run. Once he reached the chubby pug, he found his wife. Her head popped up out of the door of the cap that covered the truck bed. Because of the odd angle, the truck sat nearly vertical and the rear door opened out like a mailbox.

"Erin?"

She had something in her hand. "Did you find the keys?"

"Got them." He lifted the chain.

"Try the fob," she said, and scrambled out, sitting on the closed tailgate, legs dangling.

He hit the unlock button and the truck chimed.

He glanced down the bank and saw the truck sat nose down on the hill with the front tires resting on the incline and the grille buried in the ground beyond.

Erin tossed something from the truck. She dragged a length of chain from within. It rattled over the closed tailgate, extending to the ground. She looped the hook, at the end, around the ball-mount trailer hitch beneath the bumper.

"How did you even get up there?" he asked, looking to the truck's tailgate now above his head.

"Lulu boosted me."

He chuckled and looked at the dog, who sat on one hip, tail between her legs and eyes closed in the bright sunlight.

Meanwhile, Erin scrambled like a monkey over the top of the truck and slid down the cap roof to the cab and then dropped to the ground.

"Keys?" she asked, and he tossed them down.

Erin disappeared into the cab and emerged a moment later.

"They're in the ignition and the truck is in neutral."

Dalton lifted the chain and gazed at the truck. Whatever she had in mind, he knew they would not be able to tug this truck up that incline.

She appeared up the hill a moment later.

"Riding beats walking when you are in a hurry," she said.

"How you planning to get that truck back on the road?"

She grinned. "The SUV has a winch on the front. "I figure we attach the two and see which one makes it up the incline and to the road first."

He pressed his lips together and nodded. "Let's go."

The chain reached across the road and the winch cable easily reached the chain.

"We don't have the keys for that SUV," reminded Dalton.

"City boy," she said. "This winch is electric. You don't need to turn on the vehicle to run it. Step back now. Where's Lulu?"

He lifted the dog and moved up the bank. She proceeded to flip a lever and then flicked a toggle switch.

"Holler when the truck is on the road."

The cable began to move, stretching taut. There was a hesitation as the cable vibrated, and then the SUV dragged on its side, inching to the hill below the road. The whine of the winch was momentarily obscured by the scrape of gravel and rock beneath metal. Once the SUV reached the incline it paused as the cable continued to reel.

Dalton glanced across the road, following the cable to the upended pickup and saw it teeter. The back tires thumped down to the road and then the truck rolled with slow inertia up the hill. Since the SUV was lighter than the truck and not anchored, it was dragged up the incline as the truck crept along. By the time the pickup was on the road, the SUV was nearly up the hill.

"Good," he shouted.

The winch motor cut and the whining ceased. Erin instructed him to start the truck and drive it toward the SUV until the chain dropped so she could release the winch safely. He did and the SUV slipped back down the hill as he rolled forward. But the winched vehicle came to a stop before he left the road. Erin scrambled up the embankment and then released the winch cable, tossing it back into the culvert. She gathered the chain and threw it into the truck bed. A moment later she climbed into the truck. Lulu was ecstatic to see her, wiggling and wagging and then throwing herself to her back.

"Jet is going to eat that dog," he predicted.

She gathered up the little tan lapdog into her arms. "Where to?"

"That way has no outlet, just a loop to the gun club that will bring you back here," he reminded her.

"Right. Minerva it is."

He put the truck in motion. "You still have your pistol?"

She patted her jacket pocket. He flicked on the heater, hoping the air would help dry his clothing and warm them.

"I hate bogs," he mumbled.

She laughed and settled Lulu on her lap. Then she clicked her seat belt across her middle.

"Think we can make it to your partner in North Creek?"

"I doubt it. But that's where I'm heading."

She peered out the open window, gazing at the blue sky.

"They still up there?"

"Probably."

They did not even slow down in the town of Minerva and he was surprised that no one stopped them.

"How many people do you think are up here with Siming's Army?" she asked as they cruised past a gas station that advertised firewood and propane.

"Six fewer now," he said. "But I don't know. That could be all of them in one sleeper cell."

"Our attackers weren't in uniform," she said. "But the truck is DEC."

Erin busied herself searching the glove box. She found a bag of trail mix, the kind with chocolate mingled in with the nuts and raisins. She offered it open to him and continued her exploration while he munched.

"Nothing but the paperwork and some tools." She pocketed the universal multi-tool. Just as well, as she clearly knew how to use one better than he would.

He pulled into a KOA and drew up to the office. He handed back the half-empty bag and she lifted it, pouring some of the contents into her mouth and then offering Lulu a peanut.

"I need to make a phone call," he said.

She nodded and held Lulu, who tried to follow him out of the vehicle. Dalton used the office pay phone to call Henry Larson, who had not left the area, despite not being allowed to see him or, perhaps, because of it. The two made arrangements on how and where to meet, and then Dalton returned to Erin.

"Let me guess," she said. "You called Henry."

"I did."

"NYPD to the rescue," she said.

"I get it. You don't like Henry." He set them back in motion, pulling out of the campground's lot.

"True."

"Because when I'm with him, I'm not with you?"

"Because he thinks strip clubs are an acceptable form of entertainment and because he has a different girl-friend every time he comes to a party. Where does he get them all?"

Dalton wisely did not answer, but Erin's eyebrows rose, making the connection.

"So he's dating strippers?"

"They weren't *all* strippers."

"Oh, that makes me feel so much better."

"I don't want to fight."

"We aren't fighting," she said, as she always did. But they were.

"Do you know why I came up here after you?" he asked.

"To convince me to come home or at least not to ask for a trial separation."

"True. And because I don't want to become like Henry. I wanted to try, to keep trying."

This revelation had an effect that was the opposite of what Dalton had intended. Erin blew through her nos-trils and turned her head to stare out the window at the homes that had cut grassy plots out of the surrounding woodland. They were off parkland, he realized.

Dalton tried again. "Henry is a good guy. A solid guy. He loves his kids. He's a good father, but he has nothing but terrible things to say about his wife. He thinks that she's the reason for him losing his house and only seeing his kids on weekends. All his problems start and end with his ex."

She turned to stare out the front window. Listening, her face revealing nothing.

"I know how many cops are divorced. The statistics. I know the stats on drinking and drug abuse. It's a tough job. Stressful."

"On families, too," she said in a voice that seemed faraway.

"But I never thought that would be me. Be us. We were rock solid. I came home every night I wasn't working. I shared what I could instead of keeping it bottled up inside. Now I think that might have been a mistake. Telling you—I mean, because it frightened you. Some of the guys said I was stupid, letting you know the risks we take. The close calls. That this was the reason they didn't share work stories at home. Kids don't need to hear it and wives freak."

"I never freaked."

"You did. You left me and came here."

"Not because I was listening but because you weren't."

"I listened. But this is who I am. I'm a protector at heart. I live to get those criminals off the streets. To stop them before they can hurt anyone and see they never get the chance to try again."

"Which is why people are still shooting at us."

"Erin, I thought you agreed."

"That was before they ditched us. We have no backup or none that I have seen. I understand why we are here and I accept that what you do is important. I just can't live like this anymore."

"Erin. Please."

"I'm scared," she admitted.

She had good reason. The way this was heading, saving their marriage might be the least of their problems.

"We'll get through this."

She shook her head. "If we do, what then?"

"You come home. We work this out."

She stared vacantly at her scabby knees and offered no reassurance.

He extended his hand but, instead of squeezing it back, she just stared at it. He rested it on her leg, feeling the warm skin and firm muscle beneath. After a millennium, she moved her hand from the dog and covered his.

It was a start. Or he hoped it was.

"Are we going to get out of this?" she asked.

He set his jaw and nodded. "Yes, ma'am, we surely are."

"That just wishful thinking? Telling me what you think I need to hear."

He shook his head. "I can't believe there are this many of them. Erin, the woods are crawling with these terrorists. And I don't understand why we haven't already been picked up and brought back in."

"Because we didn't get a member of Siming's Army, not a living one anyway."

He shook his head again. Something was wrong. The Feds had not held up their end of the bargain, and that meant the deal was off. All men for themselves. He needed to look after his own and get Erin to safety.

Lulu shifted position, groaned and lay down on Erin's lap.

"Do you think she knows what happened to Percy?"

"No."

"Dogs grieve the loss of their owners, you know."

"I suppose." But Lulu's bulging eyes made her look more hungry than grief stricken.

"Are you regretting coming out here?" he asked.

She stared straight ahead, and he had the feeling

something was really wrong. Mostly because she wasn't angry and she had a right to be. He'd trusted the system and they'd been dumped in a bog as reward. Finally, she spoke, and her voice was flat calm as the eye of a hurricane.

"I would have preferred that they put out an APB that we'd been picked up and processed and released, so everyone would know we don't have that darn black case."

She cut a sidelong glance at him and then rested a trembling hand on Lulu's back. She stroked the resting dog, seeming to draw comfort from the tiny creature.

That other woman, the Homeland Security agent, would not have known to take them out on the bog, and he very much doubted that Hockings knew how to use a winch. Maybe she could have shot and killed that second man. But he'd never know. He was happy to stay with the one who had brought him to the dance. But was she happy about it?

They reached an actual intersection and a stop sign. The dirt road ended against NY 28 and he turned south, away from Minerva and toward North Creek. The southern route flanked the Hudson on the opposite side from where they had walked yesterday over the trestle and all the way to North River. They covered the four miles in less than five minutes and crossed the river. Groups of rafters drifted by on the calm section before the upcoming set of rapids. Next, they journeyed through North River, with its white-water rafting outfits perched directly across the road from the launching sites.

Dalton didn't slow but continued toward North Creek. Henry was waiting.

"Did you speak to the CIA guys?" she asked.

"Yeah. They took the drive and samples."

"Tillman was okay. Seemed nice enough but that other one. What was his name, Danielson?" she asked.

"No, that's not it. First name was Cliff, I think. Or Clint."

"I don't think it was Clint. I can't even remember what he looked like." She rubbed her chin, thinking.

"There were a lot of federal agents. Two from the FBI. Agent Shaffer, also CIA and the Homeland Security agents."

Why had he mentioned them? Now she'd be thinking of Hockings again.

"Were you questioned by the guy? Forester?" she asked.

"Foster, Lawrence," he said. He thought of the agent he had met in the men's room realizing then that the guy had said he'd join him in interrogation but never showed "I met him, but we didn't have a formal interview. You?"

"Yes. He gave me the creeps."

"Worse than Clint or Cliff?"

"Different. He was the only one who showed up alone. After the other agents left. I felt, not threatened, but cornered, I guess. He was with me until just before you arrived. He didn't ask the same things as the CIA men. He wanted to know about the pilot. Where he was and how he died. What happened to the woman who owned the dog and where we had been last night. He was the only one who asked about the contents of what we carried."

"They have the contents. Why ask you?"

"Maybe that's what bothered me. He also was the

first to ask where we had been heading and which of your colleagues you had contacted."

Dalton's radar popped on and he scowled. "Where we were heading? Did you tell him about Henry?"

"Of course."

Dalton stepped on the gas.

Erin sat forward, grabbing the overhead hand grip. "What? What's wrong?"

Lulu startled awake as she nearly fell off Erin's lap to the floor mats.

"You see his ID?"

"I... I don't remember. I didn't see Hockings's ID. I know that."

"What if Foster is not DHS?" he asked.

"Then he wouldn't have been in the troopers' head-quarters."

That wasn't necessarily true. All they had to do was to get someone to buzz them in and mingle with people in the building. It was alphabet soup in there.

"If he was legit, then he'd know that the CIA recovered the flash drive and vials."

"So?" she asked.

"He'd also know we aren't carrying anything. No reason to attack us back there."

That was true, unless their attackers had not gotten word from him or it was a different cell.

"But he asked about Henry?"

"Yes. All he knew was that Henry was NYPD SWAT. Not his name, even." She shook her head. "But Henry doesn't have anything they want."

"Neither do we, but those men by the bog still tried to kill us."

She didn't argue with that, just held on as he flew

along the highway passing a Subaru with bikes fixed to the back end and a family SUV with canoes strapped to the roof racks.

Chapter Eighteen

"I don't understand why we didn't have any backup out there," she said.

"That's just one of my questions," said Dalton.

They tore into the parking area of a chain hotel. Dalton leaped out of the truck and charged through lobby doors that barely had time to whisk open. Erin lowered the windows and told Lulu to stay. Then she followed him inside in time to see him leaning over the desk of the petite receptionist dressed in a polyester blazer with a gold-toned name tag.

"I can't tell you his room number." She lifted the phone. "But I can call his room for you."

Dalton flashed his shield to the receptionist. The wallet was soggy and much worse for wear, but the receptionist's reaction was instant. Her fingers started tapping on the keys.

"He's in 116. First floor, right down that hallway."

"Call 911. Tell them NYC detective Dalton Stevens requests backup for possible B and E."

"Yes, sir."

He pointed at Erin. "Stay here."

"Like hell," she said.

She'd seen enough cop shows to know how to enter

a room with a gun. And if Rylee Hockings could do it, she could, too.

Dalton dashed down the hall toward his colleague's room and she followed at a run. When he reached the door, he motioned her to halt, and he stood to the side to try the handle. The door was locked. Then he lifted one booted foot and kicked in the flimsy hotel room door.

He entered with pistol raised and the grip cradled in his opposite hand. Erin watched him disappear and then heard nothing.

She crept farther down the hall and made out her husband's voice.

"Larson?"

Did he see his friend or was he just looking?

There was no reply. Erin peeked around the doorjamb and saw Henry Larson sprawled on the floor, his hands secured behind his back. Dalton squatted at his side.

"Is he dead?" she asked.

Before he could answer, Dalton rose to face her and his eyes went wild. He reached and took two steps toward her. Then she felt it, the hand clutching her jacket from behind, dragging her off her feet, across the hall and into the opposite hotel room. The fabric choked her, sending her hand reflexively to her throat.

Dalton reached the hallway as her captor kicked the door to the opposite hotel room closed and threw the bolt. The impact of Dalton's body against the door vibrated through the soles of her kicking feet.

On the second attempt Dalton crashed through the door. His gun was up and raised as he advanced with measured steps.

"Far enough," said her captor. She felt the hard pressure of the pistol pushing into her temple.

Dalton paused, as if playing some deadly game of freeze tag, but his weapon remained up and pointed at her captor.

"Foster, isn't it?" asked her husband.

"For now," said the man who had spoken to her in the darn troopers' headquarters just prior to Dalton's arrival with the three federal agents, Hockings, Tillman and Shaffer. He had identified himself as Lawrence Foster, an agent with the Department of Homeland Security.

"Lower your weapon or I kill your wife." He said it as a cashier might tell you to hold on while they print your receipt. The effect was chilling. The man was cold-blooded as a garter snake.

Dalton said nothing but his eyes were on her attacker. The gun barrel moved to her eye socket.

"All right. It's down," said Dalton. "What do you want?"

"To interrogate the two remaining witnesses. Find out how much they know about us."

"We don't have the package. It's with the agents at the troopers'—"

Foster cut him off. "I know that. Which is why I blew that building. That virus is now airborne. Anybody sifting through the ashes has a great chance of contracting our little superbug, and the vaccine, well, that doesn't go airborne." He made a *tsking* sound with his tongue on the roof of his mouth.

Was it true? Was that why there was no backup? Were they all dead?

The chill shook her. Was it really just her husband and her and this madman?

"Out," said Foster.

She didn't know where they were going and, right this second, she didn't care. What she did care about was seeing that Dalton did not get shot by some maniac terrorist. She and her husband were going to take Lulu and Jet home to Yonkers and give them a home. Dalton was going to make good on his promise to become a supervisor, and she was going to see that they spent every free minute trying to start that family.

If Foster didn't shoot her and her husband first.

What would Dalton do?

Something heavy pressed against her side. The pistol, the small one that she'd carried since Jet's captor tried to kill them. Her hand slipped inside her jacket pocket and she gripped the weapon. Her thumb flicked off the safety. He marched her forward. Sweat ran behind her ears and into her hair. It rolled between her breasts and down the long channel of her spine.

Dalton retreated to the hallway as they reached his discarded weapon. The man stooped and his pistol dropped toward her neck. He motioned with the gun to the floor.

"Pick that up," he ordered her. "Barrel first."

Erin slipped the pistol from her pocket and met Dalton's gaze. She'd never seen him afraid before. But that was what she saw now. Stone-cold terror in the hardening of his jaw and the hands extending reflexively toward her.

DALTON HAD STOPPED backing up when he saw Erin's hand moving in her pocket. His breath caught. His jaw locked and he saw stars.

No. No. No.

He'd only set down his gun to keep Foster from killing Erin. But she had other plans, as always.

Had she remembered to flick off the safety of her weapon? His gaze dropped for just an instant to the small silver pistol in her hand, but it was enough.

Foster's eyes narrowed on him and he lifted the handgun that was now pointing across Erin's chest.

Dalton took a step forward. Foster hesitated as if deciding whether to aim at Erin or back at him. Erin lifted the gun under her opposite armpit and fired back at Foster hitting him in the chest. He released her, staggering backward, still aiming at them. Dalton made a grab for Erin and missed.

Erin spun to face Foster and stepped between them as Foster fired a single shot.

Chapter Nineteen

Every hair on Dalton's body lifted and his heart stuttered before exploding into a frantic pounding. Erin spun, staring at Dalton's shocked expression as Foster aimed at him. But he'd reached him now and grabbed Foster's wrist, then used his opposite hand to break Foster's elbow as he retrieved the man's pistol from his limp hand.

Dalton pointed his attacker's pistol at Foster, but his gaze flicked from his target to Erin, who sank to her knees, gasping. In that moment, Foster ducked past the doorjamb and out of sight.

The small pistol dropped to the carpet as his wife lifted her hand to her neck, pale fingers clamping down as blood welled from beneath her palm.

His head swam and he shook it in a vain attempt to wake from this nightmare. Erin stared at him, her eyes wide and round, showing the whites all about her brown irises.

"Erin. No," he whispered to himself as the truth ricocheted through him like the bullet that had struck her.

Erin was bleeding.

She toppled, her hand dropping away from her

neck, allowing blood to pour out of her body, staining the carpet.

A wild shrieking came from the man darting down the hall to the lobby, his ruined arm flailing, his elbow jutting out at an odd angle. It took a moment for Dalton to realize that part of the screaming was the wail of approaching sirens. Help arriving too late.

Dalton let his suspect run as he dropped to his knees beside his wife. He gathered her limp body in his arms. She was going to die, leaving him after all but not in the way she had planned.

He tore back the jacket from her neck and saw the bullet hole at the point where her long neck gave way to her shoulder. A gentle probing told him that the collarbone was intact, and from the way the blood exited the wound he was certain that the bullet had not struck her carotid artery because there was no spraying of blood. But it had hit some blood vessel because the hole was a deep bubbling well of red.

She was going to leave him like his men back in Afghanistan. Like his partner, Chris Wirimer. Why was he still here when everyone he tried to protect…

"Dalton?" Her voice was weak, but her gaze fixed him steadily. "You okay?"

She was worried about him. Always. And suddenly he understood. This was exactly what she had feared, only their roles had reversed. How many times had she imagined him bleeding out at some crime scene?

This was what he'd done to her, year after year, because he couldn't stand being the one who made it out.

His broad hand clamped over her wound and pressed hard. He would not let her bleed out on the hallway like some…some…hero, he realized. She'd saved his life, possibly Henry Larson's life as well, if he wasn't already dead.

"I'm here. Help is coming. Hold on, Erin."

"Did he shoot you?" she asked.

"No."

She closed her eyes then, and relaxed against him.

"Thank God," she whispered.

Dalton felt the tightening in his throat, the burning as his eyes watered, vision swimming.

Then he started screaming for help. Doors cracked open as people crept cautiously out of their rooms.

"Bring help," he shouted. "Get her help!"

She had wanted to leave that package behind. Put it on a red T-shirt with a note, she had suggested. But he had to bring it along.

If Foster could be believed, he'd destroyed it anyway, and by bringing it out of the woods, possibly Dalton had jeopardized who knew how many lives, begun some Siming's pandemic for them. But now, the only life he cared about was Erin's.

He stroked her damp hair and stared down the hall until, at last, the EMTs arrived, charging toward him in navy blue uniforms, their bulky bags flopping against their thighs.

"Hang on, Erin. Don't you leave me."

THEY LET DALTON ride in the first ambulance with Erin but did not let him into the operating wing. He was directed to a waiting area as Erin disappeared down a long corridor, followed by his partner, Henry Larson, on a second gurney. The waiting room had wooden chairs with mauve cushions set in a U-shape around three coffee tables holding a smattering of torn magazines and discarded paper coffee cups. There were two other men already there, and he was surprised to find both CIA agent Jerome Shaffer and FBI agent Nolen Bersen waiting.

"So it's true then," he said. "Troopers' headquarters is gone?"

Bersen nodded. "Agent Heller suffered injuries. He is in surgery now."

"So is Erin. Gunshot wound to her neck."

Shaffer stood and placed a hand on Dalton's shoulder. "Sorry to hear that."

"Anyone else hurt?" asked Dalton.

"Mostly minor injuries. The troopers have a K-9 dog. Former marine, and he found the explosives. They were clearing the building when it went off. Heller was hit by part of the ceiling. He's got a spine injury."

"What about the…" Dalton looked around. "What we brought in?"

"Long gone. Shaffer and Gabriel had it out of the station well before the blast. It's safe, Stevens."

Why didn't that make him feel any better?

"She's in there because of me."

"This isn't your fault, Dalton."

"I agreed to go back out there. I let her come along. Of course, it's my fault."

"I understand you're upset. With good reason. Your wife is injured and your colleague, Detective Larson, suffered head trauma in an attack," said Shaffer.

"Yeah, they just brought him in with her."

"What happened?"

Dalton's eyes widened as he realized that Shaffer didn't know about the impostor and therefore the agent from Siming's Army was getting away. "At the troopers' headquarters there was a man. We both met him. Said he was DHS, name was Lawrence Foster."

"Foster?" asked Shaffer. "I don't know him."

Dalton explained, finishing with, "He shot Erin. Don't let him get away."

Both men lifted their phones.

"So there is no Lawrence Foster of DHS?"

Shaffer lifted the phone from his mouth, pointing the bottom toward the ceiling. "No."

"Then how did he get into trooper headquarters?"

"I'll be checking that."

"What about the other one, Rylee Hockings?"

"She's DHS. On her way back to her offices in Glens Falls."

While Dalton paced, Shaffer and Bersen made calls.

He didn't realize that Agent Shaffer was speaking to him until he touched Dalton's shoulder.

"We got him."

"Who?" He'd been so lost in thought and worry that it took a moment to come back to his surroundings. Dalton was in the hallway now, standing on the wide tiles before the doors that read No Admittance.

"Lawrence Foster, or the man claiming to be Foster. Troopers caught him trying to board an Amtrak train in Glens Falls. Arm injury made him easy to spot."

"Sweating like a marathon runner," added Bersen.

"He had the proper ID for DHS. Either real or a very convincing fake."

Dalton felt none of the elation that usually accompanied a collar. He didn't care. Not unless they'd let him see him alone so he could settle up. And he knew that would never happen.

How many victims had asked him for that same thing?

"He alive?" Dalton asked, his voice mechanical.

"Yes, in custody. His real name is Vincent Eulich. He's a physicist, college professor in Schenectady with a bomb-making hobby."

"We already have agents at his home and office. But we have to go slow. Already found one IED," said Bersen, referring to the improvised explosive devices most commonly in use in the Middle East.

A man in blue scrubs emerged from the swinging doors and all conversation ceased.

"Anyone out here waiting for word on Henry Larson?"

"I'm in his department," said Dalton. And Henry was his best friend.

"Any direct family?" asked the surgeon.

"Not here. He's got an ex-wife and two kids."

The surgeon pulled a face.

"I'm Dr. Howard. Your colleague has suffered a spine fracture in three places. The rest is cuts and bruises and a mild concussion as a result of a head injury. The back injury is most serious. But the pressure is off the spinal cord and I've repaired a herniated disk. His prognosis is good. Barring complications, I'd say he'll be able to use his legs again after some physical therapy."

That news hit Dalton in the stomach like a mule kick.

"Walk? The man's a former Army Ranger. He bikes all over Westchester and runs Ironman contests."

The surgeon shook his head. "I doubt he'll be doing any of those things again. He'll need a spinal fusion once the swelling is down."

"Fusion?" Removal from active duty, Dalton realized. Just like that.

Dr. Howard nodded. "Got to get back at it."

Dalton grasped his elbow and Howard's expression showed surprise.

"Any word on Erin Stevens? She was shot in the neck?"

"Different surgical team. I'm sure they'll be out to you as soon as they can."

"Anything?" Dalton said, his voice gruff.

"Still in surgery."

He gave Dalton a tight smile and backed through the swinging doors.

Dalton walked slowly to the waiting area and sank into a chair. Bersen and Shaffer took up seats opposite. Dalton folded his hands and bowed his head. He had not done this in some time. Praying felt awkward and uncomfortable. Still he muscled through, asking God's help in saving his wife. When he finished he found both agents regarding him.

"You two waiting on someone?"

"Yes," said Shaffer. "You. And your wife. We need to be sure Siming's Army knows we have the intel they tried and failed to recover and that you two are safe. We've also got two agents outside of the operating room."

"After they know that, you think they'll try to hurt Erin again?"

"They seem determined to kill you both. So we've called some friends from WITSEC."

Dalton straightened at the mention of the witness protection program.

"That's extreme, don't you think?"

"Temporary placement. Until we get this organization shut down."

Dalton sat back in the uncomfortable little chair.

They didn't think it was too extreme. What would Erin say? What about him? He had a mom, a dad and step-mother, plus two older sisters. Erin had a brother she rarely saw and a sister who lived on the same block.

His job… He'd have to leave his job and, even after relocation, he would not be able to work in law enforcement again.

A voice came from the edge of the carpet just outside of the waiting area.

"Mr. Stevens? I have an update on your wife."

Chapter Twenty

Erin woke in pain and in the company of strangers. She asked for Dalton and a nurse's blurry face appeared above her. When the nurse didn't understand, Erin tried to pull the mask off her own face. There was a sharp sting on her hip and she sank back into blackness.

The next time she roused, fighting every inch of the way back to consciousness, it was to a room of light and sound. Machines bleated and chimed. Alarms chirped and she squinted against the blinding lights above her.

"What time?" she tried to ask the attendant who checked the fluid bag that hung above her on a metal pole.

"You're doing great, honey," said a female voice.

"What time?" Her voice was the scratch of sandpaper on dry wood.

"It's nearly 9:00 p.m. You're out of recovery and in ICU. Your husband just left. He's a handsome fellow. Needs a shave, though."

"Dalton?"

"That right? I thought you said *Walton*. Anyway. He seems nice. You'll be here tonight and tomorrow. You do okay and you'll get a room. You in trouble, honey?"

"Trouble?" Other than getting shot? she wondered.

"There are two US marshals right outside. I know they aren't for me. So you in trouble?"

"Not anymore." Talking hurt so badly she had to close her eyes.

"You hurting?"

She nodded and immediately regretted it. The nurse used a syringe to add something to her IV line and Erin's body went slack. The pain dissolved like fog in the sun and she slipped away to a place beyond the needs of her body.

"Erin?"

She knew that voice.

"Erin. It's Dalton."

She tried and failed to open her eyes.

"Can you hear me?" He lifted her limp hand. "Squeeze my hand."

She tried, failed and swallowed. The pain was back. Her throat throbbed as if she were a tree trunk and a woodpecker was knocking a hole into her with repeated stabbing blows.

"Your sister, Victoria, is here."

Another voice, female murmuring. Erin tried again to open her eyes, but the deep pain-free well beckoned.

She let go and dropped. Just like rappelling down a cliff, she thought as she glided into blackness.

DALTON DIDN'T SEE the surgeon until the following day. The guy had sent a physician's assistant out to see him in the waiting room yesterday, and his visits during the night had scared him silly. Erin had a bandage the size of a football on her neck. And she was on a ventilator.

Her sister, Vic, had arrived at nine and the physician appeared at bedside during the fifteen minutes they allowed Dalton each hour. Vic had stepped out at the MD's appearance so Dalton could step in.

"The loss of blood resulted in your wife suffering a cardiac arrest. To reduce her energy expenditure, I ordered a drug-induced coma. The medication is keeping her body from using any extra energy, easing the burden on her heart."

"How long will you keep her like this?" asked Dalton.

"Until her blood volume is normal and her bladder is functioning again." He motioned to the empty clear bag hanging from the bed rails. Had her kidney's stopped working?

Panic tightened its grip upon him.

"Days?" asked Dalton.

"Likely we'll wake her up later today. Your wife lost a lot of blood. It can damage organs. We need to be sure everything is working."

"If it's not?"

"One thing at a time."

The next twenty-four hours were the longest of his life. Because of him, his best friend had suffered a spinal injury and his wife was in a coma. As minutes ticked away, Dalton had lots of time to make promises to God and curse his own foolishness. Nothing was as important to him as his friend and his wife. He just hoped that he'd have a chance to tell them both.

ERIN'S EYES POPPED OPEN. It was as if someone had just flicked a switch and brought her to full awake. Tentative movement told her that she had not imagined her injuries.

Four unfamiliar faces peered down at her.

"Mrs. Stevens? How do you feel?"

"Thirsty," she said.

They asked her a series of questions that seemed designed to test her mental acumen. The day, month, who was president? What holiday was next on the calendar, and math problems.

"Is my husband here?"

"He is. And anxious to see you. But a brief visit. Right?" The physician looked to another attendee, who nodded. Brightly colored cartoon illustrations of popular candy bars covered this man's scrubs top.

Three of the gathering wandered out in conversation as the one male attendant remained.

"I'm Will. I'm your nurse today."

"Hi, Will. Um, water?"

"Ice chips for now." He fussed with the IV bag and then disappeared, returning with a plastic cup. "I did one better. Lemon ice. Okay?" He handed it over with a plastic spoon.

Erin discovered that she could not really work her left hand without waking the dragon of burning pain in her shoulder.

Man, it hurt to get shot.

Dalton arrived, hurrying forward and then slowing as he saw her. He looked as bad as she felt.

"Oh, Dalton!" she said.

"Erin?" He got only that out and then he did something she had never seen him do. He wept.

Both hands covered his big, tired face and his shoulders shook. She reached her good hand to him and called his name.

He peered at her beneath his dark brows and raised

hands. The circles under his eyes startled and he looked thinner. Then he took her hand and allowed her to draw him to her bed, where he sat awkwardly on the edge.

"You're awake," he said.

She smiled. "They gave me an ice. But I can't manage holding and scooping."

Dalton took over both jobs, offering her wonderful sweet, cold bits of frozen lemon. Nothing had ever tasted so good, though the act of eating and swallowing hurt her neck. She didn't say so but was relieved when Will came to roust Dalton back out. The weariness tugged at her features and pricked at her skin.

"I'll see you soon."

She held her smile until he was out of sight and then groaned.

"Pain?" asked Will.

She nodded and then flinched. Will returned with the pain medication and then the throbbing ache retreated like a receding tide. She breathed a sigh.

"Thanks."

"Your sister is out there. I'll send her in after you take a little nap."

She murmured her acceptance and closed her eyes. What choice did she have? For the rest of that day and through the night, she had short visits with Victoria and Dalton. The following day she felt so much better that they removed both catheter and infusion bag. She ate solid food for breakfast. Victoria visited her at noon and then told her that she was heading home.

"You know there are armed guards outside your room?" Victoria asked.

"There are?" Erin asked.

"US Marshals, they said."

"Gosh. That's not good."

Victoria looked at her. "They do witness protection, right?"

"I'm not sure."

"I am. Dalton told me what happened out there. It's a miracle either of you is still alive. I don't know what I'd do without you."

Their embrace was tentative, but Erin survived it without too much discomfort.

"I'll see you soon," said Erin.

"I hope so. Love you." With that, her sister was gone.

Erin followed her with her eyes, stopping when she saw Dalton leaning on the doorjamb, obviously giving them time to say goodbye.

Something in his expression made her uneasy.

"What's happening, Dalton? Victoria said there are police out there."

He came in and sat in the padded orange vinyl chair beside her bed, the one she was supposed to be allowed to sit in this afternoon.

Erin offered her hand and Dalton took it in both of his.

"Are we still in danger?"

"We are. The FBI has turned us over to the US Marshals."

Her heartbeat pulsed in the swollen tissues at her neck, sending sharp stabs of pain radiating through her shoulder and arm.

"Witness protection services. Right?"

He nodded grimly.

"We have to go?"

"It's voluntary but until they know who is after us and if there are more…" His words trailed off.

"Does my sister know?"

"She saw them sitting there," said Dalton. "They frisked her."

"They did not!"

Dalton made a face that said he was not teasing.

"Have you spoken to your parents?"

"Just Helen. She's going to bring Mom up to see us."

"Your father?"

"If we decide to go, they'll bring him, too."

"What have we gotten tangled up in, Dalton?"

"Some very bad, very dangerous people who are unfortunately also well financed. Our guys don't know who is behind them yet. Have to follow the money. Large corporation or foreign government, I suppose."

"Are we going to have to leave?"

"They're recommending it."

She drew a breath and held it, studying him. "Together?" she asked.

He gripped her hand. "Erin, I know I put you in danger out there and I'm so sorry. You might not believe me, but you are the most important thing in the world to me and I hope you'll let me prove it."

"How?"

"I'm thinking I should see a counselor. See why I keep doing this."

"You think maybe that psychologist you were required to see after that deadly force thing might be right? That this has to do with your military service?"

His head dropped. "I was their platoon leader, Erin. It was my job to look out for them. Keep them safe."

"An impossible task."

"Maybe. But I failed." He met her gaze, and his eyes glittered with grief and helplessness. "They trusted me to look out for them."

"It was a war," she reminded.

"Military action."

"With bombs and gunfire and schools used as shields."

"Yes. All that," he agreed. "I just keep feeling responsible. That I don't deserve…"

"What?" she asked.

"You. My life."

She gasped at that. In all the time since he'd left the service, he'd never said such a thing before.

She thought about all the chances he'd taken since discharge from the service. He'd only ended his military career because of her and her threats of separation. Now the pieces began to snap into place. Was he looking for a second chance to save his men? Or a second chance to die with them?

How was it that she'd never realized that his risky behavior coincided with the loss of so many of his men over in what he called the Sandbox?

"Counseling sounds smart," she said.

"A beginning place." He dragged a hand through his hair and then let his arm drop wearily back to his side. "The marshals, if we choose relocation, told me I can't be involved in law enforcement."

"All I've ever wanted was to keep you around," she said, the tears burning her throat and making her shoulder throb.

He chuckled. "Funny way of showing me that. Throwing me out, I mean."

"I tried other things first. You didn't hear me. Then

after you got shot, I just couldn't stop worrying. Couldn't put it aside. It was consuming me. Eating me alive."

"I'm sorry. I don't think I understood that. I just thought you were being overly protective. That you'd get past it like all the other times. But seeing you out there, watching you get shot, well, it scared me to death."

Their eyes met and held. She knew it instantly. He understood. Finally and irrevocably, he comprehended what it was like to face the death of the person whose loss you knew you could not survive.

"I couldn't live if something happened to you, Erin. I'm sorry I didn't understand. That I didn't listen."

Tears streamed down her face as she gripped his hand. She wanted to hold him, but she could not lift her arm without hitting that morphine button and she needed a clear head.

"I just wanted you safe. It's all I ever wanted."

He gave her a sad smile. They'd come to an understanding, she thought.

"Dalton, I want to go home."

"It might be a new home."

"With the dogs?"

"The…" He laughed. "You *are* feeling better. I'll see if we can arrange that."

"Are they both all right?"

"Yes. Lulu has a new dog bed and Jet has already devoured two Frisbees."

"Where are they?"

"Your sister took them back home with her."

"I want to keep them. Lulu and Jet. Can the marshals arrange that?"

"I'll ask."

"So, the relocation…is it permanent?"

"Shouldn't be. Just until they sort out this group."

"Siming's Army."

He nodded.

She tentatively moved her arm and winced. "That will be hard, losing everyone, my family."

"It's a big decision."

Someone stood at the door and cleared his throat. They turned and Erin saw a man in green scrubs holding a clipboard. Was this the surgeon who had stopped the bleeding and saved her life?

"How are you feeling, Erin?"

She smiled at him as he approached the bed. He was handsome, with symmetrical features, of average size and above average physique. His brown hair needed a trim and the manicured stubble of a beard covered his face.

"I'm Ryan Carr," he said, and offered his hand to Dalton, who rose to shake his hand. The two released the brief clasping of palms and Carr continued around the bed, looking at her IV. She no longer had the solution dripping into her arm, but the needle remained in her vein.

"Did you say 'Carr'?" asked Dalton. Where had he heard that name before?

"How is your pain level?" asked Carr.

"I haven't used the morphine this morning."

He smiled. "That's good." He turned to Dalton and motioned to the chair. "Would you like to sit down, Detective Stevens?"

Her husband now had his hands on his hips and his brow had descended low over his dark eyes. She knew the look. Her husband sensed a threat.

Chapter Twenty-One

Dalton realized that Ryan Carr, though dressed appropriately for hospital staff, with the Crocs, scrubs and ID tag on a lanyard, gave off a totally different vibe.

Less like a healer and more like a predator.

"What did you say your position here is?" asked Dalton, not taking a seat and instead moving to stand between Carr and his wife.

"Very good, Stevens," said Carr. "You really are very good. Most people don't even notice me."

His wife spoke from behind him. "Women would notice you."

That made Dalton's frown deepen. He was attractive if you liked pretty boys.

"You need to back up out of this room," said Dalton, keeping his attention on Carr's hands, which held only the clipboard.

"I just wanted to warn you. Mind if I get my ID? My real ID?"

"I do mind. But go ahead. Slowly," said Dalton, prepared to body slam this intruder if he even looked at Erin again. He had touched her arm, checked her IV and demonstrated very clearly how easy it was to get to them.

And then he remembered. "Ryan Carr. The chopper pilot said you gave him the cooler."

Carr nodded. "That's right."

He removed his wallet. "The marshals checked my ID, bless their hearts. But they apparently don't have a list of hospital staff. If they did," he said, taking out his identification and passing it to Dalton, "they'd know that I don't work here."

Dalton glanced at the ID with a very prominent CIA in blue on the plastic card.

"How do I know this is real or that you are who you say you are?"

"Feel free to call in and check after I go. I'm here for two reasons. First to warn you that leaving for WITSEC sooner is advisable. You are not secure here."

"And second?" asked Erin.

"To thank you. I was the one who collected that intel from a foreign operative. And I *was* the one who put it on that helicopter and gave instructions, instructions that were passed to you, Mrs. Stevens. If I understand correctly, you swam out to the pilot, attempted a rescue and took what he offered as imperative to our country's safety. Is that right?"

She nodded.

"And I'd like to thank you, Detective Stevens, for not doing as your wife requested and leaving it behind...on a red T-shirt, is that correct?" He smiled.

Dalton knew that only the FBI and CIA who had interviewed them should know these details. Was this guy for real?

"I am who I say, Detective. A fact that Agent Tillman will verify."

"We've already been lied to by someone claiming to be DHS, so excuse my skepticism."

"Lawrence Foster, yes, he proves my point—about your safety, I mean. The Justice Department is a fine organization generally. Good for moving career criminals into nice new neighborhoods after they testify. But this group, Siming's Army, they are not your typical wise guy looking to get even. They are organized and funded, backed by foreign nationals, according to my contacts. The information you rescued will be instrumental in making my case and it has already reached its terminus. The CDC is analyzing the virus and vaccine. And all because of your bravery, Mrs. Stevens." He bowed to Erin and then turned to Dalton. "And your dogged determination. Thank you both. Your country owes you a debt."

"You're welcome," said Erin.

Carr backed away from the bed and then headed for the hall, pausing to meet Dalton's troubled stare.

"Call Tillman. Tell him Carr says we need to relocate you today."

"The CIA relocates people?" asked Erin.

"We are a full-service organization, ma'am. Best of luck to you both."

He disappeared into the hall. Dalton followed him as far as the seated marshal. Carr had vanished.

"Get your boss in here now."

ERIN'S STITCHES TUGGED as she transferred to the wheelchair under heavy guard. It turned out that their visitor, Ryan Carr, was exactly who and what he claimed. The real deal, apparently. An honest-to-goodness spy who had done exactly what he claimed, rescuing the package from repeated attempts at recovery by members of Siming's Army and then finally reaching the airlift location, only to watch the chopper be shot down.

Erin thought that he must have been only ten or twelve miles from where the helicopter crashed.

But right now, Erin's main concern was to not throw up as she was wheeled down the hall under the protection of a ridiculous number of men armed with rifles. The hallway to and from the elevator was absolutely devoid of people.

"Did we just go up?" she asked Dalton.

The elevator was making her sour stomach more upset.

"Yes."

"Why?" She swallowed back the bitter taste in her mouth.

"Evac helicopter is taking us out of here."

"Like the one that Siming's Army already shot down?"

Beside her, Agent Kane Tillman leaned close. "Appreciate it if you don't mention them."

She nodded her understanding.

The next twenty minutes were a blur. She only threw up once and the attending EMTs seemed used to this sort of disturbance. They gave her something that settled her stomach and something for the pain. But the analgesic made her sleepy. Now she struggled to stay awake.

The sky was a deep blue and the lights below them flicked on. Streets glimmered with lines of red taillights and white headlights, strung in parallel ribbons.

"Where are we heading?" she asked, watching the Adirondacks resume custody of the land now stretching below in darkness. She stared out at a complete absence of lights and land broken occasionally by the soft glow of dusk gleaming on a lake or river. Her stretcher pressed against one window and her incline allowed her to see forward to the pilots and down to the emptiness between them and the wilderness. She searched for familiar landmarks and saw what could only be the Hudson River, larger now and dotted with the occasional river town. She saw the Mohawk merge and the twin bridges that told her they were headed south. What was their destination?

She did not have long to wonder.

"Are we descending?" she asked Dalton.

"Seems so."

"Dalton?"

He held her hand. "Hmm?"

"I can't stay awake."

He kissed her forehead. "I got you, Erin."

The drug was seeping into her bloodstream like tea in warm water. She blinked and forced her eyes open, but they rolled back in her head and her muscles went slack.

"No," she whispered, or merely thought she spoke. Had her lips moved? She drifted, torn loose from the mooring of pain, knowing that if danger came it would find her defenseless.

DALTON HAD A long night and now sat on the front porch as the birds began their morning songs. They had arrived at the temporary safe house on a country road in a little village in a county called Delaware. He'd never been to central New York. Their hostess was a woman who ran an orchard. Peaches were in season and the bees already droned in the honeysuckle bush that bordered the porch.

Erin was in an upstairs room with Roger Toddington, a former army paramedic and an EMT who was also their hostess's son. Somehow Dalton had dropped into a crazy world of espionage and he felt like Alice slipping through the looking glass. Everything seemed so normal here, but it was not.

The outside of this farmhouse looked typical enough, but the adjoining outbuilding was not the garage it appeared to be; instead, it was a fully equipped operating room with an adjoining recovery suite that rivaled the ICU where Erin had convalesced from her surgery.

Their hostess, Mrs. Arldine Toddington, offered him a cup of black coffee. The woman was fit, thin and muscular with hair that was snow-white on top and red and white beneath. She looked about as much like a spy as Mr. Rogers, God rest him. But according to Tillman she was a former US marine, a nurse practitioner with unique experience with gunshot wounds and was, it seemed, even tougher than she looked. She also made an amazing peach-and-walnut coffee cake.

But if Agent Tillman was to be believed, they were safe here and would remain in Mrs. Toddington's care until Erin recovered enough to travel without drawing attention to her healing bullet wound.

"Estimate that will be twelve to fifteen days," said Arldine.

"Do you have a location?" Dalton asked Tillman.

"Two, actually." Tillman set aside his coffee to accept a fork and a plate with a large piece of coffee cake littered with sticky walnut bits. "Thank you, Arldine."

"We'll have a choice?" asked Dalton.

Arldine and Tillman exchanged looks, and Arldine withdrew to lean against the porch rail facing them. Tillman nodded and she took over the conversation.

"We understand your wife has asked you for a legal separation."

Dalton lowered the plate to his lap and forced himself to swallow. The moist cake had turned chalky in his mouth, and the sticky topping made the food lodge in his throat.

Tillman filled the silence. "Safer for you both if you go separate ways. You are a big guy. Distinctive looking. Erin is more attractive than most women, but with a change of hair color and wardrobe, she can fit in just about anywhere."

Sweat popped out behind his ears and across his upper lip.

"Now you're saying that if we stay together, I put her at risk?"

"We are," said Tillman.

"But a few moments ago you said you could keep us safe."

"Carr has uncovered more information on this outfit. Seems to be heavily funded from offshore accounts, and we do not have a handle on the number of recruited members or even how many more sleeper cells can be activated. The speed of their response is daunting. They definitely have our attention."

"Erin and I are no threat."

"But you are on a kill list."

Dalton sat back in the rocker, sending it tilting at a dangerous angle. He knew what a kill list was. Crime organizations used them. It was a bounty list of sorts with a price on the heads of people who had betrayed or wronged them in some way.

"How do you know?" asked Dalton.

"We've gotten that much from Lawrence Foster. It was why Carr made his appearance. He doesn't usually get involved with civilians. But you two protected the information he had carried. So he felt a certain debt. He was at the hospital when I arrived, watching over you and your wife."

The man gave Dalton the creeps, and that was saying something when you considered all the types of criminals and military badasses he had come in contact with over the years.

"Where will you send her?" asked Dalton, getting back to the crux of the situation.

"I'm afraid I can't tell you that. Only the location we plan to send you."

Dalton would not even be allowed to know where she was.

"We will give you regular updates on her condition and will notify you both immediately when we neutralize the threat."

Neutralized, he thought. Also known as dead, killed, KIA or otherwise squashed.

"I need to talk this over with Erin."

"Of course," said Arldine. "You should."

"But remember that the threat increases if you stay together."

Chapter Twenty-Two

Dalton dreaded this conversation. He had come up here to win back his wife and save their marriage. Now he was going to blow it up again. Only this time he had a good reason. He was doing it to save Erin. To protect her, he had to leave her.

Impossible. Necessary.

He rubbed a knuckle back and forth across his wrinkled forehead trying to prepare for the conversation. She was just recovering, only off the morphine for one day, but he did not have time to waste. The longer he waited, the higher the chances that he would back out. Thinking of the look on her face and of never seeing that face again might just be enough to kill him. According to her, he'd been trying to do that—kill himself—ever since he came home from the Sandbox. He realized she had been right all along and so he would see a mental health professional ASAP. Or he could throw himself right back into the action. He could decline relocation and reenlist.

He felt as if his stomach was filled with tiny shards of glass, cutting him apart from the inside. He stood before her door, an upstairs bedroom of Arldine's farmhouse with southern exposure, lots of light and a fine view of the hayfield across the road.

Dalton rapped on the door. Roger called him in. When Dalton did not enter, the EMT appeared at the door, his face fixed with a gentle smile.

"Come on in, Detective. I'm just finishing." Roger looped his stethoscope around his neck and held the ends as one might do with a small towel.

Dalton stepped in on wooden legs. Would she believe him? He had to make her believe him.

"Hey there," Erin said.

She sat up in the hospital-style bed, a bouquet of sunflowers in a blue ceramic pitcher beside her on the bedside table. Beneath them rested a pill bottle, a half-empty water glass and a magazine.

"How are you feeling?"

"Lonely. I asked Roger to let me move back with you. I understand you have a queen mattress and a view of the barn."

He hadn't noticed the view, except that there was easy access to a flat roof beneath the window and a short drop to the ground from there.

The thick bandage on her neck was all the incentive he needed to do what he must. Dalton drew up the old wooden chair and placed it backward beside her bed. He sat, straddling the chair back, using the dowels as a sort of barrier between them because he feared that if he touched her, he'd never let her go.

Dalton cleared his throat.

"Honey?" asked Erin. "What's wrong?"

Erin felt the worry creeping up her spine like a nest of baby spiders, their tiny legs moving over her back, lifting the hairs on her body and washing her skin cold.

Dalton's expression was unfamiliar and deadly serious. She hazarded a guess.

"Are they out there?" She motioned toward the window and winced, forgetting not to use her left hand. Her head was clear thanks to ceasing the narcotics, but the pain pulsed with her heart, and her healing skin and muscle burned with the slightest movement.

"No, they're not. Erin, we are going to different locations."

"What?" Confusion mingled with the fear, landing in her stomach and squeezing tight. She sat up, leaving her nest of pillows, ignoring the pain that now bloomed across her chest. "No."

"It's what you wanted. A separation."

"Trial separation and I explained that to you. I don't want a separation. I want you to stop taking unnecessary risks. To see a counselor as you said."

"I changed my mind."

Her mouth dropped open. She could not even formulate a reply.

"I'm not leaving the force."

"But…wait…no…" She was stammering. "You have to leave the force. We're relocating. You can't… Dalton, this makes no sense."

"You said I have a death wish. I'm agreeing with you."

"This is suicide."

He nodded.

"You have to come with me."

"I'm not."

"What are you doing, Dalton? Are they using you as some kind of bait again? We got them Foster. They cannot expect you—"

"They don't. Haven't. I just thought you deserved to

hear it from me. I'm leaving *you* this time. I'm sorry, Erin. People don't change. Sooner or later, I'm catching a bullet. I'm ready. Ready to join those guys I promised to protect."

"Oh no, you don't." She reached for him.

He stood, looking down at her with regret. But not love. Somehow that was gone. The coldness in his dark eyes momentarily stopped her breathing, and her hand dropped to the bright pastel quilt.

"Goodbye, Erin."

The pain solidified like the surface of a frozen lake. She pointed a finger at him.

"Dalton, don't you dare walk out that door!"

But he was already gone, and the door slammed shut behind him.

DALTON MADE IT only to the top of the stairs. Tillman stood on the landing a few steps below him. Dalton sank to the top step still gripping the banister.

"She believe you?"

He nodded, thinking he did not have the strength to rise.

"Good. You can leave now. I have your location information."

"Where?"

Chapter Twenty-Three

Erin adjusted the wide-brimmed ranger hat on her head and proceeded toward her truck, the radio clunking against her hip with each stride. She paused to pass out a few stickers to the children in a visiting family who had stopped to read the nature trail board at the start of a gentle two-mile hike.

"Thank you!" piped the middle child. The youngest was already trying unsuccessfully to affix the sticker on her shirt without removing the backing and the eldest squatted in front of her to help.

Erin waved, feeling just the slightest tug in the stiff muscles of her neck. The cold in the mountains seemed to creep into the place where she had been shot.

She crossed the lot to her truck. Her new location was Mount Rainer National Park where she spent more time outside than she had on the East Coast. Unfortunately, she did not teach rock climbing or lead nature hikes for groups visiting from all over the world. That would be too much like her old life. So she did patrols, taught classes to youngsters in the nature center and manned the admission booth. At night she presented educational programs in the outdoor amphitheater for the visitors camping on-site.

Once in her truck, she unzipped her heavy jacket and headed back to the station past the yellow aspen and spectacular views of the ridge of blue mountains. She lived close to the station in the housing provided by the park to the rangers. Lulu and Jet greeted her at the door, as always. She had spent many nights alone back in Yonkers while Dalton worked his cases. And, though she had worried, she'd known he was out there and hoped he would be home eventually. Now that hope was gone. The cabin had a hollow feel and if not for the dogs, she didn't think she could take the solitude. Even with the other rangers she was alone, sticking to the story they had given her that made her five years younger and an only child.

September in New York was cool and lovely, but here in the Cascades the high altitude changed the seasons early. There was already snow predicted in the Cascades. In downstate New York, the earliest she ever saw snow had been November, and often just flurries, but here it was September 7 and predictions were for an accumulation tomorrow.

She didn't mind, could not have asked for a more perfect relocation. And the Company, as they self-identified, were optimistic that she would not have to stay here for more than a year. The information she and Dalton had furnished was likely to stop a pandemic.

Agent Carr kept in touch, appearing erratically to join a hike or as a solo camper applying for a wilderness permit. He said they were in the process of finding the three Deathbringers that were mentioned on the thumb drive.

The three Deathbringers, according to Carr, came from Chinese folklore, though even in myth form they were still considered dangerous by many. These "corpses" were believed by some to enter the body just after birth and determined the life span of each individual. Each corpse attacked a different system, brain, heart and organs. More specifically to the CIA, they would attack US citizens. The virus that she and Dalton had carried attacked the internal organs, causing a massive shutdown of the renal system. That was corpse number one and steps were underway to locate and intercept a shipment of this virus before it reached US soil. The second corpse, which attacked the brain, referred to a cyber attack, already in place, the brain being a metaphor for the infrastructure that kept communication open. Their people were working on that one now, as well. And the heart? Carr said that the Company believed this was an airborne toxin in production somewhere in New York State.

At the cabin she glimpsed a rental car. A man stood on the porch beside Jet, and for just a moment her heart galloped. But then she recognized that the stranger was too small to be Dalton.

She didn't look over her shoulder or jump every time she heard an unfamiliar sound. She just was not living her life like that. Erin was out of the vehicle and greeting Jet before she recognized the man in the cowboy hat.

"Mr. Carr," she said. "That hat makes you look like a Texas Ranger."

He slipped down the stairs to shake her hand. "A pleasure to see you again."

He smiled. "And you."

"Staying for supper?" she asked.

"No, unfortunately. Just wanted to tell you that the tech team has located the computer virus their hackers

installed. It was set to disrupt two different systems.
The rails in NYC, including subways, and the gas and
electric grid in Buffalo."

"Can they stop it?"

"Working on that now."

She finished stroking Jet's head and the canine
moved off to explore around the cabin. Erin hoped the
porcupine she'd seen last night was now sleeping in a
tree somewhere.

Lulu barked from inside. Erin let her out and Carr in.

"Can I fix you some coffee?"

He nodded.

She didn't ask if he'd like a beer, knowing he always
turned her down.

"We are working to shut down the cell that came
after you. Early indications are that they did not pass
on any information about you or Dalton."

"What does that mean, exactly?"

"If we can ascertain that no other cell of the terrorist organization is aware of your involvement, it would
mean you could return to your family."

It took only a moment for the coffee to brew. She
used the time to force down the lump in her throat.
To be able to return to your life would be wonderful,
but one member of her family was absent. She missed
Dalton so much her body ached from the sorrow. Erin
forced her shoulders back and she passed Carr a mug
of black coffee.

"Erin?" he asked, his face showing concern as he
accepted the mug.

"That's good news." She managed the words, but her
voice quavered. "How are my parents?"

"Missing you. But fine."

"My sister?"

"Said to tell you that the middle one lost a front tooth."

Erin smiled. "That's Patrick. I hope he didn't knock it out." He was in second grade, and all his classmates had that same gap-toothed smile and whistling disability.

She never asked about Dalton out of a mixture of sorrow and fear. They would tell her if and when he was killed. Wouldn't they?

The panic that they wouldn't forced her to tip heavily against the kitchen counter. Summoning her courage, she fixed her gaze on Carr.

"What's the word on Dalton? Is he still with the New York City Real Time Crime Center?"

The mug in Carr's hand paused at his lip and he regarded her a moment in silence. Then he lowered the mug to the counter.

"What was that?"

"I'm asking if he's back with his unit?"

"Erin, we told Dalton that joint relocation was dangerous because Dalton is so…" He extended his arms, indicating Dalton's unusual size. Carr's hand then went up to indicate Dalton's above-average height. "So…distinctive. You both agreed to separate locations."

"I'm confused," she said. "Dalton turned down relocation."

Carr arched a single brow that told her instantly that she had something wrong.

"Yes. I was aware he told you that," said Carr.

"Turned it down," she said, trying to convince Carr as the panic constricted her throat. "He told me that he couldn't change and that he would miss the action, the danger. He told me…" She made a fist and scrubbed it across her forehead. "He said…" She lifted her gaze to Carr. "He relocated?"

"He was. He just didn't tell you."

Her knees went out and she sank down along the lower cabinets, stopping only when her backside hit the floor.

"He lied to me."

Carr was beside her in an instant, squatting before her. "You signed the papers agreeing to separate locations."

She glared up at him. "Clearly, I didn't read the fine print."

"That was unwise."

She rested her forehead on her folded forearms supported by her knees. She spoke to her lap. "I would never have agreed…"

And that was why Dalton had not told her.

"Exactly," said Carr his expression showing regret.

She concentrated on breathing through her nose until the dark moth-like spots flapped away from her vision. Then she lifted her head.

"Why tell me now?" she asked.

"It seemed wrong to me. And you are unhappy."

"I want to see him."

"Marshalls service will tell you that is impossible."

"Really?" she said. "Then I'm taking out an ad in the *Seattle Times*."

"That will get you killed."

"Want to stop me? Take me to Dalton."

"I can't do that."

She was up and snatching the keys from the bowl beside the door. Jet trotted after her. Lulu came at a waddle.

Outside she opened the truck door and Jet jumped in.

Lulu needed a boost. She was behind the wheel when Carr reached her, on the phone, talking fast to someone and then to her. "Where are you going, Erin?"

"Yonkers."

He stood in the open door, keeping her from closing it.

"I could arrest you as a threat to national security."

"You told me what happened. Now you can take me to Dalton."

"He did this to protect you. If you leave WITSEC, his sacrifice is for nothing."

"The heck with that. I only agreed to this arrangement because he lied to me."

"Which is why he did this."

"I'll sue."

"You can't sue us."

Erin turned the key in the ignition. Carr reached in and flicked the engine back off.

"You knew what I'd do when I found out."

Carr shrugged. "Surmised."

He was playing her. Why did he want her to break cover?

"Why?" she asked.

"He's unhappy, too. Seems poor payment for your service."

"Take me to him," she whispered.

"All right," said Carr.

Chapter Twenty-Four

Dalton returned from his monthlong job on an offshore oil rig in the Gulf of Mexico on calm waters. The transport vessel slowed to dock in Mobile, Alabama. The replacement crew was behind them, and he and his new coworker were off for four glorious weeks. The gulf was the color of the Caribbean Sea today as they reached shallow water, and the sky was a pale summer blue. Though fall had taken firm hold up north, here the summer stretched long and warm.

He let the young ones hurry off the vessel first—those with girlfriends and new wives who still cared enough to greet them upon disembarking. The older men and the single ones had no one waiting and could make their way leisurely to their trucks and Harleys to head to wherever they went when not working thirteen-hour shifts. Dalton wondered where Erin was today. Was she looking at a blue sky or gray clouds? Was it raining where she was? Was she safe? Did she miss him?

"See you soon, Carl," said one of the roustabouts he had come to know.

He touched two fingers to his forehead, tanned from all the outdoor work, and gave a sloppy salute.

His roommate, a motorman from the Florida Panhandle, slapped him on the back as he headed down the gangplank, which led to the receiving area where family sometimes waited.

"Bye, Carl."

"Safe drive, Randall," he called after him.

His position as an offshore installation manager was made easier by the real manager who was teaching him the job. Dalton's own experiences working on so many task forces definitely made the transition easier. And he was used to getting off duty only to be called back up the instant he fell asleep because that part of the job was exactly the same.

But he'd always had Erin to come home to.

He adjusted his duffel bag on his shoulder and exited the gangway over the pier and headed into the arrival facility. His body had healed, leaving only the entrance and exit wound from the bullet that had broken his marriage.

"Wasn't the bullet. It was you."

Had Erin's wound healed?

He crossed the lobby, passing the couples reunited after their offshore stints. He was surprised to see so many children here on a school day, greeting dads.

Nice, he thought.

The bureau had furnished him with a three-year-old red pickup truck and he headed to the lot, hoping it would start after sitting in the blazing sun for a month.

Dalton cleared the lobby of the company's dockside offices and was hit by the heat and humidity. Without the boat's motion, the breeze had ceased and he began to sweat. He hurried down the sidewalk toward the lot, anxious to reach the air-conditioning of his truck.

But where was he going? Back to his empty condo? Not likely. He'd have a meal first. One where he could pick what he wanted from a menu. And a beer. He'd missed having a cold one on a hot day.

He caught motion in his peripheral vision, his brain relaying that there was an animal running toward him. He turned to give a knee to any dog stupid enough to jump on him. Dalton dropped his duffel as his hand went automatically to his hip to find no service weapon waiting.

The dog was black, a skinny Lab with a new pink collar. The dog seemed familiar and wagged frantically as Dalton stared in confusion. It whined and bowed and fell to its back kicking all four feet.

That almost looked like…impossible.

This dog could not be that dog. But then, waddling around between a pigmy palm and a hydrangea bush awash in hot-pink blooms, came a fat pug dog.

"Lulu?" he asked. He turned back to the black dog as he dropped to one knee. "Jet?"

Jet's reply was a sharp bark. Then she threw herself into Dalton's arms, wriggling and lapping his face with her long, wet tongue.

Dalton scooped up Lulu and stared at her. The dog seemed to smile and panted as if the walk had been taxing. Dalton returned her to the ground and she dropped to one hip as he shot to his feet.

Erin. She had to be here. But that was impossible.

Dalton scanned his surroundings, fixing on the only running vehicle that had dark tinted glass.

He turned to see a woman stepping from the rear seat of a large, dark SUV, the sort you might see in a presidential motorcade. Sunglasses hid her eyes and her hair was shorter, darker and much more stylish. Her mouth lifted in a familiar smile. Was she wearing red lipstick?

"Hey, sailor," she said.

She slammed the door shut, giving him a view of the flowery, sheer halter top and short cutoff jeans. The pale skin told him that wherever she had been it was cold, for it looked as if she had not seen the sun since he last saw her.

Jet darted back to her and then reeled and dashed back to Dalton. Lulu sat looking at her mistress, content to wait for her to catch up.

From the opposite side of the SUV stepped CIA agent Ryan Carr. "I got a delivery for you," he said, tipping a thumb toward Erin.

"Where do I sign?" asked Dalton.

"We have an escort in the lot. They'll take you to your new location."

"Where?"

"New Mexico. Tourist town outside Sedona."

Erin lowered her glasses and studied him, taking a moment, it seemed, to absorb the changes. If he'd known he would have cut his hair, shaved his face. He rasped his knuckles over the stubble that was well on its way to becoming a beard.

He blinked at her, trying to understand and then taking two steps in her direction before the truth struck him.

They were blown.

Dalton turned to Carr.

"When?" he asked as he strode toward Erin. He needed her back in the car. Out of sight. What was the agent doing letting her be seen out here?

"When, what?"

"We're blown," he said.

Carr shook his head. "You're not. Just a change of plans."

Erin reached him now, slipped her arms around his middle and pressed herself to him. He gathered her up in his arms and lowered his head, inhaling the familiar scent as he took in the changes. She was thinner.

He drew back to look at her, seeing the puckering red scar at the juncture of her shoulder and neck. A shot through the muscle that had torn into a major blood vessel and nearly taken her life.

Erin flipped her sunglasses up to her head and stared up at him. The look was not longing or desperate unrequited love. It seemed more like a smoldering fury that he had seen too many times in their marriage.

She lowered her chin. "You said you wanted a separation."

"I said that."

"You never told me the reason. So what is it, exactly?"

He pressed his mouth shut, not wanting to spoil this. To see her again, it was too sweet, and even having her mad was having her.

"Dalton?" Her arms slipped from his waist and folded before her. One slim sandaled foot began tapping the hot sidewalk.

"They said you'd be safer away from me. That I stand out."

She threw up her hands. Then she slugged him in the chest. He absorbed the blow. He knew from experience that she had a better right than that. This was just a mark of displeasure.

"You were protecting me?"

He nodded.

"You still love me?"

He nodded again.

"Then get in the car." She motioned to the SUV.

"Yes, dear." Dalton slipped into the rear seat. Erin retrieved Lulu, who had collapsed to her side, and then snapped her fingers for Jet, who bounded onto the rear seat and sprawled across Dalton's lap.

Then Erin climbed in and closed the door, ordering the dogs off the seat.

In the front area Carr was already buckling into the driver's seat and put them in Reverse.

Erin touched a button on the armrest and the privacy window lifted. Once it had closed completely, she tossed aside her glasses and grasped his face between her two small hands. Then she gave him the sort of kiss that had his eyes closing to absorb the perfection of the contact.

When she drew back, they sat side by side, breathless, hearts racing. She curled her hands around one of his arms and lowered her head to his shoulder.

"I missed you every minute. I can't believe you'd do this without telling me."

"Would you have gone?"

She shook her head. "I love you, Dalton. And marrying you was my way of letting you know that I wanted to spend the rest of my life *with* you."

He closed his eyes as he wondered if being apart, safe and miserable was preferable to accepting the increased risk and being with his wife. Then he decided it was not.

"I was wrong," he said. "I know it. I knew it almost immediately after I left you, but it was too late."

"Apparently not."

"How did you get them to come for me?"

"Threatened to walk away, tell the papers all about it."

He sat back, stunned. "You can't do that. You signed an agreement."

She shrugged.

"You threatened the CIA?"

Erin's cheeks turned pink. "I did."

"They make people disappear for that."

"We're small fish. Best to just let us go."

"I'm glad you did," he admitted. "So glad. I've been miserable without you, Erin. You're more than a piece of me—you're my heart."

She hugged him. "Oh, Dalton."

They drove in silence behind the escort car and trailed by another, winding through the streets and toward the highway.

"Where are they taking us now?" he asked.

"Airport first. And then, who cares? As long as we are together."

He gathered her up in his arms, dragging her to his lap for another kiss. She was right again. It didn't matter where they went. It mattered only that she had never stopped loving him and that he had her back in his arms once more.

* * * * *

COMING SOON!

We really hope you enjoyed reading this book. If you're looking for more romance, be sure to head to the shops when new books are available on

Thursday 8th August

To see which titles are coming soon, please visit

millsandboon.co.uk/nextmonth